LATE QUARTET

The Story of an Obsession

By Maria Jacob

 **New Generation Publishing**

Dedicated to Mary and Dominic,
With love and thanks

ACKNOWLEDGEMENTS

To Susan Anglin and to the staff at Woodburn Cottage for their advice about dental reception work

To the officers at Nailsea police station for information about road accidents

To the past leader of the Liberal Democrat group on Bristol City Council for his ideas, shamelessly purloined.

To my Orthodontist friend and one-time lodger Niall McGuiness, for advice on a dentist's professional commitments and dentistry in general.

To the senior nursing staff at the Bristol Royal Infirmary for information and advice on head injuries.

To my late and very dear friend and actress Nanette Stratford Johns who knew all about television soaps.

To my late, ex-husband for inspiration.

To Catherine and Suzanne for their encouragement at the very start.

To all my political friends at the sharp end for up-to-date information on procedures.

And to all my other friends in all the other spheres who have stayed around while this tale was being born.

ONE YEAR LATER

WHEN Miss Hannah Pascoe, smiling, suitably tanned and just turned 60, stepped from the S S Oriana onto the wet quay at Southampton Dock, she was met by her daughter Lucy with several actors from the television soap, Wayside Walk, plus a dozen or so fans braving the rain in the hope of autographs. She was also presented by Lucy with a large bunch of daffodils ("to welcome you back to showery Britain") and a bulky brown paper parcel.

This was marked "Not to be opened until seated comfortably with feet up and large G and T in hand." So, having at last been restored by friends and family to her Padstow cottage, Miss Pascoe dutifully kicked off her shoes, provided herself with a full glass, took a first sip and ripped open the package.

Inside were a computer disk, a USB memory stick and a pile several inches thick of email print-outs, with a covering note from Mrs Christabel Fraser.

"Dear Hannah," said the note, "Since neither you nor I wish to overload our hard drives indefinitely, I thought you might like to have it all on disc, as a record of the Hannah-that-was. And because I know how much you like books and things written on real paper I'm sending the hard copy as well. So now you've got both. Meanwhile I am dying to meet the new Hannah, the Hannah-that-is. I haven't included my own replies because that would have been an unforgivable waste of time and trees. But thank you for trusting me with the best read of my life. Enjoy!

Love as ever, Chrissie.

1

To: Christabel Fraser

FROM   Hannah Pascoe
TO: Chrissiefras@coolmail.net
SENT: 1 January 2008
SUBJECT: Hurrah!

Chrissie, I've done it. Made the decision and told Robert and the cast. They didn't believe me at first. Robert said "But darling, you'll be bored out of your mind in two months and begging for scripts. In any case, this is just the result of over-excitement. You'll feel better after Christmas." And Tom said actors don't retire, they don't know how - which only goes to prove what I've been telling everyone all along – that I'm not really an actress at all, just a sort of idiot machine into which one places Maisie Mitchell scripts, presses a starter button and waits for words to plop out. Scatty, harebrained Maisie is becoming me, or I am becoming Maisie, holey jeans and all, and I'm getting very sick of wondering who I am every time I wake up in the morning.

But the gauntlet has now been run, I have endured all the "Oh Buts" and the "You can't *possiblys*," – and fought down the panic. My panic, that is. Odd that after so many months of deep thought and desperate decisions, I should now be filled with such frightening feelings of insecurity. When I think it through, though, I realise that of course it has to be like that. Six years of Maisie are enough to set anyone in aspic. In this case, it feels more like concrete!

But what a splendid way to start a New Year.

Michael wasn't best pleased and still isn't. I've told him he will have his house cleaned and his meals not only cooked but set before him *on time*, but the prospect of coming home to a domesticated wife doesn't seem to compensate for my loss of minor stardom. I think he prefers froth-headed Maisie to me. Sometimes I think I do too. There's something very innocent and honest about her. I hope they don't kill her off under a bus, but send her away to Fiji or Outer Mongolia. She should have a romantic exit.

There's to be a Party. With Presentation. Woo-hoo! I hope they don't take too long to write me out as having decided on Freedom to Do My Own Thing I want to be out there Doing It.

Unless one's heart and soul is in it, Fame never quite satisfies, does it? What little fame I've had as Maisie would be as a pale and misty shadow to the joy of seeing one little book with my name on the cover, on a library shelf or in the window of a bookshop.

Incidentally, although you can't see it with the physical eye, you are at this moment witnessing more than one historic event. This is being composed on a lovely new laptop (*mine!*), since Michael and I always seemed to need his computer at the same time. So now I not only have the freedom of the World Wide Web, I can also be peripatetic. Have laptop will travel! An excellent idea. You, my dear Chrissie, are the first to reap its rewards.

My love to Peter and the kids, and hope to see you all soon when my time belongs to me instead of to 'Wayside Walk'. HAPPY NEW YEAR! Hannah.

P.S.Lucy has a part in 'Dear Brutus' starting next week in Bristol. It's good news but I shall miss her dropping in to empty my fridge, eat all the jam and use up all the bath oil. Andy doesn't seem to mind her going, but he's a phlegmatic young man. Happy to be left with his camera and tripod, which Lucy says he loves way more than he loves her. (The lying jade – she knows perfectly well he adores every inch of her!) She sends love and promises you a programme. Haven't had news of Timothy for a while, which means he's happily occupied and doing well, as normally he only contacts his mum when he wants something. Paris suits him perfectly (Well, it would, wouldn't it? I think I could manage to put up with it quite happily myself). Hopefully I shall be invited to hop over there for visits, now that I have time to spare. An attractive thought!

P.P.S. Do you remember the piano I bought last year with Maisie money? Yesterday we moved it from the musty corner of the glory hole, where it had been sitting forlornly ever since it arrived. It is now against the dining room wall opposite the window and underneath my favourite picture of The Lady of Shalott. Mind, that's all I've done – move it and stare at it (the piano, that is, not the picture, although I quite often stare at that too). As with all instrumental devices and workable machinery, the idea of actually using the thing is something I prefer to put into practice tomorrow rather than today.

ooOoo

2

To: Christabel Fraser

FROM   Hannah Pascoe

TO: Chrissiefras@coolmail.net
SENT: 3 January 2008
SUBJECT: Thanks

Many thanks for your card. I love the eagle (at least I presume it's an eagle – the drawing was a trifle on the impressionist side so it could have been just about anything with wings) soaring off to God knows where. Freedom, I hope. "Enjoy!" you say.

I shall, oh I shall. I can smell it, like horses smell the stable. This afternoon I sat for three hours, feet on a stool and head on a cushion, listening to all my favourite CDs as a foretaste of pleasure to come. I chose them with the greatest care, as the moment was somehow significant. And waves of Beethoven and Sibelius and Schumann and Tchaikovsky broke magically over my head until I was swimming in sound, floating, tossing up through a frothy crest. The usual miracle was very present, though as wonderfully mysterious as ever, that vibrations, travelling on air waves and hitting parts of my eardrum, can be decoded by my brain into an experience so emotionally engulfing that I am lifted up on billows of it. Blown about on eddies of it. And occasionally kicked in the guts by it. I don't know whether to laugh or cry and often do both.

What do you do when kicked in the guts by music?

Authority (in the form of Producer Robert plus writers) has decreed that Maisie Mitchell be given the sack and retired *pro tem* to her sister's in Haverford West, while they decide whether to leave her there or restore her to Soap life after a suitable interval with a Hannah Pascoe substitute (is this possible?). So I have one more episode to do this week then *"finito."* Party fixed for Saturday. Champers and caviare? (What? On this budget?)

Michael is not sure he wants to go to the party, but probably will in the end as it is (he hopes) the last. He enjoys my Maisie persona with its fan mail and its mild fame, but sidesteps the social life. I suspect peering into mouths and prodding teeth all day could give one a rather specialised view of people stuffing themselves with plastic beef. But although I am not a dentist, parties can pall on me too. I won't be sorry to lose some of them. Not all of them, of course – Scrabble and slippers warming by the fire are not for me just yet.

Meanwhile, take care and come over Real Soon. I haven't seen you for far too long. Glad Suzie's passed her driving test but I imagine your nerves will now twinge nastily every time she asks for the loan of your car.

Love to Pete and Stew and, of course, to yourself.
Hannah.

P.S. Michael has bought himself a fancy new jacket. It fits him perfectly, shows off his shoulders and makes him look taller than ever. He is really a very handsome man, so what more can a wife ask? Perhaps that he wears the new jacket at my farewell party? We shall see.

P.P.S. Email sent to Timothy in Paris. He replied rather tersely, asking if I knew what I was doing and saying he'd be over shortly.

ooOoo

3

Christabel Fraser

FROM   Hannah Pascoe
TO: Chrissiefras@coolmail.net
SENT: 11 January 2008
SUBJECT: Photo
ATTACH: Lucy

I'm attaching the photos of Lucy you asked for. She's still with 'Brutus' and I miss her, but thank God she doesn't live here any longer. The more I see of her haphazard standards the more I admire her wonderful indifference to comfort, and the less I wish to share it. My advanced age (at least I think it's that) rebels at the sight of odd socks draped dismally over cups of cold coffee and a sticky jam jar, and I am convinced one muddy trainer has been under her kitchen chair since last Christmas. And why does everything look either mud brown or mud grey? I buy her colourful clothes from time to time but she dyes them all black, or they somehow take on the same mud patina. Is there a new brand of mud washing powder?

Have made fresh contact with my neighbours. We used to nod in friendly fashion on dustbin day and exchange pleasantries if we met on the pavement, and we are occasionally invited to peoples' parties, but soon I shall be home all day and no doubt they'll pop out of hedges and call from windows. Yesterday I started my new life by going next door for coffee. Her name is Mary Quintrell. An agreeable youngish woman, though tense and anxious with a permanent, placatory smile. I suspect her of being horribly law abiding. Or maybe her husband bullies her. It's my turn for the coffee next week.

Also enclosed is the latest photo of Maisie, which I have carefully edged in black for her (professional) demise. I shall now HAVE MY HAIR CUT.

Only one more day to go. Michael suggests that I pilfer Dustin Hoffman's scene in 'Tootsie' and reveal myself as a man in the final moments. What an amazingly seductive thought. Unfortunately – well, fortunately really – everything I have is attached to me so I can't even take my teeth out let alone wig or boobs. As for revealing parts of even greater intimacy, I suspect the studio would burst spontaneously into shocked flames, this being a Family Show. But now I come to think of it, maybe not, in view of the way we all seem to be heading.

How comforting that after tomorrow I shall be ME.

See you soon, I hope.

Love, Hannah.

ooOoo

4

Christabel Fraser

FROM   Hannah Pascoe
TO: Chrissiefras@coolmail.net
SENT: 15 January 2008
SUBJECT: Positively last appearance.

No, I didn't strip off or shout inconvenient truths or in any way jeopardise Maisie's last scene. Little harm would have come from it anyway, as the programme is pre-recorded. Robert would merely have shouted "Cut" and made me look even more foolish than usual. I did, however, get tearful towards the end of the day as zero hour approached and a six-year pattern was about to be demolished. These people have become very close. Part of my life.

The episode was boringly undramatic. I (Maisie) just pushed off to my (her) sister's and promised to write. There was talk of a claim for unfair dismissal, but this was no more than a passing idea, quickly squashed, as Maisie was nicely paid off in redundancy money and wishes only to go away and spend it. Perhaps in a few months we shall hear that she fell downstairs and broke her neck, but meanwhile the finale to my professional career was just a little tame. Robert has promised that if Maisie is ever killed off formally, I shall be invited to the wake.

He made a nice little speech as Producer, and we opened a pre-party bottle of inferior bubbly, then Tom escorted me, plus baggage, to the car park where he stowed us in our respective places – me in front, baggage in boot. The bubbly wasn't potent enough for more interesting variations. Then he kissed me goodbye. Reiterating, of course, his many avowals of undying devotion, or deathless passion, and saying how much time we've wasted all these years and how I'm *still* not getting any younger, as though at any moment he expected my lifespan to turn itself about like an egg-timer (I wish!), and he's rather surprised it hasn't.

"For God's sake, Han," he said, "If you don't want to do yourself a favour, at least do me one. I've fancied you for six years and now you've left me, and I don't even know if I'm ever going to see you again."

I said that of course he'd see me again, tomorrow. "The party," I explained. His eyes glazed momentarily. "You know, P. A. R. T. Y. with champagne and caviare."

"Ah!" he said, and I knew he wasn't listening, in fact

gazing deeply into my soul at fairly close range. There is a very small mole on the left side of his nose. I considered the time had come to take self and baggage out of closer reach, so I switched on the engine and pushed the button to wind up the window through which the nose, plus mole, was peering. He removed it.

"I am a happily married woman, Tom," I mouthed, giving him a sweetly sad smile, but I think he missed some of it because he was hopping out of the way. Driving out of the car park I glanced in the rear view mirror and he seemed to be saying something. I think it was rude.

Not that I believe for a moment that he means it. He's been playing this game for too long. Mind, it was very pleasant having such a charming and attentive stage next door neighbour, and he is after all quite personable. There was a time when I might have fallen for it and taken him seriously, and then what would he have done? Run like a hare for safety? Or hurl me to the ground and ravish me on the spot?

Of course I know it isn't too late, and that tomorrow evening could see the start of a new adventure in more ways than one, but my days of looking for candyfloss love are past and done. Besides, he's already been divorced twice, and I have no desire to be Mrs Tom the third, or even Girl Friend No 47.

But to greater things – I have to decide which stunning outfit I look most stunning in, and who precisely it is that I wish to stun. As for the aforesaid champers and caviare, the former may be faintly possible but the latter certainly, definitely, positively *is not*. See if I care! I don't much like the stuff anyway.

Michael is still making up his mind.

Looking forward to seeing you within the next two to three weeks.

Till then, all love, Hannah

ooOoo

5

Christabel Fraser

FROM   Hannah Pascoe
TO: Chrissiefras@coolmail.net
SENT: 18 January 2008
SUBJECT: On my way!

Yes, Thursday would be perfect. Then I think I'll drive down to Cornwall for the weekend. I rather fancy being alone in the cottage to cook or not cook, sleep or not sleep, walk, run or stagger as the whim takes me. I have become over-peopled and will fly to you next Thursday like a pigeon, knowing you will hide me away in your loft and feed me best birdseed.

The party was quite pleasant, very standard and in parts rather boring, but redeemed half way through by a nice little drama in which Mel Kendrick pulled off an equally nice little one-liner and then wished he hadn't because from then on he was pursued by a relentlessly stage-struck teenager. I recognised the girl. She had thrown herself at me outside the studio one day last week and had nearly knocked me down, over-enthusiasm seeming to do something funny to her feet. True, she apologised sweetly at the time and shyly requested my autograph, and, true, she particularly asked to be introduced to me properly last night and gazed adoringly when Janine (her aunt) obliged. But following an unwinking stare at the door, and a pretty blush and start when it opened upon Mel, she vanished from my side in a flicker of jeans. Can jeans flicker? It depends on who's inside them, I suppose.

15

I was not jealous. Mr Kendrick is thirty-five, disgustingly handsome and understandably has the edge.

The evening began normally enough, in the hospitality room as usual. There were more speeches. Janine was amazing in wonderful, floaty, gauzy black and orange which, topped by the black plume of hair and forceful nose, gave her the look of some delightful tropical bird. In fact she seemed in imminent peril of rising in a swirl of robes to hover above us, but she tethered herself by placing a firm hand on my arm and saying "Hannah darling, someone here wants to meet you."

I was at the time choosing between cold beef and smoked salmon, with Tom and Myra doing the same thing beside me. And having decided only seconds earlier that they all looked the same, like highly coloured plastic, I said so.

"Why do they?" I asked. Do they have special factories churning out pretend meat?"

"Perhaps they do," said Myra, "Who's going to put it to the test?"

Tom daringly forked a piece of pretend beef, folded it between two chunks of French bread and bit it. Then he clasped a hand over his mouth. "Oh God, my new dentures!"

For some reason Myra and I found this exquisitely funny. I expect it was the sparkly wine.

Having pulled myself together I told Tom he was very reassuring.

"Am I?" he asked, "Why, what have I done?"

"You said something real. Normal. I was afraid we'd all stopped. Gone into some sort of two dimensional robot land."

"You mean like toons?"

He was absolutely right. Cartoon figures come to

life.

Myra, obviously fascinated, asked Tom if he really did wear dentures. He smiled ferociously, lips closed and bulging. Then he shook his head and Myra lost interest.

We stood sipping and chewing, watching the assortment of people standing about doing more or less the same, chewing, sipping and talking. Certainly, always talking.

"Don't we ever stop?" I mused. "Are we afraid that if we don't keep mouthing words at each other we'll vanish, cease to exist? I'm glad I'm going."

Tom said: "You are going through a phenomenon called Disenchantment, and you know quite well you'll be praying for scripts in six months, and devastated if they don't come."

"Maybe," I said. I knew I was being unjust. But my feelings of mixed relief and rebellion were growing too fast to be talked down.

Janine, who had materialised as only she can, gripped my arm firmly and interrupted.

"Hannah darling," she insisted, "Please come and meet my niece. She's stage struck and star struck and for some reason appears to worship you. You don't have a photo handy do you?"

"Sorry," I said, "I don't keep them about my person. Is it necessary for the introduction? "

"Like an ID card?" Myra leaned hard against the table and shouted with laughter. She had gone rather pink. "Are you really and truly the great, the famous, the awe-inspiring Hannah Pascoe?"

I smiled mirthlessly at her, showing my teeth. "Only to my public," I replied and swept off behind Janine in her elbowing and shoving progress across the room. Not that I had any choice, really. She still had my sleeve firmly between her fingers. From behind us I heard Myra's floating voice telling me I was expected to fish a photograph from my knickers. "That's if you're wearing any," she finished. I put my free hand behind my back and gestured with two fingers.

We emerged before a softly young, slight, pale girl with long straight blonde hair and round blue eyes, whose hand was confidingly upon the arm of a pugnacious youth in jeans and a black tee shirt. He seemed vaguely to be living up to something, possibly an aggressive jaw.

I recognised the girl who had nearly knocked me down outside the studio.

"Karen, my pet," Janine said, "Here is your Hannah. Never say I don't do anything for you."

I said hello and was rewarded by a worshipful blue gaze.

One day I won't be recognised any more. Will I mind? Vanity, and of course a sense of fitting reward after years of hard work, tells me all this reverence is quite right and proper (oh boy!), but it came home to me then, as it often has before, how simple and naïve people must be who offer it. I wanted to pat this child on the head and tell her that Hannah Pascoe is an illusion. She doesn't exist. "Don't waste your admiration," I wanted to say. "The real heroines are elsewhere doing real things like emptying bedpans."

But I didn't, because (I confess to you, Chrissie) such admiration is delicious and there will come a time, quite soon probably, when I won't get it any more. While the sun still shines I shall make my hay! Besides, Karen was obviously enjoying the giving, and who am I to spoil anyone's fun?

She said she thought I was marvellous.

"Really?" I asked politely, and with suitable modesty. "I'd have thought you'd be more interested in the younger ones."

"On *no*!" Her mouth was a circle of anxiety, as round as the eyes above it. "You've got such *experience.* You've *learnt* so much. You and Mel Kendrick," she added, her voice now breathless with awe. "He isn't here yet, but Auntie Jan says he's coming. I do *hope* so."

I know my place, Chrissie. As I said, Mel definitely has the edge.

"You seem to admire us," I said, "Is it just the actors, or are you keen on acting yourself? I mean, do you do any?"

It was the right question. Joy lit her like a torch. She loved it, had loved it all her life. She turned for confirmation to the pugnacious youth, and it was then I realised that confirmation was exactly what she was not going to get. He was slowly freezing her, his jaw elongating itself into a hatchet.

"Get as much experience as you can," I told her. "Go to Drama school. Then, if you're any good…"

"Don't encourage her," The pugnacious youth (hereinafter to be known as Hatchet Jaw) interrupted with a horrid frown and looked as if at any moment he might grow horns and charge me. "She can't act for peanuts."

The silence that followed was filled with sudden, tangible pain, and Karen's eyes misted with hurt. Indignation gripped me. I dripped ice at him.

"Oh? I assume you're qualified to judge?"

Hatchet Jaw and I stared eye to eye. "I know a good actress when I see one," he said, and I understood that the description did not extend to myself.

"I'm happy for you," I told him, "but opinions in this are apt to be subjective. Many people may not agree with you. You sound like the sort of man who looks at pictures and says 'I don't know anything about art but I know what I like', which is fine so long as you're not an art critic or, in this case, a drama critic."

It was a duel.

"I'm a member of the audience," he said, "We pay for our seats and we decide whether plays are any good or not, not the fucking critics. They're just jumped up intellectuals who play a sort of game: 'Let's have fun and pull this one to pieces, lads', and 'Who shall we turn into a star tonight, then?' It's all a load of fucking crap. It's bums on seats that matter, and the bums know who's worth staying there for."

I was tempted to ask whether his bum was where he normally kept his manners, but by this time Karen was a pretty puce colour and staring at the floor as if she wished herself anywhere but standing on it. She tugged at his sleeve from time to time and whispered "Mark," but Mark was into his stride and going nicely. He would probably have continued for quite a while longer had the door not suddenly opened, framing Mel Kendirick artistically within it. He was wearing his best naughty-boy smile.

Karen let go of Mark's arm and vanished. I heard the "Shooooosh!" as she trembled and was gone.

"Sorry to be late," Mel was saying as we all, somehow, found ourselves drawn around him. To be one of the surrounding mob was against my principles, but there I was nonetheless. "There was an accident on Stoney Hill and I was held up."

"Oh dear!" Janine handed him a full glass. "Was it a bad one?"

"I didn't actually witness it, but I arrived probably thirty seconds later and saw the result, and that was nasty enough. Some kid on a bicycle. The chap who knocked her down was in one hell of a state. He'd cut his head rather badly, to judge by the blood, and was obviously suffering from concussion. By the time I'd phoned for an ambulance he'd passed out, so he and the girl went off at the same time. Then of course I had to stay and make a statement for the police."

"How was the child?"

Mel paused. "I'm not sure. She was still alive, I think, but only just. Didn't look too good anyway. In fact I would guess she'd probably be dead on arrival."

There was a silence, Karen gave a small hiss and keeled over at my feet, knocking the glass out of my hand and myself sideways against a chair back. What is it about this girl and me? That's the second time in two days. I picked her up – she is so light I could have done it with one hand – and stowed her in a chair, where she came muzzily back to us. I persuaded her to lean forward, and held her head down between her knees. Janine brought a glass of water and squatted by the chair.

"So delicately put," she murmured to Mel.

I looked down at Karen's long, silky hair and felt she was having an unfairly painful evening. But at least she would have the reward of Mel's sympathetic attention, for he was now faced with the unpleasant result of a nicely timed piece of histrionics. After all, how could he possibly know if the girl died or not? It was just a guess, and an unpleasant one.

"But you don't *know*, do you?" I said at last. "You're only guessing."

From his elegant pose on one knee beside Karen's chair Mel looked pained. "Of course," he murmured, "I was only telling you what I saw. And you did ask!"

"True!" I said, and took to wondering about Hatchet Jaw. He was standing just a little apart from the small huddle of guests around us, within hearing but detached. I returned to Karen, who was now sitting up, pale and a little damp but otherwise rather enjoying herself.

"I am so terribly sorry," Mel was saying to her, all

charm and remorse. "It was stupid of me, stupid and thoughtless. Please forgive me."

Karen gazed into his face. Romantic novels describe heroines as drowning in the hero's eyes. Well, that is precisely what Karen was doing in Mel's.

"Oh please don't apologise. You weren't to know."

"Of course I should have known what a sensitive little thing you are. Good God, I should have more sense."

"No, I didn't mean...."

The pugnacious Mark moved swiftly and suddenly towards her and she was silenced. But not for long. His star had been eclipsed and Mel, a brighter sun, hung gallant and glorious above her, obviously waiting for her to continue.

"You see, Mark and I saw it happen."

There was another shocked silence. Karen had produced a perfectly timed *tour de force* of her own.

"You saw it? You actually *saw* it? You didn't say anything when you got here." Janine sat back on her heels, more than ever like a fairy-tale illustration.

"Well yes, we saw...," but Karen now looked at Mark, faltered, then stopped. He stared stonily at her. After a short pause she continued. "Well, I suppose we didn't *actually* see it happen, I mean we didn't see the car actually...I mean, we only thought we might have but by that time we'd gone past and we were going to be late and Mark said not to stop, so..."

The air about us grew chillier. We all looked questioningly at Mark who lifted the hatchet jaw and stared back.

"Sure, I said not to stop," he said. "It's always a bad idea to get involved in accidents. Anyway, you said yourself she's sensitive." He glared at us. "You saw what happened when you just told her about it. Effing 'ell, if we'd stopped she'd have needed an ambulance

22

herself."

I gazed thoughtfully at Karen's ingenuous face and thought perhaps he had a point. Then I fell to wondering about the dependence of personality upon personality. This frightfully rude young man was indefensible in his rudeness, yet that might be the very quality she liked about him. Could it perhaps give her the feeling of security and power she needed? Whatever one thought of his values, he certainly had the strength of character to stand up for them against a hostile audience.

But Mel was imprisoned for the evening. I was not sorry for him. Personable, romantic leads have to pay for the adulation of their fans, and Mel was paying for his.

"Let's get another drink," Myra said. "We need it," and Tom steered us both to a convenient corner, leaving Karen in better hands than ours. "I've had enough drama for one evening."

"I've had enough drama, full stop," I said, and meant it. "I've finished with it"

Drama was not, however, quite finished with me.

After a suitable time spent comforting his little patient, Mel joined us and kissed me on the cheek. He looked penitent, but I noticed that he was also very pale.

"Hannah sweetie, I'm so sorry. Have I spoilt your farewell party?"

I smiled and told him he had ruined it utterly, then relented. "No of course not, you mutt. Not for me anyway, and you've given Karen a wonderful few minutes. Almost worth it, I'd have said. But what really did happen?"

Mel frowned. "It wasn't pleasant. I happened along so soon afterwards I swear the bike wheels were still turning. She was only a kid, but from the way she was

23

lying it looked pretty bad. The chap was still in the car when I got there, but he got out and looked down at the bike. His head was cut and there was blood all down his front, but it was his face I'll always remember."

He stopped talking and stared down at his glass.

I prompted him. "What did you do?"

"Called the ambulance on my mobile and stayed with them. What else was there to do? I covered the girl with my coat and gave the chap my handkerchief to wipe the blood off his face and hold against the cut. But I don't think he knew what to do with it. Kept saying "Oh my God! Katy!" I asked him if he knew the girl and he sort of stammered. "Yes. No. No. I don't know." His car was wrapped around a tree, so he couldn't get back in, but I tried to get him to sit down before he fell down. He wouldn't. He just kept crying "Oh my God, Katy!" and crouching over the girl crying his heart out. It was ghastly, Hannah."

I touched his arm and said: "Don't go on if you'd rather not"

"No, it helps. I asked him if he remembered what had happened and he said somebody was passing him too closely on the right, and there was nowhere to go except into the tree. Then he passed out. When the ambulance came there were two bodies to be picked up. They're pretty fast, I have to say. The paramedics were astonishing. Extraordinary people. I couldn't do what they do to save my life. The police came at the same time and I gave them my statement, but as I hadn't actually seen the thing happen I wasn't a proper witness. By the time they'd let me go the bodies had been taken away. Then I came here, expecting a drink and consolation and looking forward to telling the story. What I did not expect was another witness fainting all over me, poor little sod. Bit of an oddball, her boy friend?"

"Yes," I agreed. "Personally I think oddball is too kind a word. Let's hope she'll have seen him in a new light after tonight."

Mel raised his glass to me in a toast. "I wish you weren't leaving," he said. "We're going to miss you."

"And I'll miss you all," I replied. But would I? I'm ready, ready to go, Chrissie. Jan and Myra I won't be leaving behind because we've grown closer during the past year. In any case the three of us and Nick Wadham are the only members of the cast who live locally. The rest commute. You've met both Jan and Myra but I don't expect you to remember them, except the inimitable Janine, our look-alike Audrey Hepburn who wears exotic clothes. She's kind, generous, intelligent and funny, and she plays Trish Hamilton, who lives at Number 11 with a commuter husband and rebellious teenagers. Myra plays Mrs Binny with a pronounced, meals-on-wheels conscience. In real life she's tall, blonde, inclined to plumpness and lazily sardonic. They're both divorced. Jan has daughters abroad, Myra has cats and seems to be constantly surrounded by the soft, fluffy fruits of their carnal appetites – any generations of which could have been mine had Michael ever overcome his bizarre fear of the things. Strange, but I suppose no stranger than my fear of spiders. The fact that we're both a good 500 times larger and more powerful than either of those creatures doesn't seem to make any difference.

Anyway, apart from those there are other people I shall be sorry to lose. They've been my almost daily companions for six years. Sally Marx, Lynne Jones, Andrea Thorne and Beatrice Rudge who has been my screen mother for so long we both believe she's my real mother.

I want to write books. I want to be free. But leaving The Walk is like leaving my own family.

Oh well, one can't have it all ways.

Anyway it was quite a day, taken all round, and now I can't stop thinking about the little girl and her devastated parents.

Meanwhile, love to everybody,

Hannah.

P.S. No, Michael wasn't there. "Not his kind of party," he said in the end, and really he was right. He would only have moped in a corner. A pity, though, as he can be good company when he puts his mind to it.

P.P.S. Yes, they gave me a present. Flowers and a very posh leather document case with my initials in graceful capitals. To put my manuscripts in, they said. I promised signed copies of the result.

P P P S There was a brief email from Number One son Tim in my inbox to say with luck he'd be arriving sometime in February. It will be good to have him home again, if only for a few days.

ooOoo

6

Christabel Fraser

FROM   Hannah Pascoe
TO: Chrissiefras@coolmail.net
SENT: 21 January 2008
SUBJECT: From Padstow

Thank you, thank you. Two days with you began the

process which Cornwall, I hope, will complete – the restoration of Hannah to her true self. That is, of course, providing I know who and what that is.

It wasn't until I left home *en route* for Marlborough and you that I realised how very tired and frustrated and overstretched I'd been for so long. Maisie and the conflict of living her life unwillingly week after week took more from me than I, or anyone, ever knew, and the situation with Michael growing slowly worse year by year (lately month by month) seems to have alarmingly used up my ghost. Here in the cottage, solitary at last, I can begin the stock-taking.

The old exasperating ability to 'act happy', with the awful brightness and the often second-rate wit which issues from despair and exhaustion, is so efficient a cover that I, too, am taken in. All the world but you, and a very few others, think me cheerful, collected, efficient and enjoying myself. Only in the privacy of bathroom or car or midnight darkness can I admit to being none of those things. I am an ageing actress (sorry – ex-actress) with hair going grey and elbows getting crepey, and I have chosen to throw away familiarity, security and a small share of limelight in a risky bid to start a new life.

But what do I really want from this new life, and does Michael want the same?

The time with you helped to clarify some things, if only because you have experienced them too, in one way or another. I remember your divorce as if it were last week. Does it seem like last week to you, despite the wonderfully consoling bulk of Peter today?

As I write I can see a woman in a headscarf plodding down the pavement below me. My table in the window overlooks the street and the entrance to Ruthy's Lane, and the archway to the public footpath is immediately beneath my feet. Odd how strangers can walk right underneath where I'm sitting at any time, night or day, completely unaware of my breathing body overhead.

The room is tiny, a microcosm of living, with everything within reach, kitchen, dining table, sofa, front door. The only necessity is to be an octopus. Buying it last year was an inspiration, especially as Maisie Mitchell paid for it, so she has given me something very special as a memorial, a small, convenient and peaceful haven that's mine alone. Down the hill lie the harbour and shops. Up the hill stands the church. Body, mind and spirit all catered for.

All of those need catering for, believe me! I realise now, properly and for the first time, how my soul has been gasping for peace. This morning I went to the old parish church and sat serenely among the usual regular, out-of-season worshippers who smiled and offered me hymn books, and together we all sang energetically if not always tunefully while I gazed at the rood screen and thought about Life and God, and wondered why the woman in front had chosen a shade of acid green for her knitted woolly hat. I decided, most positively, that God is uncontainable and that any attempt to put him in a denominational box – or a doctrinal one come to that - will only result in him seeping out again in all directions. The thought was comforting. If he is that big, he is certainly equal to me and my rather haphazard concerns.

Tonight I shall go to my chaste bed with a library book, How to choose between 'The Client', 'Mr Finchley Discovers His England' or 'A Morbid Taste For Bones'? Who was it said everything about a person can be discovered by studying his or her bookshelves?

With that disconcerting thought I shall leave you. Many, many thanks, and hugs all round. Thanks especially to you for listening to my self-absorbed

ramblings. It was delightful to see Suzie looking so
well. A special kiss for Peter, for giving up his new
wife to my company for so many hours, and for not
demanding reasons for our hysterical mirth. It was like
those boarding school nights when we stuffed our
mouths with pillows to stifle the giggles, dreading the
footsteps outside the dormitory and the sudden rush of
light when the door opened. Peter was no Sister
Martha, though, to say "Now girls, what's all this
noise?" although I'm willing to bet he felt like it often
enough.

So extra hugs to make up, and meanwhile,
Love, Hannah.

ooOoo

7

Christabel Fraser

FROM   Hannah Pascoe
TO: Chrissiefras@coolmail.net
SENT: 23 January 2008
SUBJECT: Guess who?

Please thank Suzie for her card, and yes of course she
can stay overnight on Thursday. And no, I won't make
her doss on the floor in any old corner. She can have a
whole room and a whole bed to doss in.

Guess who I bumped into this morning? Do you
remember Bill Box? You'll have to cast your mind back
about 15 years to my first tour in West Yorkshire, with
a final short season in Leeds and time to spare at the
end of it. I was introduced to this rumbustious person

up to his hairline in local politics. He was agent for a Liberal candidate (that's what they were then, not LibDems) in one of their Borough Council elections. Can't remember which.   We met in a pub after the show and he talked me into delivering leaflets and knocking on doors. God knows how!

You have to hand it to him. Anyone who gets me knocking on doors must be a megasalesman *extraordinaire*, and to add to the wonder of it all, I enjoyed it. Not that much talking was necessary from me, I just carried the clipboard and Bill talked for both.

His candidate won, which confirmed all I suspected about Bill, since in those days Liberals generally didn't. Then he threw this blazer of a thank you party at his home. It was both entertaining and educational, being surrounded by a colourful assortment of local activitists, some predictably wearing beards, some wearing sandals and one or two wearing both. This was some time ago, you understand, when these were *de rigueur* for the Liberal Party dress code and I daresay not at all as it is now. A few were more anonymous, indistinguishable from party activists anywhere I suppose, and one or two hairstyles were debatable. In fact I felt just a smidgeon too tidy! But they all shared one marked, identifiable characteristic – enthusiasm for their political party or their candidate or both. Since on this occasion they were also jubilant, the result turned out to be just a bit noisy.

Bill was an exhilarating companion, if not always a comfortable one, and I was never quite sure that I liked him – but as he seemed rather manifestly to like me I enjoyed his entertainment value and looked no further. Certainly he infused those last few days in Leeds with marvellous zim and zest and I remember them with real pleasure.

Anyway, there we were, and there I was feeling

rather disjointed, and Bill said I ought to go into politics myself. "You're a natural," He said.

"A natural coward," I replied, "so no thank you. Not enough skin."

He pulled a face, took away my empty glass and appeared a minute later with a full one which he handed to me with heavy courtesy and an ironic twinkle.

"That's rubbish and you know it. You've got personality with knobs on as well as brains. All you need is the motivation."

"Which is precisely what I haven't got," I said. "Honestly, I'm not the least bit interested in politics. Not really. I've been doing this for fun and because it's different, something I haven't done before."

He is a large man with a hefty paunch, a thick wadge of white hair and bushy eyebrows, a fairly prominent (everso slightly spongy) nose and thick, fleshy lips. At that moment the thick, fleshy lips were pursed in disapproval.

"You don't really mean that, of course," he said, a trifle dismissively I felt. "Politics comes into every area of your life, including your profession, so if you want any sort of say in how it's run you have to be interested in politics or you might as well close the door on the world – shut up shop and never complain again."

At that point his son wandered past, apparently looking for someone. His father grabbed his arm and presented him to me.

"This is Alan," he said, and Alan smiled with what can only be described as shy charm. He was probably about 35 but looked less, and I should state right now that he was also impossibly good looking, with dark curling hair and soulful brown eyes.

I wondered why I hadn't seen him before, his father being agent, and he explained that he'd been helping with the election in his own ward some miles away in Ossett. "Dad didn't need any help, but my own lot did," he smiled.

"Did your lot win?" I asked.

"No, I'm sorry to say we didn't. My father's the one for that, and there aren't too many of him about. Unfortunately," he added, giving me another shot of the charm from under long, dark eyelashes.

"This is Hannah Pascoe. She's an actress," Bill explained, almost, I felt, as an apology for my ignorance. There was no gleam of recognition from Alan. I was hardly surprised. A not very well known theatre company does not give one world-wide appeal, or even local appeal most of the time, and Maisie Mitchell was still only a distant, as yet unborn creation in her author's imagination.

"Really?" the eyes and the question were polite but entirely uninterested. I might as well have been introduced as a bus driver, though now I come to think of it he might have shown more enthusiasm if I had. Women bus drivers were not at that time two a penny. Actresses always are.

The shy charm drifted away, I suspected in search of more nubile prey among the younger, high-energy helpers. Bill watched him with pride.

"He'll be candidate next time," he said. "Chairman of the constituency party this year and a bloody good one. He'll make a cracking good M.P one day, you'll see."

"That's nice," I said, rather lamely I felt. "What does he do?"

Bill was puzzled. "Do?"

"Do for a living?" I explained.

He grinned and made quotation mark signs in the air with his fingers. "You mean has he got a 'Proper Job'? Yes, he's a teacher, and he's married with two children, a boy and a girl."

"I'm surprised he has time for politics, especially if he wants to get into Parliament. Teaching is usually a full time commitment, or so my teacher friends tell me."

Bill nodded several times over his glass, lips pursed. "It's like everything else, once you get the bug you'll always find the time."

"Doesn't his wife mind?"

He had the grace to hesitate. "Well, yes, to be honest I think she does. It happens sometimes. She's not interested herself, you see. Not here tonight, for example."

I felt a wave of sympathy for this absent and apparently neglected wife, but was allowed no further opportunity to discuss her as someone banged a table and Bill went away to announce a victory speech by the successful candidate.

"Here he is," he shouted. There was a burst of clapping and much stamping of feet. "*Councillor* Tony Watkins."

I don't remember the speech, nor do I remember much of what was left of the evening, but I certainly remember going back to my digs in the early morning afloat with adrenalin and euphoria. I left Leeds within days and never saw Bill Box again, though we sent each other Christmas cards for a while.

This morning he came galloping out of the bank and knocked my handbag out of hand. It emptied itself into the gutter and we bent together to gather up the horrid assortment of bits. (Why does one never drop a handbag when it's tidy?), and he said, "Good God, if it isn't young Hannah Pascoe."

"Some things never change," I laughed and retrieved a lipstick and some supermarket receipts from his hand, relieved he had made no remark about the rest of the bric-a-brac – which he certainly would have done years before, being the sort of male who can be expected to make patronising jokes if given the sniff of a chance. Then I realised he had been too preoccupied to notice the bric-a-brac.

He said he was down from Wakefield to see Alan, who was in "a spot of bother." Accused of dangerous driving, he said, and could he, Bill, give me a ring?

I said yes, of course, and gave him my phone number. "What happened?"

He said he'd explain fully later, but Alan had knocked a girl off her bicycle and injured her so badly it had been touch and go for a few days whether she'd survive. Luckily she was out of danger now, but the affect on Alan had been deadly.

"Good heavens!" I was astonished. "That's the second I've heard of in a couple of weeks. Some people I know actually went past something of the sort on their way to my leaving party."

"Really?" Bill was frowning, staring at me, his brain obviously engrossed in high speed calculation. "What date was that, and where was it?"

I told him.

"That," he said slowly "is interesting. *Very* interesting. In fact I think it might be a godsend." He leaped suddenly into life. "Look, I must dash, but if you give me your phone number I'll ring you later today. You can help."

I gave him my mobile number but was too surprised to ask any more questions, and in any case wasn't given the opportunity as Bill raised his hand in brief salute and vanished round the corner.

I expect all will be revealed in course of time. Meanwhile I've been playing the piano, which was so surprised at the sudden attention that at first it declined to open its lid, and then some of the keys rebelled and refused to utter at all. I shall defer to its reproaches and call the tuner, but am pleased to find that while technique is definitely shabby, I haven't quite lost the touch.

Michael, however, is sulking. Not sure why. That too, I imagine, will be revealed in course of time.

Till then, all love, Hannah

ooOoo

8

Christabel Fraser

FROM   Hannah Pascoe
TO: Chrissiefras@coolmail.net
SENT: 26 January 2008
SUBJECT: The Boxes

It was good to have Suzie here last night. She gave me a ride in her car. Delightful and irrepressibly joyful she is. How has she come through your horrifying divorce with so few obvious scars? She brought the Grieg lyric pieces (which I'm trying hard to play) and the whodunit (which I began to read immediately) and left a feeling of space behind her. The house is suddenly too quiet.

Lucy was sorry to miss her but will be away for another month yet. Michael was very taken with Suzie, impressed with her common sense (because Lucy hasn't got any, he says) and we all had a very good time. Quite by chance Timothy rang from Paris to say he hopes to come home for a weekend very soon (*sans* Francine, who stays in Paris because of her job). He rang to make sure we would be here when he comes. It will be extraordinarily nice to see him after what seems a very long time. I hardly dare complain. I was an absentee mother for most of his important years, pursuing my own iffy and chancy career, and now that he's establishing himself in his, the biter is bit!

I am becoming that social hazard – a Proud Mum – my son in demand as a gifted lighting designer and my daughter with more acting talent in one fingernail than I ever had or ever will have in mine – plus the vital quality I definitely didn't have – a love of acting for its own sake.

Poor Michael, to suffer a wife and **both** children in the theatre, yet though I've retired from mine now he doesn't seem particularly happy with that either. I suspect he doesn't quite know what to do with me.

Bill Box rang the other day as promised, inviting me for a drink, so we went to the Buttress and sat warmly inside the lounge bar watching the weir, (with its resident heron perched miraculously on one leg, of course, and looking exactly how herons are supposed to look). The Buttress is the most enchanting pub in the world, but why is the sound of rushing water so soothing? A running tap is merely infuriating.

Bill told me a long story about Alan which I only half understood because he was too worried to be succinct. But although the situation sounds a bit complicated, I understood he was telling me because I might be in a position to help.

"It's obviously the same accident as the one I heard about," I agreed.

"There couldn't be two like that on the same night," he said, "so your finding witnesses could be really momentous. But in any case you know a lot of people and have influence outside."

A small surge of anxiety made me glance at him over the rim of my glass. I felt he was putting too much weight on my purely illusory power as a *celeb,* and would be disappointed.

"Exactly what do you want me to do?"

"For a start, you can tell me as much as you can about the story you heard. Who told you, and why, for example, and do you know anything about the witnesses who didn't stop?"

"Yes I do. One of them is my friend's niece."

Bill put his hand over mine. He seemed genuinely concerned so I gave him the benefit of the doubt and left it there.

"Well then," he said, "Could you chase them up a bit?"

Realising this was coming I considered the matter, recalling the hostile young man in the black tee shirt who declared one should never be involved with the pig police. Persuading him to co-operate seemed as likely as getting his police pigs to fly. But Karen, free of his repressive influence, might be more amenable.

"Tell me exactly what happened," Bill said again, so I related as much as I knew – or remembered!

"But where is Alan now?" I asked, "and what is he doing here anyway? I thought he lived somewhere near Wakefield."

Bill removed his hand from mine and rubbed his face in perplexity. He sighed. "He did. In Ossett. He's been here six months now. Split up from Elizabeth. Divorce was finalised a couple of months ago. What with one thing and another he's low, very low."

"I'm sorry. This won't be helping, will it?"

"No m'dear, it isn't helping at all. I want him to come back with me to Wakefield, but he won't. Rather stay and face it out, he says, but I confess I'm worried about him."

"But if his job is here….?"

"He's been off sick since the accident."

We were both silent, thinking of the implications, then I asked: "Is there anything else I can do? I'll do what I can, of course."

Bill put his hand on mine again. "Tell you what," he said, "You could give him a ring and perhaps call on him."

"Of course I will," I exclaimed. "There are things I shall need to ask him in any case."

Bill wrote a number on a slip of paper and handed it to me. He seemed relieved. "You'll be good for him," he said, "Buck him up. Lucky chance, bumping into you the way I did."

We finished our drinks and left the weir to the heron standing peacefully in the shallows. Bill explained that he was leaving for Wakefield in the morning, and asked if he could keep in touch with me. "You can tell me how Alan is," he said, "since he doesn't always come out with it himself. Doesn't want to worry me, apparently."

I said yes, certainly, and we went back to our own lives, myself not sure precisely what I had let myself in for and mildly resentful of possible disruption to my new lifestyle, but flattered all the same at being thought of in terms of rescuer of politicians in distress, personable or not! Besides, there is the Curiosity Factor. What will the charming 35 year old look like 15 years on?

I know what his father looks like now – well into his seventies, a paunchy, raunchy sort of man with still-young ideas, a high colour and the same full mouth. And the same driving energy. I found myself regarding him speculatively, deciding that as a piece of male pulchritude he was too fat and too old, which is, of course, unfair – especially the 'too old' part. After all, what does age matter? And how dare I, at 58, write off as *passé* anyone older than myself? I mean to say, in not too many years time I shall be where he is now, and decidedly miffed if and when someone 20 or so years younger than me makes the same judgement about myself.

Strange how that thought has only this minute occurred to me. Be that as it may, Bill Box is a man whom I would prefer as a friend rather than an enemy – disconcerting and a mite intimidating notwithstanding the faint gleam which still lurks in a mildly lascivious eye. Right now, though, whatever tiny spark smoulders there is being snuffed out by worry over his son.

I shall let you know what happens when (or if) I visit Alan Box, which for some reason I seem to be putting off.

Till then, all love,
Hannah.

P S. I told Michael later about meeting Bill. He remembered my brief incursion into politics, and the desire to change the world which followed it, and smiled into his newspaper. But he was genuinely shocked about Alan's accident. "What a terrible thing!" he said. It is indeed a terrible thing.

ooOoo

9

Christabel Fraser

FROM   Hannah Pascoe
TO: Chrissiefras@coolmail.net
SENT: 29 January 2008
SUBJECT: More Boxes

How very self-centred my emails have become. I am secretly ashamed of them. Only your repeated assurances that you enjoy getting them, *and* reading them, gives me the confidence to continue.

After all, you did ask!

But even as I write it I wonder if this is true, or if Pascoe Speaks With Forked Tongue. For somewhere there is the horrid suspicion that I would write them anyway, whether you read them or not. As a lifelong, compulsive writer-downer, I just have to hope you get around to reading a word here or there when there's nothing better to do.

The writer-downer instinct has landed me in scrapes in the past – some funny, some not – and no doubt will again. I have strong memories of seeing loving but strict parents and a lordly older brother picking up pieces of paper on which I had, at a very tender age, composed romantic little stories, and feeling very hurt when my family fell about with merriment. There is a sort of residual horror even now at the sight of anyone peering at stray documents. I have quite a to-do not to snatch them out of their unsuspecting and (usually) innocent fingers!

But in you I am reposing full trust that if my communications ever graduate from merely indiscreet to downright nuclear, they will be sent where they belong – into limbo. Even that, though, isn't always as final as one would wish, is it? I have been reliably informed that items seemingly deleted forever can still be retrieved by those with the know-how to do it – so I promise not to endanger your reputation by adding libel or pornography to whatever indiscretions I may be guilty of.

You ask if my novel is progressing. Well it isn't. As always, whenever I intend to get down to it, a thousand other things scream to be done first and I put it off.

'Twas ever thus.

Meanwhile, I give in to the temptation to write long emails to you instead, as you have so nobly and generously suggested, and hope to do so with more than usual care although, I fear, at more than usual length.

Upon your head be it.

Since giving up Maisie (sounds like a comedy film title), I have become aware of the astonishing number of acquaintances I have these days. Lucy once said I knew 70,000 people. Well, maybe not quite 70,000, but the mail on my desk seems to prove something of her point – letters from colleagues, old school friends, college friends, fans (a great many of those, I'm happy to say), all saying how much they enjoyed Maisie and how sorry they are that she isn't still among those present. They also tell me of their affection for me personally, though how they manage that is a mystery. Maisie and I seem to have become inescapably mixed up in the general mind. So although I may have retired, it doesn't feel like it yet. Rather like picking all the fruit from our apple tree. When one has baskets and baskets of the stuff one is not aware of having stripped the branches bare. It's only when the apples are either eaten or have gone soft and rotten that one notices the empty tree.

At some point I am going to notice my empty fame tree, when strangers stop recognising my name or face, when friends no longer bother because I'm only one more ordinary person. And even that statement is hypocritical as I don't regard myself as in any way ordinary, and have no intention of becoming so.

Whatever the truth of it, I now have to find out who I really am. Don't know yet, as my personality has always been mangled and enmeshed in Michael's and

Timothy's and Lucy's, in a hundred jobs followed by a series of small stage parts and ultimately in Maisie. But mostly it's been what I thought people wanted it to be, or how I felt was most flattering to Hannah. If I'm only attractive when I smile, I will be an indefatigable smiler. If my friends want to be entertained I shall entertain them. And if, as often happens, they like a sympathetic ear for problems, an ear is what they'll get.

Why? Because I need them to like me? Or love me? Is that it? Do I only ever see myself in the mirror of other peoples' responses? To a certain extent I suppose that's what we all do – perpetually pass down a hall of reflecting glass, most of it distorted like the ones in a funfair sideshow.

Incidentally, some of my fan letters include proposals of marriage. Even more lately, which is not only extraordinary but very heartening.

I've put off telling you about Alan Box because I don't know what to say. He is at once an interesting anecdote and a disturbing event, not so much by disturbing me personally as by my awareness of being involved in something, committed to something of wider significance than would seem at first glance. His problem is legal, political, emotional, spiritual and deeply psychological all at the same time, and I don't know which strand to pick up first.

Please note, I am not asking myself whether to pick up any strands at all. That's a decision I seem to have arrived at already, almost without conscious thought. Perhaps I feel challenged, or perhaps the problem has appealed to so many facets of my own persona that in helping Alan get his back together I shall be straightening out my own.

He is an intellectual exercise. He is also a psychological one.

I rang him last night, after looking at his telephone

number so many times during the afternoon that in the end I dialled it from memory! But of course there was no reply – an anticlimax after all the puttings-off-until-after-tea, or coffee, or Martini or after I'd listened to the news.

I had to drive out later to pick up some bread and potatoes, so I studied my A-Z guide, drove the car in the direction of Church Street and parked not quite outside his door, clutching a pre-written note in case he should still be out. He wasn't. For a few minutes I wished he had been.

He is, of course, older. I'd have spotted him in the street as someone I knew without quite knowing why or how, with that maddening half-recognition which stops one from going to sleep. But apart from a curious young-old quality in his face, there is an even more important factor. He has a fresh scar running from his left cheek upwards into his scalp, with a patch around it where the hair has been shaved. The sight is disconcerting at first, making it almost impossible to focus on anything else.

After a first, surprised glance, I called up the old stage tricks and looked into his eyes instead. They were polite, puzzled, large, deep and luminous. I explained who I was and why I was there, and he let me in. Then he preceded me into a tiny sitting room where a sofa covered in a red blanket entirely filled up one wall, bookcases filled another, and books, pens and piles of papers lay on a small rectangular table in the middle. Two shirts and a pullover were tidily draped across the back of the sofa. The room badly needed painting and the wallpaper was a thundery orange.

"I should explain this is not my house," he said, "It belongs to a friend and I'm renting it while he's away. Perhaps you'd like some coffee?"

I said that would be nice, to give him something to

do and me time to recover. Bill had said nothing about an injury, although from what Mel Kendrick has told us I should have been expecting it.

By the time he had returned with two mugs and a bag of sugar, I'd looked around the room, noted as much of his book selection as I could read from my perch on his sofa, not quite feeling up to peering more closely so soon after arrival, and felt sufficiently at ease to smile my thanks and point to the loaded table.

"You look busy," I said, "Am I disturbing your work?"

He sat at the other end of the sofa, there being nothing else to sit on, and regarded his hands, which were resting on his lap. "No, I'm not busy," he said, "in fact I'm glad. It's nice to be disturbed."

Silence fell while we sipped and each waited for the other to speak.

"I hope you don't mind me calling on spec like this," I said at last, "but I tried ringing and you were out, so I thought...."

He looked up suddenly, and there was the shy charm, fresh minted with no years between, only today I saw it as natural, not a thing put on to ease guests or facilitate the chase. It was there. As much part of him as the curl of his hair or the curve of his top lip. "Yes, I had to go out to the shops in the end. There's a limit to the length of time one can stay indoors without tea, coffee, bread and milk. And cigarettes," he added, pointing to the packet beside him. He picked it up and gestured an invitation.

"No thanks, I don't smoke," I said.

"Neither did I until this month. I'd given it up two years ago and now I'm trying to give them up again. Not very successfully I'm afraid." He put a cigarette in his mouth and lit it.

"You don't have to tell me anything," I said, "but

your father seemed to think I was in a position to help you, possibly as a valuable witness, though I'm not sure how to go about that."

Once again his eyes were on his hands, twisting the cigarette from side to side to make the smoke curl in patterns.

"I don't know either. It isn't simple."

I waited in silence, not moving, trying to breathe peacefully. I wanted his confidence, and signs of stress or impatience from me might send him away like a strange cat on a wall. Then he took a breath, squared his shoulders and turned both palms upwards.

"I knocked a young girl off her bicycle and almost killed her. It was dark and I don't remember much. I do know I was driving along this B road into Bristol. It was quite bendy, with not many straight stretches. There was a car behind me trying to overtake. He was tail-gating, flashing his lights at me. But there wasn't much I could do on a strange road at night, so he had to stay where he was"

He paused and took another deep breath. "Except that he didn't. He pulled out. I don't remember much after that, except thinking he was a fool to try it with a bend coming up, so I slowed down a bit to give him enough room. Then something shadowy flashed in front of me and I had nowhere to go. So I swerved to avoid whatever it was and that's all I know. I do vaguely remember standing in the road shouting about Katy, and I think there was someone else there. But then it all gets mixed up again." He paused. "I must have passed out, because I came to myself properly in hospital. They gave me some tests and the police breathalysed me." He touched his head, "They stitched all this up." There was another even longer pause. Then, so quietly I could hardly hear him, he said "I thought I'd killed her, but don't know how I knew."

He looked at me briefly and away again. "I was going to stand for the City Council next May, here in this ward, but I've told them I can't do it. It wouldn't be fair. They'd suffer as well as me from bad publicity and I couldn't do that. Not under the circumstances. I know what happens in these elections. Besides, you'd have to agree I'm not exactly in the best condition at the moment."

He paused and waited. Finally he looked up again, directly into my eyes as though only in that way could his next words be fully understood or appreciated. "Five years ago my daughter was knocked off her bicycle and killed by a hit and run driver."

We sat eye to eye for eternity. Then I closed mine and put a hand on his arm.

"Oh my dear," I said. My lashes were filled with tears which eventually spilt down my face and onto my chin, but I didn't try to wipe them away. He smiled his irony and, I suppose, his thanks for my caring.

"So I don't really see what you can do - what anyone can do."

The grief in the room was so tangible and engulfing that for a moment I was washed over by it. Then suddenly I became all practical, uncrossed my legs and sat square.

"Well, out of three problems I might at least help with one," I said at last. "It's a long shot, but I just might be able to produce witnesses to tell us just what did happen, although I must be honest and admit I don't know what they'll say, or even if they'll want to talk about it. But at least it's a beginning."

"Witnesses? As far as I know there weren't any, which is a problem all by itself."

"At a party last week there were three people who had passed an accident exactly like yours on the way there. Two of them seemed to be pretty close to the time it happened, but the third arrived immediately afterwards. He called the police and the ambulance on his mobile. Do you remember anything at all?"

He shook his head. He seemed much struck by the coincidence. "But that's extraordinary," he said. "There can't have been two similar accidents at the same time. But how do you come to know about both?"

I smiled. "No, I'm not psychic. I bumped into your father, or rather he bumped into me, and explained why he was down here to see you. And the story rang bells."

"I'm glad they did," Alan said, "but nothing your friends say can alter the fact that I nearly killed a child."

"Rubbish!" I said stoutly. "For a start you didn't kill her. And anyway you have no idea what happened and you mayn't have been responsible at all. What's the position so far?"

"I've been charged with dangerous driving, but they haven't set a date for the hearing yet." He paused again, kneading the back of one hand with the fingers of the other. "I've rung the hospital, where the little girl is, several times, but they won't tell me anything. You have to be a relative before they give you information. Last time, though, they said she was "comfortable." It's better than nothing, I suppose. And a million times better than dead." He paused. "I wanted to send flowers but the hospital doesn't accept them."

We stared at each other without smiling, and I suddenly felt it was time for me to leave. We had both had enough.

"I'll make a start," I promised, "and I'll ring you as soon as there's anything to say."

We stood up. "Thank you," he said. He escorted me to the door and waited for me to drive away before going back into the house.

What have I promised to do, Chrissie? Whatever it

is looks like taking up some time, so it's as well there is some to take up! Meanwhile, Michael is due home in ten minutes and I haven't even started to cook yet.

Love in a panic,
Hannah

ooOoo

10

Christabel Fraser

FROM   Hannah Pascoe
TO: Chrissiefras@coolmail.net
SENT: 31 January 2008
SUBJECT: Garbo Lookalike

Many thanks for your card. You are perfectly right, I'm getting rather tired of this "Jokey Hannah" image. Really I'd love to be like Greta Garbo, beautiful of skull and soulful of expression. One can then be glamorous asleep as well as awake (I wish!) and wouldn't need this ghastly smoke screen. Happily for me, you are not taken in by it, for which I thank the God of surprises.

Andrew, my youthful admirer, turned up today bearing gifts in the form of several pounds of potatoes and a cauliflower, produce from his market garden.

A serious young man, he handed me the cauliflower with grave courtesy and for a second or two it took the form and colour of priceless orchids. He did not, however, declare his love like the troubadour he is, but simply ate his way through my chocolate cake. If he ever finds out I'm 59 he will probably forget about being a troubadour and concentrate solely on the cake, since he is only 26.

I jest! He may well have a girl friend tucked away somewhere, though he never mentions one, so it's once again a case of fame being an aphrodisiac – which won't last long because unless I become a famous writer the glamour mist will melt in a twinkling. He will then see me with eyes of truth.

There is a fairy dust about "celebs" (Why do I use jargon words when I hate them?) which invests them with more intelligence, beauty, romance of soul (and of course talent) than it's possible for any one little body to contain. I have had my opinion courted on all kinds of esoteric topics (Try saying that quickly. It rolls around the tongue like a plucked guitar string), most of which I knew nothing whatever about. And I was only Maisie Mitchell. Had I been a real, proper, top-notch STAR would I have come to believe myself as omniscient and wise as people said? A frightening thought.

As for Alan, I began my researches at once by ringing Janine and asking for Karen's name, address and phone number. I explained why, and enlisted Jan's support and sympathy. She agreed that Karen on her own is a safer bet than Karen plus Hatchet Jaw, but as K moved in with him some time ago it will now be a question of timing. I'll ring her at work this afternoon. Her work, not mine – she's a receptionist for a big insurance firm.

I also rang Mel Kendrick but found myself speaking into his answering machine, so am now waiting for him to get in touch. I shall try him again later today, but could, of course, leave a note for him at the studio. If I can't get him any other way I'll do it tomorrow.

Meanwhile, many thanks again for the card and note and words of encouragement. Next time you see me I promise not to smile.

    All love,

    Hannah

P S. Lucy tells me she's sick of being away from Andy and has asked her agent to find work nearer home. So even she finds enthusiasm for a stage career coming second in the end to LERV.

ooOoo

11

Christabel Fraser

FROM   Hannah Pascoe
TO: Chrissiefras@coolmail.net
SENT: 2 February 2008
SUBJECT: Not a lot!

Are my emails getting too long? I'd hate to bore you into insensibility – easy to do in written form because one can't see the yawns. Talk is such a different matter. What you might call real audience participation. The instant one sees a glazing eye, or the glance drifting off around the room in search of diversion, one knows it's time to wrap up. Not that everyone wraps up when they should, but at least the signs are obvious to anyone with half a brain.

    Fortunately for you, there is a 'Reply' button on my messages via which you may communicate your own vital information and risk boring *me* into semi-paralysis instead, although I must say you never do, never have and almost certainly never will. So I can carry on being as self indulgent as I please.

There is, however, very little of startling import to tell. A simple diary of events should suffice.

Lunch yesterday with Anne (red hair, runs a boutique in our local Shopping Mail), followed by tea in an Olde Tea Shoppe with Alice, and an evening with Myra watching Miss Marple on the telly. She wasn't sure if I wanted to watch Wayside Walk, and seemed quite relieved when I said a very definite, positive NO. Not yet anyway.

She, Myra, says they are all missing me and it isn't ever going to be the same again. Tom, she says, mopes and will not be comforted, which I refuse to believe. He is a card, and cards do not mope. I asked if I had been supplanted yet, and she said not to her knowledge, but Tom has apparently phoned me countless times to no avail. Where am I? he wants to know.

Michael went to his monthly L.D.C. meeting and currently has two patients with exceedingly complicated problems, so comes home even more tired and even less communicative than usual. He's been extravagant with wine this month. Last night we got through two whole bottles each. I do not complain, you understand, except insofar as wine makes me talk more and Michael talk less, so my words tend to bounce unrewarded from folded hands and two closed eyes.

My agent rang with the offer of a part in a TV commercial. I was tempted but remained firm. Told her for the 70th time I had retired and meant to stay that way, and she said "Yes, yes! Of course you do!" I now know it's possible to pat someone's head from long distance. I also know when I am not being believed.

I rang Karen at work and arranged to meet her tonight. She has no transport, so, not wishing to become entangled with the pugnacious Mark, I'll pick her up at 7.30 and take her wherever she wishes to go in search of food and drink – but mostly, I confess, drink. Quite heartlessly, and with incredible ruthlessness, I hope to loosen her little tongue. At present there is no pity in me for any girl silly enough to fall in love with so catastrophic an object as Hatchet Jaw.

There – this is a shorter message. I feel virtuous. Perhaps in future my missives can be restricted to a ten minute read instead of 30, and so avoid filling up beyond redemption not only your hard drive but at least two memory discs and whatever spare time your lifestyle grants you.

Love, Hannah.

ooOoo

12

Christabel Fraser

FROM   Hannah Pascoe
TO: Chrissiefras@coolmail.net
SENT: 6 February 2008
SUBJECT: The softening-up of Karen

Thank you. If your preference really is for long, long emails, then I will certainly oblige and you will be happy to get this one! There is much to say.

Mel Kendrick responded with gratifying speed to my message on his answerphone. He rang back within hours, to tell me they were all missing me and ask when the hell I was going in to see them. I reminded him of the party and the accident and he said God yes, he'd never forget it. So I asked if he could remember as much as possible, in the greatest possible detail, so he asked why and I explained. Then he said he'd try. I told him I was out to investigate little Karen and needed him, Mel, to add reassurance and persuasion if and when she could be brought to make a police statement against tough opposition from her beloved!

He groaned.

"You see, we have to circumvent this poisonous boyfriend and the only person in the world who can do that is you. She adores you, poor little mutt that she is."

Mel made suitable noises down the phone, which deceived me not at all. "Come on Mel, there's a dear," I said, "Save a fellow human being from injustice and despair, and at the moment I think he's convinced he'll land up in gaol for manslaughter, or because the girl hasn't died, at least dangerous driving. Karen may be the answer. At least let me tell her you're on our side, even if you can't bring yourself to tell her personally."

Mel agreed, of course, as I knew he would. The prospect of giving Hatchet Jaw one in the eye would have been enough all by itself, but there is the added lure of playing the brilliant new role of Mel-To-The-Rescue. He promised to ring Karen herself over the next day or so.

Meanwhile I started the softening up process by whisking her to the pub of her choice. Mark was not at home, so there was no embarrassment – this time anyway. I anticipate plenty in the future! He plays darts and goes out fairly frequently which, if I were in Karen's shoes, would not worry me one bit. (For preference I'd arrange for him never to be home at all.) But this seems to upset little K. Oh well, each to his own! She was no end flattered, which was of course the intention, and kept saying "No really, you choose." So in the end I did, feeling rather guilty because I was about to abuse in abominable fashion all this overwhelming gratitude.

We went to the Buttress again, the pub by the weir to which my soul seems to fly, since I obviously have a penchant for sipping a G & T to the sound of gushing torrents. Karen chose beer, which surprised me. She looks more like a lager or Bacardi-and-coke girl, but perhaps she's intent on muscle building. She might need it!

I began by asking if she had thought any more about acting and how, if she did, I may be able to give her some advice. I have no conscience. This went down almost too well, since for a little while the conversation stayed obstinately on Stage when I wanted it diverted to Alan. However, I did manage to remind her (two beers and many words later) about the party and the accident.

She went awful quiet, Chrissie. *Awful* quiet. I then explained, in graphic, not to say ghoulish detail how this poor chap was in a dreadful state because his own daughter had been killed in the same way, and how there were apparently no witnesses etc. And how she was *the only person in the world* who could save his sanity, his political career and, of course, his job which could be hanging in the balance.

There were tears in her eyes when I'd finished, which was only right and proper. Otherwise I would have considered myself seriously lacking in expertise. The point then was to cash in on them. I did.

"Would it be a relief to talk about it?" I suggested gently, and she gulped. Then she nodded, gulped again and blew her nose.

"Miss Pascoe," she began.

"Hannah please," I corrected, and touched her hand with my finger. The eyes, now swimming entrancingly, were lifted to mine in fervent admiration. She murmured "Thank you," and sniffed.

The story came out in a tumble. She and Mark had

54

been driving back to Bristol, rather fast because they were late and she didn't want to miss even five minutes of my party.

"It was my fault," she said, "I kept saying 'Oh please hurry,' and then we got behind this car and the driver wasn't going fast enough for Mark, so he kept trying to overtake him. It was quite dark by then and the road was a bit bendy and not very wide, but Mark knows that road really well, and we were on that straightish bit of Stoney Hill before it bends to the left, and there's that little lane off to the left somewhere. So Mark took a chance and moved out to go past the car, but just as we got level there was a…."

Here Karen paused, as if conscious for the first time of the full significance of what she was telling me. "There was a….."

I said "Take your time, Sweetie."

Karen took a breath and began moving the salt cellar to and fro on the table.

"There was a sort of bang and a…sort of scrunchy noise. The sort that gives you nightmares. We had to pull out very fast not to hit him, and by that time were coming up to the bend, but I looked back. I told Mark I could see something on the ground and the car was all over the place, and something really awful must have happened so hadn't we better stop. But Mark said no, there was plenty of traffic about and we'd be there for hours. He said 'Do you want to get to this party or not?'"

Karen looked up, directly into my eyes. "Miss Pascoe, the awful thing is I didn't really want to stop. I didn't want to see it. So I didn't argue with him, I just wanted to forget all about it." She smiled dismally, "But of course I couldn't because it all came out at your party. I dream about it and it's on my conscience. In fact I've had nightmares every night since then."

I had felt sorry for Karen before, but I felt even sorrier now. I smiled back and a removed a stray lock of hair from her forehead. There was a temptation to suggest she ease her guilt by doing something positive now, like giving evidence, but I decided against haste and in the end she made the suggestion herself.

"I've been feeling so awful about it," she said, "You've no idea. Especially when Mel came and told us how bad the girl was...." She gulped again and took another sip of beer. "So if there's anything I can do, I think I'd like to help."

I beamed, and felt like shouting "Geronimo!", but instead I said "Wonderful! I expect it will just be a case of telling that story to Alan's solicitor, and the police as well, of course, but I'm not sure of the procedure. We'll have to find out. But what about Mark? Won't he object? I don't think he much cares for the police."

"No, he doesn't," Karen said, looking subdued.

There was silence for a while as we both considered the problem. Then I said, rather more briskly, "How brave are you, Karen?"

Considering the choice was between her conscience and her love for Hatchet Jaw, I wouldn't have put money on her reply.

"Not very." She stared into her glass, swilling the beer gently round and round. "Is this why you wanted to see me tonight? Because of your friend?"

I understood the implication and went for the truth. "Do you mind?" I asked gently.

She looked surprised. "No, why should I? It's just lovely to be here with you."

I was both touched and silenced, marvelling again at the simplicity of those who value me simply because I'm an actress, and waiting hopefully for the day when I'll be valued for myself alone. All else is false, an illusion, and ultimately a disappointment. No-one can successfully pretend for long to be anything other than who and what they really are, and I have this horrid feeling that discerning people can see clean through me to the maggoty core within.

Karen, however, was obviously not one of them. She was in fact both overwrought and overawed, so I thought it better to relax the high drama.

"That's all right, then," I said at last. "Let's get something to eat it. I'm quite peckish myself."

By the time the beer and ham, salad and pita rolls had washed themselves down together, Karen was looking better, hardly the same girl in fact, so I gently re-introduced the topic, knowing the success or failure of Alan's case hung on the courage she may or may not possess.

She'd been chattering happily about the wonderful Mark, so I asked what affect the accident might have on him. "Will he try and stop you?"

"Giving evidence, you mean?"

"Well, at least making a statement," I nodded, watching the large round eyes, the smooth cheeks and the small pointed chin. She looked no more than fourteen years old.

"I'm not sure," she said. "Probably, yes."

"And would he succeed?"

She caught my gaze and didn't smile.

"I don't know. He might. I'd like to think he'd agree, or that I'd be strong enough anyway, even if he didn't. But…would you be around to help?"

"Of course."

"I don't think Mark likes you, but it's got nothing to do with you personally. It's because I do and you're in the theatre. He thinks I'm silly and stage-struck mooning over actors. Just a silly kid!" She pulled a face.

I smiled at her. "He sounds jealous," I said, "Perhaps

he'd like you to moon over him instead."

She giggled suddenly. "He *hates* Mel. He thought it was disgusting an old man of 40-something making up to a young girl like me just because I fainted. He said I made a fool of myself and he was ashamed of me."

I smiled and wondered how Mel would like her description of himself. "I must say you don't sound very repentant."

"No, I'm not," She sounded surprised

"So perhaps you're braver than you thought."

She smiled, looking brighter by the minute, so I left the subject and we finished our drinks and rolls in comfortable agreement. When I delivered her to her door, an hour later, we agreed I should set things in motion and then see what she was prepared to do. Privately I was thinking "Mel, where are you? Come to my aid!"

Now I must contact the relevant authorities, whoever and whatever they are. Simply finding that out is a challenge. The obvious way is to ask Bill or Alan, but I feel inexplicably shy about doing that. Maybe raising their hopes for nothing?

Another part of me is feeling desperately sorry for the child's parents. The nightmare image of Tim or Lucy in that position even now, let alone when they were small, is one I prefer to push away. We just have to hope she carries on recovering without suffering long term injuries.

Life, however, goes on and Mary Quintrell came from next door this morning to drink my coffee and eat my biscuits. She seems nice – helpful and interested but rather timid. I get the impression that crossing our threshold is a brave and daring enterprise, and that she hurries home afterwards to a familiar husband and a strong cup of tea.

Meanwhile Michael is still sulking, but politely. He

spends more time nowadays in his workroom, coming to meals when called but often just late enough to be awkward (When is food cold enough to stand re-heating?) We're perfectly friendly, but conversing less and less. Even his culinary urges have dropped off, though he cooked a delicious Pilaf on Tuesday and promises a chicken and sherry casserole for the weekend.

I am being less than fair. He deserves better than me.

Love to Peter and Suzie.

Hannah

P S. Our beloved son Timothy will be here on Friday for the weekend. Perhaps that will rouse Michael from his present mood.

ooOoo

13

Christabel Fraser

FROM   Hannah Pascoe
TO: Chrissiefras@coolmail.net
SENT: 15 February 2008
SUBJECT: Clever Hannah's come-uppence

I haven't been reading the local papers. I should. This morning Clever-Cloggs here bragged to Janine about my enormous skill in finding Karen and persuading her against gigantic odds etc etc. Now I learn that the local paper ran half a page on the local politician who was involved in a collision with an innocent girl cyclist etc

etc etc.

What's more, not only are the girl's parents grief-stricken and vengeful, they are also politically motivated. Her father is Chairman of one of the opposing parties and her uncle is a local councillor. The paper concerned, one of the more scurrilous of the freebies, referred to Alan as Prospective Candidate, which is incorrect and would have been so even if he **had** been standing, since no candidates are officially named until the start of a campaign. So the poor chap will not only be miserable and angry and conscience-stricken, he'll feel even more guilty in all sorts of directions at once. As if he hasn't got enough to worry about!

Thank you for sending your copy of "The Ladies of Missalonga". If you are really coming over next weekend, will you be able to spare me a little of your time or will it all be taken up with interviews?

Michael and I went to Sam and Meg's for supper last night and it was pleasant – good food, good company and, even better, being "out" together. But I grow more and more tired of *trying*. Trying to please, trying to be intelligent, trying to look the part, whatever that happens to be at any one time.

The rhetorical questions in my last email, asked in fun, struck me as unexpectedly pertinent only after they were written and sent. "Who am I and where have I come from?" I have asked them before but am no nearer the solution. Nor am I any closer to answering the question following logically on – "Where am I going?" I've been too busy playing the lead in my own home soaps "Hannah the all wise, all efficient, all caring Working Wife and Mother", "Hannah the successful, the witty, the elegant", "Good old Jokey Hannah always ready with a merry quip", and of course "Hannah the Strong".

What a load of old codswallop!

Chrissie my old darling, I am looking for someone to love me because I'm a failure, thus putting you on the spot because you can't reassure me without also admitting the failure, which you won't want to do. So I absolve you from comment.

Michael is at a meeting tonight and won't be home until quite late. I shall have a soapy, scented, luscious bath and go to bed.

All love, H.

P S. Shall I ring Alan and Bill before or after the soapy bath?

P P S. That is of course another rhetorical question.

P P P S. Timothy came and stayed till yesterday. It was lovely to see him again, but heaven knows when the next time will be. I invited myself to Paris, since I now have the time for flitting here and there, but can't go yet as he is travelling about, up to the eyebrows in new productions. This freelance life may be precisely suited to his personality but it makes him annoyingly hard to pin down.

ooOoo

14

Christabel Fraser

FROM   Hannah Pascoe
TO: Chrissiefras@coolmail.net
SENT: 17 February 2008

SUBJECT: Oh vision of loveliness!

I've had a busy few days. I rang Alan, who told me his father wanted him back in Wakefield, but he (Alan) had some hospital appointments, and had decided in any case that to leave the city just now would only give credence to the newspaper report. He was of course distressed and angry, and seemed grateful for my call, but when I asked how things were going and if the solicitor or the police had contacted Karen he said rather more was involved than could be explained over the telephone. There was a short pause. Eventually he asked if I would like to visit him, or maybe go for a drink somewhere. I gathered from his tone that the second option wouldn't be his own choice. In view of the scar on his head and face, if I'd been in his position it wouldn't have been my choice either, so I promised to call on him one day soon. He didn't press for a date.

For all I know his hesitation may have nothing at all to do with his scar, and everything to do with me. Suddenly I am uncertain of myself, of my welcome, aware of the awful possibility of being suspected of trapping him into a date.

Surely a first for confident, jokey Hannah – but taken all in all, and quite apart from the existence of a very dear husband, I would prefer a date with fewer problems.

There is something about this man which fires warning shots across my bows.

Karen tells me Alan's solicitor has been in touch and wants to see her. He has also offered to smooth her path further by (a) helping her make her police statement and (b) by talking to Mark himself. So her problem is now imbued with the romantic glow of ADVENTURE.

Suddenly I am very tired. How long does it take to retire? Not that I've been very successful so far, as circumstances seem to keep me trotting, trotting round and round like a donkey on a turntable, and in some puzzling way the stress has remained. The peace I promised myself has not yet materialised, and now my face has come out in a rash all over. It started with an itchy place on my chin, then it spread everywhere and now I'm all red and blotchy and beginning to peel. Yuk!

I shall definitely *not* call Alan until it has all subsided.

To Michael this is all a mystery. Oh, he can see the fatigue and the rash but not enough cause for them. Have I not officially removed myself from the fountain of all this stress? Am I not now a free woman?

His failure to understand is worrying me, and now I'm too weary to argue. I'll write again at the weekend.

Love, Hannah

P S. Sad that we only had a short hour together the other day, but thank you for making time for me, however brief. Your life is now so much busier than mine that I'm ashamed of complaining. I am lucky and ought to shut up.

ooOoo

15

Christabel Fraser

FROM   Hannah Pascoe
TO: Chrissiefras@coolmail.net
SENT: 23 February 2008
SUBJECT: ???

Thanks for the phone call and yes, the rash is past its first startlingly horrid stage and reached something which can be camouflaged by tinted cream and the right sort of powder. At least I'm hoping this is true. It was stupendously awful, first itchy patches, then swollen, shiny patches, and finally flaky, peeling patches. I didn't leave the house, and could have done with a yashmak. Until yesterday, that is, when I felt better enough to make the promised visit to Alan Box.

I might not have gone even yesterday, only Karen called me to say she'd seen Alan's solicitor and actually agreed to make a statement for the police. I told her about the current state of my beauty and she was all concern and understanding. And when she arrived on my doorstep later I hadn't been at the camouflage creams, so she saw the remains of my affliction in all its hideousness.

"Oh Miss Pascoe," she breathed, "It must have been awful for you."

I said it hadn't been very nice but everything was clearing up nicely, and we had a comfortable coze – tea and cakes by the fire on a wet and rather miserable afternoon.

She told me all about her chat with the solicitor and how he'd said she was a "very public spirited young lady," and I said Mel was impressed with her too, which impressed *her.*

So yesterday morning I looked hard in the mirror, decided my appearance had returned to as near normal as anyone could hope for in the time, sloshed on some cover-up and phoned Alan. Please note that I put on the makeup *before* phoning, which didn't strike me as odd until afterwards. Is there a deep psychological significance in there somewhere?

On being told about Karen, he invited me to his

house again, so I went and was again plied with coffee out of unmatched mugs. One was inscribed "Don't bother me," and the other with musical notes and what seemed to be Beethoven's signature. A fair indication of character, I'd have said. I drank from Beethoven.

He told me about the accident. He'd been to a party conference in Weston-Super-Mare and was driving home along a B road to keep an appointment with some constituents at 8.30pm. He was helping them with a claim for compensation. He hadn't had anything to drink, wasn't in a vast hurry and was preoccupied with ideas from the conference, and wondering how to solve the claims problem. He said he noticed a car coming up very fast behind him, flashing its lights, but as there was a bend coming up and a side lane just ahead on the left, there wasn't much he could do about it.

What happened next is a jumble in his mind. He remembers the car overtaking him, and after that nothing except for little surreal images, like illustrations or cinema flashbacks. At one point he can see himself standing in the road looking down at something, but his mind shies away even now from any recognition of what he saw. The policeman told him he was shouting "Katy, Katy", which confused everyone for a while because they assumed he knew the child. What they didn't know was that he was reliving his own tragedy.

Apparently he was pulled away, sobbing and shouting. Then he woke up on a trolley being wheeled down hospital corridors, miles and miles of them he said, and the overhead lights were mixed up in his mind with cats'-eyes in the road. He thought he was upside down and couldn't understand why he hadn't fallen into the cat's-eyes, but decided his safety belt must have been holding him up. It took a while to adjust to reality and he lay for hours in a permanent nightmare, knowing that Katy was dead and believing he had just killed her himself. The truth when it dawned didn't help much, for now there were two children to grieve about – and this one he believed he really had killed. He only found out later that she'd survived.

His head was injured when he hit the tree because a low branch went through the windscreen. Unfortunately his car was too old for the sophistication of an airbag, but at least the safety belt stopped him from worse damage, although it gave him a few bruises. The doctors in the hospital kept him in for a few days while they stitched up the cuts and tested him for various things. They'd shaved the front of his head, but told him the scar would fade in time and the hair grow back. I have the impression he doesn't much care.

As there were no witnesses and the overtaking car hadn't stopped, the police had to charge him with dangerous driving, but are still looking for clues in the road and on the girl's bicycle. There are no houses on either side of that particular stretch of road, so until Karen's testimony there was nothing to convince him personally that he wasn't entirely to blame. He just didn't remember enough to know! He understands that the police have made a long and detailed study of the road for skid marks, and took the bicycle away. The lamp was broken in the accident, of course, but it seems they can find out whether it broke during the accident or was faulty before, and they can do the same with the brakes. Technology is a wonderful thing! Anyway, the girl had come out from a side lane into an unlit B road, with a nasty bend not far away. I keep wondering why a ten year old girl should have been cycling along unlit roads at 7 o'clock on a dark, winter evening. Where were her parents for heaven's sake?

I am inexpressibly sorry for him, even more than for the girl's parents, because his daughter really did die.

But how easy is it to point out all the arguments against his guilt, yet how difficult not to make those very arguments sound trite and unbearable.

He is a hard man to assess. On the one hand his eyes hold a kind of solemn honesty, almost an apology for the truth – "This is my opinion and I won't waver in it even though you may disagree and it may even hurt you, and if it does I am deeply sorry..." And on the other, he tends to be cautious, so one is obliged to base one's verdict as much on what he doesn't say as on what he does.

I think he's no longer absolutely sure what is fact and what is dream, and he's afraid he's going mad.

I didn't stay long. Bill returns tomorrow or the day after. I believe he would like all three of us to meet. Presumably he'll contact me when the time comes. Meanwhile I am sorting out my bureau and have found ancient photographs. Plenty of you and me at school, and there's an album belonging to my father. He looks a forbidding man, quietly daunting, but he wasn't. He died when I was 20. According to the photos I was a cute child. Not in the least pretty. Just cute.

I shall now continue this beguiling trip into the past and leave you in peace. Till next time. All love, Hannah,

P S. I've been practising some Chopin nocturnes and a bit of Beethoven, interspersed with South Pacific and West Side Story. But nothing sounds right. It's been too long. Yet I'm on fire to improve. How about a recital next year?

ooOoo

16

Christabel Fraser

FROM   Hannah Pascoe
TO: Chrissiefras@coolmail.net
SENT: 2 March 2008
SUBJECT: What is there to say?

I don't know how to start this email. The past week has been spent in a strange and unfamiliar state and I'm not sure I have the words to express – what? Shock? Bewilderment? Excitement? Intense anxiety? And at the same time a quite euphoric bliss?

Bill Box arrived and promptly rang to invite me for lunch next day at his hotel. I had arranged to meet Myra but did a little tactful reorganisation, agreeing to meet her on Monday instead. Then I trotted to keep my appointment with Box Senior (wearing mint green with a black scarf) and found Box Junior there too, looking casual in a dark blue pullover and jeans. Bill was large and confident in a grey suit, fit and robust and only the slightly spongy nose and the loose folds under his chin betraying not so much his age as a boozy lifestyle. They were both waiting for me in the hotel bar.

Alan was quiet and thoughtful. I was aware of him but whether as a personality or because he has already taken up so much of my attention I didn't know. He says little but the little he does say is to the point.

There was another man at the bar, slim, blonde with a moustache, who was introduced as Steve Hobday, Alan's solicitor and an old college friend. He seemed extraordinarily pleased with me and Karen, and I learned a bit about police procedure and what will probably happen next.

He said the Road Policing Unit go to a great deal of

trouble to establish the facts. What was the weather like? Were Alan's lights working? What was the state of the road, how fast was he travelling and what would his stopping distance have been? Alan was breathalysed, of course, and they took a blood test in hospital. Both negative. He was kept in hospital, under sedation at first because of the state he was in when they found him, but also for tests.

They can do very clever things now, so we hope Karen's statement will establish his innocence beyond any doubt. The only trouble with that being that getting Alan off one hook looks like landing Hatchet Jaw on another, and I'm not sure Karen is quite up to that yet. The question is – how besotted is she, really and truly? A really, truly besotted young person may well be thinking "My lover right or wrong." And jib at betraying him.

Only time will tell. Meanwhile Alan is in a bad dream.

Mr Hobday (I've been told to call him Steve) was so full of admiration at my producing new evidence like a rabbit out of a hat that I began to glow gently in the warmth of their collective esteem.

He also seemed a tad influenced by the idea of Hannah Pascoe aka Maisie Mitchell because he then went on to ask questions about my life in general, but mostly about being a quote star unquote, which I felt was probably a welcome change for him after discussing just another boring case of dangerous driving and possible manslaughter should the child die. Actually, he is taking Alan's case very seriously, but then I suppose he would, being an old friend as well as a conscientious lawyer. He left us eventually, presumably to go back to work, and we followed a hovering waiter to our restaurant table.

During Steve's little inquisition I had become aware

of Alan's deep attention, and as the lunch progressed there stole across the table such concentrated interest that I found myself telling the true story of how I became an actress almost by accident when I wasn't even sure I wanted to be one. How I'd spent years and years as an audio typist, acting in amateur shows for fun. And how, when a producer friend offered me a small part in one of his plays I leaped at it, since anything must be better than audio-typing. Besides, Michael seemed pleased. "It'll be fun," he said. And I thought "Just for a while, I won't stay long", but Michael grew even more pleased, so I stayed – and stayed.

I told them how I got myself an agent, and how when Robert Mackenzie wanted some new characters for Wayside Walk I auditioned for Maisie, and there I was, concreted into my profession.

Finally I told them how it was eventually borne upon me that there were other, more important things I wanted from life than pretending in front of a camera, and that there was never enough *time.*

The precise conversation that followed has gone from my memory. The deep and growing sense of communication has not.

When Alan began to speak I found myself looking directly into his eyes. His questions were concise, clear and searching. What was my real reason for doing it in the first place? What had I gained from it? Had I been more interested in the fame, or had I enjoyed acting for itself? I had said there was more to life. Had I found it? What was I looking for?

From some inner cache I discovered answers I didn't know I knew, dredging them up from far corners of memory, of subconscious, until all I was aware of was the touch of another mind on mine, a tangible thing. And at the same time there was an indescribable desire, almost a compulsion, to leap across the table and throw my arms around him, as truly touched as if he had laid a physical hand on me.

We carried on talking only to each other. I think I ate ice cream and drank coffee. Eventually we rose to leave, and stood beside the table while Bill handed his credit card to the waitress and signed the receipt. Then I opened my handbag to find the complimentary ticket for "Gaslight" which Janine had given me last week. I offered it to Alan. He looked somehow both grateful and apologetic at the same time. "It's very kind of you," he said, taking the ticket and staring down at it. "but I don't go to the theatre much".

"Well, there's always time to start," I smiled, "but if you really don't want to go I'll have it back." I put out my hand. He shook his head, whisking the ticket out of my reach. "Thank you," He said.

I stumbled to the door, received a fond goodbye kiss from Bill and was helped into my coat by Alan. Together they saw me into my car and I wound down the window.

"Enjoy the performance," I said, "and don't worry. It'll all sort itself out."

Alan smiled courteous thanks. Bill called "Keep in touch", and they waved me away.

"Don't worry?" How had I come to say anything so stupid and inane? And why was I driving without knowing where I was going?

I arrived home and somehow there was nowhere to sit, so I lay on my bed, thinking, remembering, remembering, thinking. I tried to read but Alan's face and voice kept superimposing themselves on the words. I listened to Tchaikovsky and Brahms but didn't hear a note. On Radio 2 every song was a love song, breathing passion and desire. And Radio 4 was no better than the useless books – every voice might just as well have been intoning "fish and chips."

That night I slept not! And all next day and the days after I strove to rid myself of this extraordinary incubus. Each time the infuriating image imposed itself on me, which was about once per thirty seconds, I tossed it out. "Go away," I told it repeatedly, re-addressing myself to the job in hand, and repeatedly the image returned to torment me, arousing me to a fever of – what? Exasperation? Longing? Compassion?

No, there was little compassion. The desire was not to enfold him protectively like a hen with one chick. It shames me to say, Chrissie, that I was consumed by a passion of lust, and the instant his face was allowed to appear I was on fire within! It was totally beyond my experience and infuriatingly beyond my control.

I speak in the past tense, but the experience continues and gathers force and momentum by the minute. This morning it occurred to me how fortunate it is to be female. No embarrassing telltale signs on my person to show how strongly I'm gripped. How do men manage? Cold showers every half an hour?

Please allow me one paragraph of eulogy and then I'll shut up.

His eyes are brown, large and speaking, with long, dark lashes. His hair is soft, very curly and still thick except for where it's growing in again around the scar. Until last week I'd have called it black, but now I realise there are colours in it of copper and chocolate. Very little grey, but then he is still only in his 40s.

His face is thin, intelligent, almost ascetic and just a trace Byronic, with lines round his eyes and on his forehead. His mouth is wide and expressive, neither thick nor thin but curly at the corners. Left to itself it would smile. His smile enchants me.

He is taller than average, slim and springy. Nervous energy is apparent and, at present, reveals itself in small ways – a tic in his left jaw muscle, tension in his shoulders, and most of all in his eyes.

He is deeply distressed.

Bill has gone back to Wakefield. The next move must now, I feel, be up to Alan since I no longer have the courage to make one for myself. Until then I am chained to the telephone. He may ring while I'm out, and as yet he doesn't have my mobile phone number. I must give it to him.

Michael sees, I think, that something is wrong but as I can't explain he no doubt assumes I am regretting Wayside Walk and Maisie. He too is withdrawn, but he's been so for weeks, maybe months. Too long anyway.

So many new thoughts about my life are surging up to confuse and bewilder me. I am only now beginning to understand how little Michael and I have been giving to each other through all these years. A torch has been pointed at me from a fresh and unexpected angle, to light up all the dust and aching fantasies, all the empty spaces and wishes unfulfilled.

My dearest Chrissie, I must go, though I hate to leave my letter.

With much love, Hannah.

ooOoo

17

Christabel Fraser

FROM   Hannah Pascoe
TO: Chrissiefras@coolmail.net
SENT: 5 March 2008

SUBJECT: What fools we mortals are.

After our telephone conversation two days ago one would expect there to be nothing new to say, yet of course there is. The rash having returned in even greater force, I went to the doctor yesterday as you and Michael had commanded, and he gave me some ointment which hasn't done anything very much except make me look shinier and more bizarre than ever. I now stay resolutely AT HOME. To set foot beyond the garden gate takes more courage than I've got.

Until now I would have described myself as reasonable and normal – probably a false assumption, and anyway what *is* normal? And by what yardstick do we measure reason or reasonableness? But however we look at the matter, one has to admit that here and now I am neither.

Am I going insane? Are Alan's neuroses catching, like a sort of disease?

The more his face appears in my teacup or on the box hedge or among the rather stylised roses on my bedroom curtains, the more exasperated and guilty I get, and the more I try abortively to kick him out the worse I feel about Michael, to whom I have lately given a great deal of serious thought.

This man has shared my life for 35 years. I ought to know him. Mostly, I believe I do. He is on the whole kind and honourable, careful, conscientious and generous, inclined to be serious, a lover of the Quiet Life (except possibly, in a vicarious fashion, through me), and possessed of a sharply acute brain. There are no flies on Michael Pascoe.

However, though there may be no flies on him there are some in the ointment. Communication between us almost nil. Sometimes I feel he is speaking Italian when I'm speaking French, or Russian to my Greek.

I love him very much Chrissie, admire, respect and (most of the time) like him. What is it then that makes the *reality* so difficult? It's as though my head runs through all his qualities, sums them up and finds them excellent, yet the moment I am faced with them in the flesh there's little to say.

Not that I don't talk. You wouldn't believe anything else, would you? But the talk is chatter, froth. He himself says little, preferring to listen to my stream of inconsequential words through the filter of bookprint or heads on television.

Sometimes I wonder if he filters out the person of Hannah in the same way, and if so why. He says he likes my chatter and if I stop he asks what's wrong. He is possessive of my time and company, resenting evenings spent with friends, though never seeming to resent time away as Maisie Mitchell. I understood his resentment in the early years of acting because starting such a perilous career so late turned me into the archetype of a demented teenager straight from school and having *adventures.* (Sister Martha would have been revolving briskly in her coffin.) Do you remember Paul Griffin and Ben Woodishore? And the rather odd young man with red hair and a beard who could set up eight pints for himself and then drink the lot apparently without taking breath – if he had, he'd have certainly drowned.

These are just names from a colourful snatch of past living, and after one or two disasters – which I'm sure you haven't forgotten – I became at last a model wife. Remorse for my misdemeanours has enabled me to avoid these occupational tripwires with hard-won ease.

So why is it that after so long in Michael's safe, if difficult, company, and with these flirtations tucked away in history, I am now obsessed in a totally new way? This is an unfamiliar world, yet it's startlingly familiar too, for the imagery of poetry and love songs, that seemed up to now just the exaggerated fantasy of artists and songwriters, *is all true.*

This morning, after ten days of desperate flinging away of thoughts which stubbornly refused to go, I gave in.

I am in love. For the first time in my life. I am 59. And married. He is 49. And in deep trouble. Oh boy! Am I in deep trouble too or am I not?

Alan hasn't contacted me since our lunch, but even if he does, one thing is clear, certain, sure. Looking as I do, like a tomato that's begun to go off, he is coming nowhere within sight.

But frustration is growing, because although Bill rings me when he wishes to know something, I won't be told things myself because I have no status. So far as everyone is concerned I am just an ex-actress who happened to be in the right place at the right time and was kind enough to help out. Steve Hobday, however admiring he might be of the theatre and its personnel, won't give me another thought because I've done what I had to do and am no longer necessary.

Till next time, of course. Actors, even ex-ones, have their uses – especially when it comes to publicity.

I do, however, have at least one source of information. I rang Karen. She is pleased with herself and aghast at what she's done to Mark, all at the same time, because the police look as if they are going to investigate *him.* He is furious and there have been so many rows that, with the choice between his rude and ungenerous self on one hand and the diamond studded Mel Kendrick plus a social conscience on the other, I don't hold out much hope for their future life together. Put it this way - with odds like that, who's going to bet?

It's a funny old world. Love, Hannah.

18

Christabel Fraser

FROM   Hannah Pascoe
TO: Chrissiefras@coolmail.net
SENT: 13 March 2008
SUBJECT: Moving on

How long is it since I asked you how you were? Or how Suzie is, or Peter? It can't be right, spending so much time and creative energy talking exclusively about myself, yet this is all I seem able to do for now.

However, since I have obviously become so obsessed that everything else exists only in a mist of irrelevance, I shall bring you up to date.

Yesterday, just after breakfast, Bill Box telephoned. He said he was "worried about Alan."

I said "Oh dear," while my heart moved down somewhere to the region of my toes and stayed there like an icy compress. "Has something new happened?"

"Well yes," he replied, "but some of it's good. The police look as if they're taking Karen's statement seriously, plus the fact that the headlamp appears to have been faulty before the accident, and they're doubtful about the brakes too - so Steve is quite hopeful. The trouble is, the girl's family are jumping up and down and talking about trying to get him on a civil action, even if the police drop charges, and even though little Celia is getting better. She broke her leg and had some internal injuries, but she's at home again now. Unfortunately the whole thing's even more of a mess because of who the father is, (Chairman of Council no less) and it puts the whole political thing on the block."

"Ah! Another worry for Alan on top of everything else."

"It's difficult because he knows he injured a young girl and seems overwhelmed with responsibility for little Katy's death as well. He keeps saying he killed her. There's no arguing with him."

There was a pause. "Can you do anything, Hannah?"

Heart and organs turned a somersault and I blinked into the phone. "I don't know," I said, "I don't like to push. He may not want my help."

"Oh, he does." Bill sounded firm and positive. "But even if he doesn't, I do, and I'm asking you. He's not in a fit state to know what he wants."

I thought for a few seconds, but not for long. My answer was predetermined.

"Okay," I said, "What would you like me to do? Ring him in the morning? Will he be there?"

"Oh, he'll be there. He isn't going anywhere, which is one of the things that's bothering me. He just sits in that room all day staring at the wall – or that's the impression I get anyway."

"Okay, I'll ring right away," I said.

"Good girl," said Bill, "You're an angel and I'm beginning to wonder what we'd do without you. Please keep in touch."

I sat and looked at the phone. Then I made a cup of tea, washed my hair, had another cup of tea, and stared again at the phone. Finally I made a third cup of tea, took a deep breath and dialled Alan's number.

"Hello," he said. His voice was deeper than usual and very flat.

"It's Hannah Pascoe," I said, feeling some kind of necessity to add my surname in case he knew half a dozen Hannahs.

"Oh! Hello," he said again, and this time there was a

faint dawning of some kind of life.

For a horrid moment I thought he was going to ask: "What can I do for you?" which would have silenced me. Don't you hate it when people start off like that? As if you only ever ring people when you want something. But he said nothing, just waited for me to continue.

"I just wondered how you were and what the latest news is," I said, with a new and unfamiliar kind of breathy tremble which I could do absolutely nothing about.

"Up and down," he said, "but thank you for asking."

"You mean you're up and down, or the news?"

"Both."

"Is there anything I can do?"

"Not really, no, and anyway you've done plenty already."

I felt deflated, at a loss, but something made me push a bit further. Perhaps I was afraid of reporting a failure to his father.

"Are you visitable? Do you want to see anybody? I could call, if that would help."

"You're very kind. I don't like to put you to any trouble."

Half amused and half frustrated, I closed my eyes and spoke rather more firmly than usual. "Forget about putting me to trouble. Would you like to see me or not?"

"Yes." His voice was suddenly positive, definite.

"Right. When?"

"When can you come?"

"When would you like me to come?

"As soon as possible."

I tried to make my smile inaudible. "In that case, how about coffee time?"

"Fine. Thank you."

I stood before the mirror, staring at the skin which

79

had lost most of its puce shine and a great deal of the flaky top layer, and knew I'd ceased to care. If I could tolerate (tolerate? What a strange word to use in this context?) his damaged face, he could maybe tolerate mine. I dressed carefully to appear careless, as if the visit were of no importance. Newly laundered jeans, blue polo-necked sweater and heeled boots, covered by a faux-suede jacket and with long silver tulips dangling gently from each ear.

He opened the front door and preceded me once again into the tiny living room. We stood looking at each other.

"This is very kind of you," he said.

"No it isn't," I replied, "I'm dying of curiosity, and anyway I have a vested interest." I nearly added that his father had requested the visit in the first place, but didn't because I didn't want to humiliate Alan by giving the impression I was merely doing as I was told, out of duty.

"Oh yes, of course." He smiled, and waved me towards the settee. "I'll get the coffee." But I followed him into the kitchen. He hadn't washed up for some time. "I'm afraid I've rather left things a bit," he apologised, rinsing two mugs under a running tap.

I restrained myself from snatching a dishcloth, allowing myself merely to watch him find the coffee jar and the opened, rather old-looking milk carton. We stood in silence waiting for the kettle to boil, and I studied him out of the corner of my eye. His hands were shaking and the tic in one cheek and jaw muscles were worse, yet it was excited kind of tension, as if that alone were keeping him alive.

He leaned against the work top and closed his eyes, then turned to give me his peculiarly sweet smile.

"It's nice to see you," He said.

I smiled back. "Good."

Hot water was poured onto spoonfuls of coffee but the milk carton only produced two drops of liquid. "Oh, I'm sorry." One hand went to his head. "I seem to have run out."

"I quite like it black," I lied. He smiled his gratitude.

We sat one at each end of the settee, nursing our mugs, waiting for the right words or the right moment. Then he reached down and picked up a photograph to hand to me. It was of a young girl with long, silky-straight fair hair.

"Katy," he said, "a few months before she died."

I studied it in silence, then handed it back. "She's lovely," I said. "But you didn't kill her, someone else did. And you haven't killed the other girl either, she's getting better."

"Didn't I kill Katy?" He turned towards me, suddenly fierce. "Didn't I? How do you know? And if Celia is recovering it isn't any credit to me, is it?" He closed his eyes. "The impression I have is that Karen would probably remember whatever you wanted her to remember."

My own eyes opened wide with surprise and I gasped. "Are you accusing her of perjury just to please me? You're joking!"

He shook his head, impatient with us both. "No, no, of course not, of course I'm not doing that. But she may want to remember what would please you, and if she's suggestible, which I think she probably is, then half consciously...." He spread his hands.

We stared at each other in sudden despair, on my part born of an urgent desire to shake him.

"Look," I began, as reasonably as I could under the circumstances, "Karen told part of the story the night it happened, at a party, and I was there and heard every word. The rest of it came out without any prompting from me. In fact she was rather scared that Mark himself might get into trouble, and she certainly wouldn't have risked that just to please me, or anybody else for that matter. Not even for Mel Kendrick," I added, screwing up my nose. "Furthermore, the police have checked with their own findings, which seem to be pretty exhaustive, and Steve thinks they'll probably drop the charges. So if they think you're not to blame I would definitely say you're not."

He stared at the carpet, then gave the sort of audible smile one gives when one is not amused, just conscious of the farcical nature of life. He looked up and raised an eyebrow at me. "I seem determined to take the blame, don't I?"

I nodded. He continued to scrutinise me, puzzled, almost bewildered.

"You're being very kind to me," he said. "I don't understand. Why are you helping me like this?"

The question should not have taken me by surprise, it could have been foreseen. I tried to shrug it away, saying his father had asked me to keep an eye on Alan in his absence, but that explanation, even if I wanted to give it, sounded thin. As if my relationship with Bill were closer than it was. There was an embarrassed silence. I broke it eventually, hesitatingly.

"I'll tell you the full reason one day, but not now."

He nodded, looked away and sat forward with his head in his hands.

"I seem to have gone to pieces," he said eventually. "Up to now I've always been positive − I like to think effective − sure of where I was going and what I wanted and how to get it. But look at me. A whingeing mess. Spineless." He smiled suddenly. "A self-pitying, whingeing, spineless mess who runs out of milk."

I jumped at it, half laughing. "But yours isn't a normal situation is it? Nothing about it is normal. Accidentally knocking a child down must be bad enough at any time, but with all the politics and nastiness..." I paused, then went on. "And especially with what happened to Katy."

"Ah yes, Katy." He paused. "But then, you see, I wasn't a good father even while she was alive. She died because of my neglect."

I frowned and sat very still, hardly breathing, hoping the stillness might encourage him to continue.

"I was always out, you see. Work, Family, everything came second to politics. Second, third, fourth in fact. I was a councillor then, Party whip, Chairman of local party groups. Very important it seemed in those days." He stopped, leaning back in his chair with his eyes closed, and I wondered if he intended to say any more.

"She hadn't had the bike long and wasn't supposed to cycle on the road by herself. I had promised to go with her. But I had to go out. To a meeting."

The sentences hung in the air. There was so much more now that I wanted to know, but was afraid to ask. Years of experience with Michael and the children have taught me that direct questioning rarely results in information, the gaining of which is usually like pulling teeth (Sorry Michael). I wondered if the accident had caused the divorce, or whether they were divorced already. Did the girl's mother also blame him? I knew I would never ask those questions, but felt one or two might be acceptable.

"How old was she?"

"She was ten."

I waited for a minute, then asked: "Have you always blamed yourself for it?"

"Not really, not at first."

"Do you mean this second accident has brought out your feelings about the first one?"

"I was angry that anyone could have let a young girl

83

out on a bicycle after dark, and then I realised I had done more or less the same thing. Now I can't expect the girl's parents not to blame me, because in just the same way I blamed the chap who killed Katy."

"Was Katy out at night?"

"No."

"Was she on a leafy minor road?"

"No, round the corner at the local shops."

"At the local shops in broad daylight?" I pondered. "There's quite a difference. One has to let children take some risks. We think they're controlled risks, but how much control do we really have over anything? School playgrounds, the swimming pool, bus trips? And mightn't she have gone without you anyway even if you had been home?"

"She was nervous."

I risked another throw. "What about her mother? Could she have taken her?"

"Elizabeth hates bicycles. She always did. She didn't want Katy to have one, but I persuaded her."

I digested all the implications of these flat statements, and watched Alan open his eyes and sit forward with his arms on his knees. He looked directly at me.

"You're trying to absolve me, but you can't," he said.

I leaned forward too, and stared back. "You can absolve yourself," I said, "of this accident at least, if you will believe Karen's story. The two accidents are not the same. They are different, different incidents. What will it take to convince you?"

His eyes softened, warmed, and gently he touched my hand and smiled. "I don't know."

Then he looked at his watch. I picked up my shoulder bag and began to leave. He didn't stop me.

"I'm sorry, but I have an appointment at the doctor's

this afternoon," he said. "I expect he'll just write out another prescription. Or tell me I'm scarred for life!"

"I'm quite sure he won't, but you're obviously not in the mood to believe anything good today, so I'll shut up."

I smiled up at him, wanting very badly to kiss the scar."I wish I could inject you with some of my optimism."

"I wish you could, too. Believe me, I'm not usually this much of a misery." We studied each other for a moment, then he turned away to open the door for me. "I mustn't keep you any longer."

As I went to step onto the tiny front path he said: "Shall I see you again?"

"Of course. If you wish."

"When?"

I thought fast and hard. Today was Monday. "How about Wednesday morning? Would you like to drive out somewhere, since you haven't got your car?"

"That would be very nice. I've been stuck in this place far too long, not wanting to go out. It's time I did. I shall have to soon, anyway, because my friend will be back and I'll have to look for somewhere else to live. This was only supposed to be temporary, but with everything that's happened I just haven't got round to looking."

I stared at him. What an exasperating man he is, to open up a fresh packet of problems just as I'm leaving.

"I'll pick you up on Wednesday," I said, firm and brisk now, as this was not goodbye after all but a prelude to a further challenge. "Eleven o'clock, if that's okay?"

"Thank you."

He watched me climb into my car and raised his hand in salute as I drove away. Through the driving mirror I saw him vanish into his home. It wasn't until I was more than half way home that I realised he hadn't smoked.

Tomorrow is Wednesday. I know I am getting into deep and dangerous whirlpools, but don't' seem able to do anything about it. You will just have to pray for me.

Love, Hannah.

P S. (It is one o'clock in the morning). I sat for a long time after Michael had gone to bed, meditating on the strange interactions of family life. Alan is an only son whose mother died many years ago, which gives an exclusive quality to his relationship with Bill. Now he has divorced his own wife, or she has divorced him, for reasons so far undisclosed, and lost one of his two children in a particularly shocking way. Just a son survives. Is the problem of a father with one son about to repeat itself?

ooOoo

19

Christabel Fraser

FROM   Hannah Pascoe
TO: Chrissiefras@coolmail.net
SENT: 15 March 2008
SUBJECT: Yet another update

Many thanks for the reassurances that my emails are engrossing you both. The thought of you and Peter gasping for the next instalment is not only gratifying but very funny.

Today it is even more than that. The events of

yesterday need assimilating.

I picked Alan up as arranged, having spent the first part of the morning, if not the whole of the day before, either lost in dreams or restlessly clock-watching. I was very aware of Michael, conscious that his comings and goings have become less predictable – that he, too, is wrapped up and uncommunicative. The overwhelming intensity of my feeling for Alan has brought into focus the lack of such intensity in my feelings for Michael. As if I have had to live for 59 years and be married for 35 before discovering what the word love means. Certainly nothing which has ever come before has prepared me for such an experience, and I am shocked by it. Shocked that I have so little control over my actions, or over the emotions that are causing them.

I am like my own adolescent children, yet entirely and utterly convinced that what I'm trying to do is right – consumed by a longing to see Alan happy and confident and back in his world, no matter what that may cost me. I can see the possible cost, but only dimly because at present I see only from day to day, minute to minute, and the next objective may be the last I am allowed to pursue.

How is it possible to be so filled with longing yet so *sacrificial?* This morning I went to church, hoping to find an answer there. I sat alone and preoccupied, wondering where this absorption in someone else's life and emotions was leading, wondering if God intended it or merely allowed it – whether it is a *good thing* and I am to have a share in its outcome, or whether I have simply made the whole thing up. The fruit of an actor's fantasy? The wish dream of a middle-aged matron fearful of age? An unfulfilled longing flying to the first beacon it sees? How much of my own frustration am I putting onto God and how much onto Alan himself?

In the end, after a long conversation which was

really a monologue because I did all the talking, I simply left the whole matter with God to sort out, for I certainly can't.

Meanwhile I drove to Alan's house and he was ready, waiting for me outside the door. Then he was in my car. A strange sensation. He told me his own was a complete write-off and he would now have to get himself another. He said the police had crawled all over it testing the brakes and lights and looking for clues. Because he had to swerve to avoid Celia, there was nowhere else to go but into the tree. The thought is pretty horrific. Not one to dwell on for too long.

"Not that being car-less makes much difference at the moment. I'm not exactly what you'd call road-worthy myself," he said simply. "I've lost my nerve." He asked where I was taking him.

"Home," I said, "to my house. If you feel like going somewhere else, of course we can, but at least we can sit in comfort while we decide. In new surroundings," I added.

He asked no questions. It occurred to me that he had shown no curiosity about whether I had a husband or not, and assumed that either he wasn't especially interested or had learned all he needed to know from Bill. I hoped this easy acquiescence showed, at least, a trust that I wasn't going to drop him into any embarrassing situations. Or perhaps he felt that asking if a husband, if any, would be home as well would be in rather bad taste. (How tortuous life has become in so short a time. A few short weeks ago I was worrying about what to wear for a party.)

In fact, I felt no hesitation whatsoever about taking him home. The only difference between Alan Box and the scores of distressed friends who have sat in my house drinking coffee (with or without Michael) is that I am in love with this one. I suppose that alone could be a huge argument against what I was doing, but I chose to ignore the little tinkle of warnings bells and carried on driving.

We said little on the way, except for a warning from me that both car and home were strictly no-smoking zones. "Although I have to say you've been very good so far."

He smiled, a tad ruefully I thought. "I'm trying to give it up again," he said. "Doctor's advice." I nodded but said nothing more. I drove through my own gates with a sudden rush of pride, wanting him to see my home - to open the front door, as I was doing then, upon a hall polished and fresh with early daffodils, and into a sitting room where the late morning sun warmed the colours and softened all the details into a mellow, welcoming whole.

"Coffee or tea?" I asked. It should really have been nectar or, at the very least, Madeira or mulled wine.

"Coffee please." He followed me into the kitchen. "What a lovely house."

"Thank you, I like it most of the time. It's been my home for twenty years."

He watched me absently, his thoughts elsewhere.

"Do you like music?" I asked.

He said yes, he certainly did, so I handed him his mug, picked up my own and carried it back to the sitting room where I gestured him into an armchair and knelt on the floor by the CD rack, choosing.

"What have you got there?"

"You name it," I said, "and we may have a small selection of it. Our tastes can be said to be catholic. Mine anyway," I added.

He smiled and came to join me on the floor, to peer at the CDs. He chose one of Beethoven's late quartets, then sat back in his chair. "You're being very good to me. Why?"

I took the disc from its cover and slipped it into the CD player, but instead of pressing the start button, I sat back on my heels and stared at the carpet.

"You asked me that before, and I said I'd give you the answer later."

"What's wrong with now?"

I looked up at him, making up my mind. His eyes were on me with serious intent. He was waiting for my answer.

I decided to give it. "I love you," I said.

He neither moved nor spoke and the silence began to do funny things with my diaphragm.

"I'd better tell you," I continued "that I have no intention of breaking up my marriage or leaving my husband, for you or anyone else, but all the same, for better or worse, I love you."

"What do you mean by love?"

I pulled a face. "No-one has ever been able to answer that question, but in my case it means I'm in love and will do everything in my power to help you."

His eyes were warm but troubled, and he sat watching me for several minutes, elbows on his knees and hands clenched between them.

"I'm afraid I'm not very good at loving," he said. "I've never given much time to it and I don't really understand it. Apart from my children – child – I think I'm probably incapable of loving anyone at the moment."

I said simply: "I'm not asking you to love me. I'm just telling you the truth, that I love you, which is more than enough to be going on with, believe me. And you did ask!"

I picked up the remote control and pressed the key to begin. The room was filled with sound. We listened in silence, then the strong, intoxicating notes of the quartet rose like eucalyptus mist to unlock his brain and his tongue, and he talked.

With pauses, and in a quiet voice, he told me something of his marriage, of his preoccupation with politics, which he described as his first love – and his desire for eventual power. "Not so much for myself in particular. At least I don't think so, although I suppose there's always something of that in it. But in order to get things done which so desperately need doing, like restoring our crumbling schools, housing the people who sleep in doorways or live in B and Bs. Redressing some of the terrible injustices that happen every day. I've been in the wrong party for power so far, I know that. If I'd chosen one of the other parties I might be at Westminster by now, but it was a simple choice to make. I don't like their parties' principles and I do like the one I'm in.. It's a matter of integrity. All the talk about joining a party to change it from within is, in my opinion, simply rubbish because it is almost impossible to achieve. Unless you get into the cabinet or become Prime Minster there isn't much one M P can do on his own. It's a bit like pitting a Mini against a juggernaut. I'm not sure what my father would have done if I'd have chosen a different party from his. He is very ambitious for me."

He smiled suddenly. "I'm ambitious for me too. Burningly so. But he's worse, probably because he never managed to get elected himself. He found it hard to forgive me when I didn't stand again last year for Wakefield, but I couldn't. I had to leave it."

He was silent again. I hoped he would carry on, but asked no questions because I didn't know the right ones to ask.

"It's an odd experience," he said at last, "finding you can't do something you've always taken for granted. I was always in there fighting, enjoying the battle for its own sake, the footwork, guessing what everyone else is going to do so one can outsmart them. I enjoyed it all and I was good at it. Then one day I stood up in the Council chamber to make a speech – and I forgot what I was going to say. My notes were meaningless. Nothing mattered. We were all playing silly games, like kids holding mock trials in the playground, only there were real people on the receiving end. What we decided in our power games made a difference to tens of thousands of people who had no power at all to change anything. It wouldn't have bothered me before. One gets to expect things like that. But this time it was deeper, a kind of disenchantment. From then on I limped through to the next election, about nine months later, and told them I wasn't standing again. There was a bit of a battle, but I meant it. And then I moved here."

"Disenchantment," I repeated. "That's the word Tom used when I left Wayside Walk. He said I was disenchanted. The situations are different, but I think I know what you're saying."

We smiled at each other with sudden fellow feeling. "But you were going to stand again here," I said suddenly, "At the City elections next May."

He raised one eyebrow at me. "I was like an old horse going round and round on its circle, doing the same old things because that's what it always did. My father again – he wrote to party friends on the council and told them I was here, so I could start off with a social life, he says. But I knew better than that. They arrived on my doorstep full of ideas and expectations. Said my reputation had come before me and took it for granted I would fall into their arms with whoops of joy. I said no at first, of course." He smiled and made an impatient movement with his hands. "I was depressed and lonely and weak enough to be pleased. It was the wrong thing. That goes without saying. Bad timing all round. But once you even look as if you might say yes you're caught in a sort of mesh and it's hard to get out. So I gave in and went for total immersion. There was no-one to please but myself, and it's something I know how to do, so I sort of hurtled about from meeting to meeting. Electioneering is fun, you see, exhilarating, and there's a shared kind of busyness. A bonhomie. It's hard to match. But once the election is over and won, the terms of reference change. It's like being trained as an electrician and then being asked to fly an airbus."

I laughed. He was more alive and interested than I had seen him so far.

"I'm not ready to fly yet, not even a biplane, and I'm not sure I ever will be again. Or even if I'll be given another chance. Standing down in one place and giving up entirely in another a year later isn't exactly going to inspire confidence in the Party. Not if they've got any sense. I'd be turned down."

"Are you sure? What's that saying about a week being a long time in politics? And you had a very good reason this time."

It was the wrong thing to say. "Yes, knocking a child off her bike. Hardly an attribute. And anyway think what the other parties could do with it."

I wished my tongue could have been cut off there and then, out of harm's way, but after a short pause he spoke again. "In any case I've lost confidence. I'm not sure I could make a speech again, or even if I want to try."

I smiled at him from my place on the floor, leaning back against an armchair. "I can see that nothing I say will convince you."

"It's good of you to have a go."

Unexpected warmth in his eyes unnerved me, leaving me with nothing to say except, after a pause, to ask if he was hungry.

"Yes, I think I am a bit."

"The choice is sandwiches here or a pub lunch by the river."

He looked around him. "I'm very happy here," he said, and I replied: "Good!"

We ate our ham and cream cheese baguettes in front of the fire, which I lit because despite the sunshine the room was growing chilly. He stayed for the rest of the afternoon and I told him about Lucy and Timothy and a little of my early working life as a Temp, and of some of the shows I'd been in before Wayside Walk. We talked about music and books and discovered the same taste in both. Then I began to describe my dabble in electioneering with his father, and the stories made him laugh."

"I remember you at the Thank You party afterwards," I said. "You were being frightfully charming. Mostly to the younger females, as I recall."

"I expect I was. I'm afraid that's what I do. Power again, and the joy of the chase. Challenge. I'm not a nice man, Hannah."

"Are there any?"

He smiled. We finished with tea and cake and then I drove him home. Outside his door he leaned over and kissed me gently on the lips. Every part of me melted.

"Oh my dear," I said.

He looked me directly in the face, surprised and scrutinizing. "You really do love me, don't you?"

"Yes," I said.

"Shall I see you again?"

"Yes," I said.

He opened the car door. "Same time next Monday?" he asked.

How could I wait so long? How dare I suggest an alternative – like, for instance, tomorrow? Both were impossible.

I nodded. "Okay. Same time next Monday," and

drove away.

I am full of confusion, and have only now realised, too late, that we didn't talk about his appointment with the doctor. Or even about his having to look for somewhere to live. How remiss of me. How odd that he didn't volunteer it..

I am too full of wandering thoughts tonight. I don't think I'll ever sleep again.

Meanwhile, all love, Hannah.

ooOoo

20

Christabel Fraser

FROM   Hannah Pascoe
TO: Chrissiefras@coolmail.net
SENT: 20 March 2008
SUBJECT: What is there to say?

Thank you for not telling me off, not telling me to be careful or be my age, for you know too well that I wouldn't take any notice. I'd have listened to your good advice and known it was good, but it would still have saddened me and made it harder to send these emails to you – for nothing would, or could, make any difference now to my feelings. Sadly, I seem to be in their grip.

Nothing in my life so far has prepared me for this, not even the romantic and passionate roles I've played in the past, so I flounder and thresh about in a sea of confusion, hope and despair.

It's agony, isn't it? This love business?

My biggest comfort is that you have been through it

all yourself and understand every hyperbole. You have not only suffered the torment but come through in the end to win. You are the person without whom I would now go quietly demented, for the luxury of expressing thoughts and emotions inexpressible to other people is itself inexpressible. Especially since I don't understand any of it myself.

These few days have lasted two years. I saw Janine and Myra for lunch at The Swan. Neither was needed at the studio so there was no hurry, and I saw Jan again later in the evening. I love her cockatoo brightness and shrewd honesty. I like Myra too, most of the time, but one has to side-step her sides-wipes! Her sharpness of wit can leave one reaching for the elastoplast.

Tom sent a message through Myra to say he keeps ringing and ringing but I never seem to answer. He leaves messages and hopes I will at least reply to those. I can see I'll have to give in and answer at least some of the calls. I suppose I could give him my mobile number.

There was more fan mail in the post and a proposal from a gentleman in Weston-Super-Mare who seems weighted down with cash which he is apparently anxious to spend on me, though whether he'd still have done so had he seen my face recently is debatable. It (the face, not the cash) has gently but steadily improved. Now I can at last be seen by Alan *au naturelle*, that is, with proper flesh-tinted flesh. I don't think he likes cosmetics much.

Monday finally came about and I duly turned up at his house in a state of nerves reminiscent of a First Night, only worse because this play is unscripted and there are no prompts or stage directions.

We decided to go out for lunch, which I took to be a good sign, as so far he's chosen *not* to be seen in public – a sentiment with which I am now fully in sympathy.

So I drove him to the Buttress and opened Act One by asking how his hospital visit had gone, and he said results were both bad and good. Scarring would be so faint as to be hardly noticeable. Then for the first time he mentioned the headaches. These have been with him since the accident and are now growing worse.

"You've had them all this time, and never said!"

Her stared into his glass. "Other things seemed more important. In any case I imagined they were part of the injury and in time they'd go of their own accord. They haven't, that's all."

Spring isn't far enough advanced yet for drinks outside, so we sat in a conservatory restaurant and ordered lasagne for Alan and a jacket potato with tuna mayonnaise for me, with only fruit juice and mineral water to drink, as he is still on medication and I was driving. And do you know? I could think of nothing to say. Me, Hannah, mute and speechless. Normal chatter dried up like a stream in a drought as I chewed my potato and green salad. And wrack them as I might, my brains came up with nothing. Nil! Zilch! I thought "If my friends could see me now!"

Just as I was thinking he would write me off as the most boring lunch partner he had ever known, I remembered to ask if he heard further from the solicitor or the police.

"Yes," he said, "Steve thinks the police will drop charges"

"Alan, that's wonderful."

"Is it?"

"Well, isn't it?"

"I still knocked a young girl off her bike and seriously injured her. Nothing can change that. I've been trying to think of ways to make it up to her and her family, but now that her father has made it political, it's become very messy."

"Yes, but it wasn't your fault."

"Maybe not, but he's threatening things like civil action."

I re-addressed myself to the potato, exasperated and compassionate at the same time. Not sure how to continue, I changed the subject and told him about my dates with Janine and Myra, and spent twenty minutes or so describing them with much gusto and detail. He seemed very entertained and livened up noticeably, which shows promise for the future. Living on his own with only his problems to think about, everything must now be thoroughly out of perspective.

I asked if any of his political friends ever call or offer help.

"Yes they do, occasionally," he said. "One or two of them have been very kind, but there isn't much they can do at the moment. It's comforting to know, though, that some heavy guns could be brought in on my side, if necessary."

"That sounds good," I agreed, wondering why this piece of information should have disturbed me and why I hadn't considered the possibility before. Why hadn't I? Has the Hannah Pascoe image grown so puffed up that I could ignore such an important part of his life simply because I saw myself as the big Mrs Fix-It? There was also the realisation that had I thought of the political aspect in the beginning, I could have persuaded Bill to try that avenue for help, instead of coming to me, thus saving myself cosmic problems and certain heartache. And the fact that he had apparently done so without prompting didn't help me in the least!

I retired to digest it all, looking through the window on a grey river, on patrons in heavy pullovers and children in anoraks, and on one empty and abandoned tankard left on a wooden table with two bright plastic wrappers from salt 'n vinegar crisps, and the white polystyrene foam from take-aways. Apparently there were hardier folks than ourselves who were prepared to eat outside.

"Did you have time to get to know these people?" I asked at last.

"Not really. On a superficial basis mostly. That would have come later. We hadn't worked together long and May is still two months away. I hated letting them down, but knew I'd have let them down even more if I'd stayed. Think what the opposition would do to a civil action by the chairman of the council!"

"Ouch, yes! They've offered help?"

"Oh yes," he said, surprised. "Of course."

So much for the alone and friendless Alan Box! Then he said: "But the one sure way of helping me was to come up with new evidence, which they couldn't do and you did." He reached out a hand to touch mine. "Thank you."

I smiled, recognising soothing balm when I saw it. "Sheer luck, and putting two and two together."

"And putting yourself out in order to do it. Don't forget that."

He withdrew his hand and I felt bereft. I was also struggling with the first faint twinges of jealousy.

"Do these people come and see you?"

"One or two have, but it's coming up to a busy time, and I'm not a rewarding person to visit, am I? Not what you'd call a bundle of laughs."

"It's quite easy to make you smile. You've been smiling today. And laughing."

"You've been working hard at it."

"Oh dear," I laughed. "Is that how it looks? Actually, I haven't been working hard at all. I just like telling stories."

"So do I normally."

"I'm looking forward to hearing them."

"I hope you don't have to wait too long. The way I feel at the moment I can't imagine being normal ever again."

"What about your job?"

"I was supply teaching and that would have finished at the end of term anyway. There might be something after Easter if the doctor signs me off."

"Are you looking forward to going back?"

"Not really. I don't know."

A hesitant beam of sunlight fell on the table and lit up scraped potato skin and small pools of sauce, somehow investing them with new and romantic importance. I finished my glass of orange juice and lemonade, and looked over the rim at him.

Alan ordered coffee for us both, so we put on our coats and took the cups outside to drink, sitting on a bench beside the lock gates. I looked down at the water, mesmerised by the flashing dots of light which winked jauntily back at me. "I love this place," I said.

When it was time to go, I stood straight and faced him. "I want to make you believe," I said, "I want you to believe you're going to be all right. This will all be a bad dream one day." His eyes were large and serious, fixed on me but revealing nothing. "Believe it," I said again. I put a hand on his arm and we stared eye to eye. A sense of complete, overwhelming conviction was giving my words an urgency so strong I felt it couldn't fail to communicate itself. "Believe it, Alan. I've never been so sure of anything in my life. You – are –going – to be – all –right." And I leaned forward to gently kiss the scar on his cheek.

His eyes were so deeply warm I was in danger of leaping into them.

"Nobody's ever loved me like this before."

I don't feel any loss of dignity or pride in telling him the truth. Maybe I should, but he really needs to know.

In a world of guilt and recrimination, accused by others but even more by himself, where physical and mental pain and insecurity and loss of identity are drawing him down and down, he needs an entirely unconditional love, someone to love him whatever happens to him, not because of anything he does or doesn't do. Simply because he *is.*

We went for a drive in the country and the sun grew so warm we opened the sunroof to the fresh light. As I turned the car for home, I asked if he would like to drive.

He was very surprised. "Are you sure?"

"The insurance is fully comprehensive, any driver."

"You trust me?"

"Of course or I wouldn't have offered."

He thought about it, then thanked me and said he'd like to try. I handed him the keys and he drove all the way back to his front door, enjoying it more and more as he went. And as he pulled up at the kerb he turned, placed an elbow along the back of my seat and leaned sideways to look me long and hard in the face.

"You are an extraordinary woman," he said.

"Well of course," I said.

He laughed and shook his head, then kissed me on the lips. His were like silk.

"Will you come in for coffee?"

I said no, not today. There was a meal to be cooked.

"When shall I see you again?" he asked.

"When would you like to see me again?"

"As soon as possible."

I wanted to ask if tomorrow were sooner than possible, but was afraid of being rebuffed, so instead I asked what "soon" meant.

"When are you free?"

There was no need to look in my diary to know I could be free whenever he wished. I would simply switch whatever was in it to another day, to suit his convenience.

"Well actually, I'm free tomorrow," I said lightly.

"That would be nice," he said, and I found that holding my breath had made me light headed.

"I'll ring you," I said, "to see what time. There are one or two things I have to do, but they won't take long." (Oh fie, but I'm a liar!)

"Don't let me upset your arrangements."

I gurgled. He was playing havoc with them. "Will you be in at half past ten?"

He nodded.

I wondered if he would kiss me again, but he merely laid a hand on my arm before opening his door, climbing out and coming round to help me out of the passenger seat into my own again. He had already vanished inside his house as I drove away.

It is now 1.30 in the morning. Again! Michael is in bed, presumably asleep, and I am as wakeful as ever. It's tempting to hold this over until tomorrow, but I've grown so prolific that another day's writing would jam up both our hard drives.

All love, Hannah.

ooOoo

21

Christabel Fraser

FROM   Hannah Pascoe
TO: Chrissiefras@coolmail.net
SENT: 21 March 2008
SUBJECT: Back again

This morning I told Michael about Alan's problems and he showed real concern, though saying at one point "Be careful, don't get saddled with a lame duck. I know you, and he could get to be a nuisance."

I was just reassuring him how unlikely this was since Alan has never pestered me (in fact it's always been me making the running, although I didn't of course tell Michael that) when the telephone rang and it was Alan.

Isn't it always the way?

"Sorry to ring at breakfast time," he said, "but I have to see the doctor this morning as well as Steve, and don't know how long it's all going to take. I was afraid you'd ring when I was out, and think I'd forgotten."

"That's all right," I replied, embarrassingly conscious of Michael drinking his coffee three feet away. "Perhaps you could ring when you get back. I shall be interested to know what they say."

"Yes, of course. You're sure it's not putting you out?"

"Quite sure. That will be fine. Thanks for letting me know," and I rang off rather more abruptly than usual. Michael raised a sardonic eyebrow.

"Okay," I nodded, "I'll be careful."

"You know what you're like. They can spot you a mile off."

I laughed. "Will you be in for tea?"

"No, I'll be late. There's another L D C meeting."

"Really? It doesn't seem a month since the last one. How time flies when you're having fun! How late is late?"

He considered, wiped coffee from his mouth, aimed a kiss somewhere in the region of my own, and made for the door. "Ten-ish? Eleven-ish?"

"Okay," I waved a hand. There's been an increasing number of ten-ish, eleven-ish nights.

His departure left me with a morning in which to do *all* the washing, the shopping, the ironing and the cleaning that should have been done yesterday and the day before – and the day before that. Needless to say they weren't done today either. I certainly pecked at them but achieved precisely nothing. I rather think I mooned. There is nothing so eternally aggravating as a silent telephone.

At twelve o'clock it gave voice, but it was only Janine to ask how things were going. At ten to one it rang again, this time being a colleague of Michael's to leave a message. But at half past one we hit the jackpot.

"What would you like to do?" Alan asked. Since I didn't care what I did as long as he did it with me, I asked if he had any preference himself.

"Shall we go out again?"

I was pleased. His scar phobia was obviously dwindling.

I said I'd pick him up in half an hour, and he said "Lovely."

We drove to the forest at Westonbirt. The day was grey and not very warm, but we had the trees to ourselves and as we wandered we talked. The paralysis which attacks my brain and vocal cords on first finding myself in his company melts the instant any conversion begins, and then I – we – can't talk fast enough. One idea flows into another, diversifies and becomes twenty, so I have to choose which thread to follow and, having chosen, lose the other nineteen – only to remember them in passing later and grab their tails as they flash by.

"Stop!" I cried at one point, halting mid-path to clutch my hair with despairing hands. "We keep going off at tangents. Will we ever remember what we started off talking about?"

"Does it matter?"

I laughed happily and threw my arms in the air, twirling myself round and round and looking up at the patchy sky between the misty green of tiny new leaves.

"No!" I shouted, "Of course it doesn't. Nothing matters, nothing, nothing, nothing."

I stopped gyrating and found him smiling, watching me. I smiled back, perfectly happy, and the smile turned itself into a wide, ecstatic beam of pure joy.

He is going to love me, Chrissie. He must. He won't be able to help himself.

We ordered tea and cream cakes at the little café, then he drove us back in my car and pulled up outside his door. This time I accepted his invitation and went in for coffee. And over our coffee we talked more and he played one of his Shostakovich CDs. (Do you know the Jazz Suite? Brilliant! I must get it at once).

Then Alan said: "I haven't got much of my stuff here because this place isn't permanent, as you know. I'll have to leave soon."

"Yes, you said. When is your friend coming back?"

"In a few weeks. He's been in Sweden for a year, but he'll want his home and there isn't enough room for us both. Besides, he has a girl friend, and there definitely isn't room for three."

I laughed and agreed, but once again was taken aback by the almost inconsequential dropping in of last minute information. We had been together all afternoon without discussing this at all.

"Have you anywhere in mind?"

"No," he said, "All this business has knocked it out of my head. In fact until lately I haven't been able to concentrate on anything at all except surviving. But I had a letter from him the other day, and I hadn't realised how time was going by. The trouble is that everything seems so uncertain I simply don't know what I'm looking for."

Chrissie, I have to say Mrs Fix-It rose instantly to the challenge.

"What would you really like, if you had the choice?" I asked, feeling omnipotent, as if by taking thought I could produce a dwelling from the air about me exactly suited to his requirements.

"That's the problem," he said. "It would help if I knew." He spread his hands. "I don't know how this case is going to go, for a start, and I'm not even sure I shall find a permanent job quickly either. I was only doing supply teaching, and may not get signed off until the headaches are sorted out, which means I can't afford much."

I was quiet. Obviously he needed somewhere cheap and quiet and preferably supportive.

"How much can you afford?"

"Not much. I'm sending some to Elizabeth and Dominic every month, and most of our capital is tied up in the house." Then he touched his face. "There's this, too, as well as the headaches. I'm not everyone's choice of tenant."

I leaned across and traced the line of his scar with my fingers. For a few seconds he didn't respond, then he put one hand over mine and stroked it.

"I wish I was better at loving," he said.

I smiled, certain that he would improve in time. "Don't worry about it," I said, "You'll get better." Then I removed my hand and stood up.

"I must go. Shall I come again?"

"Please." He held out a hand to me and I took it. "I need you, Hannah."

He kissed me goodbye at the door, and this time he hugged me too. We rocked gently and companionably, arms round each other, then he kissed me again.

"Tomorrow?"

"Tomorrow," I said, mentally relegating whatever

was in it to some future date.

My car wheels never touched the ground. Together it and I floated home.

Now we have to find somewhere for him to live. Meanwhile I must go to bed. Michael came in at ten thirty, ate his cottage pie and switched on the television, leaving me free to write as I wished – lengthily!

He went to bed an hour ago. I am about to join him.

Goodnight, Hannah.

P S. The doctor was pleased with his face but concerned about the headaches, which should by now be getting better. He has pain killers but doesn't like taking them. At least stress hasn't turned him into a junky or an alcoholic. H

ooOoo

22

Christabel Fraser

FROM   Hannah Pascoe
TO: Chrissiefras@coolmail.net
SENT: 25 March 2008
SUBJECT: Life goes on.

The police have told Alan they are not charging him. As well as Karen's evidence, they'd already tested the girl's headlamp and brakes, and decided the lamp had been faulty already, if not broken altogether before the accident. There were serious doubts about the brakes as well. What could her family have been thinking of to let her out on it? Unfortunately, right now they seem to be thinking in terms of revenge – some kind of legal action - although Steve says if their solicitor has any brains at all he will advise them against it, as they would certainly lose.

The biggest threat now is Karen's Hatchet Jaw, who had a nasty few minutes with the police. It was only the lack of concrete evidence that saved him from being charged with dangerous driving and losing his licence as, according to Karen, he already has nine points on it. Another three would have finished him off, and there would have been either a massive fine or a spell in gaol. Fortunately for him, by the time the police got around to investigating him it was too late for him to be breathalised, or the book would really have been thrown at him. Consequently he is now hell bent on revenge as well, especially since little K is seeing him with new eyes (Mel-tinted, as it were) and has withdrawn her affections forever. She is now staying with Auntie Janine.

Alan and I have been meeting almost every day and Bill rings me most evenings. They are beginning to treat me as Guardian Angel Number One, which is rather pleasant but has its drawbacks, since it's only a question of time before they find that my wings are made of *papier machè* and that my halo is simply a toothpaste advert.

I have, however, managed one or two flutters with the *paper machè* wings. I remembered that Nick Wadham lets one of his rooms. He is one of the Wayside Walk regulars but as his role of travelling rep doesn't take up much of the plot, he has plenty of free time and uses his house in Waterloo Road as a second income, a fact which came to me as a lightning bolt and which sent me hot-fingered to the telephone.

Result – Nick Wadham lets a room and yes, it will

miraculously be free in about two weeks time. I told him that would be perfect, provided he gave me (Alan) his first refusal. He said he would.

Mrs Fix-It strikes again!

On Thursday I asked Alan if the plan appealed to him. It did. He rang Nick that same evening and arranged for us all to meet last night at the Black Lion.

Nick, as you may recall, is a youngish man somewhere in his late thirties or early forties about whom I know little, except that as a rule he was charming and friendly, a colleague with whom I would pass a cheerful time of day on set. He always kept his private affairs quiet, but as he is moderately handsome in a fair, pale sort of way he presumably has a love life of some kind. In the usual spirit of research, I hope to find out. Meanwhile, he seems kindly enough disposed and should make a friendly and amenable landlord.

He and Alan made friends at once and we spent a pleasant evening over a pint or two while Alan arranged to visit the house to look at the room. If he likes it, he can move there as soon as he's warned his present host. "I can't just go," he said, "as if I'm doing a moonlight flit!"

I am aware that continuing to make Alan grateful is not the best way to his heart, so am acting against my own best interests. But since I have already decided that my role is simply helper and guardian angel, my own best interests have no right to be considered in the first place. As I told him firmly two weeks ago, I have absolutely no intention of breaking up my marriage for him or anyone else, so love versus gratitude is an irrelevant issue.

Lucy is out of work again but doesn't seem to mind. Andy being away in Plymouth, she came here for the day and instantly littered every surface from floor to mantelpiece with diverse objects peculiar to herself –

striped socks, badges, old letters, still older magazines, one sweater with holes in and another with "SAVE THE WHALE" across the chest, plus one trainer (muddy) and a large Sainsbury's carrier bag full of clothes to be washed in my machine. Oh, and a tin of tuna and a packet of Tofu, which we are doubtless about to sample. Among the garments whirling happily in the tub is the most feminine set of underwear, thongs and bras like wisps of lace, so the black, baggy image is obviously confined to surface dressing. I seem to remember proceeding in the reverse order when we were her age – the top layer intended for seduction and the bits underneath giving way to economy. But then we didn't expect the bits underneath to be seen quite so early on – at least until the top bits had achieved our longer term designs!

Do you get the impression our generation has missed out somewhere?

Normally the question of age and generation doesn't bother me, but now I find myself more and more giving the whole subject a fearful second glance, the paranoid glance of a woman who is about to be sixty and a Senior Citizen but who has been bewitched by a younger man.

A recent remark of Bill's has brought it very much to mind. On the phone yesterday he thanked me (again) for all I was doing, adding "It's particularly good of you as he's so much younger than we are."

"Gee thanks," I replied, amused at first by what seemed a bitchy remark (I don't suspect him of being gauche – this man hasn't been gauche since he was in nappies). He partly recovered by saying "But then you're a bit younger than I am, so I suppose you're nearer his age than mine."

"I've never thought about it," I lied, feeling slightly winded, as though someone had just punched me gently

110

in the ribs.

I'm fascinated by how often Bill refers to the subject in his everyday conversation. He seems to have a set of pigeon-holes marked off in numbers, into which he consigns his acquaintances and according to which they are expected to regulate their behaviour. A sort of "act your age" fixation. Is this the preoccupation of someone who doesn't want to grow old himself?

However, now that it is continually being brought to my attention, this gap of ten years has made me more nervous than usual. I looked harder and longer in the mirror last night and decided that bearing two children does absolutely nothing for one's bodily charms. Parts of mine look a bit like scrambled eggs, though fortunately those bits are not generally on view.

Happily, my face has escaped the worst and has relatively few lines, though in present circumstances I fear they are multiplying by the minute, and apart from some tension around the mouth which everyone gets in time, the skin seems to have recovered its bloom and I occasionally look quite radiant. It's love isn't it?

So why am I disturbed? So far as I can tell, the advancing years don't worry Michael and haven't yet appeared to worry Alan. They certainly don't stop Tom from active (if not altogether serious) pursuit, and only yesterday Andrew the troubadour brought courgettes, a large cabbage and the nicest new potatoes, which I cooked this evening in a lavish supper for three.

Michael enjoys having Lucy in the house again and has been laughing quite boyishly. At times like this I realise what a lucky woman I am, ageing tummy notwithstanding.

Lucy sends love to Suzie and says she has a present for her. I send love to everybody and wish you were all nearer. I could do with a sight of you.

Love, Hannah.

P S Lucy's agent has offered her some telly commercials That would bring in the cash and allow her more time with Andy. I hope it comes off.

ooOoo

23

Christabel Fraser

FROM   Hannah Pascoe
TO: Chrissiefras@coolmail.net
SENT: 26 March 2008
SUBJECT: Life still goes on.

This is following hard upon the heels of yesterday's because I'm confused and need to talk.

I drove to Church Street this morning as arranged and found a man and woman there from another ward, soliciting Alan's help in the May election and trying to overcome his resistance by saying how impressed the electorate would be if he canvassed with scar and romantic tale of political harassment.

Alan was rising cautiously to the bait, aware of the implications and also of the possibilities. I could see that he found the invitation quite seductive. "Although I'm not convinced I wouldn't do more harm than good," he said, "The opposition would certainly use it against you, and we couldn't really mention harassment by the chairman, not even accidentally, as that would be laying *us* open to harassment – impugning the reputation of the child's parents, which would go down like a lead balloon. I'd really like to help, but seriously

112

I'm not convinced it would work."

The man with him was stocky and solid, with wiry dark hair on the back of his head and outlining his face in a short, well manicured fringe. He was wearing a polo-necked pullover and pale blue jeans. His name turned out to be Max and he regarded Alan thoughtfully, tapping his teeth with the end of his biro. "I don't know though," he said at last: "You've been absolutely cleared and the girl's father should be feeling guilty as hell, letting her out after dark with a faulty bike. He may not even try to use it against you, knowing he could be in trouble if he did. Something tells me he could be as afraid of adverse publicity as you are."

Alan frowned and the woman shook her head. "No," she said, "We leave the bad taste alone, I think, and carry on as if nothing's happened."

Max gave a hooting laugh. "It's a pity we can't use it, but we'd better be good I suppose."

Alan looked across at me and smiled. "Lib Dems have had a name in the past for dirty fighting," he explained, "and to a large extent it was valid, although we try to be pure as the driven snow nowadays if we can. The other parties are usually so busy slagging each other off and trying to ignore us that we can afford to leave them to it. They do a great job of mutual destruction without any help from us."

The woman, who was introduced as Ruth and who was as chic as Max was not, in black sweater and skirt with a gold and white scarf in an elegant knot beneath one ear, suddenly belied her sophisticated appearance and grinned at me.

"Everybody has to use everything they can in this game" she said. "Nobody's whiter than white, but there's no need to descend to the pit. Anyway the voters usually spot bad taste so it can work against you."

I looked from one to the other, feeling shy and out of my depth. Alan returned to the matter in hand.

"Okay, I'll help, but only low key and if we keep the accident right out of it."

"Do you really think that's possible?"

"We can try."

"Even if you're not being charged and come out of it without a stain…?"

"No, sorry."

There was a pause while Max and Ruth looked at each other and then we all looked at Alan. He studied his fingernails. Then he said. "Too close to home."

Ruth became brisk. "Fair enough. And we don't need it anyway. You're courageously supporting your candidate fresh from a bed of pain." She screwed up her face at me with what in a less elegant person could only be described as rather naughty glee. I was definitely warming to her.

"The point is," said Max, leaning forward and giving a hitch to his pullover. "What are you prepared to do? Door-to-door canvass? Actually we do a lot of telephone canvassing, now, if you really couldn't bring yourself to ring doorbells."

"No, I'll do door-to-door. I don't enjoy the other kind. I know I hate to have people asking me questions on the phone."

"Brilliant! Have you got a Focus delivery round?"

"I had, but gave it back after the accident. I'll take it again now."

"Better and better!" Ruth was scribbling happily in a notepad. Then she turned purposefully to me. "And how about you?"

I was taken aback and fell into the classic reply "Who, me?"

Alan twinkled gravely at us both. "Hannah hasn't got that far yet," he said. "She's here as a friend, not a party activist."

"Yet!" Max breathed meaningfully, and Ruth tucked her lower lip neatly beneath her top teeth. Then she smiled sympathetically. "You're not going to say 'I'm not a political animal' are you? You look far too intelligent."

"No, I'm not and I don't," I replied, falling for it. "And to put the record straight, I have been a party activist in my time and even went canvassing once, to help Alan's father in Wakefield. So there!"

I crossed my legs and folded my arms in a gesture of finality.

"So there!" echoed Alan, nodding at Ruth. He turned back to me. "Be careful what you say. Once these people sniff out a helper there's no end to what they'll ask you to do."

I looked suitably warned, silently praying they wouldn't ask me any questions about Bill's campaign because what little I'd understood at the time had now been wiped clean from my mind. I had done it for fun, and wondered if I should confess. But I could see from the resolute gleam in Ruth's eye that she was about to pin me down, so I said as innocently as possible, "People do say that, don't they, about not being political animals. It amuses me, as if you can only go into politics if you're a rhino or an orang-u-tang."

Max snorted, "And they'd probably make better politicians than some we've got," he said.

"Oh absolutely, but it's an excuse," Ruth agreed. "Most people think of politics as something out there, something other people do, nothing to do with ordinary life at all."

"Whereas," said Alan "there's nothing that isn't touched by it, and if voters realised exactly how their lives are affected by quote politics unquote" and he made two little gestures in the air with his fingers, "they'd be out there joining parties and campaigning on street corners."

I suddenly had a sharply clear memory of Bill at a party fifteen years earlier saying the same, and for the first time recognised the father in the son.

"But they don't," he continued, "and they don't listen when you try to explain. They just say things like 'Oh, you politicians are all alike, can't trust any of you'"

"Or 'All you do is slag each other off,'" said Max.

"But isn't that true to a certain extent?" I was suddenly a target for three pairs of eyes.

Max said "Of course it's true".

"Depends what you mean by slagging off," said Ruth.

"It's a competitive business," Alan explained, "the best way of competing is to have the best policies and stand on the best record, but if other parties are pushing lies or policies we think are wrong or unfair, of course we have to say so."

Ruth spluttered. "All in the best possible taste,"

"Of course"

I laughed suddenly. "You enjoy this."

They smiled back.

"Exhausting but exhilarating," Max said, "There's nothing to beat a good fight."

"All good clean fun," Ruth added.

"But deadly serious," said Alan, and I had a *frisson* of nervous excitement, of unease, almost of fear. This was a new Alan, joined with the other two in a purpose I had no part in and which threatened to exclude me. I looked from one to the other. "You sound alike a Greek chorus. "What can I do to help?"

"Good girl," said Max. Ruth beamed and Alan put out a hand to cover mine, and a beatific warmth spread from it down to my toes and up to the top of my head, with its core somewhere round about my waistline. I didn't know what I'd put my name to, but didn't care one jot.

"By the way," Ruth explained. "I'm the candidate, so perhaps you'd like to change your mind?"

I laughed, surprised without quite knowing why, but she carried on talking. "We all know you're Hannah Pascoe of Wayside Walk."

"*Late* of Wayside Walk," I corrected. "I have left it, you know."

"Okay, late of. We didn't need telling, we'd have recognised you anyway. But how do you feel about using it as publicity for us? You know – local celeb throws in her lot with Lib Dems and is actually out on the streets campaigning for their candidate Ruth Baker. That sort of thing?"

"Don't if you'd rather not, Hannah," Alan said quickly.

"I don't know," I said. "I did retire on purpose to leave that sort of thing behind, and I'm not sure I want to come out of hiding yet – if at all. Do you mind if I think about it?"

"Not in the least, and I personally won't mind either way, and there are things you can do out of the public eye. It's up to you."

I was grateful but unconvinced. I know how useful an identifiable name can be, especially from the pervasive world of television.

By the time the visitors had gone I'd agreed to deliver leaflets in a road I'd never heard of and to do something called 'Telling' on polling day. Alan carried the mugs through to the kitchen and refilled the kettle, then he took my face in his hands and kissed me. "Thank you", he said, and I could have bathed in his warmth.

"They're nice, those people," I said.

"Yes, Ruth especially. She's bright and intelligent

117

and the voters like her. She deserves to get in and probably will."

"Is she standing instead of you?"

"Yes, and she's better than me. I'll keep for another time."

I was tempted to ask if she was married and what her husband thought about it, but refrained, and our lunch was pleasantly cheerful with Alan far brighter than he'd been two days earlier. We told each other funny stories and swapped limericks, and laughed idiotically at our own witticisms. Then he told me he'd seen Nick Wadham's house, and liked his room, and his friend was happy for him to move out of Church Road next Sunday.

"That's wonderful," I said, wondering if I believed what I'd said. "It is wonderful, is it? I mean, you are glad?"

"It will be convenient and a bit cheaper," he said, "which is extremely important at the moment. Besides, I've spent too much time alone lately with nothing to think about but my own problems, so it will be good to have someone else in the house. Company on tap, as it were, with my own space to withdraw to."

I said nothing, my mind was crowded with too many images all at once, speculations about the changes that must take place from now on.

"And I must see about getting signed off," he continued, "so I can work again. I've been cruising for the past few weeks, depending too much on you. That isn't good."

"I'm not complaining," I said.

"I know. You've been unbelievably generous, with your time, your company – even your car. But it isn't good, and I'm determined to get myself a car in the next few days, so you'll be relieved of one burden at least."

His company, his presence in my car a burden? And

118

a car of his own so soon? I was silent, trying to absorb and digest all this new information. He put his hand on mine again, "And it's thanks to you I've got my driving nerve back. It was your offer that did it."

"What sort of car do you want? And where will you get it?

"Something small, cheap to run and reliable, and I'm not sure yet where I shall look. The papers? The nearest garage forecourt? But I shall start tomorrow."

There was a pause. Changes were coming too fast, tumbling over themselves like waves encroaching onto my newly patterned life. They would wash away the symbols of our relationship.

"I shall have to go home for a few days to my family," he continued, "I haven't seen Dominic since Christmas. Elizabeth came to see me in hospital, but I didn't know much about it at the time."

"That will be good," I said. He smiled at me and I tried to smile back, but peculiar things were happening inside me and I was preoccupied with the effort of breathing.

"When will you go?"

"Home?"

I nodded, disliking the word.

"As soon as I've got a car, so I can be back for the election. I rang Elizabeth last night and it should be within the next few days, but we have to confirm it."

"So you won't be away long?"

"God, no. There's too much to be done – by both of us," and he touched my hand again.

"And the job? Will you still be teaching?"

"Supply teaching for now", but I'll start looking for a permanent job as soon as I get back. I'm not trained for anything else."

"Except politics."

"Except politics, but to live by politics one has to be

in Parliament."

"Are you trying to tell me you're not aiming that high?"

He smiled, then grew serious and frowned without seeing me. "Yes, that's where I'd like to be. Eventually. Where the power is."

"And the headaches? Are they better enough for all this activity?" I tried not to sound maternally anxious and negative, but rather think I failed.

"It looks as if I'll have to live with them, so I might as well start learning how."

I studied him carefully, the dark hair newly grown over his forehead, the rather long nose, the scar which was losing its pinkness. He saw my eyes rest on it, and touched it with his finger.

"I don't want to worry Dominic with this," he said,.

"You won't."

"How can you be sure?"

"He loves you."

For what seemed many minutes we gazed directly at each other across the table, in silence. Then he said, "You're an extraordinary woman."

"Yes, so you've said before." I answered lightly.

I arrived home in time to pour myself a cup of tea and listen to Grieg's Holborn Suite. It seemed many weeks since I had last done so, which made me wonder at the changes in my life in so short a time.

I am not looking too closely at the changes to come, seeing only positive facts like Alan's new independence, the car in which I shall be his passenger rather than he in mine, the house which would be his new home shared with a friendly acquaintance who would surely give him hope and encouragement.

I thought of all the advantages, but still there was this unease, this sense of encroaching pain, almost of foreboding.

When Michael came home he said he was going out again. To a meeting, he said. "What meeting?" I asked, surprised that there had been so many.

"Only something to do with work. You're not going out, are you?"

"No. Would it matter if I were?"

"No, no, of course not," he said, and vanished to change his shirt.

I began to feel abandoned. It's been that sort of day.

Love for now, Hannah.

ooOoo

24

Christabel Fraser

FROM   Hannah Pascoe
TO: Chrissiefras@coolmail.net
SENT: 28 March 2008
SUBJECT: Explanation required.

What's happening to me Chrissie? Where am I going in this relationship and what do I want from it? Even more to the point, what am I likely to get?

I read that love is an illness, a disease, a form of insanity. Certainly only those in its grip can understand the power, the illogicality and the effect of it as a life force, the inspirational zest by which everything and everyone is transformed.

Because I love this Alan Box I now love the entire population of the world – the galaxy – the universe. And because the God whom I have come to perceive as a personal God has made the population, the world, the universe and, of course, Alan Box, I now love Him too with a quite amazing fervour. It is because of this very perception of God as the creator of beauty and justice (and Alan Box) that I am so bewildered by the strength of my emotions, for while they are certainly beautiful, are they also just? How far would I go in this relationship? Would I be unfaithful to Michael? Despite my protestations, would I ever leave him for Alan?

At the moment, the former is conceivable, the latter is not. Michael has been in my life too long. Even at his most difficult moments, there has been an instinct to protect him, to anticipate his unhappy moods and want to change them, sort out his problems, nurse him through colds and laugh at his jokes. I never want to hurt him, so how I could seriously think of leaving at all, let alone doing a bunk with another man?

Besides, he is the anchor chain in my world's harbour, so the idea is somehow preposterous. And yet I remain obsessed, and as the relationship with Alan grows closer, so I am forced to recognise the one with Michael as not being close at all. I don't know what goes on in his mind and never did, because we have never shared our mental workings-out like you and me, or Alan and me, coming back minutes later with "I didn't say exactly what I mean" or "I've been thinking, and now realise that…"

Because of this I am attracted more and more to someone who talks to me about his deepest thoughts and feelings, his fears and guilt, his past and his problematic future. This intellectual intimacy is almost closer than a sexual one, and there is, besides, a gentleness and a subtlety which truly is the touch of mind on mind.

He has the power to lay a delicate finger on my thoughts and draw me into an awareness I never knew I had.

But though this closeness has a kind of mental sexuality, it's no substitute for physical love – at least not for me, though perhaps it is for him. And the closer we become mentally the more I desire him sexually, so that sometimes when we sit in the half light, or stand together under the trees, I become temporarily unhinged. This positive but ephemeral unity needs to be translated – preferably in bed!

I am now ferociously protective and at the same time filled with reverence. Not long ago there was a news report of a group of men being taken out, stripped to the skin and then shot. And I knew without doubt that to save Alan from such humiliation, from the awful vulnerability of nakedness and from the final degradation of death, I would certainly die myself. But even without the death threat, nobody is to degrade the body which is his alone and must be inviolate (though I have to admit that, while not enjoying it myself yet, there's this overwhelming feeling that such is my right).

What he feels about this I really don't know. I swing from hope to despair. He holds my hand, touches my cheek, kisses my lips and often hugs me for a long time, yet after every demonstration he will withdraw and seem to avoid touching me at all. Then I realise he has regretted the impulse and may never touch me again, that the relationship will never be deeper or wider than it is now.

Then, next time we meet, he will hold my hand tightly or grip my arms and tell me how important I am to him, and his eyes will tell me even more. I have, after all, lived long enough and flirted often enough to be capable of recognising signals when they're there. So why do I keep getting mixed messages?

Is he waiting for me? Is he waiting for the right moment? Is he holding back because I'm married (the perfect gentleman and all that)? Is he just a flirt and not waiting at all, because there's nothing to wait for and he's simply grateful?

And what happened to the protestations at the start of this letter that I wouldn't be unfaithful to Michael? Can they be forgotten in a couple of pages? It's obviously an empty premise if the temptation is never to be put in my way! Certainly I'm safe for a few days, since the object of all this has bought himself a Ford Fiesta and driven up to Ossett. He won't be home until Friday.

Yesterday I had a visit from Ruth Baker, the Lib Dem candidate whom I met on Monday. She came to bring me the usual pile of leaflets, all neatly folded into a rubber band with a typewritten slip showing the street name and the number of houses. She was also, I suspect, sizing me up as a potential activist, the real sort, not the off-and-on kind I appear to be at present. She was, I think, also endeavouring to find out in the most diplomatic way exactly what my relationship is with Alan.

Naturally I didn't tell her. How could I? I don't know what it is myself. She is attractive in a personable but zany way, with an infectiously quirky smile and a grin that splits her face, and though there is no proper classical beauty, she has a natural sort of grace about her and somehow contrives an air of style. Perhaps it has to do with the clothes she wears, and the charming carelessness with which she wears them. Perhaps it's the length of her skirt or the fit of her trousers, or perhaps she's just one of those infuriating women who could look graceful in a black bin liner.

I like her but my heart misgives me, for she is 25 years my junior and will be seeing more of Alan than I care to contemplate. I now know she's married, so why these stirrings of jealousy? The sensation is unfamiliar and quite horrid, since I've never been a jealous person before, and have always enjoyed and appreciated the company of younger women, attractive or not!

Anyway, she delivered her leaflets, exchanged a few witticisms, assessed my work potential and then departed. Whether she was satisfied on all counts I can't say, but I shall now put on my trainers and depart also, to fulfil this newly acquired duty while the sun is shining.

It's a long time since I went around sticking pieces of paper through letterboxes but I expect that, like most things, once learnt the knack is never lost.

I shall of course let you know. Love, Hannah.

ooOoo

25

Christabel Fraser

FROM   Hannah Pascoe
TO: Chrissiefras@coolmail.net
SENT: 31 March 2008
SUBJECT: He's back.

Alan is back from Ossett and moves into Nick's house tomorrow. I have told myself he's busy with removals and that I can't reasonably expect to hear from him until he's settled in, but all the same every separate minute of time until I do is like twenty four hours.

His visit home must have affected him quite deeply under the circumstances, but whether happily or not is beyond guessing, and the lifting of the fear of criminal proceedings must be like having a bear taken off his back, so his mind will have plenty to fill it besides myself.

But how long can I go without ringing him? More to the point, how long will he let me go before taking action himself?

At least Nick Wadham is an old and friendly colleague, so my welcome there shouldn't be in doubt, and at least Bill rings me regularly – seemingly not just because of Alan but for my sake too.

If you can't talk to the man you love, the next best thing has to be talking to his dad.

He, Bill, will be coming to help with Polling Day in May.

Michael and I were invited to a party at Janine's the other day. M didn't go (why was I surprised?) but it was good to see friends I've been neglecting for too many weeks. Tom was his usual attentive, irreverent self, but for me flirting is now an effort. Karen was there, hoping for a sight of Mel, who wasn't. Hatchet Jaw wasn't mentioned, being definitely *persona non gratis* now.

Her mother lives in Reading but her father vanished years ago, so Aunty Janine has a important role to play. Her stage career has properly introduced little K to the bright lights and she's mad to join in, although Jan, more or less in *loco parentis*, hasn't liked to encourage her into something so hazardous and unpredictable without K's mother's support, so Karen has taken the bit between her teeth and applied to Drama school starting next October. Her immediate wish-dream is for a small part in Wayside Walk.

Jan was unhappy about Hatchet Jaw from the first, but says very little could be done at the time to stop it all developing. "Like a lot of small, sweet, fragile-looking people," she said, "somehow or other she manages to get her own way in the end."

I have to agree. Karen will probably go far.

2.30 pm. Nick has just rung to ask if I'd like to call this evening. Don't know if he's nervous or simply being friendly, or maybe just courteous, since I introduced them and set up the arrangements.

Michael had some Saturday morning patients but came home for lunch. He seemed abstracted and made a phone call from his study, then went out again saying there were a few things he had to get. We usually go shopping together at the weekend. The world is going just a little crazy.

3.00 pm. Alan rang. Could he drive over in his nice new car this afternoon. I said yes of course, rejoicing to hear his voice after having convinced myself that I wouldn't, but wondering if the visit would interfere with my invitation to Waterloo Road later. To be caught snooping round his room would be embarrassing, but why do I so badly want to see it before he changes it with his presence? If necessary I shall cancel this evening's visit. At least there's an opportunity for Michael and Alan to meet, to establish a basis of straightforward honesty and respectability to a rather equivocal situation.

He, Alan, is due here in twenty minutes.

I'll write again tomorrow. Love, Hannah.

ooOoo

26

Christabel Fraser

FROM   Hannah Pascoe

TO: Chrissiefras@coolmail.net
SENT: 1 April 2008
SUBJECT: Who's the fool today?

Alan was obviously pleased with himself yesterday, driving his own car through our gates with an air of nonchalance which deceived nobody. It's a nice little car, a sort of metallic dark green, taking the journey up to Ossett and back quite happily it seems.Alan told me about the job applications he made and a little, but not much, about the trip home, and we discussed teaching, its problems and possibilities, practicalities and job satisfaction, and whether cash-on-a-Friday jobs would ever have enough meaning for either of us. He had come back from Ossett with serious doubts about whether he should be teaching at all but should accept supply work while looking about for something more permanent – either in schools or out of them. He was just finding his feet here and coming to conclusions about career and politics when the accident happened. But since, by its very nature, the job would have come to an end anyway quite soon, the crash merely hastened its demise. But now what? And where? And when?

I asked why he had chosen this place to fly to, and he said because of two old college friends, one of whom had offered him his house to live in. The other was Steve Hobday.

"I don't know where I'd have been without either of them," Alan said. He told me there were a few things he must take to Nick's house before tomorrow, so to avoid embarrassment I mentioned Nick's invitation to me.

"Really? Perhaps I'll see you there then. That would be nice."

He didn't suggest our going together.

Michael arrived home just as Alan was about to

leave. They met on the doorstep and exchanged a few politenesses, then Alan drove away in his smart green Fiesta and I opened a bottle of wine and began preparations for tea. Michael followed me into the kitchen.

He leaned against the work-top, looking very tired. I saw brown circles under his eyes and little pouches under his chin which, so far as I knew, hadn't been there before. But perhaps they were. Such has been my preoccupation, I may not have noticed them.

Irritation, which is a fairly common sensation in our relationship, gave way to remorse. What have I been doing?

I poured a glass of wine and handed it to him, studying his face.

"Are you all right?"

"Yes, why? Shouldn't I be?"

Some people always answer questions with questions, leaving one wrong-footed.

"You look tired," I replied.

"No more than usual. It's been a tiring day."

"Have you any meetings tonight? Will you be able to have an evening off?"

"Yes, I'll be in," There was a pause, then he turned away. "How about you?"

I knew then that I shouldn't go to Waterloo Road, but would be quite unable to stop myself. I temporised. "Only for an hour," I said, "I'm going to see Nick Wadham. Do you remember him?"

"Vaguely. What are you going there for?"

I mentally shut my eyes and dived in. "He's agreed to let Alan move into his room tomorrow and he's asked me round this evening, presumably for a chat but I'd like to talk to him anyway."

"Would you? Why?"

I hesitated, not sure of the truth myself. "Because

I'm nosey, I suppose," I admitted, "and because I introduced them and feel responsible – for both of them in a funny sort of way. Nick's an old friend and Alan has been in so much trouble and isn't really better yet."

Michael finished his wine, refilled the glass and stood staring out of the kitchen window. "I've already warned you to be careful," he said. "You can't resist people with problems."

I laughed, "I don't think he'll hang on, if that's what you mean. He's more likely to cast me off," I added, half joking until I realised the words rang with a rather painful truth.

Michael shrugged. "Where does Nick live?"

I told him. "I won't stay. Just a quick whizz round and a brief chat."

I fried two pieces of rump steak, added chips and mushrooms and poured more wine, and we ate in a preoccupied kind of silence. My conscience taxed me with deceit and subterfuge, although I'd said nothing that wasn't true. It had simply not been the whole truth. I kissed him goodbye when I left, promising not to be long.

27 Waterloo Road was a pleasant surprise. It has an air of comfort. Not a large house, but appreciably larger than the one at Church Street, with a cosy sitting room, a large, bright welcoming kitchen and a small but tidy bedroom for Alan. It's previous occupant is now on his way to Massachusetts. Nick said little about him, but I gather Alan's presence in the house will be welcome. And although Alan will be catering for himself, Nick's friendly sympathy suggests that he might have fallen on his feet.

He left me to browse, so I spent a minute or two in the bedroom, taking its ambience to myself so that even if I never enter the room again I shall remember every detail and every nuance.

I briefly described Alan's accident and the present legal position, and gave my opinion that A would almost certainly be okay now, but if by any chance he wasn't then Nick was welcome to call on me for help at any time.

"Thanks Hannah," he said, "I know I can, but I think he'll be all right with me."

He offered me coffee, which we drank in the little sitting room, with neat leather coasters on a little round table on which we rested our mugs, and we talked about Wayside Walk, the latest developments and new ingredients in the story.

He asked why I never watch the show myself.

"I did once and didn't enjoy it. Not sure why. Probably don't like the thought of it all going on without me. Besides, I never watched it while I was in it so I don't see why I should start now. And anyway, I'm trying to start a new life, not stay in an old one."

So far as Nick knows, Maisie is to stay with her sister, but my TV niece Anne is to be married for the second time, and Mel is shortly to be surprised by the advent of an illegitimate daughter, a little waif from the past.

As we bade each other a cheerful goodnight, with the prospect of meeting again in the future, I took myself out into the Spring evening and wondered if he might be gay. Girl friends had not been specifically mentioned, and his style of living and his manner towards me had recalled gay friends from my own past. Then there was also the equivocal lodger who had left for Massachusetts, to Nick's obvious regret.

The suspicion has made me uneasy. I'm not so innocent as to overlook the possibility that Alan's gentlemanly behaviour might not be so gentlemanly after all. I may simply be the wrong sex!

I don't really think this is true. He has talked of past

girl friends, and as not all these stories are to his credit, there seems little reason to doubt them. His astounding reluctance therefore to hurl me to the floor and ravish me stems, I hope, more from shock, injury, depression after his accident or simply because I have a husband and he doesn't want a relationship with a married woman. I vastly prefer that explanation to the ultimate one – that he just doesn't fancy me!

I came home but couldn't sleep. Michael had gone to bed. It is now 6.30am, and April Fools Day, and Alan will move into his new home. Without my help. I ought to be happy that he's independent at last. Instead I feel uncomfortable without being able to identify the cause, and nameless fears are scratching at my peace, shifting suspicions that Nick will somehow damage this subtle and as yet fragile relationship with Alan, or that Ruth's infectious charm and powerful personality will seduce him away, or merely that he will drift from me through simple force of circumstances. All these thoughts are making me sad and fearful. Who is the fool on this April Fool's Day?

I shall have a bath and dress for a new day, and hope that action will in the end rescue me from any more of these woeful thoughts.

ooOoo

27

Christabel Fraser

FROM   Hannah Pascoe
TO: Chrissiefras@coolmail.net
SENT: 3 April 2008

SUBJECT: He's in!

Well, he's in. Stowed, fitted, snug, though his sparse belongings don't exactly add up to luxurious living. He has furniture scattered about the country 'twixt friend and friend, although he rarely mentions these friends to me. It's Bill who talks, at length, about the beauty of this one or the incredible talent of that one, or the commonsense of a third, with the gusto of a proud father showing off his progeny and at the same time warning interested parties that they're not the only pebbles in the sea (or fish on the beach).

If his intention is to make me feel inadequate then he is succeeding beyond his wildest expectations. Never in my life have I been so aware of my deficiencies, and especially aware of my Advancing Age. It colours everything I see and hear, for always, at the deepest level, is the consciousness that in nine months time I shall be sixty, while Alan will only just be fifty.

Sixty is such a landmark, a watershed between ordinary everyday people and Senior Citizens and however bus companies and theatre managers dress up the truth, the tactful word "concessions" simply means that Old Age Pensioners – holders of pension books – can buy tickets at a discount.

In nine months I shall be a Concessionary Fare, entitled to my bus pass. And the world will be populated by girls with youth in their bodies and elastic in their skin, with dewy faces and clear jaw-lines and the promise of years and years (and babies) to come.

What chance have I against such a promise? Yet I continue to believe in Love as opposed to Lust, and know that I have more to offer in experience and depth of commitment then any girl half my age.

Am I deceiving myself? Misled by my own

fanmail? Surely not, when there are friends about who seem to love me with or without a bus pass. Do they love me for past fame, such as it was, or am I just Good Fun To Be With?

Some years ago an old acquaintance, newly met again after many years, told me how little I'd changed. "Same old Jokey Hannah," she said. I was horribly disconcerted and temporarily short of anything to say. The image she had evoked was anything but the one I wanted.

Chrissie my old dear, please tell me you don't love me just as Jokey Hannah.

Alan was exceptionally nice to me yesterday. I was invited to supper, and the three of us sat down to a casserole cooked splendidly by Nick himself. Michael was out again. A lecture this time, he said.

After supper Alan and I sat for a while in his room. We talked until the light grew less and vanished altogether, and still we sat on in a thoughtful dimness. And when I rose to say goodnight he put his hand to the back of my head and for the first time kissed me passionately.

"I need you," he said.

"That's good," I sighed. "I need you too."

He smiled me to the door and his lingering look followed me all the way home to Michael and a late supper.

Michael is still pale and tired looking. He seems to have withdrawn into another life. Because I am now so riddled with guilt and conflict, I either fail to see him altogether or see him with a new and painful clarity.

Impossible to contemplate hurting him, yet if Alan said he loved me, what would I do?

Michael looked at his watch when I arrived home, but as the hour was not late he nodded hello and asked how the house visit went.

"Fine," I said. "I think he's going to be okay there."

"I should think he is, and I hope he's grateful. Not only do you get him off a charge of dangerous driving, even manslaughter if the girl had died, you find him somewhere to live. He has much to be grateful to you for, and I hope he behaves accordingly."

I pulled a face. It was good to have Michael's support, but I don't want Alan's gratitude. It's an encumbrance. Besides, what does Michael, as my husband, mean by "accordingly"? I am confused and filled with more misgivings then ever.

When we went to bed Michael decided to be affectionate and although I responded I didn't know how I felt or what I wanted.

Alan needs me, but I am beginning to dislike myself.

Love, Hannah.

ooOoo

28

Christabel Fraser

FROM   Hannah Pascoe
TO: Chrissiefras@coolmail.net
SENT: 6 April 2008
SUBJECT: Decisions, decisions!

I really should read the local papers. Yesterday I rang Alan, to ask how he was and if there'd been any news, and he told me the story had appeared in the local press. Not too disastrous, as it also mentioned that the police were not charging him.

"Sounds okay," I said, "Could have been a lot worse anyway. Maybe we should celebrate."

He asked if I were busy and invited me to Waterloo Road, an invitation I would find impossible to refuse even if I hadn't been impatiently kicking my heels, so off I went to eat cheese salad in the kitchen (the owner of it being engaged in slaving in front of hot studio cameras.

Alan described his new life there and said how happy he was in it. "This house is exactly right and Nick is exactly right," he said. "I can't thank you enough for finding them for me." Then he went on to talk of the election and his applications for work, and once again I felt a mysterious sense of unease, of exclusion not only from his future but also in some strange way from his present. As if I were in the process of lifting him with tender care from my own life and planting him in someone else's instead.

So for the first time I talked about Michael. I needed a response, an indication that Alan cared about my situation and perhaps wished to change it, but although his sympathy and concern washed over me like a warm shower, he made no practical suggestions. And when I left for home in the afternoon, his kiss was as it had been before, loving and gentle. The passion had melted into caring tenderness, and I should be happy with that. As indeed I should be happy with his improved circumstances.

Unfortunately I am not.

As I was leaving the house Nick came up the path, released early from W. W. He said "Hello again," and then "Goodbye again," and then, to Alan, "Cuppa tea?" Alan waited to see me drive away and then followed Nick through the door and disappeared. I felt shut out.

When Michael came home I told him about the result of the case so far and his pleasure seemed quite genuine. We talked it all through in detail and listened to some Gilbert and Sullivan, and I played some Chopin and some Grieg on the piano for him to exclaim over (which he obligingly did, being unable to play a note himself and therefore being in no position to criticise!)

I felt closer to him than I'd done for some time. Weeks, maybe months! I have no right to play ducks and drakes with his life. He is much too nice.

I awoke this morning to new decisions. They are painful ones, but they're bringing a certain peace.

I'll write again when I've sorted them out.

Till then, all love, Hannah.

ooOoo

29

Christabel Fraser

FROM   Hannah Pascoe
TO: Chrissiefras@coolmail.net
SENT: 12 April 2008
SUBJECT: OK!

Yes, I agree. The decision was made immediately after sending the last email. I shall devote myself to repairing whatever is slipping or sticking between me and Michael, and spend less time skidding about after a full grown man who doesn't need me, like a cat with one kitten. (And skidding is the right word. I don't seem able to keep my feet).

This full grown man is now on his way, self confidence mending, energy levels rising, eyes looking out to people and action instead of within himself and his inadequacies.

In short, he doesn't need me now for what I can do, and I'm not sure how much he truly needs me for what I am. His words and his behaviour change so quickly and are so often at odds with each other that I shall retire for a while, cultivate a casual helpfulness, and let him get on without me.

There is an aphorism I have always remembered and which I believe to be true: "If you love something let it go. If it comes back it's yours, if it doesn't it never was." So if Alan cares enough he will come back of his own accord.

I spent the weekend alone with Michael. We gardened and pottered and ate lamb and mint sauce and watched television. We did plenty of pottering things, but we didn't talk much, and when we did the conversation was once again difficult to pin down. I had the familiar sensation of trying to eat custard with a knife and fork.

Is it a constitutional thing, an inherent difference between us, or is he putting up a wall that gets higher and firmer each time I succeed in levering a brick from it? If I don't provoke him the talk stays safely with dogs, teeth or television, or my inconsequential prattle. Perhaps it's dealing with captive audiences all day which makes him laconic, for after all his audience can't answer back or even argue. With a poised drill under one's nose, who would dare?

If there is a wall, is it my fault? I only know I don't want it to be there, that the sharing of myself, in trust, with someone very beloved, is something I have always deeply wanted. The nearest thing to God. I had come to believe it was impossible with any man, but Alan has proved how wrong I was. He has opened doors and windows on a fresh landscape full of Spring and hope.

Yet I too keep my secrets, do I not? To share my feelings for Alan would destroy whatever there is left with Michael, and that is something I'm not prepared to do. Besides, there's no need, since I am now leaving Alan to his own devices and to God (who knows all about how I feel because I've told him and he knows everything anyway).

But I'm beginning to miss him. The first flush of glorious resolve is giving way to a sick feeling of loss. Besides, I have to see him before long on canvassing missions. What do I do next time he rings? I shouldn't have given him my mobile number. And should I give up the canvassing too?

Help! Hannah

P S   Tomorrow is Good Friday. What an appropriate time for Giving Things Up. Lucy and Andy will be here on Easter Sunday and perhaps we will have a resurrection of our own.

ooOoo

30

Christabel Fraser

FROM   Hannah Pascoe
TO: Chrissiefras@coolmail.net
SENT: 18 April 2008
SUBJECT: Pulling a dentist's teeth

I'm glad you had a happy Easter, and many thanks for your card and for the nice things you said about mine.

Lucy and Andy came round for supper. We are

seeing her a little more often these days, mostly at mealtimes. Andy's photography keeps them comfortably in toothpaste and takeaways, but for solid food and washing machines they usually come home to mum – in harder times anyway. When times get softer again they revert to Waitrose, Marks & Spencers and good wine, but I'm doing them an injustice (truth being sacrificed to a neatly turned sentence). Lucy is turning into an adventurous and often inspired vegetarian cook.

Michael was away in Bournemouth all yesterday, not appearing until past eleven. A conference, he said. When I asked what conference he said "If I told you, it wouldn't mean anything to you."

"Try me," I said.

He did and he was right. It didn't mean anything, but when I asked what and why and how it was that he'd been there, he frowned, sighed and regarded me patiently over the tie he had just taken off.

"The trouble is," he said "that for years you've been out yourself, working most days and a lot of evenings, so you've never noticed. Now you're here more so you do notice, but life didn't stop with Wayside Walk."

I thought about it too. After a pause I said, "Michael, I'm sorry I've been too involved in my own affairs and missing out on yours. I'm trying to make up for it, and would really, truly like to know more about what you do."

His smile was a tad frosty. "Right now I think we both need some sleep," he said, and I felt a bit like a too-early crocus.

I did, however, continue the conversation next morning. "Got any more good conferences today then?"

He laughed shortly. "No, thankfully."

I was surprised. "Don't you like having days off work?"

"Not really. It means patients are missing out, and

anyway they're still all about teeth."

"Doesn't anyone interesting go to them?"

"Sometimes."

"Oh? Who else goes? Anyone I know?"

There was a fractional pause while he selected a clean shirt from the wardrobe. "Oh, different people on different occasions."

I was intrigued, and laughed. Extracting information from my husband has always been like pulling teeth, which is rich, considering his profession. "Well, at least some of them might be congenial," I persevered. "Who went yesterday for example?"

Michael dealt briskly with buttons, lifting his chin so that his reflection in the mirror had a screwed-up look, nose wrinkled, lower lip thrust forward. "Margaret Anglin was there," he said.

I was surprised. "Oh, is she back? I thought she left the practice years ago."

"She did. She was at the conference under her own steam. She's a self-employed hygienist."

I remembered her. Quiet and rather dignified, she was as reserved as I am not, and usually made me feel overdressed and too highly flavoured, a bit like a flamboyant curry. She must be nicely into quiet, dignified middle age now. "Not exactly sparkling company," I sympathised.

I watched his fingers negotiate a brown and gold tie and was amused. "What do you find to talk about?"

Michael finished tying his tie, turned his head from side to side to make sure there was no stubble on his cheeks, then patted his pockets in a final sort of gesture.

"Well, I'm off," he kissed me briefly. "You are funny," he said, "Has it ever occurred to you I might like to leave my work behind when I come home?" Then he was off down the stairs, calling "See you at the usual time" as he went. And I was left to my own reflections, both externally in the mirror (which was far from satisfying) and internally with a sudden gust of longing for Alan (which was even less so).

I am trying hard to concentrate on Michael, but A's face and body keep obtruding in a most unsportsmanlike manner. I find myself gripping the bedclothes and stuffing pillows into my mouth.

It's so long since I've seen you. There is a great urge to get away from all this conflict. Please when may I come?

Love, Hannah.

ooOoo

31

Christabel Fraser

FROM   Hannah Pascoe
TO: Chrissiefras@coolmail.net
SENT: 20 April 2008
SUBJECT: The press does it again

Many, many thanks for last night. Perhaps you'd like to pin a "Reserved for HP" notice on your spare room door, for that cosy little room is fast becoming a refuge.

To talk things through, to have your response *now*, your opinion which, though partisan, is at least one step removed from the heat of the fire, was not only a luxury but a release. I hadn't realised quite how *lonely* the situation was making me feel, and without these missives to you I would by now have become even more deranged than I am. But quite apart from the relief of unloading some of the angst, it seems I needed the respite in readiness for further onslaughts.

Ten minutes after I arrived home, the doorbell rang and an unidentified girl handed over the next load of leaflets to be delivered. It seems they come with quadrupled force and speed at election time.

Ten minutes after that, the phone rang and Bill told me, in a voice low with worry, that there had been an attack in a campaign leaflet put out by another party. He wanted to know how recently I had seen Alan.

"Not for about two weeks," I said, "I thought I'd leave him to get himself settled in."

"Will you get in touch, there's a good girl? I'm coming down myself very soon, but he needs an eye kept on him."

I hesitated. "All right," I said in the end, "although Nick is there and he seems very supportive. But I'll give him a ring. I'd have had to contact him anyway, because I'm supposed to be helping with the election."

"Thank you darling. I'll see you soon. Take you out to dinner."

I said I'd look forward to that, then stood looking at the phone and biting my nails. And as I gazed at it, the instrument suddenly sprang to life again all by itself and I was shocked into biting my tongue instead. I picked up the receiver but was too startled to speak.

"Hello?" said Alan.

Thoroughly shaken, I could only manage a breathy "Hello," in reply.

"Hannah? Are you all right?"

"Yes," I said, smiling with relief. "Yes, I'm fine. I'd only just put the phone down when it sort of went off. It startled me, that's all. I was going to ring you later."

"Were you? That's nice."

"To say I've been to Marlborough for a couple of days, and to ask how the campaign is going and when you want me to do something."

"The campaign's doing nicely, except that the opposition are using me for target practice."

"Oh no!" I moaned, "Is it bad?"

"Bad for me because it's unpleasant and rakes up things I'd rather forget, but Ruth and Max don't seem to mind at all. Actually, they think it's rather a good thing."

"I can't think why. Alan I'm sorry. Are you okay, though?"

"Not very. It's too close."

"Can I do anything?"

"It would be nice to see you."

"Okay. When did you have in mind?"

"Are you busy now? May I drive over?"

I was amazed. Only half an hour earlier I had returned home prepared for an Alanless week and here he was, practically falling over my doorstep.

I laughed. "I'll put the kettle on."

There was a smile from the other end.

"Thanks. See you in a minute."

I stood with bouncing heart, not knowing what to do next. My suitcase was still in the hall waiting to be unpacked. I hadn't looked inside the kitchen or opened my post. Doing none of those things, I brushed my hair instead, washed my hands and cleaned my teeth, dabbed perfume behind my ears and faced the day, ready for whatever life, in the form of Alan Box, chose henceforth to throw at me.

When he saw me he opened his arms, gathered me up and kissed me on the mouth.

"Hannah," he breathed most satisfyingly into my neck, "Thank you for letting me come."

What could I say? He had been pushing at an open door.

So I murmured lightly, in a heavy American drawl, "Y'er welcome," then silently cursed the penchant for flippancy which time after time reduces moments of high romance to eye-crossing bathos.

He smiled and let me go.

"Sit down and tell me what's wrong," I said, turning once again (for after all, what else is there for me to do?) into the all-efficient Mrs Fix-It.

"It sounds ridiculous," he said, "You'll think I'm making a fuss about nothing."

"Have a go."

He thought for a moment, frowning at his hands in what had become a familiar attitude.

"Every time this comes up it brings everything back and I know all over again that Katy was killed and Celia was seriously injured – by me. There's nothing I can do to undo any of it. The trouble is, Ruth and Max are pleased. Angry, but pleased really."

"Pleased? Alan, I'm not sure I understand. How can anyone be pleased?"

He shook his head. "Sorry," he said, "It's this – this *stuff* that appeared in the local paper, and now in an election leaflet," and he held out a cutting and a folded piece of coloured paper. "That! That is what Ruth and Max seem pleased about."

I read the cutting first. The headline was "Child killer helps election campaign." Then it went on:

"The driver of the car which knocked down and seriously injured the 10 year old daughter of Councillor Wimbrook last month is now helping the Liberal Democrats with their election campaign in Quinton Ward.

"Alan Box, a past county councillor in West Yorkshire, who only recently moved to Bristol, has not been charged with any offence, but is understood to have resigned from his teaching post.

Councillor Wimbrook said: "As there were no witnesses, it is impossible to know at this stage whether

Mr Box is guilty of careless driving or dangerous driving, but all this has put an intolerable strain on my wife and myself, and it's rather a kick in the teeth to have him campaigning for another party in the same election."

"While the police have assured him that a witness has, in fact, established Mr Box's innocence, Cllr Wimbrook said he had only one comment to make on Mr Box's actions.

"He said: 'Although I am up for election myself, I am taking no personal part in the campaign but am leaving it to my very efficient team. I would have expected Mr Box to have had the sensitivity to do the same.'"

I pulled a face and opened the folded election leaflet.

"LIBERAL DEMOCRATS TEAM TO INCLUDE THE MAN WHO KNOCKED DOWN AND NEARLY KILLED THE DAUGHTER OF CLLR WIMBROOK," It said.

I looked up quickly. "Isn't that libellous?" I asked.

"Not really, unfortunately." Alan replied, frowning. "Borderline maybe, but the fact is I did knock her down and did nearly kill her. It happened."

"Yes, but…" I said.

"Not but…anything," Alan interrupted . "You can't argue against that. No-one can."

I almost stamped with frustration. "But you're not the candidate. You're not standing yourself, like the girl's father is. And no matter what he says, he's using it against the Lib Dems while promoting his own virtue. It's not fair. If he had any sensitivity himself he'd have kept quiet"

Alan gave a small, tight smile. "That's what Ruth and Max are saying. But carry on reading. It gets better."

The body of the story in the leaflet was more or less word for word the same, even to the quote from Cllr Wimbrook about how although he is standing for election himself he is taking no personal part in the campaign but was leaving it to his very efficient team – finishing with 'I would have expected Mr Box to have had the sensitivity to do the same, especially since we understand his own daughter was killed in the same way only a few years ago, and the comment: 'The Lib Dems must be hard up indeed for helpers.'"

I frowned and let my breath out in an angry "Ppfff!"

"Why are Ruth and Max so pleased? How can they possibly be?"

"It's not so much that they're pleased, but they can see how it can be used to our advantage. Operating a smear campaign is dodgy tactics. The voters don't like it and it often rebounds on their own heads, so public sympathy tends to go to the victim – in this case me, and of course Ruth. But I'm not the candidate, which can be refuted straight away, and am apparently being asked to use my so-called crime to get someone else elected. I don't like it and I don't think I can do it. But how can I tell them that? How can I tell them not to use something when they have the chance?"

"What do you mean, use it? In what way use it?"

"Oh you know, offer our deepest condolences to Cllr Wimbrook and suggest that his family will hardly be consoled by the publicity, especially under the circumstances. Then give public thanks to Alan Box after having gone through such a sad and horrifying experience, especially after having lost his own daughter in such a tragic way. Now, having been exonerated from all blame, he has braved his own mental and physical anguish to do what little he can. Etc etc.. That sort of thing. Sympathetic and dignified. And in spite of all this they want me out canvassing, not to talk about it but to show what a lovely chap I am. Max says if I stay skulking at home I'll simply be confirming what's been said, but I don't agree."

"But why should they pick on you? As you said, you're not the candidate. And won't this and the newspaper just bring everything back to them? It's not fair. Their daughter didn't die. Yours did. It's cruel and hateful and whoever's responsible should be hauled up and…and…and castrated."

Alan laughed. "I never knew you were so bloodthirsty! Max will complain, of course, because the leaflet makes no mention of Karen's evidence, and I know for a fact this was put together *after* her statement to the police. But the damage is done. To me." He took the paper from me, looked at it in disgust and flung it down. "Yuk!"

I said nothing.

"But in this game one uses whatever comes to hand," he added. "So I suppose I can't altogether blame them. The person I do blame, though, is the girl's father, but I can't do anything about him."

"Did Ruth and Max know about Katy?"

"Only that she'd been killed, that's all. No details."

I thought for a moment. Then I asked: "What are your options?"

"My options?"

I answered for him, ticking my fingers.

"You can carry on and do what Ruth and Max want you to do. You can carry on helping but out of sight, and forbid them to use the situation in any way that affects you. Or you can drop out of the whole thing. Which do you feel most comfortable with?"

"I'd like to drop out."

"Would you really? Are you sure? How would you feel afterwards?"

"Of course I'd feel a louse, but I shall feel a louse

anyway."

He stared again at his hands and a black cloud hung about him, almost a tangible thing. Then he looked up and met my eyes. "I'm sorry Hannah. I shouldn't inflict this on you. I'm very bad company today."

I sat quite still, forcing myself to be calm so that the stillness might pass from myself to him. Neither of us spoke for several minutes. Then I said: "You once told me there was nothing you could do to bring Celia and Katy back. So does it matter then what you do?"

"It matters to me."

I thought myself into his position. How would I feel if Timothy had been killed on his motorbike years ago and I had nearly done the same for a boy of Tim's age? Something bled inside me. I went to kneel beside his chair, took his hand and held it.

"It's bloody awful," I said. "I want to help you."

"I know you do."

"I love you, Alan."

"I know."

I looked up and met his scrutiny, deep and loving, and knew I would do anything to see him through a situation which, like a nightmare recurring, came back and back to torment him and colour whatever he tried to do. It wasn't fair.

He pushed the hair back from my forehead. "Hannah," he said, "It means a lot to me to hear you say that. What would I do without you? I'm getting very dependent on you. Too dependent perhaps."

I smiled slightly. "Call it interdependence. I'm dependent on you too."

"I can't imagine how," he frowned. "You're always giving. I never give anything back."

How could I explain that there was nothing I needed from him except his continuing presence, his existence.

"I'm afraid you'll get bored and give up on me," he

149

said, "I drag you down."

"Well of course there's always that," I smiled, rising to my feet and looking down at him. "But honestly, do I look dragged? Or bored? Or ready to give up?"

He smiled back with genuine amusement for the first time, and gave my hand a little shake. "No," he said, "You don't look any of those things. You are too full of life and zest and courage."

I pulled a face. "You're joking! Inside I'm a shivering coward."

"That makes two of us."

We bathed in mutual appreciation. It was like diving into the same hot spring.

"Anyway I don't believe it," he said. He stood up, put his hands on my shoulders and regarded me solemnly. "If you're a coward my name is Stanley Livingstone. Now let's go and find a pub and I'll tell you what I've decided to do."

"Oh well done, that was nice and quick," I nodded, and laughter filled my spirits and the room and heightened the sense of sunshine.

We drove to our Buttress by the river and Alan's cloud lifted. His changes of mood are so quick and so complete that I have to consciously hold still, to adapt to the new person whoever that may be, like a surfer keeping his balance while the board rocks and sways between breakers.

He told me he had decided to continue the campaign, to let Max and Ruth publish the facts as simply as possible without resorting to their own smears, and that he would certainly canvass for them but no more than he felt capable of doing. If he found it too difficult he would stop.

"Sounds all right to me," I said, "Let's drink to it." So we did.

I arrived home in time to cook for Michael, whom I

150

hadn't seen for two days and who was even quieter than usual. We said little all evening and at bedtime he turned out the light immediately. I didn't sleep much. I don't think he did.

It seems at least a month since I left you, yet it was only this morning.

Love, Hannah.

ooOoo

32

Christabel Fraser

FROM   Hannah Pascoe
TO: Chrissiefras@coolmail.net
SENT: 23 April 2008
SUBJECT: Day out.

There's definitely something wrong with Michael. Conscience has been having a fine time, pointing out that my overpowering feelings for Alan must have transmitted themselves and been obvious to anyone with half an eye, however hard I try to cover up. Am I nicer to Michael or less so because of it? Am I preoccupied, or talking too much to fill up the silences?

Last night, towards the end of the evening, he said he was taking today off work. His habit of throwing me unexpected pieces of information, like bread to the ducks, is one I've never grown used to, so never foresee.

"Why do you always leave telling me to the very last minute?" I asked, "I might have arranged something."

"Does it matter? You can still go ahead."

"Yes, but…" I began, knowing before I started that the sentence wouldn't say what I meant it to say, that it would be inadequate and probably inconsistent and even incomprehensible. "When you have a day off," I continued slowly, thinking very hard before I spoke, "I like to be able to enjoy it with you or it's a waste. And if I don't know beforehand I might have fixed something with someone else which I then would prefer not to do, and that would be a pity."

I stopped and waited.

"Well have you?"

"No."

"Then that's all right then. What are you upset about?"

"I'm only upset about the principle. Next time you may not be so lucky. And why tomorrow? What have you done with your patients? Forbidden them not to have toothache?"

"Don't be sharp," Michael said, and I rolled my eyes in exasperation. "Of course I've rearranged the patients."

I gazed at him in wonderment. "So you knew well enough in advance to be able to reorganise your appointments and yet you haven't told me till tonight."

"Tomorrow is convenient. One can't take days off just when one happens to feel like it. There are other people to consider."

I was wrong-footed, knowing my discomfort would seem out of proportion to his crime, and knowing, too, that the discomfort was partly due to the realisation that I was the last person on his list of 'people to consider' — but also because I would now be prevented from seeing Alan if he needed me. And because I felt guilty, I didn't notice until too late that, as usual, he had not only changed the subject and thrown the onus back onto me, but hadn't answered my question either.

"What would you like to do?" I asked in the end, disconcerted and vanquished, knowing that if I pressed him to a reply he would only side-step it again. "Have you any plans?"

"I thought we might have a day in Cheltenham," he said, "We haven't been there for some time."

I wanted to be enthusiastic. I concentrated hard on the pleasures of Regency Cheltenham, the shops, the parks, and as I did so found myself wishing to be away from here, away from a telephone which might ring and away from the complications life has acquired over the past few months.

This morning I was eager to be gone but couldn't explain my restlessness. Michael was in relaxed holiday mood ("Why should he hurry on his day off?") and it was difficult not to bite my nails. If I were going to be out all day I wanted to be gone before the phone rang. Just to make sure, I switched off the mobile phone too.

Michael drove us in his Peugeot and the motorway was clear and easy, so we listened to one of his jazz CDs. We didn't talk very much. Or rather, I chattered and Michael grunted his replies, and we finally drove through the wide streets to the multi-storey car park, nipped a ticket from the machine and walked into the town.

Cheltenham was warm and busy, full of Spring and flower baskets. People like ourselves ambled from shop front to shop front, getting in the way of serious-minded pedestrians who knew where they wanted to go and lost no time going there. We visited the Assembly Rooms, newly opened for the season, and walked around Sandford Park with its daffodil beds, yellow and mauve primroses, and heady, sweet-smelling shrubs. We had coffee in one place and lunch upstairs in another, looking down on the shoppers in the High Street below. We bought books from a wonderful second-hand bookshop, where lovely, faded, dark red cardboard covers evoked memories of a childhood spent with Edgar Jepson and Jeffery Farnol, and where boarding school stories bore absolutely no relation to the reality of yours and mine at St Mary's. I had read those books lying on a large and battered sofa, listening to music with my silent father. And now here I was with an equally silent husband whose remoteness was all the more daunting for his denial of it.

"Talk to you?" He had said in the car. "What do you want to talk about?"

A familiar impasse. Over how many years had I made similar requests and received similar replies? Yet I have always tried again, as I tried again today, until I recognised the impasse for what it was and gave up.

So instead I snatched paragraphs here and there from old books smelling of musty paper so ancient that minute insects journeyed across the pages like tiny dusty dots, and part of me wanted to hold onto this silence. It was familiar, safe even in its discomfort. For after all, don't the latest books tell us that men only talk when they want to exchange information, while women talk in order to feel connected? Who am I to even think of changing the way Michael is constructed?

The trouble is, Chrissie, that this theory has thrown up an exception, and I found myself keening for the joy and satisfaction of sharing myself with someone who not only receives my sharing but also shares himself. No one-way traffic, with confidences disappearing like stones into a duck pond but a wholeness of experience.

As we wandered mutely around Cheltenham, I hungered for Alan, wondering how he was and if he was trying even now to contact me.

We came home in time for supper of sausage and

chips and an evening with the television. Just as we were about to go to bed Michael said: "There's a farewell party tomorrow for Roger. Do you want to go?"

I was touched. Roger has been a dentist in Michael's practice for some years.

"Oh, yes, of course. I didn't know he was leaving? Where's he going?"

"Nowhere, he's retiring."

I nodded, thinking he must be about the right age and wondering about Michael, who would be retiring too within a very few years. And although I'd always known the time would come, and had in fact rather looked forward to it as a new kind of freedom, I now found myself seriously considering what would happen to our relationship when it did.

"Will he just retire, or will he get himself a part time job doing something else?"

"No idea. Jobs are not so easy to find, even for efficient, mature professional people."

I laughed. "How about inefficient, immature, ex-actresses?"

"You could have stayed on as Maisie. You wrote yourself out, nobody did it to you."

There was a familiar edge to his voice. I understood that my jobless state was rankling and felt it may be time to look for gainful employment.

"So where's the farewell party?"

"It's at the Swan, and do you really want to come?"

Now is the time, I thought, to show real interest in my husband's working life. "I'd love to come. I've always liked Roger."

That was several hours ago. Michael is in bed. I am now about to give in to the despairing plea of my closing, crossing eyes and join him there.

Good night, Hannah.

P S Tomorrow is Roger's party.

ooOoo

33

Christabel Fraser

FROM   Hannah Pascoe
TO: Chrissiefras@coolmail.net
SENT: 24 April 2008
SUBJECT: What can I say?

Once more I'm beginning with "How do I begin?", because fortune has turned yet again in a totally unforeseen direction. That is, unforeseen by me, though when I look back over the past I realise all the clues were there. I just didn't have the wit to see them.

What else am I not seeing?

Last night Michael and I went to Roger's farewell party. Margaret Anglin was there. She has that ageless air, neither old nor young. Some years ago she came here once or twice to supper and we met occasionally at social functions, then suddenly she wasn't there any more and I forgot about her. And although Michael had told me she had come back, her presence at the party was for some reason a surprise.

Why was it?

The Swan was full of -people I knew slightly but not very well. One or two knew me by sight, or thought they did, or thought they should but couldn't remember why. Some knew me because they watch W W, but they were in the minority. Obviously dentists don't go in for soaps - just toothpaste and formalin!

Margaret seemed suitably and politely pleased to see me, but I was aware of a *frisson* of disturbance, in myself but possibly transmitted to me, which for the first time made me notice her. And as Michael came from the bar with drinks for us both, I also noticed him.

They were easy together, passing small comments, laughing at each other's jokes. And as the wine flowed and the talk flowed even faster, I saw they were a unit.

It was a shock. I became subdued, curling myself into a defensive ball, longing to go home. But roles were reversed and now it was Michael who was enjoying himself and wanted to stay.

I talked to strangers and tried to hear what they said, discussed Maisie and Wayside Walk and the world of theatre with the ones who were interested, but beneath the same old platitudes truths were dawning on me and I wasn't ready yet to face them.

We drove home in artificial good humour, undressed and went to bed, and as we lay together in the concealing darkness, Michael said "You don't mind if I have lunch with Margaret sometimes, do you?" I turned my head to regard his faintly visible profile. "Why should I mind? At least you've asked. You could have been doing it all along and I'd never have known."

"Yes I could, but now I'm asking you."

"Is there any reason why I should mind?"

"None whatever. It's only lunch."

"Then of course I don't mind. Have fun!" and I turned over onto my side and wondered what was happening to us.

Next morning Ruth rang to ask if I would like to go canvassing with Alan. "Just to see what it's like," she said. "On the other hand you could always try telephone canvassing. That way you wouldn't have to meet anyone."

"No thanks, I hate the idea of disturbing people at home. I know it's disturbing them just as badly to call at the door, but it's different somehow. I don't know why."

"Right then, are you up for a bit of door knocking?"

Still hesitating, I said: "I'm not sure I have the nerve."

"What you? No nerve? Pull the other one. Anyway it's a knack you don't lose, so I thought you might go round with Alan to sort of break yourself in gently"

"Is he good at it?"

"Brilliant. Charm the birds off the trees. That's why you should go with him. Once you've done it you'll be just as good, having bags of charisma of your own."

I was amused. "You're not doing badly yourself. You certainly know how to flatter a girl."

There was a gurgle. "But that doesn't make it not true. You're a gift to any candidate."

"After that how can I refuse? When do you want me?"

"Tonight?"

"Have you asked Alan?"

"Of course. It's as much his idea as mine."

I said okay and where and when did she want me.

"Max's house, 6.30," she said. "35 Station Road. Thanks Hannah, you're a star. See you tonight."

I shook my head, feeling as if I'd been hit by an intercity train. A forceful person, Ruth!

The morning was spent in a state of anxiety, excitement and tension. But there were things I must do, so I buried my feelings, rang Janine and arranged lunch for next day. And at half past one Alan rang to suggest we may as well go together tonight and only take one car.

"Yours or mine?" he asked.

I promised to pick him up at 6.15, since I more or

less had to pass his door *en route* to Max's house.

"How are you anyway?" he asked.

"Fine thanks," I replied cautiously, since I didn't know the answer. "And you?"

"So-so. I'll be glad when tonight's over. I'm not looking forward to it."

"Neither am I, but you'll be okay. All your training will come to the fore. By this time you must have coped with just about everything voters can throw at you."

"Hannah, you're wonderful," he laughed. "You always have an answer."

I was busy eating pizza and salad, changing my shoes and putting supper on a dish for Michael when he came through the hall and into the kitchen.

"Going out?" he asked pleasantly.

"Yes, canvassing for Ruth." I was cheerful because the explanation was both simple and true.

"You'll enjoy that. What time will you be back?"

"No idea. In Wakefield there was always a sort of *après-canvass* with coffee or beer and a post-mortem, but I don't know the form here."

"Do they give you a rosette?"

I laughed. "I should think so, I imagine it's *de-rigueur* but I'll let you know". Then I studied him in sudden surprise. "You look happy. Have you had an especially nice day?"

"Not bad."

I stood mentally on one foot, waiting for him to continue but realising how unlikely that was. Instead he departed to the living room to switch on the television while I took myself out of the front door and into my car.

Wondering about Michael put me onto automatic drive until I realised I was almost at Alan's door without really knowing how I'd got there. With Alan in the passenger seat to guide me, I drove with rather more care to a long rising street bordered on either side by tall, Victorian houses.

There were two people already in the dining room of Max's very long, very narrow home which belies its outside appearance. We were all given cards and rosettes and a map, and were sent cheerfully out by a business-like Max to do our bit for the Party. Alan produced a rosette from his pocket.

"Where did you get that?" I demanded. "It's bigger than mine."

"It's mine and you can't have it."

"How very ungallant!"

He sighed. "Never let it be said…" and with care he pinned his rosette onto my lapel.

"Oh Alan!" I cried, overcome.

Max laughed, handed us posters and ushered us out. I'd been told we must work quickly and accurately, with no time for playing. So, following Alan's directions, I drove us straight to a road of 1930s semi-detached houses with neat front gardens full of daffodils and early bedding plants. and at least one car in each driveway. The trees planted at intervals along the pavement were pale green and delicious. We parked the car outside No. 1 and looked at each other speculatively. Then we opened our doors and stepped out into the Spring evening.

The first house was an ordeal for both of us. As we walked up the path I could feel Alan's painful awareness of his quickly fading scar, and told myself how unlikely it was that any of these people would know who he was. As for knowing who I was, I doubted that too. The idea of a soap actor appearing at their front doors would not occur to them – unless of course they read their local newspapers. Even then they would probably have me down as a Maisie look-alike.

I applauded Alan's courage and told him he didn't have to do this. "Nobody's putting a gun to your head."

"Yes, somebody is. I am."

I clutched my clipboard and stood beside him as he rang the bell. A thin, middle-aged woman opened the door and gazed at us blankly. Alan politely held out his hand and said "Mrs Whiting? My name is Alan and I'm calling on behalf of Ruth Baker, who is your Liberal Democrat candidate. You do know there's an election coming up, don't you?"

As his hand was still extended and he was smiling at her with a sort of beguiling trust, Mrs whiting had little choice but to wipe her own hand surreptitiously on her dress and place it in his. She nodded, a bit bemused.

"You know Ruth Baker from the Focus leaflet," Alan went on. "You do get your Focus regularly?"

The woman nodded again. He continued. "Good, so you know how hard she's been working for you for a long time. Will you be supporting her, Mrs Whiting?"

She shifted her gaze to the hydrangea bush beside the door.

"I don't know yet. Maybe. We'll have to see."

"That's fine," nodded Alan approvingly. "It's good to give it some careful thought. Does your husband feel the same?"

"I don't know what he votes. We never talk about it."

"Well thank you very much for your time," Alan smiled again, more brilliantly this time, and moved away. Mrs Whiting stayed in her doorway watching us. At the gate Alan turned to wave to her. He ticked his card and moved to the next house.

"What did you tick her as?" I asked, intrigued. He showed me the card. "Nothing very clever, I just put her down as Undecided," he said.

The man at Number 3 was large and bald. "No,

we're Labour," he said, and was gone.

The third and fourth houses were closed and obviously empty, despite the one light left burning to deceive burglars, but at the fifth was a young man who leaned on the door post and folded his arms. "Go on, then, convince me," he grinned, but Alan told him if he read the literature put through his door, common sense would do the convincing.

"Whose literature? They all say the same."

"Oh, do you get more than one?"

"Not often."

"And then only at election time, I suppose. Well, we're the ones that deliver stuff all the year round, and we tend to talk about what we've done, not what other people haven't done. But perhaps you don't read it."

"Sometimes."

"In that case you must know the answer. Vote for us."

The young man grinned again and stood upright. "Yes, I usually do."

We all laughed. He watched us walk down the path and waved briefly as I closed the gate.

Alan turned and looked down at me. "And now, my dear, I'm going to send you off on your own. The sooner you get started the better."

I pulled a face. "But I don't feel qualified. I don't know the answers," I whined.

"You've got your crib sheet, you've got bags of charm, and if people ask you questions you can't answer, refer them to Ruth. Tell them she'll call on them personally if necessary. Cheerio," and he gave a little wave and set off across the road towards house Number 14.

So I took a deep breath, reminded myself that nothing can be as terrifying as a First Night, and walked purposefully through the next gate.

162

The rest of the evening was a vividly detailed dream. I went from door to door creating my own patter, culled and adapted from Alan's, and occasionally we stopped on the pavement to compare notes and exchange advice, or simply to laugh. On the whole the reception had been friendly, but a large number had expressed complete disillusion with politicians of any and every colour, and said categorically that they had no intention of voting for anybody.

"You're all alike," they said.

Another paid good dividends by nodding, agreeing that Ruth did indeed work hard. "She got our street lights working again."

"Oh excellent!" I replied "We try our best to look after you."

The last man began an aggressive diatribe. "Can't believe any of you. You promise the earth and then when you get in you don't do anything you promised."

"Do you know," I said thoughtfully, "You sound as if you'd be really good at this yourself. You've got strong views and you could get things done the way you want them. Have you ever thought about standing? Perhaps you'd like to meet the candidate personally. You know – get the low down."

The man, who was wearing his slippers and an old, comfortable pullover, frowned at me, not sure whether to be flattered or offended. Whichever it turned out to be he was undoubtedly silenced, so I smiled reassuringly and suggested he gave our party a try. "After all, it's the only way you're going to get any change at the moment isn't it? You never know, you might even find we're trustworthy after all."

The man came to life again by shaking his head and making a sort of shishing noise through his teeth. "No thanks," he said and firmly closed the door. At least it wasn't slammed, which I took as a hopeful sign.

I relayed the conversation to Alan. It made him laugh. "Poor chap," he murmured. "It might even keep him awake for five minutes tonight."

I also told him of the repaired street light and he nodded. "That's how we win," he said, "by solving peoples' problems for them. Even if we can't solve them altogether we have a pretty go at it, and it pays, believe me. Casework is more important than most people realise, but in fact it's vital."

There was. a surprising number of friendly door-openers who declared themselves quite joyfully to be our committed supporters. But the rest shook their heads and refused to commit themselves. One or two of them I promised a personal phone call or even a visit from Ruth. Generally, however it was borne on me how sadly the dishonest few can dishonour the whole.

Dusk had fallen by the time Alan and I climbed into my car to sit in peaceful darkness. I was tired but filled with adrenaline.

"It was another First Night," I told him. "Stagefright and wondering if you'll dry or forget some vital directions, then the concentration and the exhilaration of doing it all with an audience, and then when you come off you want to go straight back and do it again. I'm shattered, bushed!"

"You were very good."

"Was I? How do you know? We were at different houses."

"I kept an eye and ear on you," he smiled, then he took my hand in a firm clasp. "I certainly had a good pupil. Now let's report back and have a drink."

Max offered us coffee so we stayed for half an hour sitting around on cramped chairs or on the floor, comparing experiences with the other canvassers who drifted in in ones and twos. Then Alan suggested the local pub on the way home, so he and I sat on stools and felt glowingly self-righteous, and eventually I drove him home and he kissed me goodnight outside Nick's door."

"Coming in?"

I shook my head.

"Will you be out again tomorrow?"

I said I may, but wasn't sure. He squeezed my hand and kissed me again.

Michael was reading a book. The television was switched off.

"Well? Did you enjoy it?"

I relived the evening, describing the houses and the people and the funny things they said..

"You're very bright and cheerful," I said at last.

"Yes, I've been out for a drink with Margaret." I said that was nice.

"Yes, it was rather."

We regarded each other in silence. After a while he said: "I was in love with her years ago when she worked with us. She was in love with me too. She wanted me to divorce you and marry her, but the kids were too young. So I didn't go. I should have done. I've been regretting it ever since."

There was another pause. "Now we've met again and we feel the same."

The silence was solid, an audible thing. "And you're in love with Alan Box."

The room turned itself around, making me dizzy. I shut my eyes and sat down, letting out the breath I'd been holding without knowing it.

"How does that make you feel?" I asked.

"My dear," he said, "You have my deepest sympathy and my total support."

Suddenly I was crying, sobbing against his shoulder in confusion and grief. "But that's not the point," I wept. "All these years you've loved someone else and I never knew. How horrible. You must have hated me for being in the way. And I didn't even know. Michael, all those years!"

We went to bed and lay in each other's arms, crying and holding each other in sadness and support.

I woke early this morning, exhausted and very frightened. I lay in bed watching the dawn and thinking:"This isn't happening. It's unthinkable. I don't want to change my life." There is still too much to comprehend, too much to digest and ponder over. When the shock waves have settled perhaps I'll know what it all means.

Until then, Chrissie, I am your stunned but loving Hannah.

ooOoo

34

Christabel Fraser

FROM   Hannah Pascoe
TO: Chrissiefras@coolmail.net
SENT: 26 April 2008
SUBJECT: That seems to be that

After sending the last email, and still bemused, I rang Jan and Myra and arranged to meet them both at the café on the High Street. And such was my state that most of the story came rushing out with the first cup of coffee. I'm not sure if I told it coherently, but I certainly told it with panache – and more than a touch of levity. Never have I been more conscious of this near fatal urge to turn tragic events into funny ones, and to laugh when I'm in pain. I've been doing it for most of my life and would find it hard now to change what has become almost an automatic response.

It was a relief to tell them. Their eyes opened in shock and I prayed they wouldn't put their fingers too rudely on the soft parts of my soul – the parts I am not eager to reveal but which I feared might be showing themselves only too clearly. Both Janine and Myra have known Michael, in a vaguely social sort of way, for some years, but Alan is a new ingredient in the mix, and as I tried to describe him and his situation their uncertainty grew. They obviously felt I had gone over a precipice into something deep and dangerous.

"We don't want you to get hurt," they said. I thanked them, but knew that the fear of getting hurt would never keep me from doing stupid things (it had never done so yet!) – and that one howl of distress from Alan and there I'd probably be, handcuffed and ready.

Finally, hesitantly, for I had barely acknowledged it myself, I told them about Michael and Margaret, and the tears came at last. "It's hard to take in," I said, burying my nose in a coffee cup.

Janine touched my hand with her forefinger and Myra said "It's a bit of a smackeroo!"

"Hasn't done much for my self esteem," I agreed.

It had been a relief to talk, but the relief wore itself out, and I was left like the lover who carves a name on a tree and ends up carving the name even more deeply into her soul. Talking about Alan and Michael had relieved me of nothing, had simply established the whole story as *fact!* And I could no longer avoid the fact since the story had just been described as a "smackeroo!"

We drank our coffee and I changed the subject, asking them for the latest gossip from W W and asking what they knew about Nick. As this turned out to be not much more than I did, the conversation lapsed.

"What are you going to do?" Janine asked after a silence.

"I don't know," I replied. "What is there to do? I can't stand in Michael's way *again*, can I? He stayed with me against his will once, how can I ask him to do the same thing now? It's up to him in the end. And as for Alan, I can't do anything much there, either, because that's up to him too. All I can do is wait and see – be there for both of them." I shrugged and hauled my coat from the bench seat beside me.

Myra picked up her bag and looked me in the eye. "What do you want?"

I sat still. I only knew what I didn't want.

"It's a puzzle to know," I said in the end. "I really don't want to divorce Michael. In a whacky sort of way I love him to bits, but I've got this thing about Alan and feel I must help him while he needs me." I gathered up my coat and stood up. "Oh well," I said "At least you know the score. I suppose it's a case of 'Watch This Space.'"

Then we all departed to our cars and I came home to do wifely things like cleaning the kitchen floor and preparing Michael's favourite lasagne, and when he arrived he was nicer, happier and more loving than he'd been for many years. I asked after Margaret and he asked after Alan. I replied that I didn't know how he was because I'd been out for most of the day.

Michael asked if I were going canvassing.

"I don't think I'm capable of it," I told him. "All I want to do now is sleep. Anyway, there's nothing arranged."

After supper we unplugged the telephone and talked for hours into the night, explaining, describing, at last telling each other the truth. I made a last offer by saying I would give up seeing Alan if he would give up

Margaret, but he said "Oh, I'll never do that. I'll never give up Margaret."

The offer had been totally genuine, and I was deadly serious. I love him better now than I've ever done. There has been more real communication between us in the last two days than in a lifetime of marriage, and I understand, now, why it's been so hard to get through to him. He had given up his chance of happiness once because of Tim and Lucy. He must have spent all those years resenting me, trying to make the best of second best! But I also know that now, with this new binding power, all the fun we have known could become a solid, safe base for a new structure. But it's too late. Beneath it all, like a dye staining everything it touches, is the certainty that Margaret is dearer to him than I am, and that if I made him stay he would very soon come to resent me more than ever – and life would become untenable.

But he talked of Alan as though there's a real chance for us to be together, and said that if the chance arises I must take it.

I shook my head in the darkness. "I don't know," I said, "He gives such mixed messages. One day I'm certain he loves me, the next day I'm just as sure he doesn't. It's getting me down."

Michael put his arm round me and I felt warmed and cloaked. Safe.

"But what about you?" I asked. "You must follow your star too."

He agreed he must, and would, and I fell asleep eventually in a world where the following of one's star was a romantic and exciting prospect in some hazy and distant future. Tomorrow all these things might come to pass. But not today.

Today I'm tired. Love, Hannah

35

<u>Christabel Fraser</u>

FROM   Hannah Pascoe
TO: Chrissiefras@coolmail.net
SENT: 27 April 2008
SUBJECT: Day One of new order.

Alan didn't ring yesterday. He turned up instead, smiling at me from the doorway in positive expectation of a welcome. Astonished, I stared blankly back for several seconds before convincing myself he was no apparition but a very material person.

"Good God!" I said, "How very nice." Then, biting my lip, I half smiled. "You want something."

He pretended to be hurt. "That's unkind."

"But I suspect true."

He crossed the threshold and turned to look down at me in the now familiar attitude, very male and rather protective but always scrutinizing. "Does that mean if I do want something you won't let me in?"

I rolled my eyes. "Too late. You seem to be in." The deeper meaning hung in the air between us. He kissed me.

"I'm sorry, Hannah, and I'm really not here just for what you can do. You know that."

I didn't reply, just waited in silence for the request I knew was coming.

"I obviously don't deserve coffee."

"Depends."

He changed his tactics. Spreading his hands and smiling slightly, he turned to go.

"Oh well, if that's how it is…"

I should have let him go, knowing he was teasing and wouldn't have got beyond the doorstep, but the thought of losing him now he was there filled me with sudden, fierce panic. There was a wild pain in my inside, as if something were being physically torn from me. So I put my hand on his arm and stopped him, laughing to hide the astounding fear which had taken me by surprise.

"Okay, okay, you win. You shall have your coffee and then tell me what I have to do."

"We need the use of your car – with you driving it of course – that's all. This evening if possible. That's if you're not otherwise engaged."

I was tempted to invent an otherwise-engagement, but the request sounded reasonable and in any case what else had I to do? So I asked where to and what for.

"We have another Focus to deliver to the deliverers, and Max's car is on the blink. And anyway we can't spare him from canvassing, so would you mind driving Rosie round so she can drop off the bundles? She knows what to do and it's much quicker with two."

A little confused, I pretended to understand what he said, hoping things would become clearer if he kept on talking. "Rosie?" I asked.

"She's one of our younger activists. You'll recognise her when you see her. On the Ward committee. Intelligent and useful."

"Ah!" I said, wondering if I should like ferrying this paragon around the streets of my home town. "Yes, I'll do that."

"Wonderful! I'll tell her to go straight to Max's. You can pick her and the Focuses up together from there.

They'll be bundled and put in order and Rosie knows the route."

He looked well, alert and lively, and the scar was fading nicely. He suddenly smiled apologetically. "Thanks Hannah."

"Don't mention it. I'd like Ruth to win. She's so nice."

"I'm glad you like her. So do I."

My stomach muscles, which hadn't recovered yet from the shock of seeing him on the doorstep, had to take on the new threat of a young, intelligent and *useful* Rosie and a 'slightly-older-but - still-younger-than-me' Ruth. To overcome the discomfort inside, I leaped in with mild sarcasm.

"Intelligent too, of course."

He seemed surprised. "Indeed she is. Very."

"Aren't you lucky? Three bright and brainy women at your beck and call. Do you deserve all this good fortune?"

"Obviously you don't think so."

Without warning we were in battle lines, the electricity between us as palpable as it had been unexpected.

"You're angry because I came to ask you a favour," he said, amazed and accusing.

Tears pricked my eyes. All at once I was incapable of bearing any more blows.

"No," I said, feeling very small and frustrated. "I'm not really. It's lots of things. Sorry,"and the tears spilled onto my blouse. They were large, heavy tears and I was unable to stop them.

Alan watched me for a few seconds then opened his arms and I walked into them. His "oh!" was a long groan, deeply sympathetic, which rose to a note of compassion that tore me still further, and he was rocking me gently to and fro, my face wetly in his neck.

"What is it, Hannah? Is it something I've done?"

"No, oh no!" I held onto him tightly, needing reassurance. Needing to belong. "It's Michael. He loves somebody else and we're splitting up."

Alan withdrew to look me in the face. I gazed back, mesmerised by the closeness. "It's only just come out," I said, "We've done nothing but talk for two nights and I haven't had any sleep, and I'm so tired and *frightened!*" The last word came out as a wail, childish and imploring.

"Oh Hannah, I'm so sorry."

By this time I was so taken up with being in his arms that the reason for the fear and tiredness was rather overlaid by the overpowering present.

But the present became bleaker as he released me and led me to a chair. Then he knelt by my side and lent me his handkerchief, into which I obligingly sniffed. "Don't tell me anything if you don't want to," he said.

"Oh, but I do," I cried, and the story flowed from me in the same way the tears had done – fast and heavy and beyond my power to stop.

He listened carefully, obviously shocked, and asked questions about Margaret. How old was she? How did Michael know her? Had she been married before?

"She married someone else after she left here, on the rebound I suppose. Anyway it didn't work out. It wouldn't would it? Rebound marriages hardly ever do. I don't think she was married very long, either. In fact I know very little about her really, and I'm not sure I want to."

"What will you do?"

"Don't know. We haven't got as far as definite arrangements yet. It's all been a bit sort of… past and future, if you see what I mean."

He nodded. "Oh, I do. Unreal and happening to

someone else."

"Yes. Absolutely. I've woken up the last two mornings and haven't believed any of it. I thought I'd dreamed it in the night and it was a relief to wake up, until the truth hit me. It wasn't a dream after all."

"Will you be all right?"

"I don't know. I expect so. I usually survive."

"Where will you go? By rights you should stay here really, as he's the one wanting out."

I smiled dismally. "I don't know that either. I don't know very much, do I?"

He pulled himself from his knees and stood over me, holding out a hand for mine. "I'm sorry, my dear, but I really do have to go. I should have been somewhere else half an hour ago."

Terror rose once more to smite me, and there was a fresh sense of abandonment and disintegration, a frozen weight of loss. I stood up and he kissed my forehead and the tip of my nose.

"Are you sure you want to drive Rosie around tonight? And will you feel up to canvassing tomorrow with all this going on?"

I clutched tomorrow as a lifebelt to keep me afloat and alive for one more day. "Yes, it'll do me good. Better than moping here."

He walked towards the front door, looked back with a brief smile, and left. I felt as though he had taken a part of me with him and that I couldn't be complete again until he returned.

At half past six I drove to Max's house and a slim girl with tumbling dark hair met me with a bright smile. She looked to be in her early twenties. Her bomber jacket and long black leggings made her look jaunty and ready for life.

"I hope you know what you're doing," I told her, "because I don't."

She reassured me. Together we carried two large cardboard boxes to the back seat of my car and began a slow and involved journey around roads I never knew existed. We must have called at twenty houses, though it seemed more, and at each one Rosie found the relevant bundle, leapt nimbly from the passenger seat and rang a doorbell. She is as Alan described, both intelligent and useful. She is also pretty. I found myself regarding the tightly black-clad hips and firm jaw line with jealous, jaundiced eyes.

When the very last bundle was mine, I returned Rosie to her door and returned myself to the house which is no longer my real and proper home.

Tonight Michael and I asked each other where we were going and he told me he'd warned Margaret of our probable separation and asked her to marry him. She had said yes. She must have thought it was her birthday!

"Congratulations!" I said, "You're engaged," and we opened a bottle of wine.

I have now moved my belongings into the guest bedroom, although Michael seemed to think it wasn't necessary. I did point out to him that Margaret would *not* appreciate any other arrangement, whereupon he helped to make up the spare bed. So I am emailing this sitting up in a strange bed looking at unfamiliar curtains. I feel peculiar. perhaps I shall sleep.

All love, Hannah.

ooOoo

Christabel Fraser

FROM   Hannah Pascoe
TO: Chrissiefras@coolmail.net
SENT: 28 April 2008
SUBJECT: Day Two

This morning I woke early to find myself in a different room, and thought at first that the night before had been a dream. Then the truth dawned in a rush. It was no dream. I lay for a long time staring at the guest room curtains, through which I could see sunshine and the movement of the chestnut tree, and I was paralysed with terror. Ice cold weights pinned me to the mattress. To separate myself from Michael after 36 years had truly become unthinkable, a nightmare concept which I very slowly forced myself to think about and recognise as true.

"It can't happen," I told myself. Yet I knew it could and that now it must. To coerce him into staying would invite disaster – not only resentment but frustration and, in time, even hatred.

I could no longer interfere.

After a very long time I heard him moving in the bathroom and in the kitchen below, and then he knocked on my door. I called "Come in," and he appeared beside me holding a cup of tea. I sat up to take it, patting the bed for him to sit with me, and knew without any doubt that he felt the same. His face was white and his eyes were round and staring. We gazed at each other in misery.

I wanted to throw my arms around his neck and sob into his pyjamas. "Oh please can't we forget the whole thing? Please I want to stay with you," but Margaret was freezing me into silence. There were three of us in this, and it wasn't up to me any more. The decision had been opened out and its very opening out had made it irrevocable. How could I expect him to rescind a proposal of marriage?

So we stared eye to eye in dumb and dismal fright while I drank my tea. Then he went back to his room and I stayed in mine.

Today is Saturday and we are back in the land of shopping, phone calls and washing up. Michael is gardening. He will be having tea with Margaret this afternoon. Janine is coming here at 3 o'clock. Meanwhile, I shall be pretending to myself and everyone I meet that life today is no different from life on any other day. Is it an advantage or is it not, to be an actress, even a not very good one but still capable of fooling the whole world - including me? Especially me?

11.30 pm   I was due at Max's this evening for canvassing at 6.30, so was going out of the door as Michael came in. This pleased me. I wasn't ready yet to dismantle the cocoon I had spent all day building.

Because I arrived early, Max and I were able to spend a few minutes getting to know each other, and I found him extraordinarily easy and pleasant. His small, brightly agreeable wife brought me coffee, smiled in a cheerful but detached way and vanished again into some region where small children were being put to bed. Their normality and friendliness were a balm. I had no effort to make, nothing was required of me except to return the friendliness, and that was easy. Max didn't suggest I canvass on my own, but instead talked happily of politics until others arrived – including Alan, who greeted me as warmly as if he hadn't seen me for several weeks. I softened.

He drove me in his car to new streets where the response was gratifyingly high, so we came home fired with enthusiasm and hope. Nobody mentioned Alan's accident, though one or two had glanced thoughtfully at the scar which the power of his personality either makes one forget or brings painfully to mind, according to the state he happens to be in. And also according, I suspect, to the effect he wished to achieve. He is not only a natural politician, he is a natural actor.

Afterwards, having as usual drunk Max's coffee and exchanged news and the night's funny stories with the other canvassers, Alan and I went to the Kings Head and he asked me how I was.

"Frightened," I said.

He regarded me sympathetically, then said "I hope I don't make things more painful for you."

I stared at him. After the many and varied icy thrusts of the past few days, I would have thought my internal organs would by now be frozen and immovable. But because I didn't understand the question another two dozen ice cubes began their journey down to my feet, and I was too numb to reply. Had I done so, it would have been to say "Only if you ask damn fool questions like that", but my thoughts were defensive and circling around like trapped flies trying to escape further damage.

I don't remember what I finally said, except that it was not to the point. How could it be? The question had begged too many others – why should his company be painful? Why should he think it was?

I didn't of course ask him. I was avoiding more hurt at all costs, keeping my head beneath the parapet, holding my breath and waiting for the pain to go away.

He saw my distress and, though obviously not understanding the reason for it, set about making amends, and the evening became in the end one of the nicest we have ever spent together. For the first time he asked questions about my own family.

"Have you any relatives you can call on for support?" he asked.

I told him the truth, that my parents had died many years ago, and my only brother was somewhere in the Australian bush flying aeroplanes.

"I never know where he is. Every now and again he rings me up or sends me a card, otherwise we communicate by email, but not very often. He's a bad correspondent. So the answer to your question is no – but I have a son and daughter and some very good friends. *Very* good friends. Very supportive."

"Have you told your son and daughter?"

I pulled a face. "That's a pleasure to come," I said. It is certainly to come, Chrissie, but I doubt if it will be a pleasure! So I changed the subject and asked him what he would do when he was finally elected and how he would use power if he had it.

"What an impossible question!" he exclaimed. "Do you mean power on a local council like ours, or the ultimate power of a prime minister?"

"Start with the first and work up."

He hitched his shoulder and drew lines on the table. "It really boils down to economics – shortage of funding is a nightmare, with the cake either cut up into tiny pieces or into just a few larger pieces with everything else going hang! There are ways of alleviating it, but I wouldn't be popular suggesting them - far too controversial. The problem is the hoary old one. You can please some of the people some of the time but not all of the people all of the time."

He paused. "Go on," I said.

He grinned. "I've learned that some cities' museums have priceless collections which are never seen. They're too big to be displayed, so they moulder away in

179

basements while they could be bringing in cash."

"Who do they belong to?"

"The city they're in. Which brings up a nice little moral dilemma. Is anyone ever entitled to sell a gift? Would you sell a Christmas present from your Aunty Jane?"

I frowned. "Certainly, if I thought she wouldn't find out. I have done that in the past. Isn't that what car boot sales are for?"

"But if you knew she would find out? And be upset?"

"Probably not then, but it would depend how urgently I needed the money."

"Yes, well we need it desperately and the matter is so urgent I believe the moral balance is in our favour. I know that one particular collection is so vast it could never be displayed at all, ever, because there simply isn't room for it, but it has a value enough to build several schools and a hospital." Enthusiasm crackled about him, sparking from his eyes and his hair and from the hands which illustrated each point with fists and fingers.

"The trouble is, though, that if that sort of motion was ever brought to council, it would never be passed."

"Why not? It sounds perfectly reasonable to me."

"Unfortunately, my dear, that is not enough. One lot wouldn't agree to selling off art treasures, and there would probably a public outcry if t was tried, and the other lot might agree to sell but would disagree about what to do with the money.

"Yes, I see." I took a sip from my glass and stared out of the dark rectangle of window beside me. Then I turned back to Alan. "And what if you ran this council?"

He laughed. "You wouldn't believe," he said "the megachanges I'd make. But I wouldn't last. A few months, two years at most, then I'd be politically assassinated."

"What sort of changes, and what sort of assassination?"

"Oh, changes like turning management on its head, executives into front line desk staff, putting the people with power where they should be – dealing with the public, instead of little clerks who have no power at all. It would work, but I wouldn't be popular because management has grown used to the idea that the further up the ladder you go the more removed you are from the blunt end where it hurts. But the blunt end is where the most knowledge and expertise is needed."

"Yes, I can see you wouldn't be popular, but what do you mean by assassinated? Strung from the nearest tree, or shot like Kennedy?"

He grinned at me. "Not quite. Just unseated from office. Which raises another moral issue. How far would I go in my megachanges if there really were a chance of being chopped? Would I have the courage of my convictions then? I doubt it."

"I don't think anyone ever knows what they'd do until they get there. You might surprise yourself."

"My dearest Hannah, you have considerably more faith in me than I have in myself."

"I have faith, yes, faith in an ultimate good – faith in a God who loves me, and loves you, and faith in what I've seen of you. And I know I'm right. Look at you now, compared with how you were only a few months ago."

"You say faith in an ultimate good, and in a God who loves you, but how do you reconcile that with all the suffering we see about us all the time? The homelessness, the cruelty, the selfishness? And the natural disaster, earthquakes, tsunami. Nothing to do with Man at all."

"I think I know how I'd explain it, but then I'm only me, with a very small brain. I know that most disasters are man-made, not God-made, and that is some way or other this world is a sort of training place, and the better we are at grappling with our own suffering and other peoples', the stronger and better we become. I also know that this earth has been going through violent eruptions of one sort or another since its birth, so why should we expect anything different now? And anyway, we all have to die. Which is worse – to die in a car crash on the motorway or painfully with cancer or with everybody else in an earthquake? We'd all like to die peacefully in our sleep, but how many do? As for God, he never promised us a rose garden. Besides, is it the job of a really loving parent to give the child absolutely everything it wants, regardless? Shouldn't some training and discipline go into the process?"

I grinned at him suddenly, "I just know that God loves me like he loves everybody and that if we ask him for something specifically it's very likely we'll get it - if not what we've asked for, then a better alternative. The important thing is to believe it."

Alan gazed at me in silence, then he shook his head. "I wish I had your simplicity," he said.

"I wish I could give you some of my hope," I replied.

We talked our way out of the pub and into our cars, then we sat in Nick's kitchen and talked some more. We told each other jokes and capped each other's stories and finally we discussed each other's future – his job, his defence of a civil action if one came about, and my newly independent state and finances.

We found no answers, but there was satisfaction in sharing the problems, and his goodnight kiss was the best so far.

The second night in my new bedroom promises to

be considerably better than the first! I might even sleep this time. Goodnight - Hannah.

P S. Bill Box arrives tomorrow. P P S. No, people on the doorstep don't usually recognise me. Some of them look at me as if they ought to know me but don't know why. If they ask me I tell them, and have to admit the results are most gratifying. Dare I believe that if Ruth wins by one vote, a tiny bit of credit may go to Maisie Mitchell?

ooOoo

37

<u>Christabel Fraser</u>

FROM   Hannah Pascoe
TO: Chrissiefras@coolmail.net
SENT: 30 April 2008
SUBJECT: Confusion reigns!

I think I'm on automatic pilot. Polling Day is next Thursday, I saw my Solicitor this morning (on my own behalf this time, not on Alan's) and Bill Box arrived yesterday. All of those things I have grappled with, in one way or another, with disconcerting aplomb. It must be the adrenaline.

Bill rang at Breakfast time from his hotel and spoke first to Michael. Very friendly and cheerful the conversation sounded from this end, though Michael pulled a face as he handed me the phone.

"How're you doing, my dear?" Bill asked.

"Very well, thank you," I replied.

"Will you be canvassing this evening and are you busy this afternoon?"

"Which shall I answer first?"

"The nearest,"

"Very well, no I'm not busy this afternoon and no, I don't intend to go canvassing tonight, although there's nothing much to stop me" (and certainly nothing to keep me at home either, I added to myself).

"In that case, will you have tea with us? Alan's coming. He's been telling me of your kindness and I must say whatever you've been doing seems to have worked. I haven't seen him this bright for a long time."

I made "thank you, glad to help and all part of the service" noises and agreed to meet them both at the hotel at three o'clock. This evening, I thought, could look after itself. I replaced the telephone and Michael looked at me over his glasses.

"Watch your step with that character," he said.

"In what way?"

"I don't know exactly. Just a feeling. Sort of 'Watch your back.'"

I thought about it. Michael sometimes has witchy instincts which turn out to be reliable, so his warnings are worth noting. "Thanks, I will," I said, "but I don't think there's much Bill Box could do to me, and anyway I'm flavour of the month at the moment, having saved his beloved son from a fate worse than death"

Michael gave an unamused barking laugh. "You may be right," he said, "but watch your back all the same."

I said I would, and asked what his own plans were. He was very slightly bashful. Margaret was preparing a little supper for him.

"Oh, is she a good cook?" I asked.

Michael smiled but didn't answer. "She must be ecstatic," I went on, "marrying the man of her heart after all these years."

And courtesy of me, I thought, for I might have stopped it. I still could, perhaps, but what would be the point? Where the advantage?

"Put a good face on it, Hannah," I told myself, "Look on it as exciting, a challenge, an adventure. No dull middle-age for you." Then I rushed about, telescoping into one hour what was originally intended to take four, because the faster I worked the less time there was for thought.

Bill and Alan were sitting comfortably in armchairs in the hotel foyer. Bill rose, kissed me on the mouth, which I did *not* care for, (Is this a Box family habit?) and led me to a small table with a tea tray and a plate of assorted cakes. He looked smartly casual in grey trousers and a navy blazer with an interesting looking badge on the pocket which I never wanted to get close enough to identify. Alan stood up to say hello but didn't kiss me, probably because his father had taken a somewhat proprietorial stance and got in first! Bill talked about his journey and about the political scene in Wakefield, where his ward party would be managing their election without him for once. "I wanted to be down here," he said, "and they can't grumble. I've worked my guts off for the past few weeks." Then he said "And I hear you've been helping Ruth."

"Can't say I've done much."

Alan smiled. "Only delivered several thousand Focuses, done a delivery round and been canvassing three times. Not a lot. And not bad for someone who wasn't going to get involved in the first place."

"Ah!" I said, biting into a doughnut. "Sorry, my mistake."

Bill wasn't listening. He was studying a copy of the local newspaper. "Listen to this," he said, and read out a letter from the correspondence column. I tried to be intelligent but the words passed through my mind as a disjointed series of sounds, totally unrelated to myself. It was as if the sentences had somehow lost their gummyness. Not that it mattered, for Alan was doing all the replying necessary, leaving me happily surplus to requirements. So I thought my own thoughts and ate my doughnut and drank my tea. Obviously this was serious stuff.

Having exhausted the letter section, Bill returned rather absent-mindedly to me and asked if I had decided about canvassing later.

I said yes I had and yes I would. Michael would be supping with Margaret. What else was there to do?

"Well done," said Bill. "We'll have the place carved up by Thursday"

I wondered for approximately thirty seconds why he should be going to such trouble for a woman he hadn't met, in a ward he knew nothing about. Then I realised this was not for Ruth but for Alan, and not necessarily for his health. A success for Ruth would ensure a success for whoever followed her.

"When is this ward up for election again?" I asked.

"Next year. The other city seat."

"Why do you ask?" Alan wanted to know.

"Just curious," I said.

I watched this interested and interesting man and believed he knew very well what his father was about, and that he not only shared his plans but would see that they came about.

After a while, finding the conversation too restricting and the participants too single minded, I excused myself and rose to go. Bill hugged and kissed me and told me how grateful he was. "He's so much better," he murmured, gripping my upper arms to prove his point.

"See her to the door, Alan," he said. I bit my lip,

half amused, half angry that a man in his late forties should be given peremptory orders by a parent in front of a guest. But Alan seemed undisturbed and escorted me quite calmly to the pavement.

"See you later." He peered through my opened window, kissed me briefly and was gone.

Tonight for the first time I toiled the streets on my own, and although we all shared Max's *après-canvass* coffee, Alan and his father went home together, leaving me to return to an empty house, to pour myself hot milk and to plod upstairs to a bed fast becoming familiar. My personal belongings are now arranged around the room, my pictures are on the wall, my books on the shelves beside my bed, and a new, if temporary, haven created. A lonely haven, but mine own!

Michael wasn't very late. He came to see me, bringing cups of tea, and we talked about who should stay and who should go and on what grounds we would be divorcing.

I had provided Steve Hobday with a list of questions this morning, the answers to which I duly reported to Michael as he sat on the bed beside me. Possible grounds are two years' separation with mutual agreement, five years if contested, Adultery and unreasonable behaviour. There is also finance to be decided.

Lucy or Timothy must now be told. My heart fails me. I'm so tired.

I've thought about your suggestion that Bill might be attracted to me himself, which could explain his obsession with age, but I honestly don't know, for he seems wrapped up in his son. If anything, more jealous of my power over Alan than Alan's power over me. Perhaps he doesn't know the truth himself. I can't be the only confused person in this place! Love, Hannah.

ooOoo

38

Christabel Fraser

FROM   Hannah Pascoe
TO: Chrissiefras@coolmail.net
SENT: 2 May 2008
SUBJECT: Confusion still reigning!

Every morning is the same now. I wake to a nightmare. Something terrible has happened or is about to happen. For a little while paralysis congeals every muscle, for though I have to avert this tragedy I know it can't be done, it will come down on my life with cold, dark claws and pervert it. So I lie still, thinking myself into reason and into the prospect of freedom and the independence I always claimed to be hankering for. Then I remember Alan and the memory turns me in a fresh direction, for now I am free to love him. And he is free to love me.

Whether he does or not is another matter. I'm afraid that even if he does he's unaware of it. But how can such a powerful emotion be one-sided?

There is a destiny hanging over us. We carry on with our day to day life, the happenings and boring routines and small dramas, as though propelled by some outside force. Sometimes it seems that somebody, hopefully God, is stage-managing the whole thing. If the organiser is really God, everything should come right in the end – whatever "right" is.

Meanwhile, when the fear ice-blanket smothers me again, I am conscious of being pushed and nudged into decisions I don't want to make, yet find myself making quite easily all the same. Yesterday I emailed Timothy in Paris. I dread his reaction. Today I shall see Lucy. The thought of telling her is truly awful, for how and where does one begin?

I now have to find a job. Acting has been my profession for the last part of my life, but the thought of it at the moment makes me physically sick, and I can't possibly go back to the sort of office job I hated so much. Dental receptionist is the obvious solution, since that is where I began my career a good thirty years ago. Furthermore, after living with Michael what I didn't know then I could quite happily fill in now. The idea holds a certain seductive irony, don't you think?

Janine rang this morning. She is free today and will come over later. She seemed relieved the decision had been made.

"Not so long ago," she said, "You told God it was up to him what happened about Alan. Well he's certainly slammed one door, so perhaps he'll open the other. Make it work out for you in the end."

Make it work? With Alan? Is it possible? Part of me believes it isn't, but when I think of the heart-searching, the compulsion, the force of circumstances, that propels me into Alan's world again and again in spite of all my resolutions, I begin to think the sheer depth of my feeling for him may have more uses than just helping him out of a jam! Wouldn't you think such dedication should merit some kind of reward? Or is virtue really its own reward, like it says on the tin? All I know is that I have to carry on helping him, reward or no reward. Anything more will simply be a bonus.

He has been applying for permanent teaching jobs. There are one or two interviews, fortunately after the election. Meanwhile I haven't seen either him or his father for two days. Apparently Bill considers two doughnuts and a cup of tea sufficient for now to express his gratitude. He was happy to ring me every day from Wakefield, but Alan was in a bad way then and he himself a fair distance away. My usefulness is now in abeyance – except of course in the little matter of electioneering!

Am I being unfair? They are both extremely busy, and will remain so until after tomorrow. There's been another delivery of leaflets to stuff through peoples' doors, and then I am to sit for two hours outside a polling station taking numbers, with an option later on for some mysterious activity called "knocking up" (which I am told means something quite different in America, so it's just as well this is good old Merrie England). Fortunately it has a more innocent meaning in campaigning circles – merely the polite reminding of known supporters who don't appear to have voted yet– and I am invited to take part, providing I've enough energy left after the rigours of the day. I am assured, however, that nowadays most of this knocking up is done via the telephone but since I don't like the idea of that either it seems I am to be relieved of duties for the time being. The final celebration (or wake) is to take place at Max's house, to wait for the results.

Sounds riveting!

I have to admit that although I started out doing all this because Alan was doing it, I am actually beginning to enjoy it for its own sake. Politics has always interested me, but in a mild, disinterested sort of way. Something other people did. But looking deeper there's a kind of seductive challenge to it all, the adrenaline rush that actors crave, and one meets such an astonishing mixture of people. And not just people, for there are houses and dogs and cats and letterboxes, all encountered during an hour or so of glorious door-knocking. Especially the dogs, the small ones that leap up and snatch things, the large ones that keep very quiet until the last minute then hurl themselves against the door like ten ton trucks, Then there are the excessively tall ones with teeth. They hide with quivering impatience on the other side of the letterbox. They don't, of course, want the leaflets. Just the fingers.

There are high letterboxes, horizontal letterboxes and narrow letterboxes, ones with teeth rivalling the dog's, and vertical ones designed to take nothing but tubes. But the worst are at ground level, requiring gold medal acrobatics and the dumping of all one's goods upon the doorstep.

I suppose it's all worth it. Ruth must think so. Despite the motivated zip and vigour she is looking very tired.

All this chat is designed to put off my phone call to Lucy. She is expecting it but I don't want to make it. I shall drive over later. You'll just have to pray for me since I'm quite incapable of praying for myself. Love – Hannah.

ooOoo

39

Christabel Fraser

FROM   Hannah Pascoe
TO: Chrissiefras@coolmail.net
SENT: 4 May 2008
SUBJECT: D Day

Well, polling day has been and gone. Some of it I remember very well, other parts not at all. There are memory flashes of sitting on a chair outside a junior school wearing a small rosette (Alan took his own back after the first night and found me another, smaller one) and clutching a little notepad on which to write the electoral numbers of voters as they came and went. It was a companionable business, sitting with red and blue rosettes and discussing everything but politics – children, holidays, jobs, the weather and all stops in between. If any of us missed a number the others obliged with it. Very few people objected to being asked, which I found mildly surprising. With true British placidity they smiled, coughed up and passed on. One or two frowned and told us that voting was a private business – which of course it is, only we weren't asking them how they voted. But still, there were so few of those that it didn't matter anyway.

Later in the day I was sent out with lists on computer print-outs of names and addresses to call on late voters. I would ask if they had remembered it was polling day and they would reply that yes, they had, but they were waiting for spouse or partner or daughter to come home - or to finish his or her tea – or watch the telly news or Eastenders. One of them had been watching W W and looked quite overcome at seeing me on her doorstep. "But aren't you.....?" she murmured at last, eyes wide and pointing finger aimed somewhere around my midriff. I nodded solemnly. "I'm afraid so, but I'm not here as Maisie today. I've come about your candidate Ruth Baker." I'm not sure she took it in because she continued to smile shyly at me and merely nodded when I asked her if she would be supporting us. She said she missed me and asked for my autograph. I scribbled it on the latest election leaflet and hoped she would read the contents more carefully, since it had now become vastly more interesting. She waved me goodbye, I thanked her and left, hoping for the best.

The fact that so few people recognised me at first I

put down to the drastic change in hair style and clothes, and the strange propensity of TV cameras to fatten one's image. I may not be the sylph of the century, but at least my own particular image appears to have lost some weight.

But all said "We'll be along later." Some of them even were!

The Committee Rooms were nests of efficiency, with earnest-looking activists hunched over computers red-hot with updated information going in and out. And always the telephone rang and people came and went looking cheerful and determined, to be asked how it was going and given more statistics. And somewhere out of sight, there was a small army of telephone canvassers doing what I had been doing only from long distance.

I threw myself into it, anaesthetizing myself with the pleasant excitement. From time to time I saw Alan. He always greeted me with pleasure, but then always vanished again on purposes of his own. Everyone told me how lucky we were to have him. "It's fantastic," they said, "to find someone with real sharp-end experience. We'll find him somewhere as soon as possible. He's almost certain to get in and he'll be a real asset to the group."

I am absurdly proud of him. But he's tired and his scar shows red, as it always does with fatigue, and there is an anxious look in his eyes.

At the end of the day he went with Ruth and Max to the school hall where the votes were to be counted. I went home to change my clothes. Then I was back to sit with Max and his wife and Bill and the others, drinking wine and eating rolls and *pâté* and cheese and small strips of pizza.

I think Bill had been trying all day to be helpful without looking as if he were trying to run the show. In this he was not successful. He has spent too long running his own shows. But he worked hard and effectively and Ruth told me she was immensely grateful. She and I are getting on very nicely. I hope we shall stay friends.

During the quiet part of the evening, with a background of telly presenters offering us the latest statistics, standing in front of Swingometers predicting results we should all know ourselves within a few hours, Bill said "Alan told me the other day that you and your husband are thinking of splitting up. Is that true?"

"I'm afraid so."

He was thoughtful, scrutinizing the wine in his glass for tiny pieces of cork.

"Nothing to do with Alan, I hope?"

"Certainly not," I said firmly. "My husband wants to marry someone else."

I waited for the information to be digested, then asked "Why? Does Alan think he might be responsible? He needn't. It's got nothing to do with him."

"That's good," Bill said, "but I'm sorry about the divorce all the same. Not the best idea at our age."

I smiled. He simply couldn't resist the final age thrust. "Thank you, but please reassure Alan if he asks."

"I will."

We said no more and ten minutes later the man in front of the swingometer declared a win for the Lib Dems in St Mary's Ward, so we all shouted and jumped up and down. Only minutes later, Ruth and Alan came in with the others, full of jubilation and triumph. She is now Councillor Ruth Baker.

Alan came over quickly to take my hand and pull me out of my chair. "Come on," he said, "You're coming with us to the Council House."

"Me? Why?"

"You'll enjoy it. Besides, you'll be useful."

I asked no more questions, just picked up my coat and allowed myself to be ushered into his car. Several of us went in convoy to the centre of the city, where the council offices were bright with lights and street lamps were reflected in water from the fountains. The day had been warm and the spray was inviting. The foyer was filled with gratified winners with their exultant supporters. A board showed the latest results and reporters looked around in quest of scoops, pounced on their prey and asked earnest questions. I saw Ruth and shouldered my way towards her.

"Congratulations," I said, meaning it. "I'm really, really glad."

She made a gesture of fatigue, arms raised, hands limp from the wrists, head lolling. Then she smiled with her own torchlight beam and suddenly put her arms around me.

"Hannah, you're so *nice*," she said. "Thank you, thank you for all you've done."

I held her away to look at her. "I've hardly done a thing. You've been working like stink for weeks – months, years probably."

"Oh, I've had help; it hasn't been me alone, far from it. It's the backing, you know. Besides, I wasn't even going to be the candidate at first. It's the people who work and work and get none of the glory. They're the ones."

We looked at each other with mutual approval.

"You're not so bad yourself," I grinned.

Alan appeared beside us with a young man bearing a notebook. Behind him were two more, one of whom carried a camera and equipment and the other a fuzzy microphone.

"Hannah, may I have a word?" We retired a few

paces. "Don't if you don't want to. We mustn't impose and I know you're trying to avoid it, but wouldn't it be rather good if you could talk to the reporters? They know you're here and are keen to interview you. Of course."

Ruth put out a hand towards us. "Poor Hannah! That's not fair."

I raised my eyebrows in smiling resignation, grinned at Ruth again and turned to the reporters." "Yes?"

"How long have you been interested in politics, Miss Pascoe?" There was a flash of light and two notebooks were opened and ready.

"On and off for a time," I said, "but not too seriously up to now. I've only been active here relatively recently."

The photographer moved Ruth towards me and posed us. "One of you two together, I think if you don't mind." We smiled obligingly and leaned our heads together, as instructed.

"What made you decide to help Ruth Baker in this election?"

"I've been a card-carrying Liberal Democrat for years, and Ruth was a perfect candidate. What more can I say? She's proved it by winning."

Alan had vanished at the sight of a camera, but I knew he would remain within hearing, if not in sight.

"Why haven't you been involved before this?"

"No spare time. I was always too busy doing other things. But now I've retired from Wayside Walk I can be more active."

"Why did you really retire?"

"Purely personal reasons. Nothing to do with the show or politics."

"Will you be taking a more active part now? Would you consider standing as candidate yourself?"

I laughed. "Certainly not, I'd make a very bad

politician."

"What qualities do you think a politician ought to have that you haven't?"

I saw an escape and took it. "Ruth's," I said. "Look at Ruth Baker and you've got them all"

I heard a laugh behind me. Alan was leaning against the wall with his hands in his pockets, so I retreated towards him.

"Well done," he said, "You were splendid, and you're quite wrong. You'd make an excellent politician. It's three parts acting anyway"

"So I've noticed," I smiled, privately thinking what a pity that was. How much better it would be to have straight-forward representatives who simply told the truth – not some of the time, or even most of the time, but all the time.

The reporters had moved on, leaving us in weary relief, ready to go home.

"Let's go," said Max. "There's food and wine waiting."

I don't remember very much after that, apart from Max's television showing faces and names and percentages, and causing shouts of dismay or scorn or excitement to explode in small gusts as further news issued from it. I sat on the floor and said nothing. Alan sat in an armchair, head back and eyes closed, and I wondered what he was thinking.

Lucy, Timothy and Michael existed in a different world, and for the time being it was pleasanter to leave them there.

I saw Lucy on Wednesday. She was magnificent. She put her arms around me and said she thought under the circumstances our divorce seemed best all round.

"Go for it!" she said. She would support me in any way she could, and I could always count on her. "Come and cry on me any time".

Since I had been sobbing on her shoulder for several minutes, this was nice of her and I was grateful. She reached for the tissues. "Have you told Timothy yet?"

"No. I sent him an email, but hated having to do it. It doesn't seem right somehow and I don't know what he'll say," I sniffed. "I'm never sure where he is and a letter might not reach him for days. The phone could be even worse. You really need to *be* with someone, for that kind of conversation. I think he opens his emails regularly, even if he doesn't always reply, but I'm nervous about his reply to this one."

Lucy fished a tissue out of the box and blew her own nose. "Look," she said, "it's your life and nobody else's, and what you and Dad decided is up to you and Dad. It's nobody else's business." Then she added: "Tim'll be okay. He's a big boy now."

Andy brought mugs of tea on a tray which he placed on the floor, then he sat on the other side of me and put his arm round my other shoulder. "Lucy's right. It doesn't matter what anyone else says. You're a big grown up girl."

We all laughed and we all blew our noses and Lucy handed round the tea mugs. It was very friendly and comforting but one more seal had been set upon the truth. With every new person I tell, the nightmare becomes less dream and more fact. There is no escape.

But for twenty four hours polling day became the reality and the nightmare faded, so that I almost forgot it. Almost but not quite.

Today is Polling Day Plus One.

Where do we go from here? Love, Hannah.

P S. By the way, Cllr Wimbrook was re-elected too. I was afraid we might bump into him at the Council House, but since neither he nor Alan has actually met they wouldn't have recognised each other anyway. Max did point him out to me, though. A tall, rather thin man with a firm-looking jaw and fierce eyebrows. I can imagine him playing the vengeful parent battling for his daughter's fair name etc, etc. I wonder what will happen when and if Alan becomes a member of this august body and the two men find themselves on opposite sides of the council chamber. I wonder if this thought has occurred to Alan. H

ooOoo

40

Christabel Fraser

FROM   Hannah Pascoe
TO: Chrissiefras@coolmail.net
SENT: 8 May 2008
SUBJECT: Oh well!

I've made my first proper moves towards the future, Chrissie. This morning I told Michael I thought I'd like to be a dental receptionist again. He said "Hmmmph!," showing neither approval nor disapproval but rather a wary discretion. After a pause for thought, however, he suggested I telephone his friend Charlie. Charlie listened sympathetically and said "Leave it with me". He is aware of the situation, so there was no embarrassment and I was happy to do as he said, not feeling strong enough yet to begin hunting for myself, and not inclined right now to argue over possible nepotism. Anyway, aren't there rules about that sort of thing nowadays? Equal opportunities and all that?

Michael and I have been talking about money, a

hateful subject. We've decided how to make all the divisions, but for the time being I must work. We've always spent our money as it came, so although dentists are not among the lowest paid in our national statistics (have you ever known a poor one?) accounting for two separate establishments from one income means that neither of us will live any more in the style to which we have become accustomed (except of course that when Michael and Margaret are married, they will have two incomes while I'll still only have one. This is where an eligible millionaire might come in handy!). Maisie money paid for holidays, entertainments, luxury meals in expensive restaurants and my cottage in Padstow, but she and her money-well have now dried up forever.

I hate the idea of dependence, but at the moment it's a moot point how long I would keep up any moral stance that seriously threatened my next meal, seeing as how although I might have been short of cash in the past I have never actually starved. Michael doesn't understand my attitude. But as he will soon have new expenses of his own, he's isn't putting up any noticeable resistance. He has said several times that he doesn't want either of us to be destitute, but if I want to be the one to leave the marital home and live on my salary, that's up to me. Of course I know it should be Michael who leaves and moves in with his amour, but Chrissie I can't bear the idea of living alone in such a house of ghosts.

So I am searching under "flats and bedsitters" in the local papers. I can't stay here much longer. We are living a lie.

I rang Alan this morning but he was out. Nick answered. He sounded friendly enough, but I was aware of a *je ne sais quoi* in his voice – less a positive coolness, more a certain lack of warmth.

"I don't know when he'll be back, I'm afraid," he

said, "but if you'd like to leave a message...?" The question mark hung in the air.

I hesitated, prudence advising me to pursue no further, yet my evil demon prodded me with his loathsome fork and I found myself asking: "Any idea where he's gone?"

I hated myself.

"Yes, he went out in the car with his father. Probably to the solicitor's, but he's got a job interview too."

I suddenly felt sick and my throat closed. "Sounds good," I croaked cheerfully..

There was a pause. "Right then, I'll tell him you rang."

I put the phone down slowly and stared at the wall. Two weeks ago I would have known about those things myself. Now Nick knew them and I didn't. I felt excluded.

Worse still was knowing I had no right to feel any such thing.

I sat for a long time ignoring the work mounting up around me. His call eventually came at ten minutes past five. His voice was as warm as ever. He asked how I was.

"Looking for a job," I told him, "and looking for a flat. But apart from that I'm okay and life continues to flow. How about you?"

"I'm fine. What's this about a job? What sort of job and what sort of flat and where?"

"I'm trying for dental receptionist, seeing I know a bit about it already. That's one of the two hundred and fifty jobs I did after I left school, and it's where Michael and I met. Love among the cavities. As for the flat, somewhere near the job when I get one. Have you had any luck with yours?"

"Yes, I've struck lucky. There's a supply job going

in a school where the teacher is off sick suddenly and won't be back until the end of term. Then there's possibly a permanent one starting next September. The interview was this afternoon, and I think it went reasonably well."

"Alan, that's wonderful!" I was pleased and proud of him. "Where and teaching what?"

"Oh, economics," he said, and told me the school.

"How about the legal business? Is it still a problem?"

"Not so much for me. Karen's loveable boy friend could be in for a sticky ride though, and the Wimbrooks look as if he's dropped any idea of a civil action. For political reasons, of course. Steve was right."

"Of course he was. You must know that really."

"It isn't as easy as that, Hannah". He was sharply reproving. I closed my eyes.

"No, knowing *about* something isn't enough, is it? It's like everything else. We need personal experience."

"Anyway, good luck with the job and the flat. I hope you get both soon."

"Thanks," I said, wondering if he would suggest seeing me.

He didn't.

Michael came in for tea but went out again. I told him I must find a flat and a job as soon as possible. He insists I stay here for as long as I wish, but I explained how unpleasant that would be for everyone. "I don't think Margaret would be overjoyed, do you?"

"There's no hurry, though. Margaret understands the situation."

I doubted that. What newly engaged woman would relish the constant presence in his home of her fiancé's ex-wife? But I must no longer be the spoilt little girl having things arranged by a kindly father figure. I must start looking after myself.

Exhaustion has crept over me so I can only keep one eye open at a time. Love for now, Hannah.

ooOoo

41

<u>Christabel Fraser</u>

FROM   Hannah Pascoe
TO: Chrissiefras@coolmail.net
SENT: 17 May 2008
SUBJECT: Here we go!

Bill went home to Wakefield last week but has started ringing me again. Not so often, for it would seem more reasonable for him to speak to Nick, who after all sees Alan every day.

Yesterday at about six o'clock there was a call from Bill to say he'd been trying to reach Alan but there was no reply either from the house or the mobile. Did I know where they could be? (I wish!) I explained that Nick has a part in Wayside Walk and may well be working on set, but that I had no knowledge at all of Alan's movements.

"I heard he got a job supply teaching," I offered.

"Yes, that's very good, isn't it? It's a relief, believe me. I was afraid he'd have lost his nerve about that too."

He asked me about my plans and I explained.

"I hope that doesn't mean you'll be moving too far away from Alan," he said.

"Haven't a clue," I replied, mildly amused. Living in the same neighbourhood as Alan made no difference to our relationship, whatever that was. Nor did it matter to my availability in times of stress, since we both drove a car.

Chrissie, did I tell you that Michael suggested the other day that I move into Nick's house as a second lodger? I said: "Good heavens, no. That's the last thing I have in mind." He wanted to know why not, as it would be a very sensible arrangement and I could keep an eye on Alan properly then. "Yes, and kill off whatever's there," I said, "Besides, neither Alan nor Nick has suggested it, so I certainly won't, and even if they did I'd still say no."

Michael had raised an eyebrow and smiled his disbelief. I left him to his convictions. After all, who knows what silly thing I may do if pressed. My record hasn't been all that good so far, has it? Like St Paul, I do that which I would not do, and fail to do that which I should!

Bill, however, wished me to find Alan for him. He would, he said, be going out later that evening and needed to speak to Alan before tomorrow.

I didn't want to do this. Of course I said yes, but am growing more and more sensitive. There are strange vibrations in the air which I don't understand. Neither do I know whether they originate from Alan or from Nick and, if the latter, why they should. What is it to him whether I see Alan or not, since it was at my request that he moved there in the first place? And Alan himself is usually charming and welcoming and apparently happy to see me and talk to me. He just doesn't follow it through.

Am I getting over-sensitive?

9.30 pm Last night I rang Alan at 8 o'clock. Nick answered and said "Yes, I'll get him." I heard him ask Alan if he would like to speak to me. Not, you will notice, simply telling him I was there. I had been snubbed.

"Ah good!" Alan said, "I was going to ring you." (Yah boo! to Nick, I thought) "I'm off to Ossett the day after tomorrow to see Elizabeth and Dominic and on Monday I start work. Will you come to lunch with me? You haven't started your job yet, have you?"

"No I haven't, and yes that would be nice." I gave him his father's message and went to bed in a happier state. At last he had taken the initiative.

We drove to a new and unfamiliar pub and ate our lunch watching the rain through huge windows. We talked seriously. I told him about Michael and myself and he touched the back of my hand with his forefinger.

"You must never underestimate what you've done for me," he said, "I can't express how much I owe you, and nobody will ever be able to take that away. In the truest possible way we love each other."

We gazed into each other's eyes across a very small table, and neighbours on either side glanced at us romantically. There should have been violins. Afterwards we drove to my house for coffee, then he left to prepare for his visit to Ossett and for school on Monday. There had been no mention of seeing him again, and as he moved to go there was a physical wrench, as though a part of my body had been attached to him and was now being torn away beyond hope of recovery. Actual, physical pain. I have never felt anything quite like it before, and never wish to again. Then the door closed. He had been saying thank you and goodbye.

At teatime Michael's friend Charlie rang to ask if I would present myself at Howarth and Partners at a suitably convenient time, as there was now a vacancy for part time receptionist. I am to ring in the morning to arrange an interview. Presumably there are other applicants. The practice is in Clifton.

It's been a funny day. Love, Hannah.

ooOoo

42

Christabel Fraser

FROM   Hannah Pascoe
TO: Chrissiefras@coolmail.net
SENT: 26 May 2008
SUBJECT: What a strange life this is.

I felt very odd last weekend, knowing Alan was with his wife and son and that Michael would be spending most of his free time with Margaret.

Janine has been amazing. I speak to her or see her every day now, and her presence and your emails have kept me plodding through this morass of emotion and bewilderment. Would the situation have been easier to bear, I wonder, if I hadn't jettisoned Maisie in such a cavalier fashion, but how was I to know what would follow at such dizzying speed? It is almost like a West End comedy. In fact there's a striking element of farce about it, with exits and entrances slickly timed, idiotic dialogue and some very hammy performances.

A black comedy so far, unfortunately, and the leading lady isn't finding it so damned funny!

I rang Charlie's Howarth and Partners, and was interviewed by Mr Howarth himself on Tuesday morning. He was sufficiently impressed to ring later to offer me the job. I had apparently been on a shortlist but past experience and (?) maturity obviously worked in my favour because I start work next week. I shall be job-sharing with another working mum. The fact that there really were two other candidates to be considered allows me to close my eyes to an original suspicion of string pulling. It's so much nicer to believe someone wants me for myself and not because he is a friend of my soon-to-be-ex husband! In this case I'm fairly certain Mr Howarth doesn't want me for Maisie's face either, as I doubt very much if he has ever watched Wayside Walk in his life.

It's a relief to know there is work for me, and I may now look for a bedsitter in Clifton, but there have been other claims on my attention, and factors like *Job* and *New Home* are tending to be stowed away in a drawer marked "Automatic response only"

Yes, I did see Alan again. He came home worried about Dominic, who has become very wild since his father left. He has acquired a motor cycle and is now careering about Ossett, to the terror of his mother (and probably all other road users) and the dread of his father, who lives in fear of yet another tragedy. He is superstitious enough to quote the old saw that "things go in threes!"

He wanted to bring Dominic back here in the car, giving everyone a holiday from stress, but Dom works in a library as a Saturday helper and is apparently all too prone to taking days off, which Alan is unwilling to encourage because this one day a week is the only fixed routine in his life at the moment. He is eternally at odds with his mother, and Alan feels responsible.

I know all this because this morning I lay back against my pillows, meditating on life in general and my own in particular, and deliberately, with much pain and woe, *I Gave Him Up!*

I spoke firmly to God. "Okay God," I said, "If you don't want me to have him, I won't argue with you. I've done the best I can, now it's up to you." Then I added: "But if you really want to take him away I'd be glad to know definitely one way or another. If you don't mind, that is. And if you could see your way to giving me a sign that would be wonderful and I'd be really *really* grateful. For example, if he is to come back, a phone call would be nice."

One hour later the phone played its little tune. Alan said "It's Saturday and I'm going swimming at twelve. Would you like to come?"

Having brought my breath back from somewhere around my toes, I said yes that sounded nice, and arranged to meet him at the pool. Then I laughed and said thank you to God, and hoped he meant it.

I was exceedingly amused. The pleasure of comfortably cool water on my skin and the sight of Alan in bathing gear seemed a most direct and forthright answer to my challenge. One minute I was Giving Him Up. The next I was being presented with his almost naked flesh. As responses go, this one could hardly be called equivocal!

His legs are muscular and his swimming trunks are red. Okay? I wore my best black swimsuit with the white band across the top (the one that makes my tummy look flat!) and was glad my hair is short enough to drip dry.

I wish swimming didn't make me feel so *healthy*. Too many drives and juices can be darned uncomfortable.

We shared a companionable lunch at a nearby pub, then went for a walk in Snuff Mills, where the river winds and curves in a gorge between steep banks, under bridges and over weirs. The day was warm and sunny and the park was full of strollers in new summer clothes. Alan strolled and I strolled with him, talking, talking, talking. I knew then how much I had missed him.

The sound of the river, the sight of the gorge banks rising to tree above trees, the narrow paths and sudden sweep of turf, the dogs excited by floating sticks, and the children, pink with effort, pedalling small three-wheelers in front of hand-in-hand parents. All these printed images on my memory, and the central figure is always Alan. Alan leaning on a bridge parapet staring at a small waterfall below. Alan walking in front of me in jeans and a tee-shirt, gazing down at me from a sawn-off tree trunk.

I realised how helplessly in love I was, and I despaired. What had I become? I knew the answer - the kind of woman I had always secretly despised.

But he talked, about Elizabeth and Dominic, and about the teaching that he found harder than before. His headaches had returned.

"Have you stopped having regular checks?" I asked.

"I go back in six months. But if they carry on like this I shall go before then."

"Please do," I told him. "Don't suffer unnecessarily."

He said he wanted Dominic to visit him as soon as possible. He was, he said, feeling guilty about the boy.

"I'd like to meet him," I said.

"Of course."

I drove him back to Waterloo Road and he leaned over from his seat to kiss me. The car floated home. I think our petrol station serves its own kind of fuel, possibly called Bliss.

"Thank you, God, you're amazing,"" I said again later, as I climbed into bed, but I was too filled with thoughts to sleep.

Tomorrow I have an appointment with a bedsitter in Quinton. Meanwhile, all love, Hannah.

ooOoo

43

<u>Christabel Fraser</u>

FROM   Hannah Pascoe
TO: Chrissiefras@coolmail.net
SENT: 31 May 2008
SUBJECT: Wowee!

This, my dear Chrissie, is a BONANZA letter. The jackpot I have hit!

Yesterday I began work as part-time receptionist in Howarth & Partners. Bearing in mind how many years have gone by since I did this before, and the way science has galloped ahead ever since (with or without teeth), surprisingly little has changed. There are still records to keep, telephones to answer and patients to book in and out and watch while they turned magazine pages or bit their nails, or simply stared unhappily into space.

The one big change, of course, is that instead of mountains of files and typed notes, we now have state-of-the-art computers. These fazed me at first, but, boiled down to fundamentals, all computers are more or less the same. Not unlike cars, really – all with the same basic principles but with different twiddly bits. And since I mastered the twiddly bits on Michael's highly involved equipment and my baby laptop without much difficulty, I managed to finish the day without losing too many dental records or un-arranging too many appointments.

I was very tired at the end of it because of the excitement and the strangeness, but also because I had a date with Alan at seven o'clock and anticipation had done nasty things to my energy levels. So although the work was explained to me most carefully by a young woman called Anne, and although I paid close attention (honestly!) not much of it was left in my head by Home Time. I'm afraid Anne will have to explain it all again tomorrow. I just hope she won't write me off as a hopeless imbecile even before I've begun. The trouble with nervous excitement or anxiety, or grief, or even bliss, is that one really does temporarily become an imbecile.

I repeat - Love Is An Illness. Cynics have said the only known cures are time and/or marriage, but while in the grip of this madness it's hard to believe any cures exist at all. Meanwhile I stay bewitched.

So when Alan drove us to Blaise Castle and we decanted ourselves into the car park on a beautifully warm, glowing evening, it was hard not to stare vacantly into the distance with jaw hanging restfully open. The combination of fatigue and close proximity to the beloved was reducing my intelligence to nil.

The woods were spread before us across an expanse of dog-and-child-bedecked grass. We seemed to be conversing so I must have spoken - although, once launched, Alan is capable of a flood of words continuing without help for a considerable length of time, so maybe I didn't contribute much after all.

We set off up the hill into the trees and reached a level path transversing the way we wanted to go. Alan looked in one direction and then in the other. "I don't want to go that way," he said, "Or that way. I want to go this way", and he pointed upwards to a steep bank half covered with scrub and spreading tree roots. He glanced down at my feet. "What are your shoes like?"

I had come out for the evening in white slip-on summer shoes, not allowing for rock climbing.

"Slippery," I said promptly. "Like glass."

He grunted, then held out his hand for mine. "Let's try it all the same."

We tried it. I was right about the shoes. At several points on the way my feet left the ground altogether. Since the gradient was roughly vertical, this was not surprising, so I dangled with only Alan's hand between me and sudden, very unwelcome acquaintance with the concrete path below. Amazingly, I wasn't nervous or even put out. Life and limb were dependent solely upon the strength of Alan's arm, and between giggles I was deliciously aware of the symbolism.

When we reached the top he said: "Well done!" and we continued on our way. The path is narrow and twists among trees, with on one side a sheer drop to the gorge and a view over the tree tops to distant hills. On the left is an opening railed from the gorge face, and there we stood to watch the wood pigeons flying from tree to tree below us. It was strange to see them from above, as though they existed in a world within a world, and that somewhere down in the heart of that world was another, where one might look over smaller cliff edges to another and yet another vista of smaller treetops and smoky valleys and the wings of yet more wood pigeons. A never-ending view of mirrors within a mirror, vanishing into space.

We stood for some time in silence, Alan at the edge contemplating the view and myself sitting on a tree trunk contemplating Alan. He turned suddenly to look for me, as if conscious for the first time of the silence and, who knows? Wondering if I were still there? I wanted to bottle the moment, for there was magic in it.

To break it would have been sacrilege, though of course in the end it had to be broken, and when it was we spoke quietly and solemnly, and the young men's voices floating up from the Alice-in-Wonderland realm below made our own world even more remote. The echoing human sounds drifting upwards only added to our lofty separateness.

We moved at last, down and down a sloping path until, if we had turned to the right, we might have joined the young men and the pigeons. But we took the left path instead and found ourselves back on the grass with the children and the dogs and car park beyond. And as we went we talked of Michael and me, and about Elizabeth, and about our sex lives.

Sex has often figured in our conversations – not salaciously but with a sense of pleasure all the same in talking about what was obviously in both our minds (well, in mine for sure. And it must have been in his to some extent or we wouldn't have been discussing it!)

There was a pub close by, so we drank one glass of beer each then he drove me home, and this time he came in for coffee. We sat looking out on a garden which could still be seen in the soft greys and blues of late evening. The light from the next door garage lamps sent golden strips across the lawn, and there was a smell of honeysuckle.

"I'm sorry if I've been quiet tonight," Alan said.

I was amused. "I don't think I'd have described you as quiet. More serious than usual, perhaps, but not exactly quiet. We've been talking non-stop for about three hours, or was it all me doing the talking?"

He shook his head. "No, I know I've talked and I've enjoyed it. But then I always do like talking to you. But there's been something on my mind."

I sat in silence and waited.

"You know I've been having headaches. Now I have to have a brain scan"

"Oh Alan, no!" I said, "When?"

"Next week."

"Are you scared?"

"Yes, a bit"

He was leaning back, eyes closed, hands gripping the chair arms, and my heart gave a leap. Within seconds I was kneeling beside him, knowing that what I did was undignified but not caring one bit, for what he needed then was not pity but the reassurance of knowing he was loved.

I picked up his hand and played with his fingers..

"You''ll be all right," I said.

"You're too good to me, Hannah"

I looked up into his face and found him frowning at me, eyes large and anxious.

"You're thinking what a coward I am," he said.

I gasped. "Positively not! If you knew what I was thinking you'd be shocked."

"I don't believe that"

"Wanna bet?"

He nodded. I considered, decided he needed blasting out of his anxiety and self denigration, and staked all on one throw.

"I was thinking 'Shall I rape him now or later?'"

There was a snort of amused shock and his eyes become bright points of light. I was pulled towards him and passionately kissed. I was drawn between his knees and held there.

"I want you," he said.

My lips went soft and with infinite care I kissed his scar. "So what's stopping you? I'm a very sexy lady."

There was small sound against my neck and he drew away to look me amusedly in the eye. "I'm very glad to hear it," he said.

There are ways and ways, Chrissie, of handling erotic moments. In all the best, steamiest books, the heroine lies back in deep and sultry passion or goes at it with serious intent, but having arrived at the place where I had longed to be for many months, in a sexual embrace which looked as if it were going somewhere, I found myself so incredulous about it all that I couldn't take myself seriously.

Because it was unbelievable I failed to believe it, and therefore did what I usually do in moments of crisis. I giggled.

Needless to say, by the time I had stopped gurgling and had been taken back into his arms, the moment had slipped from a passionate one to a tender and emotional one instead.

"There is so much we can do," he said, "So much ahead."

I sighed, and wanted to merge myself into him so there would be nothing to show where I stopped and he began. Once again his mouth found mine and his hands found the rest of me, and suddenly there I was believing it after all. My mind cried out in silent desperation. I was afraid I might burst into flames on the carpet.

The telephone rang.

"Leave it," he said.

We counted the rings to six, then the answerphone clicked and Michael's voice came to us clearly from the hall.

"Hannah, it's me. If you're there will you pick it up please? I'll be home in about ten minutes and I've forgotten my keys. I'll try you on your mobile."

There was silence for half a minute while Alan and I stared at each other. Then the mobile phone in my handbag began its chirruping. I sighed, leaned over and picked it up. "Hello?"

"Hannah, where are you? I've forgotten my house key and I'm only half a mile away. Is there anything you can do?"

I was confused and disorientated. "I'm here," I said.

Michael laughed. "Yes, but where is here?"

"Oh. Actually I'm at home but I wasn't quick enough to pick up."

"That's lucky." There was a pause. "Are you all right?"

I thought about it. "I don't know," I said.

He was obviously smiling. "See you in a couple of minutes then."

I put the phone down. Alan was holding my other hand and looking lovingly at me, but the moment had passed.

"He's on his way," I said, bewildered at all the sudden changes. "He'll be here in just a few minutes." I put my hand to my hair and closed my eyes. "Oh dear," I sighed, ""What bloody awful timing."

Alan's hand slipped to the back of my neck and I was pulled forward into his arms. "Don't worry," he said, "There's time ahead," and he kissed me again. "Will I see you tomorrow?"

"Of course."

We walked to the hall with our arms around each other and stood kissing goodnight inside the front door before he opened it.

"Tomorrow," he said.

"Tomorrow," I smiled. And Michael's car headlights swept the gate and the garden path. He and Alan met on the drive and exchanged a few words. Then Alan was gone.

Michael faced me in the doorway. "I hope his departure was nothing to do with my arrival," he said. "I should hate to have spoilt a tender moment."

"Oh no, he was on his way out anyway," I lied. We didn't talk much after that. I was too full of thoughts, and decided to pursue them in a hot, soapy, foamy bath.

Tomorrow is now today. I have spent from early morning writing to you. Now I must dress to meet my lover. Love, Hannah.

P S. Shall I write to the British Medical Association with my new certain cure for anxiety over brain scans?

ooOoo

44

<u>Christabel Fraser</u>

FROM   Hannah Pascoe
TO: Chrissiefras@coolmail.net
SENT: 7 June 2008
SUBJECT: Moving on

This week has been a mite busy, Chrissie. I did my second working day at Howarth's but floated through it mindlessly, memory drawing appropriate snatches of information from more than thirty years ago, and some kind of native common sense (more than I knew I possessed, in fact) supplying the rest. Considering how little my thoughts are on the work, I am apparently making a better job of it than I deserve. The other girls are nice, some nicer than others, some younger than others, but all younger than me! Well they would be, wouldn't they?

The question of age continues to thump me with disturbing force in sensitive parts, with regularity and recently with decimating effect. What can one do with a decimated friend? There must be an answer. The pieces have to be gathered up and put back together.

I saw Alan again next day as arranged. Michael was planning an evening at home with the television, so I drove to Waterloo Road hoping Nick would be out and longing for time alone with Alan. I had, of course, thought of nothing else all day. Every love song composed, every poem penned, every storybook romance, all of them have been written expressly for me. But Nick was (alas!) at home, settled in for a convivial evening with two friends and a bottle of wine and an apparent wish to include Alan in their plans.

Alan, however, met me at the door full of a warmth which moved me so deeply I was almost frightened of it, and because I was too shaken to respond suitably, I greeted him with a rather too flippant friendliness.

Then there was no choice but to walk to the Star & Garter and sit at a small table face to face, scrutinizing each other afresh. We talked of personal things and he told me about the new school which is turning out to be unexpectedly stressful.

"Teaching gets worse," he said. "It's partly the run-down state of the building and the lack of funding, and the changes in the curriculum and emphasis, but it's also the changes in Society. How the children are seen by their parents, and seen by themselves. I hate to say it, but most parents seem scared of their own offspring"

"I'm certainly scared of some of the twelve to fourteen-year-olds," I said "They stare at me, defying me to do anything about anything, yet I suppose if I really challenged them they'd probably back down. So far I've never been quite brave enough to put it to the test."

"Some would, some wouldn't. I'm only supply teaching at the moment, which means I haven't the months behind me of getting my own messages across. They're testing me all the time. Seeing how far they can go. Nothing new about that, of course, it's always been like that. I was just as bad at that age. But there's less and less one can do about it. Very few ways left of imposing discipline, especially when you don't know the kids. It's very tiring. And it doesn't help having these headaches and the scan coming up. I'm afraid of having more time off"

"How's the head now?"

"The same. No, if I'm honest, it's a bit worse."

"At least when you've had the scan you'll know something, one way or another. I hate not knowing, don't you? It's the worst kind of torture"

I studied him carefully. "Is it really bad?"

He nodded.

"Then," I said, placing my fingers on the back of his hand "You should be at home in bed."

"Soon. I'm enjoying being here with you, but I will go before too long, if you'll forgive me?"

I grinned. "It's supposed to be the lady who has the headache, I believe."

He gave a rather sad little grimace. "I'm not very good at this."

"So you keep saying, but practice makes perfect," I replied. His face was paler than it should have been and there were dark marks under his eyes, and shadows on his cheeks. I wanted to wrap him up, send him peacefully to sleep and nurse him back to health – and happiness. Nothing else seemed of the smallest importance, not even the longing that had been overwhelming me all day and the knowledge that it wasn't going to be assuaged tonight.

"Go home to bed, darling heart," I said lightly.

He helped me on with my coat and kissed me full on the lips in front of a bar-full of patrons. Now you can't say fairer than that!

We walked home arm in arm down the brightly lit pavements until we reached his door, where he turned and put both hands on my shoulders. In the warm darkness of the porch he held me in his arms and I hoped and hoped he would ask to see me next day.

Instead he said against my ear "I'm frightened of your age, Hannah."

I stood still, quelling the shock by dealing with the question behind the statement.

"Do you mean you're frightened I'll get old and wrinkled and unattractive, or that I'll die first?"

"Both," he said.

I closed my eyes. There seemed to be nothing worth saying. Then he kissed me again and I drew away.

"What shall we do now?"

"I'll see you," he promised. "We'll be in touch with each other soon."

I nodded and left him at the gate. "Drive carefully," he said, and watched me drive away.

I knew of course that I would drive carefully. My death would not only be a devastation for Lucy and Timothy but it would be one more blow for Alan on top of all the rest. And all the way home I explained carefully to myself that nothing had changed. The age difference had always been there. Not a new discovery. And it hadn't stopped him the night before. Give me a chance, I thought, and I'll show him that age has nothing to do with love or sex or personality or communion of souls. I recalled the men who had loved and desired me in the past – all of them younger than myself and one of them twenty years younger! – and asked myself if the events of the past months had aged me beyond further hope.

I arrived home to find Michael watching television. I asked him how things were going.

"Fine," he said. "Help yourself to wine or Martini, there's both on the sideboard"

I stood in front of him. "Do I look my age?"

He raised his eyebrows. "No," he said, "You never did. Why?"

"Alan's worried about the ten years difference"

"Then he's a fool," he said shortly. "Anyway he's got nothing to write home about"

I beamed. Good old Michael. Then I stopped beaming.

"What will I do without you?" I asked.

"You can always ring me up"

I scoffed. "What? Hello Margaret, can I speak to Michael please, my confidence needs shoring up?"

I went to bed very confused. Next day I was back at the surgery, trying to motivate myself to be pleasant and sympathetic with patients, efficient with computers and dentists, and friendly to colleagues, but concentration gets harder and harder. My brain has started to gyrate.

Once we had a hamster which insisted on climbing onto the outside of his wheel and running there, instead of doing the proper thing and getting into its middle. So he was always clawing his way to the top and falling off the other side head first, or clinging with his forelegs while his little back feet jumped up and down in impressive but hopeless optimism. He never stopped trying, but he never succeeded.

I am a hamster, and life has become a wheel which inevitably, ceaselessly, throws me off either at the front or at the back.

Alan surprised me again yesterday by ringing to say Dominic arrives tomorrow for the weekend and would I like to meet him? Of course I said yes. They will come to lunch on Saturday. Michael will be out with Margaret.

I am now *seriously* flat-and-bed-sitter-hunting. The journey in rush hour across the city to the dental surgery has just emphasised the need to move away as soon as possible to somewhere closer to work. And although Michael still insists I can stay, circumstances are now painful, untenable.

I don't like it. Can't stand it any more. I must move. Meanwhile, all love, Hannah.

ooOoo

45

Christabel Fraser

FROM   Hannah Pascoe
TO: Chrissiefras@coolmail.net
SENT: 9 June 2008
SUBJECT: Dominic

I have now met the troublesome teenager. Alan brought Dominic to meet me today. He's lovely, just seventeen and handsome in a different way from his father but with the same charming, shy smile. Good teeth, nice hands and long legs. He is also unusually articulate for his age and sex. Long sentences with hardly any "er"s or "um"s or even "you know?"s.

At present his preoccupation is with mountain bikes. Since I know nothing whatever about them, he was overjoyed to find a captive novice, an audience for his obsession. And, as hostess, I naturally listened with enthusiastic and (I hope) intelligent attention. I'd have done so anyway. Having Alan's son talking to me so animatedly was a joy in itself.

The subject was evidently a difficult one for Alan but he joined in all the same, and the conversation eventually turned to Wayside Walk and my role in it. Actually, he, Dominic, had been so engaged with his gears and accessories that he'd forgotten who and what I was, so when the penny suddenly dropped it lit him up like a firework flare.

"Oh yes, of course!" he cried, "I knew I knew your face, but couldn't think why. Dad told me last time he came home but I'd forgotten. I used to watch it when I was young, but I don't so much now. It's always on when I'm doing something else"

I smiled. When he was young? "Don't worry, I don't watch it either, and anyway that's the ignominious fate of soaps. They always seem to come on when you want to do something else. Of course if you're an addict you organise your timetable around the programme, but then it ends up ruling your life. If you miss more than three episodes you could lose the thread and lose interest altogether, but Wayside Walk doesn't move fast enough for that. You could probably miss twenty and still pick it up."

"Less of a Walk than an Amble," suggested Alan.

"I'm afraid that's not a new joke," I told him sadly.

"The best ones come on at mealtimes," said Dominic. "That's how I came to watch yours. Mum likes it, so it was always on at teatime before I started my homework."

So Elizabeth was a fan of my show! Now, there's a thing!

I pulled a face. "I hope it didn't put you off your food. I always seem to get the news or natural history programmes. I don't know which is worse. I'm just putting a forkful of dinner into my mouth when bingo! there's a beautifully clear close-up of a cheetah sinking its teeth into a wildebeest. Plus all the horrid details. It almost put me off meat for life, and I stopped watching at mealtimes just in case. I decided it was bad for the digestion!"

"Talking of digestion, what are we having for lunch?" Dominic asked. "Wildebeeste Liver and giblets?"

I stuck out my tongue.

"What's it like to be an actress?"

"How long did you say you were staying? And do you want the short answer or the long one?"

I did my best, but as usual found it almost impossible to describe what, for me, had been an ordinary, routine part of an established life. To someone in a different sphere it must sound mysterious and strange, almost incomprehensible, not the mixture of excitement, nerves, slog and boredom that it really is.

"Why don't you go back to doing it now?" Dominic asked, "instead of working for a dentist? Not Wayside Walk particularly. You're a household name, so you could get a job anywhere."

"Being a household name doesn't necessarily help," I said, "In fact it's often the reverse. I expect my agent could come up with something eventually, but that doesn't answer the question. I don't know the answer. I know I didn't just give up The Walk, I gave up acting, full stop. For now anyway. Maybe I'll be tempted back in a few years time."

"But why, if you enjoyed it?"

I gazed at him thoughtfully. At seventeen his perspective on life and problems took him straight to the heart of a question which the more sophisticated of us usually tiptoe around. "Out of the mouths…" indeed.

"Only part of me did enjoy it," I answered carefully. "I enjoyed it because it was what I was doing, and it seems such a waste of time not to enjoy what you're doing while you're doing it. If that makes sense? And there's nothing quite like being in front of a live audience. There's a buzz to it which you somehow miss in front of a camera. Some people prefer that, but I never did.""

Dominic nodded.

"You get your real buzz, though, out of entertaining people, even if it is at second hand. But really I was in the wrong place. I suppose I'm just not a natural actor. Taking on other people's personalities in front of a camera or even an audience, it just wasn't what I wanted to spend the rest of my life doing. And every day was getting to be a new stress because I felt I was somehow wasting time. You know – with more important things to be done somewhere else.. I don't know what they are yet, but I expect I'll find out. Anyway, I still love the theatre and everything to do with it. It just doesn't seem to be for me, that's all. Is that an answer?"

Alan had been listening attentively. "It certainly seems rather irrelevant," he said, "and not much to do with life with a capital L. A chance to have fun and be paid large sums of money for pretending to be someone else."

"Wey hey!" I said, "Now we're coming to it. You'll listen for hours to music played by professional flautists and cellists who are doing precisely the same thing but in another medium. Being paid to entertain you."

"I know, yet I instinctively feel there's a difference"

"Politicians too," I went on, "It's all a big act, isn't it? You've said so yourself. The House of Commons as shown on TV. Full of people putting on theatrical performances, only they're messing with real lives. At least we only set out to entertain, with a bit of instruction thrown in if we're lucky. We want to raise peoples' awareness and raise their quality of life. Make them laugh. Even more important, to make them think. You want power, to change things over peoples' heads.

"Not over their heads. With their co-operation. But power, yes, to do what they put us there to do. You talk about raising their quality of life, but we're the ones who can actually do that. Give them an education, improve their standard of living, make it possible for some of them to live at all. Things like health, hospital waiting lists, preventive medicine, surgery, casualty departments, if they're not run properly people die. And without education children grow up not knowing how to be doctors and nurses and stop people dying. It is quite literally a matter of life and death, while acting is just about quality of life.

"*Just* about quality of life? Wow! But without the spiritual qualities of beauty and art people die inside, like living in bright soulless multi-storey blocks where the poor sods jump out of the windows in despair?"

"Agreed. But someone has to arrange for the right houses and flats that aren't bright, soulless multi-storey blocks, and you can't do that with just entertainment. Someone has to design the houses and put one brick on top of another. But above all, someone has to have the power to make the building possible in the first place"

"And those people have to go home after designing the houses and laying bricks all day, and watching the telly or going to the theatre gives them the mental energy to go back and do it all again tomorrow."

"You mean like watching Wayside Walk?"

I laughed. There was a pause. "Why not Wayside Walk?" I countered finally, "If it takes peoples' minds off their own troubles for half an hour every other day it must be useful and helpful in its own way."

"Actually," said Dominic, "I like 'The Simpsons' best'"

Alan and I looked at each other, then we both laughed. "You're quite right, Dominic," I said. "It leaves Wayside Walk standing."

"What it boils down to," Alan said, "is each to his own"

"Horses for courses."

"*Chacun a son gout.*"

"One man's meat is another man's poison."

I never get tired of talking to Alan.

"What it really and truly comes to," he admitted, "is that society needs us both!"

In the afternoon Alan had a meeting at school, so I took Dominic to the Downs in the car and we ate ice cream and stood on the suspension bridge, looking down at dark water below. Then I returned him safe and sound and still in one piece to Waterloo Road, where his father gave us tea and cake in the big, bright kitchen, and made us laugh by describing the meeting and the funny things the kids say.

"Will we see you tomorrow?" Alan asked me, but this time I had to say no. Dominic goes home next day.

As I stood up to leave them, Alan put his arms around me and held me close. Then he kissed me lovingly.

"See you soon," he said.

I briefly hugged Dominic, said goodbye and came home. Janine arrived at half past seven and we opened a bottle of wine and searched the evening papers for accommodation to let. There were three advertised, so we dialled the numbers. Two had already been taken but I made an appointment to see the third tomorrow at half past six. I expect that will have gone too. I now have to buy the early morning newspapers as soon as they come, and even then all the rooms have been whisked from me by a new breed of early bird which always gets there first.

We sat, Jan and I, in the evening dark with the garden just visible through French windows, and we talked about Michael and Alan, about Margaret and the morality of living only half a life, and about the basis for personal integrity. And I thought of the discussion earlier in the day over the quality of life.

What is my quality of life at the moment? What can I expect from Alan, from Michael, or even from myself?

"I'm in a sort of limbo," I said, "Not married, not divorced, nobody's partner or girl friend, neither fish nor fowl"

But Alan had embraced me in front of his son and therefore I was reassured, comforted, filled with new confidence. Tomorrow is another day. Perhaps I shall find a flat. Michael has just arrived home. He seems happy. Tonight so am I. Love, Hannah.

ooOoo

46

Christabel Fraser

FROM   Hannah Pascoe
TO: Chrissiefras@coolmail.net
SENT: 17 June 2008
SUBJECT: Flats, flats, flats

I feel more like a hamster than ever, having spent the whole of my spare time this week going round and round on my little wheel, flat hunting, working, flat hunting, sorting out my belongings and flat hunting. Then again, flat hunting. It's astounding how many hopefuls there are, all like myself queuing for somewhere to live. It feels as if I'm in competition with the whole of this crammed and sprawling city which seems to be, at this particular moment, mostly made up of aspiring and *per*spiring university students all yearning for somewhere to rest their little heads.

Meanwhile I've been sleeping at Jan's top floor apartment overlooking the Suspension bridge. Michael is friendly and helpful, but I am getting more and more disturbed. Happier at the moment away from home. Jan will be away next week, staying with her brother in Northampton, so I'll have her flat to myself.

Alan is waiting for his brain scan. His headaches are no better, so he keeps quiet and out of sight. We haven't met since Dominic left, but I've been so busy on my own account that it would have been hard to do so anyway.

I began the week full of confidence which, having ebbed, is now as a teacup to a mighty ocean. And I, like a blinkered horse, am only capable of seeing what is immediately in front of me. It would help if I could sleep. All love, Hannah.

ooOoo

47

Christabel Fraser

FROM   Hannah Pascoe
TO: Chrissiefras@coolmail.net
SENT: 25 June 2008
SUBJECT: Hey ho!

We are having a busy time. Alan's hospital appointment is tomorrow. I yielded to temptation and rang to see how he was. He seemed depressed and in pain, so I suggested he stay here for a few days while Jan is away. To my delight he agreed. He arrived last night and slept in the tiny guest room, and it was weird having him under the same roof. I was horribly conscious of his presence – only the thickness of one wall away – and felt again what a waste it is to be apart. A waste of time and warmth and companionship. But he is unhappy and strained, full of tension and anxiety, and the headaches are still there. Getting stronger, I think..

Still no further news from Timothy. It's frustrating, having him so much on the move, and for some reason I have become shy of making contact. Lucy is being cheerfully supportive. I speak to her on the phone several times a week. She's been making telly commercials for cat food and says she now knows how to be gracefully upstaged by two tortoiseshell kittens and a ginger tom.

Still no bedsitter, either, but I'm happy here for a few days. Perhaps by the time Janine comes home I will have somewhere to go. We certainly couldn't share a home for very long, not because I don't love her but because we both acquire large quantities of *stuff* and in time would vanish beneath our own detritus. We'd eventually have to be dug out by the fire brigade and forcibly removed by Health & Safety officers.

I am now longing to be on my own, to think, to re-assess, to be quiet. Quietness has become essential.

At present I'm sitting in the living room window looking down at the street, where late morning walkers are stepping briskly towards the shops, or plodding more heavily home again with bulky carrier bags filled with cereal packets and selected pre-washed potatoes in polythene. Sometimes one can see bottle tops, and the ends of long French sticks or jumbo packs of toilet rolls, but really I am only watching them because I'm waiting for Alan to wake up, and observing my fellow humans is a good way of passing the time. I took him a cup of tea an hour ago.

What a strangely all-embracing emotion this love is. On the one hand I want nothing but his happiness, and could lie protectively beside him all night asking nothing at all. He has to be free of headaches and happy and confident again before I'll risk anything more. But another part of me doesn't know how to contain the passion he's arousing. Even kettles have an outlet when their water comes to the boil, but I have to keep the lid on mine and bubble away in secret.

There were two men in my lurid past whose feelings for me were so powerful the shock waves were almost irresistible. In fact they were so strong I had to reply, even though the reply wasn't usually the one they had expected! Or wanted!

It wasn't enough, was it, my half reply? I liked them both. In fact I was fond of them, and didn't at all want to hurt either, but that wasn't enough for them. Am I in a reverse situation now?

The thought frightens me. My mind tends to shy away.

On the other hand, of course, when Alan is free from pain he behaves as if he loves me. Wonderfully gentle and protective and always with this draw of excitement and stimulation when we talk. Every comment from one inspires instant response from the other. We share tastes, we love the same music, read the same books, laugh at the same jokes and cry at the same songs. We sigh at sunsets and gaze at rainbows. I believe he must love me in the end. He may not know this now, but one day the realisation will burst upon him like switching on the light.

Anyway, how could anyone possibly resist me? (That question is rhetorical and does not require an answer!)..

I can hear him in the bathroom. This will be continued in the next natural break. Love, Hannah.

48

Christabel Fraser

FROM   Hannah Pascoe
TO: Chrissiefras@coolmail.net
SENT: 27 June 2008
SUBJECT: Now what?

The past four days have been disturbing and I am more in limbo than ever.

Alan was quiet during his stay here. He apologised for coming, for being bad company, but since that was precisely why he'd been invited, he eventually got the message and stopped apologising.

We talked everything through. His remorse over Celia Wimbrook and his own Katy, the still unresolved feelings about divorcing Elizabeth and leaving Dominic, and his confused love and gratitude for me. All these were binding him up in awful guilt and fear. And now he is convinced he has serious brain damage or a tumour. It didn't matter what I said because his fear is beyond logic, but he just seemed to like having me there.

It rained all day. We went out briefly to buy a Chinese meal, but for the rest of the time we sat watching grey sheets of rain bombard the roofs opposite and the tree outside the window. We shared a bottle of wine and gradually the talk, as it usually does given time, turned to sex. He seems afraid he will never be normal again.

The electricity between us charged my already tight nerves until I was crying inwardly for him to take me to bed. Not at some future date but *now this minute*. I didn't, so he didn't, and so far I haven't died, even though instead of taking me to bed he took a hot drink and some pain killers there instead. I followed him and lay in my own bed wishing there could be a magic wand, or fairy dust to speckle his eyes and change his view of life and love and me.

I woke early. His hospital appointment was for 10 o'clock. He insisted on going alone. As he opened the door of the flat he looked down at me with a mixture of despair and chagrin.

"I'm sorry," he said.

"Don't be. It's been good just having you here, and I hope it's helped."

He smiled a very brief, watery smile and kissed my forehead.

"I don't know why you bother," he said.

I'm not sure I know either. Love is a mysterious business all round, as I'm sure you know all too well.

I told him I would fetch him from the hospital if that turned out to be necessary, and asked him to let me know how it went and whether or not they would be keeping him for further tests.

He nodded and walked out onto the landing. I waited until he had vanished down the first flight of stairs, then closed the door. He would go straight back to Waterloo Road, as there was a meeting in the evening to which he had, as a kind of pledge to himself, promised to go. Then he would come back to me. We have tickets for a concert in three days time.

I refused to entertain the thought, even for a moment, that the hospital really could keep him. It can't happen, therefore it won't.

That was yesterday. There has been no word. It is nearly six o'clock, but I will *not* phone him. Besides, tomorrow he comes back and we're going to our

233

concert.

Love from a getting-very-screwed-up Hannah.

Text Message
From Hannah Pascoe to Christabel Fraser 29.6.08

"S O S. Couldn't get you on phone. I need help.
Desperately. Hannah"

ooOoo

49

Christabel Fraser

FROM   Hannah Pascoe
TO: Chrissiefras@coolmail.net
SENT: 30 June 2008
SUBJECT: !!

I don't know what to say. I sent you my HELP text and
you came bearing bottle and cake and flowers, and
what better friends could anyone have?

I've thought over everything we said, everything I
told you, and know that although it's more than I can
bear I *must* keep to my decision not to see Alan for
some time. The wound is too raw, I am too tender and
need what little strength I've got for other things.

It still amazes me that he could arrive so calmly last
night to tell me he wouldn't be staying here after all, as
casually as if he'd decided to change his shoes, or that
he had come on the bus to save parking.

He had come into the living room, still wearing his
coat, and I gazed at him blankly, stunned into disbelief.

So much was happening inside my head that I couldn't disentangle one thread of thought from another.

"But why?" I asked in the end.

"Well there's rather a lot to do to catch up, and besides," he looked down at his hands on the chair back, "I'm rather enjoying my life at Waterloo Road at the moment"

Jealousy, hurt, rage and a bottomless well of disappointment all rose together in my throat and down through me in a hot, dark, red suffocating blanket. Yet I could do nothing about them and there wasn't even anything I could say. Why shouldn't he want to go home? I couldn't argue. There was no point.

"You haven't told me how you are," I said at least. "Or how the scan went"

"Oh that seems to be okay," he stared.

I stared at him in wonderment. "Why didn't you tell me? I was waiting to hear"

His eyes were suddenly two million miles away, cool and spatial. "You mean report back?"

I turned away, hurt now beyond bearing.

"I don't think I'll come to the concert," I told him. "And I can't keep this up"

"Keep what up?"

"Staying stable while you're not."

"Ah!" he said, and when I turned to look at him he was nodding.

"I won't see you for a while," I said. "Too much is happening in my own life, I can't cope with you as well, so I shall withdraw to recoup my strength"

"How long for?"

"Till such time…," I said.

He came towards me and stood looking down into my face. "Yes, I think you should." There were tears in his eyes. "Believe me, Hannah, as far as I am capable of loving anyone, I love you."

Then he kissed my forehead and was gone. So I sent you my Help! Text and you came.

Thank you, thank you.

Janine comes home tomorrow. I shall stay here for a few days more and then find myself a home. Today I went to work and rang several likely numbers from the newspaper.

I have to begin again, Chrissie. Please thank Peter for bringing you. Forty miles is quite a way to come on the spur of the moment to rescue a friend, but you saved my sanity.

Such as it is! My love and thanks, Hannah.

ooOoo

50

Christabel Fraser

FROM   Hannah Pascoe
TO: Chrissiefras@coolmail.net
SENT: 14 July 2008
SUBJECT: Hallelujah!

Cheers and hallelujah! Please note the new address – "Flat D, 47 Marlbury Road, Clifton". I am *in!* Settled. Installed. Well, sort of.

In fact I'm surrounded by suitcases, black bags and cardboard boxes, but the bed is made up with its new quilt cover and pillow cases (very smart!) and there are tins and packets in the kitchen cupboard.

There is also a teddy bear on the bed. He arrived all by himself in a carrier bag, with a note attached saying he'd met me in a shop and please could he come and live with me as he was "kleen and kwiert and well brawt up."

How could I refuse? He has a red ribbon, untidy ears and a strangely challenging expression, a direct, forthright look which is quite irresistible. He is mine and I adore him.

There was nothing on him to identify the giver, but I know quite well it was Janine. There were cards waiting, too – from you (thanks, thanks), from Janine, Myra and Karen, and from Beatrice Rudge and from Tom. Even Robert the WW director, sent a message and two more arrived next morning. The landlord seems very impressed and says I must be "very well cared for," but has obviously made allowances for Maisie fame. I think he considers it a feather in his landlordly cap to have enticed me here as a tenant. Maybe I should have made more if it with all the landlords who turned me down. A sad mistake on my part. There's a communal telephone on the landing just outside my door which rings rather too frequently despite everyone here possessing their own mobiles.

I'm going to like it here. I like it already. These two rooms are closing about me like a warm blanket after a shower.

The kitchen-diner is long, thin and bright with a large window at one end and space for my put-u-up spare bed at the other. The sitting room is quiet and well proportioned, elegant and corniced. Above all, it's mine, for the time being anyway. There's a key in the door which I can turn at will, to keep the world away.

After the past two weeks the world is not a place I wish to become any more acquainted with than I am already. Rather less, in fact. Not only have I denied myself the pleasure (and the pain) of seeing Alan, I have now incurred the enmity of his dad. I don't know why. I'd made an appointment some days to ago to meet him (Bill) for coffee, and felt it would be unnecessarily rude not to keep it – even though it was the day after I told Alan I was stepping back. The decision concerned Alan, not his father. Besides, I had known Bill for many years and he had always treated me as a good friend of his own.

Another mistake! As soon as I entered the hotel I knew there was something wrong. It shimmered in the air. Bill was off-hand and abrupt, curt. Alan was, of course, missing and I was at the same time relieved and disappointed.

Bill said shortly that he had heard from Alan and that in his opinion our decision not to see each other was a good thing. Neither he nor Alan was in a position to do anything about my present circumstances and he, Bill, thought I was simply making things worse for his son instead of better. He was, in fact, obliquely blaming me for Alan's present state.

I was too shocked at first to take him seriously. Then the truth of it was hammered home and I found myself about to cry. Bill obviously saw this because he said "Oh don't give me any of your ham acting. Tear jerking doesn't work with me. You lot are all the same."

I gasped and stared at him. "I think I'd better go," I said.

"Yes, I think you had."

Next day Lucy phoned.. Her voice was shaking. "Mum, Bill Box has just rung me. He wanted me to tell you to keep away from Alan."

"Good God! Did he give any reason?"

"Well he said rather a lot of things that I don't particularly want to tell you."

"You must, Lucy. I've got to know. Honestly!"

"Well, he said Alan would have been all right if it hadn't been for you throwing yourself at him. He said Alan doesn't want you and you've been a horrible embarrassment to both of them. What a bastard! I'll kill him."

I said nothing. Lucy, worried by the silence, said urgently. "Mum, mum, are you all right? Are you still there? Mum?"

"I'm still here. Carry on. What else did he say?"

"That..." she hesitated.

"Go on."

"He said he was appalled when he realised you were in love with Alan and it's the last thing Alan needs now. I tried to say about how you'd helped him and looked after him and he said yes, they're grateful, but that's all over now and he doesn't want you to come near Alan again. And anyway you're much older than he is. He gave the impression Alan could do a lot better. Mum! Better than you? Who does he bloody think he is?"

Her voice had risen and there were tears in it. I wanted to dive down the phone to her.

"Now listen darling," I said, "Don't take any notice of the old bat. I'll sort him out. Don't worry. I'll ring you back later. Thank you, sweetie, thank you. Bye for now"

I took a deep breath, fetched my car keys, locked my front door and drove to Bill's hotel. He was in his room. I went up and knocked on his door. When he saw me he frowned.

"Well? What are you doing here?"

"How dare you involve my daughter? How dare you talk about my private affairs to *my daughter?*"

"I had to."

"What do you mean, had to? You had no right. She's my daughter, not yours."

"I haven't got a daughter."

The staggeringly irrelevant reply disconcerted me so much I could only gasp. I wanted to hit him, to stamp on his feet, put my fist in his large beery stomach, but I

239

just stared and grew colder and colder with rage.

"It's nice to know who your friends are," I said at last. "Now I know you are not one of them. Don't ever, *ever* dare to contact any members of my family again. It was a monstrous, terrible thing to do. A terrible thing. How could you? Now I'm going and I won't come back. You are a vicious, evil minded old sod and you can keep your precious son. You deserve each other and I wouldn't have him now if you paid me."

Then I left. I had spoken clearly and precisely, to make sure I was understood, then walked back to my car knowing that if I had chosen to storm and scream the hotel (and no doubt a few reporters) would have buzzed around like flies.

But I hadn't. Instead I drove to Lucy's flat awash with adrenaline.

"Mum, I'm proud of you," she cried, hugging me and wetting my neck with tears. "What a horrible old man. To say things like that about you. About *you!* How dare he?"

She sniffed and led me to a chair. "Never mind, it's over now, you're shot of him and good riddance and you can start to live your own life."

I didn't cry until I reached Park Close. Michael was there. He gave me brandy and sent me to bed, and said he'd never liked the old bastard anyway.

"Oh Michael, what will I do without you?"

He put his arms around me. "You'll be fine. You'll see."

Alan rang later. I was in bed. "I think I have to apologise," he said.

"You don't," I replied shortly. "But your father does."

"Then I apologise on his behalf."

"He rang Lucy."

Alan was shocked. "Oh God, did he? Then please

apologise to Lucy too. I'm sorry Hannah."

"That's okay,. You didn't do anything"

"Are you all right?"

"No. But I suppose I will be in time."

There was a pause.

"I'll see you some time then, I expect," he said at last.

"Right."

"As and when…?"

"As and when…"

There was another pause. "Goodbye for now, then, and thank you for apologising"

"Goodbye."

I am not too sure how I came to put the phone back on its bed. One part of me wanted to keep it in my hand. The other felt burnt by it.

I cried again. Then I slept. But now I'm here in my own new home, and nothing around me reminds me of Bill or Alan or even of Michael. Everything is clean and fresh and different.

From now on I only want good things in it, so please will you and Peter come and visit me as soon as possible, even if you have to enter over stepping stones of unopened cardboard boxes.

All my love and thanks. H

ooOoo

51

Christabel Fraser

FROM   Hannah Pascoe
TO: Chrissiefras@coolmail.net

SENT: 22 July 2008
SUBJECT: Bedsitterland

One whole week, that's how long I've been living here,
but you know what funny things Time can do. This
week has seemed like a flicker of an eyelash and two
whole months all at once. However, next weekend will
see you here in person, in my own pad, the first guests
to be offered food cooked by me on my cooker in my
kitchen/diner. But since your time will be restricted to
one evening and not two months (the time required to
bring you fully up to speed) I shall delight your eyes
once more with a written report. Only be thankful this
isn't coming by H M Mail. It would certainly have
required Parcel Post.

I love it here Chrissie. There is nothing to bring
back old hurts, no associations from the past, only those
I wish to bring into my present or my future. I have
Lucy and Tim in their frames on the mantelpiece, and
Alan on the shelf by my bed. And yes, you are perfectly
right. If there is one photograph guaranteed to bring
back old hurts, it must be surely be the one on my
bedside table. So why, I hear you ask, am I making this
one an exception?

The answer is, of course, that I am temporarily
insane and therefore not accountable, and anyway who
wants to be logical all the time?

Michael has been to see me, bearing gifts (a bottle
of Martini, another of wine to share between us and one
or two things I left behind by mistake, including my
mobile phone which had been left on the kitchen table).
He likes it here, too. In fact there was an air of
wistfulness about him as he stood in the middle of the
room soaking up its *ambience.*

"It beats rattling about in that house," he said, then
he added "and you've got complete independence."

There has been a subtle change in his attitude over the past few weeks.

Sure, I have complete independence. It's the only thing I do have with any certainty. I go and come, consulting nobody on the matter but myself. If I choose to get in my car at 10.30 pm I do so without provoking the smallest hint of a raised eyebrow. The natives are friendly, so I expect in course of time we shall all get to know each other's business. Somebody somewhere will notice if I have a bath at eleven in the morning, or go out at midnight, or cook cauliflower cheese for breakfast – or retire to bed when everyone else is watching Coronation Street. But I imagine the rest of the household will keep its curiosity to itself.

Some very good things are happening. Leading a freshly Alan-free life has left time for friends neglected hitherto. It was a shock to realise just how long they have actually been neglected. So after scattering my change of address cards far and wide (at great expense, I have to add) my mobile has been ringing without cease with demands to know what the hell I'm doing in a bedsitter in Clifton.

The shock waves have been great fun. People who haven't rung or caught me at home have sent me texts or left messages on my voicemail – some have even sent little notes or cards. As a result, my diary is now crammed with coffee dates, lunch dates, dinner dates and parties. I saw Sally Marx the day before yesterday, Andrea Thorne and Robert Spicer the day before that and Tom the day before that. And yesterday I saw Beatrice Rudge, and that was best of all. I had forgotten just how much my mother she had become, both on and off The Walk. To her I *told all*, and she gave me home-made apricot pie and cream, and tea out of china cups, and she let me cry on her shoulder. She was comforting and encouraging and I came away duly comforted and encouraged and with a large bag of apples. That's what mums are for, after all.

This is where I am missing my own. Being orphaned for many years does **not** preclude one from crying "Mum, where are you when I need you?" at intervals!

Tom, when I saw him, was beautifully attentive and made all the right romantic moves in the never-ending game, but I seem to have turned myself into a one-man woman and could only see the mole on his nose. Poor Tom! He is a really attractive, good and lovely man who deserves a better response than the one he's getting from me right now. I succumbed, in fact, to an overwhelming impulse to tell him about Alan, which did slightly change the *ambience* of the evening. I am not totally convinced he'll ask me out again, and if he doesn't I have only myself to blame. The question is, do I care?

Meanwhile, there are invitations ahead for the next four weeks. Myra has visited and so has Janine while Lucy has been here several times. She and Andy helped me transport self and belongings, then took me home for supper. Three days later she magically appeared with a shopping basket of raw materials, and I was told to sit down and shut up while she cooked a meal *par excellence* in my own kitchen for my own table. How did she know I have temporarily given up cooking for myself? Possibly the absence of the right sort of stuff in cupboards and fridge might have provided her with a clue.

She met several of the residents. This is not difficult. Seven of us share two bathrooms and one telephone and, as we are all women, someone is using one or the other most of the time. I enjoy paddling across the landing while other females in bathrobes (or less) flit past with towels round their hair, and with their firm, tanned flesh newly laundered in fragrant body lotions. Perfumed and appealing they may be, but whether dressed or undressed they always stop to chat.

One or two have been to my room to introduce themselves – and of course to find out whatever it is they want to know. Any woman of 'a certain age' moving into a rented flatlet *must* have a story to tell, and since they have cottoned on to my stagey persona they've obviously decided my particular story must be worth the hearing. I think they're surprised it hasn't appeared in one of the glossy magazines. I did actually do so in the local papers after the election, caught on camera with Ruth – the magazine naturally misquoting everything I had said.

Alan's photograph intrigues them, as it should, being a publicity shot for past elections and portraying him as vital, purposeful and eager. Had they seen him over the past few months they might not have recognised the photo, for even I have to set myself deliberately to remember how he was and should be again.

I can walk to work, and enjoy it, taking nine minutes precisely, and I have established agreeable rituals for morning and evening. What's more, I still do my exercises. So you see, Chrissie, life has suddenly become adventurous and stimulating again. Perhaps I enjoy it all the more for planning how I shall meet Alan again one day, how he'll climb the stairs to my room, how he will look and behave, and how I shall feel.

My room, or rather my rooms if you count in the kitchen/diner, are now quite charming, even to me. Perhaps especially to me because for the first time ever I am free to impress my own personality upon them and every day add something new – although that something has to cost little or nothing. Money is a bit of a problem at the moment. This makes the challenge even greater, so I design and redesign things in my head, and call up whatever ingenuity I possess to make the designs work. There is a huge ancient storage heater in the living room which is dead and an eyesore – so I've covered it with material from a no-longer-needed quilt, with neatly tailored corners and frills around the hem. (The frills were already there – I didn't make them, you understand! Ingenious I may be, but a world-class needlewoman, I am not!) Anyway, with a plant on top, this adds a touch of *je ne sais quoi* to my room, besides matching two of the scatter cushions. Pleasing to look at while sitting up in bed drinking my morning cuppa.

Colleagues at work are being as co-operative as one can reasonably expect from people who have only known me for five weeks at most. And one or two are surpassing expectations, for why should I be offered help or sympathy when whatever I feel is concealed behind this ghastly Pascoe exuberance? (You may call it *joi de vivre* but personally I think it's a pain).

'Ghastly Pascoe' has a nice resonance, don't you think?

Impatient to see you, love, H

ooOoo

52

Christabel Fraser

FROM   Hannah Pascoe
TO: Chrissiefras@coolmail.net
SENT: 29 July 2008
SUBJECT: Still in bedsitterland

Many, many thanks for coming. Thanks for making me laugh, for making me *cook*. – a big achievement for both of us, since I am in the habit of staring in bitter hatred at this cooker for many minutes at a time, unwilling even to begin using it. I never knew how much I disliked the activity of mixing and chopping and stirring and timing. As some people feel about driving – "if one must, one must" – so I feel about *haute cuisine*, or any other kind of *cuisine*. There are so many other things I'd rather do, like writing to you, or simply sitting in a chair staring into space. Chopping, stirring and mixing take up valuable sitting, writing and staring time.

But I cooked for you, and you were very nice about the result. Thank you again.

Thanks also for loving my flatlet and all the bits I have added. Of course, in view of your good taste and refinement, your approval of my new home went without saying. But listening to the flow of words which must have sounded rather like a tap with a faulty washer, impossible to turn off, now that really was going beyond the call of friendship!

Alas, until the divorce is through and Michael is married, and until Alan has faded a little more from my thoughts, the tap is likely to continue dripping. And there's the rub! I may have moved into this world of new neighbours, new job, new colleagues and new environment, but my thoughts, hopes and desires have simply moved with me. It's true that one can escape from anything except oneself.

Not that I don't long for escape. From the first day that Alan invaded my mind, I have been trying to shake him loose. But it feels now as if every inch of my bodily tissue has been soaked through. I've been marinated. And he seems to have wound himself in and out of all my vital organs so I no longer know where he stops and I begin.

The freedom and independence I have are illusions. I go home to Michael every week to use the washing machine and to eat his home-cooked Sunday roast, and Alan remains a quietly hopeful dream and a framed image on my locker. I tried getting rid of the former (dream) by removing the latter (photograph), but I knew all the time it was in the top drawer of my dressing table, so the ruse didn't work. One day I simply gave in and brought the exasperating portrait out again.

Nothing, neither jealousy nor hurt nor wounded vanity seems to unseat him. I know he and I will meet again. Until then I am content to wait.

Meanwhile my social life continues to expand in a highly satisfactory manner. I am rarely here, but when in residence I write emails or lie on my bed meditating, sending and receiving text messages and making phone calls - oh, and reading approximately two books per week borrowed from the local library. And when not doing any of those I am chatting to my fascinating neighbours. The dental surgery with its smells and procedures is becoming more familiar, and I almost know what I'm doing. Even their computer is beginning to lose its horrors. Years with a personal computer and laptop may make one reasonably literate, but they only go so far. Entering patients' records, bringing them up to date and checking appointments in and out feel to me like a nice recipe for Hannah mess-ups! But the appointments are fun. A little chair comes up on the screen when a patient goes in to the surgery (personally I think there ought to be another - a little bubble with "Ouch!" in it) and a tick appears when they arrive and depart. I wonder if the programme will extend itself to moving figures eventually. Would writhing in the chair be going too far, do you think?

Happily, there haven't been too many personal mess-ups so far, and the rest of the daily round is much the same as it was. Listening to the answerphone messages in the morning, checking today's lists of appointments, making sure our four dentists know whose teeth they will be investigating and when, and seeing to the needs of their four pretty nurses (Why are dental nurses always young and pretty? Are they pickled in formalin as soon as they start to go off?) – these are the routines which I shall no doubt grow to love. Plus the profusion of unscheduled happenings which liven up the day – and me!

There is only one full time receptionist, Anne. The rest of us are part-timers. I am at present only working 18 hours a week, so I see Alison and Megan on different days. Anne is very nice. We have established a vital link between us – i.e. we both giggle. Yesterday, though, a patient shocked me by taking out his dentures and placing them on the counter. "These are broken," he said. Transfixed, I waited nervously for them to chatter across to bite me, and all the while hysterical laughter was surging up from my toes. But Anne solved the problem just in time by removing the teeth in a tissue, otherwise I might still have been there.

Giggles and shocks notwithstanding, I am finding great gaps in my concentration every now and then, and once or twice I've been close to dissolving into humiliating tears in a public place. The very humiliation adds to the stress, which adds to the threat of tears, which adds to the stress – so it goes on! I'm happy to say nothing really awful has happened yet, but I live in fear of making mistakes. And the more frightened one is of making mistakes, the more mistakes one makes.

I have to break this chain of cause and effect. I come home so tired and diminished that I have to spend my days off shoring confidence up with a buzzing social life. This is fatally easy. Old friends have come like genies out of a hundred bottles – mostly wine bottles!

The divorce is proceeding smoothly. Too smoothly, for I hardly know it's happening at all, and the *denouement* is likely to hit me on the head with sledge-hammer force when it does arrive. The smoothness is due to Michael and I having worked it all out between us before involving a solicitor at all. And since there is only one solicitor – mine – there is no-one for him to write complicated legal letters to, which saves both time and money. Finance has caused a bit of heart-searching because we didn't have much to start with (money, not heart) as we've always spent as we went along, but have agreed about what there is and what to do with it. The grounds are Adultery, so in a very short time all will be over.

Now that Michael and Margaret are engaged there is no going back. And if one cannot go back one must go forward. Anything else is only marking time.

It is now 2.30 am. I am sitting up in my double bed listening to the radio. Before me is a mantelpiece upon which are photographs and my little Wedgwood caskets. To one side is a bookcase holding medieval whodunits, Dorothy Sayers. Ellis Peters and Tolkien, and three small but healthy pot plants which have miraculously survived several weeks in my care. The newly covered heater looks pretty, with more plants on top, and on my left there is a shelf with clock radio, music centre and sets of Jane Austen and Dickens. To my right, the bedside table holds lamp, a picture of Alan, library books and a half empty cup of cold coffee, soon to be replaced with a full cup of hot milk. I shall then close down this lap-top, this modern equivalent of quill and seal, and lie down. To sleep, perchance to dream?

Tomorrow is Saturday. I have a full weekend.

Till we meet again, young Chrissie, I remain your getting-rather-cross-eyed social butterfly. Love, H.

P S. Last time I went to Park Close, Mary Quintrell popped up from behind a hedge and exclaimed at my long absences. "It's lovely to see you," she said, "We wondered where you'd got to." It then dawned on me that we've all been so preoccupied with our own dramas nobody has thought to tell the neighbours. I have to be honest and admit that Mary Quintrell has been the last person on my mind lately, but I wondered how Michael had avoided mentioning it. Not that there is much puzzle to it, really, as Michael can avoid mentioning anything to anyone at any given time.

But I asked him all the same.

"The Quintrells?" He seemed surprised, obviously not having the first notion of who they were.

"You know," I prompted with mild sarcasm, "the people who live next door and borrow your hedge cutter"

Michael made an impatient noise. "They didn't ask," he said, and closed the conversation. Silly me!

Mary wasn't in her garden when I left for home, and as I felt no inclination to seek her out so the problem has been carried over until next time. Too late, I am now wondering what she thought of Alan's visits during the day when I was there, and Margaret's visits now when I'm not – and whose side she will take when she learns of Michael's re-marriage. Not that it matters, but all the same…!

Still no idea where Timothy is. I expect him to pop in from Outer Mongolia or Alaska any day now and be surprised that we are surprised! Love, H

ooOoo

53

Christabel Fraser

FROM   Hannah Pascoe
TO: Chrissiefras@coolmail.net
SENT: 12 August 2008
SUBJECT: Congrats!

Your excited phone call set me up for the day. Congratulations to Peter. Wonderful news to be promoted so soon, but he must be a bright lad to have married you. I'm pleased about Suzie's new boyfriend, who has to be an improvement on the last! What is it with some women that they invariably choose the most unsuitable men in sight? But maybe I shouldn't comment, seeing what a mess I'm making of my own love life!

I am not at all sure I want this whirling social life, which seems to come about whether I like it or not. I plan a peaceful restorative day to myself, but before I've finished my morning cup of tea my mobile is drowning me in texts and calls, and another invitation is logged. I could say no, but of course I never do. Most of these people are friends from the past (Theatre gossip networks can be frighteningly efficient).

Janine and Myra both keep in close touch, but it's Jan who phones the surgery to say she has (surprise surprise!) made too much casserole for herself and would I please go round and help her get through it. When we are together we talk for hours and hours. Her exotic bird image is wonderfully heightened by a solid-looking red plastic apron inscribed "Keep your distance. I'm having a nervous breakdown" which she wears over canary yellow sweaters and chequered leggings. And underneath these startling feathers she is wise and kind and very, very bright. Too wise to offer advice which would not be taken! Instead she is simply *there.* At hand. We go for walks sometimes, but I tend to avoid the river and Snuff Mills and have stopped visiting The Buttress – which is no longer my local anyway.

Jan rarely sees Nick at the studio. The story line is such that their roles don't often coincide. But when they meet she asks after Alan. Last heard of, he was "a bit up and down". It's only the ambiguity of Nick's place in Alan's life, and the fact that he seems to have taken him up as a "cause" which he prefers to pursue without help from me, that stops me from ringing to find out for myself exactly why he is "up and down", and if there is anything I can do to lift the down part up.

I won't. I am the one who backed away "till such time...", so I am the one who must decide when that time has come. And such is the perversity of human pride that I find myself waiting for his call, when under the circumstances he is obliged to wait for mine. I wrote a "keeping in touch" message last week, light-heartedly anecdotal, but said I wasn't expecting a reply. He didn't send one. If that added to the soreness of the sore places, it is my own fault for sticking my neck out.

Councillor Ruth Baker came the other day, suggesting I might enjoy sitting in the public gallery of the council chamber for the next full council meeting. She will be making her maiden speech, so I said yes of course, I'd love to be there, and wrote the date in my diary. She is delightful. We spent a good deal of her visit laughing. She too sees Alan from time to time. He is, she says, rather quiet and subdued, but he's been helping to produce the next Focus leaflet. She thinks he has a bit of trouble concentrating. The brain scan proved negative yet he doesn't seem well.

I *will not* ring him.

Bill visits regularly and stays at Waterloo Road. It's a wonder he doesn't move down here altogether.

This divorce is amazingly trouble-free so far. Papers come now and again in the post and Michael has had to write a formal statement, but I feel no pain at all. Just peculiar. Disembodied. None of it is true and soon someone will call out "Okay folks, game's over, everyone back to their own beds."

Now that I am professionally detached I can't resist going to concerts and theatres, but nothing has tempted me yet back to the boards myself. I'm as interested in politics now as in plays, but neither inspires me to positive action.

In our ancient days do we become Watchers instead of Doers? Or is it just a phase I'm going through? The other day I steeled myself to watching the beginning of Wayside Walk again, but soon switched it off. The experience is frustrating and painful, filling me with two opposing emotions – sadness because I seem to have left no trace, like sticking one's finger in a glass of water and then taking it out again without leaving so much as a solitary ripple, and at the same time confirming absolutely my decision to leave it. I won't try it again.

Tomorrow I have an appointment with my new doctor owing to a strangely unidentifiable pain in my lower region. At least the hateful rash hasn't erupted again, for which I am duly and deeply grateful.

One of the dentists in our practice mentioned Michael the other day. He'd seen him at a meeting. I asked if Margaret had been there too, and he said yes but passed rather quickly to other matters. He may be embarrassed at my presence, but I am beyond caring.

I've been thinking over what you said, that the three most traumatic events in anyone's life are Bereavement or Divorce, New Job and Moving House, and that I have just managed to suffer all three in just a few weeks. You are of course perfectly right.

I must go. Time for bed. Love, H

P S I'm not sure I thanked you for asking after The Book. You are not alone. Since I told so many people I was retiring in order to write one, that's hardly surprising, but what with one thing and another, the few chapters I achieved on my arrival here have been lost in the swirling waters of socialite living. Instead I write emails to you, but if I continue at this pace the result may well be a book in its own right, so you'd better hang onto this *magnum opus*. What a nice thought. "Ex-Actress Reveals All." Even more likely "Wayside Walk Celebrity reveals truth!"

P P S Timothy is still silent. Last night I took firm hold of my courage and rang his number in Paris. His answerphone told me he was out, so I left a message saying I hoped he was all right. No use trying his mobile. For some reason it is unobtainable from here. Lucy wrote to him a few weeks ago but he hasn't replied to her either. H

ooOoo

54

Christabel Fraser

FROM   Hannah Pascoe

How about this, then? Yesterday I was sitting in my armchair listening to Beethoven's late quartets, remembering when I'd last heard them – at Park Close with Alan – and wondering if I would ever see him again, when the phone rang and it was Himself.

"Hannah" he said. "It's Alan. Dominic is here for a few days and he'd like to see you. May we take you out to lunch tomorrow?"

I uncrossed my eyes, remembered my training and replied in a nice, calm voice that yes, I'd love to and how lovely to see Dominic and that lunch would be lovely. Conscious of too many 'lovelys', I cleared my throat and asked what time and where. He said about 12.30 and could they pick me up, so I gave them directions and then went back to my room and stared sightlessly at it. At least one of my dreams was about to come true. Alan Box would really and truly climb the stairs with my gracious permission. There's a door phone so he can't come up without it, but that is mere irrelevance. And he will sit in one of my chairs and look around him at the room I was not at present seeing.

But reality jolted me back to panic, and I became as powerfully mobilised as I'd been motionless only five minutes before. By 9.30 that evening the room looked and smelt beautiful and I was in the bath trying to be likewise. It was a hot, sudsy bath, foam to the eyebrows, and I lay back in exquisite abandonment. Tomorrow I would see Alan. He hadn't waited for me after all.

Inside and out I was aglow!

Since there is a limit to what can be achieved in a

not very large room once it's been scoured, polished, vacuumed and rearranged at least three times, I spent most of this morning beautifying me. First I put on too little makeup, then added some more, decided it was overdone and wiped it all off again. Then I stared haplessly in the mirror. Finally I decided that whatever I did would make very little difference anyway because he'd already seen me in all states of repair and disrepair and could no longer be deceived into thinking I was even remotely beautiful.

Having reached this rather depressing conclusion, I meditated on the ultimate injustice of Beauty itself. Why should a tall, slim woman with long lustrous hair and large eyes be more admirable in herself, more desirable in her sexuality, than a short, plump woman with thinning hair and little eyes? Both are accidents of nature, whims of genealogy, and perhaps the plump woman with small eyes has a beautiful mind and soul while the slim one is a bitch? Not that I consider myself to be any of those. In fact I am hoping you will now tell me that far from being small, plump and piggy-eyed, I am tall (well tallish – 5'5" to be precise) slim (well not fat anyway) and that my eyes are of a perfectly satisfactory size. Or am I asking too much here?

The whole thing is, of course, relative, since beauty is always in the eyes of the beholder – a fact that has often impressed me when looking at wedding photographs in the press, wondering what on earth the bride and groom saw in each other. But wherever our personal tastes lie, the problem remains the same. Why should a personal taste in beauty invest another human being with qualities of soul they may not even possess. Is it mostly men who fall into this, or do we women do it too?

I've decided nature isn't fair, and men aren't fair, and Society has never been fair. But all my life seems to have been spent with the conviction that beauty was not one of the gifts handed down by my fairy godmother. To be truthful, I don't seem to have lost much, except private self esteem. Society has a way of ramming home the message that Good Looks Make Us Happy. But despite Society's strictures, I have had my share of admirers and they couldn't have been after my money because I never had any – or, on the few occasions when I did have, never kept it long enough to make any pursuit worth while!

By now you must have realised that all this dizzy chatter is due to the fact that I am in a *stew*, boiling and bubbling in my saucepan.

He arrived and climbed the stairs as planned, trailing a charmingly pleased-to-see-me Dominic. They sat in my armchairs and admired my buffed-up and shining new home, and then we put our coats back on and left for a nearby restaurant where they serve pleasant food to loud and rather less pleasant music. But Dominic liked it and the pictures on the wall were deliciously different black and white 1930-style photographs.

Alan was quiet but obviously happy with his son. He is very proud of him. Afterwards we came back to the flat for coffee and I determinedly ignored the passing of time. We too often spoil the present by anticipating its end. So when they really did leave I was less prepared than I should have been, and shock gripped my stomach and stung my eyelids.

I saw them off and returned to used coffee cups and the new, changed flavour of a room which once held no memory of Alan's physical presence but now unexpectedly did.

My flatlet is inviolate no longer. Even the wallpaper looks different.

I saw my new doctor last week. I have a spastic

colon. This sounds unromantic with comic overtones, but is apparently caused by stress. At least it's invisible. She asked me questions which I found hard to answer and as I began to tell her, almost as a joke, about Michael and Margaret and the job and my removal from home, I began to cry and couldn't stop. It was embarrassing and unnerving.

The doctor was astonishingly caring and sympathetic, warm and kindly and definitely On My Side. She handed me a tissue and said I mustn't hesitate to see her whenever I wished. So I mumbled an apology for behaving like a stick of limp celery and she reiterated what you said only last week! "Good heavens!" she cried "Do you know the main causes of stress? Moving house, changing job and divorce or bereavement. You've just had all three at once."

As you and I have already agreed on the matter, I now feel entitled to my stress symptoms.

Michael came the other day, bringing the pictures I wanted for my kitchen, some videos and a bottle of wine which we opened and drank companionably while discussing divorce proceedings.

Myra says the situation is "very French". *Au revoir*.
H

ooOoo

55

Christabel Fraser

FROM   Hannah Pascoe
TO: Chrissiefras@coolmail.net
SENT: 9 September 2008

SUBJECT: Tim

Last night I actually spoke to a real, live Timothy. After trying many times and achieving only his disembodied voice on both voicemails, this was such a surprise I was about to leave a message when I realised it wasn't the machine at all but my wandering son himself. It was lovely to hear him, but he was calling from Boston in the States so we didn't talk for long. There's no point in my going to Paris at the moment as he flies to Lisbon on Tuesday. He will, however, call here on his way home in three weeks. He didn't mention the divorce, so either he is ignoring it until he gets here or Lucy's messages and mine haven't yet reached their target. I didn't mention it myself except telling him there was a lot happening here which we would talk about properly when he came home. He said that was ok with him, so we left it at that.

Little Karen has rid herself of Hatchet Jaw permanently now. She shares a flat with a girl friend, but has been staying with Janine, for safety I imagine, since the charming Mark is exceedingly displeased at having been dropped in the murk by the girl he believed lay curled up in the hollow of his hand. But he is generally unpopular. I'm not sure if stopping to help at the scene of an accident is a legal requirement, but where there is no obvious other help it is certainly a hefty moral one! So although he was probably the cause of it, barring positive proof there is nothing anyone can do about it. More's the pity!

Karen, however, has seen him very clearly with new eyes, and he is very positively *persona non grata.* So there she is at Aunty Jan's until the bru-ha-ha has blown over, with the acting virus well into her bloodstream. Two tiny parts in W W as an extra have put stars into her eyes in more ways than one, so when she came to visit me the other evening we had a great deal to discuss. No, I shall rephrase that - *she* had a great deal to discuss. I was merely the empathetic audience.

It is an odd experience, hearing things so familiar to oneself being described with the fresh, untainted enthusiasm of the very young. I saw people and events through her eyes and the sight was disconcerting. I also had to take great care with what I said and how I said it. Apart from the danger of treading on this tender little shoot of a talent, clever comments can come too easily to the likes of me, and when the wit begins to flow cruel comments are never far away.

The local Liberal Democrats, through the machinations of Ruth Baker, (whose visits have political undertones and sometimes even overtones) have introduced themselves and taken me to their combined bosoms. They sent their local secretary, Heather Coxe, to find out what I could do for them. They already knew about Ruth's election and about Alan, so I had no excuse and was promptly engaged as an authorised Focus deliverer. Heather rounded off her sales pitch by saying she wished Alan could work in this ward instead of his own, because then we'd have had our own Box and Coxe!

We parted with mutual expressions of cheerful good will. There's a fund-raising party this coming Saturday to which I shall go, as there is no knowing whom one might meet at these do's. Political characters can be strange, often vivid and interesting no matter which party they belong to.

They are particularly wonderful in full council meetings. Last week I sat aloft and aloof on a red leather bench that tilted forward at such an uncomfortable angle that my legs ached afterwards from anchoring themselves to nowhere. And I looked down upon the grand gathering of councillors and across at the red-robed Lord Mayor. He was stately and awesome in his slow walk to the dais, but sounded cheerfully ordinary as soon as he opened his mouth. There was much chatter and cross talk, plenty of coming and going, persons wanderng about and reading newspapers in the middle of other peoples' speeches. For my part I thought they were very rude, but since I didn't understand most of the speeches I decided that possibly they didn't either. I was eventually forced to acknowledge my error when first one and then another stood up with what must have been cogent replies, so at least some members knew what was going on. I was proud of Ruth. Her maiden speech was short, witty and utterly comprehensible. When she sat down we all clapped.

I stayed for tea, sandwiches and cakes, but afterwards left at once. The experience amused me. It had also given me food for thought for which quietness and peace were required..

Andrew, my young admirer with the market garden, called unexpectedly yesterday and I was delighted to push the door phone button to let him in. He didn't bring any cauliflower this time but produced a clutch of the very last of the summer tomatoes and it was lovely to see him again. He sat in my armchair shyly drinking coffee and telling me about his holiday in Dubrovnik. Then he asked solemnly what I was doing and if I was all right. I told him equally solemnly that I was.

I think he believed me, but do I believe myself?

Tom surprised me by sending another message, through Jan, that he'd been phoning and sending a hundred texts trying to contact me but I'm never here, and since that is patently true, and since I have taken to switching off my mobile to give myself a modicum of peace, I can hardly accuse him of neglect. Perhaps one day he will succeed, and at least it seems that my lovelorn state hasn't discouraged him after all. I rather thought it might.

Life is funny and the people in it still funnier,

10.30 pm.

This breath-taking composition was interrupted by the house telephone and proved to be a call for Louise, who lives upstairs. As she was coming down to take it she passed Sarah who was going up, and since at the same moment Clare emerged from the bathroom, we all fell to talking and finally held an impromptu party on the landing carpet. Sarah fetched a bottle, I provided cheesy biscuits and we all sat on the floor while Louise talked for twenty minutes to her friend in Cardiff. We all listened with the greatest interest.

She, Louise, has a relationship with George, who comes here regularly, carrying his 15 stone up the stairs like a knight in weighty armour storming his lady's tower. I hope she rewards him at journey's end, but I expect she does because he always comes back for more, and I'm sure he wouldn't if she didn't. Louise is tall, slim and fair, and I think she ought to let down her long blonde tresses to help him in his climb.

Sarah is a flighty piece, full of giggles. Her skirts are either short and tight like a cummerbund or long and flowing like a bell. Below them her legs are mostly encased in thick black tights and fluffy boots or equally tight stretch jeans ending in fashion boots with perilously high heels Her hair is very short and very dyed, in colours to match whichever mood she happens to be in that day, and her lips are often a rich, dark purple. If not purple, then occasionally black or a bright, hot pink. She has a low opinion of men.

Clare is pretty, vital and *super-fit.* She dons track suit and trainers and sprints about the neighbourhood in the most sickening way. She has an equally fit boy friend called Nigel ("Nige") and they are in the process of house hunting. The latest kind of sport. She told us they have at last found their ideal home and made an offer for it that very afternoon. It's all very exciting.

By the time we had finished our wine and Louise had finished her conversation it was time for bed and we had, between us, decided exactly what it was the male sex is lacking – though we have little hope of supplying the deficiency just at present.

There are other girls in the house – Julia and Shirley – who also live upstairs, and Liz who is a nurse and works strange and difficult hours. Everyone comes and goes. Clare lives in the next room to me, Sarah is across the landing and Louise, despite living on the floor above, prefers our bathroom to hers. Result – frequent parties, often draped in bath towels.

That was yesterday. This evening was the Lib Dem party at a house not far away. As expected, I met some lively and fascinating people who promised to visit me. There is to be a Bring and Buy sale next week, and, untrained and ignorant though I am, I have offered to help and now look forward to another New Experience – which I assume involves my bringing something to sell as well as bringing a full purse for the 'Buying' part..

My spastic colon (the name of which conjures up so many delightful images that writing it down is almost more than I can seriously manage) continues to ache, but as I am assured it is caused by stress, I refuse to add to the stress by worrying about it!

It's at least two hours since I came home from the party and sleep is as far away as ever. I shall go to bed with a book. Love for now, H

56

Christabel Fraser

FROM   Hannah Pascoe
TO: Chrissiefras@coolmail.net
SENT: 14 September 2008
SUBJECT: Shock horror!

The *timbre* of my social life is changing by the day. Heather Coxe came this morning to check that I am an official party member. I said yes, certainly, fully paid up and with a card to prove it – not to mention the rosette given to me by Alan in a previous existence.

And tomorrow is the Bring and Buy sale. I fetched some clothes from Park Close yesterday, so Heather left with pieces of Maisie Mitchell's wardrobe which will be auctioned at probably exorbitantly prices. The trouble is, I was fond of Maisie and don't like to think of her clothes going to the highest bidder, poor chick! Still, it's all in a good cause, and she was a sucker for those! Besides, there must be some mileage in having once been a minor Celeb.

Last night Clare, Sarah and I held another impromptu party in my room. They wanted to know who was the dishy man in my photograph, so I told them about Alan. I described him as someone I am potty about but who has problems of his own and seems rather less than potty about me. They commiserated. The tale has an air of romance which hangs nicely with the rest of me, so far as they know. "Middle-aged actress leaves home so husband can marry again and cherishes hopeless passion for politician still scarred from accidentally injuring a ten-year-old girl"

How much more melodramatic can a story be? Surely 'tis the stuff of flashy novelettes!

I shall miss Clare when she leaves here.

4.30 pm Saturday

Have just had a shock. The Bring and Buy sale was a relatively peaceful New Experience. Seven of us arrived early to arrange the "Bring" part, placing a large variety of items attractively on long trestle tables, with Maisie's best pieces artistically draped or on hangers in their own special space. To my relief and in deference to confessed bashfulness in selling my own stuff, Ruth Baker herself volunteered to be auctioneer and did a magnificent job. I have yet to learn how much Maisie raised all by herself, but suspect it was a fairly significant sum. Good for Maisie!

At the end of what seemed like six hours but wasn't really, regaled as we were by sandwiches and non-stop cups of tea and coffee, I was more tired than I expected to be and sat down to rest my feet, close my eyes and dream of a hot bath and a change of clothes.

Unfortunately this was not to be my time for resting. Within the last ten minutes the whole complexion of the day changed abruptly. One of the customers left a copy of the local paper on a vacant chair, which Heather picked up while tidying the room, glanced at and then brought it to me. The headline was "Scot free!" It continued "A SUPPLY teacher not long arrived in the city has caused serious injury to a young girl in a road accident but apparently is not being charged with any offence.

"Alan Box, (48)", it went on "who was Liberal Democrat councillor for a West Yorkshire ward, is already politically active here. The victim of the accident was the ten-year-old girl daughter of Councillor Wimbbrook, and friends of the family are asking why Mr Box should be allowed to go scot free.

"Little Celia's godfather is asking why Mr Box has left a wife and son in West Yorkshire and believes his move is related to a scandal in his home town. Mr Cuthbert-Wright, party spokesperson, said: 'I feel very frustrated about it all, and very angry. As far as we know there weren't any real witnesses to this accident and I personally would like to see some justice here. Besides, what's this new scandal about a pupil in his school? There has been an accusation about a sixteen-year-old girl? I understand that she said she didn't want to complain about him, but we all know there's no smoke without fire." Apparently the girl, who cannot be named for legal reasons, is not pressing charges.

"We believe, however, that a witness has come forward recently with new evidence to clear Mr Box's name. He has also been helped in this matter by two of the cast from Wayside Walk, notably Mel Kendrick and even more notably by Hannah Pascoe, who recently retired from her role as Maisie. We understand Alan Box and Miss Pascoe are now very close. (The exclamation mark was unstated but undeniably there).

"Mr Box suffered injuries to his head in the accident, and the tragedy was compounded by his own daughter dying in a similar way two years ago, knocked off her bicycle by a hit-and-run driver. Meanwhile, he has been actively helping Cllr Ruth Baker win the seat for St Mary's Ward in the recent council elections"

Mr Cuthbert-Wright said: "Mr Box has been a lucky man. Sadly, Celia was not so lucky."

Chrissie, it was all horrible, no actual accusations but so nicely worded that one can't help jumping to conclusions. The bit about me was only to be expected, and doesn't amount to a row of beans, but what will it do to Alan? To be grateful for past help is bad enough, but to have his name so unpleasantly linked to mine could kill off any future between us, and there was little enough of that already. And what's this about the girl student? Alan hasn't said a word so far. But then, would he if he were guilty?

There is so much there to hurt him and damage his career, just when he is beginning to recover. I have to decide now what to do. I'm torn. The paper was two days old and Alan may not have known about it at once. He may not even know now, since he certainly doesn't buy the paper. Perhaps some kind friends will tell him.

I wish I knew what to do. Love, H.

ooOoo

57

Christabel Fraser

FROM   Hannah Pascoe
TO: Chrissiefras@coolmail.net
SENT: 17 September 2008
SUBJECT: Off again!

Nothing stands still for long, does it?

I didn't ring Alan, I drove to Waterloo Road instead and buzzed the buzzer. He opened the door and stood staring for some seconds. Then he gasped and let me in. His eyes were black holes in a white face.

"Hannah! How did you know?"

"I read it. At a Bring and Buy sale."

"A Bring and Buy sale?" he frowned, concentrating. "I don't understand."

"Never mind, it's not worth trying. I've come to see how you are." But I knew how he was.

"Not very good, I'm afraid, but come in."

He looked awful, seeming to not quite know what he was doing.

"Are you going to do anything? I mean, is it possible to sue the paper?"

"Suing costs a lot of money. Besides, they haven't really *said* anything, just hinted. It's the old no-smoke-without-fire thing."

We went into the kitchen and he sat down, leaning forward to scrutinise his hands in a now familiar gesture. "Hannah," he said "You've given me so much and I not only don't give you anything back, I drag your name into the papers as well"

I sat in the chair opposite and scoffed. "Rubbish! Don't you think I'm used to that? The papers love to maul celebs about, and if they can drag them through the mire so much the better. Not that we mind, as a rule. Publicity is life blood to actors, didn't you know? Like politicians? The only bad publicity being no publicity?"

I considered him. "Where's Nick?" I asked. "Is he working?"

Alan looked vague, as if he wasn't too sure who Nick was. "I don't know." Then he shook his head, impatient with himself. "Yes, of course I do. He's gone to see one of his friends. He's usually here at this time"

I mentally sent up a prayer of thanks, then asked if everything was all right. "With him, I mean?"

"Yes, fine. It's very good. Thank you for finding it."

I leaned back in my chair and waited. At some point he would have to offer some explanation. After a minute or two he looked up and studied me.

"I'm feeling very bad about it all. You knew I would. That's why you're here."

"Yes."

"You still love me then?"

"Of course."He closed his eyes and relapsed into stillness, only it was not so much immobility as a kind of death. I felt I had to call him back, that his soul was sliding away and that if I wasn't quick he would go beyond reach. So I began to talk. About anything or nothing, its only requisite being that it made a story. I told him about the girls at home and the parties on the landing. I described the surgery and the nurses and my struggles with the computer there. I even told about the bring-and-buy auctioning Maisie Mitchell's clothes, and he very slowly came up from his blackness and started to listen. Occasionally he smiled and once he even laughed.

I stayed for about an hour. When I stood up to leave he was alive and almost normal.

At the door he said: "Can you come again?"

"Of course, if you want me to." Alan nodded. "I'm working tomorrow but I'll ring you when I get home at teatime."

"Thank you," he said. When he saw me into my car he closed the driver's door and thanked me again.

My few months respite seems to be over with no change at all. Our last meeting might have been yesterday. But despite all the shocks and difficulties I am singing inside like the little blackbird in our plum tree.

Adieu, H

ooOoo

Christabel Fraser

FROM Hannah Pascoe
TO: Chrissiefras@coolmail.net
SENT: 20 September 2008
SUBJECT: More shocks

Yes, your questions are relevant but hard to answer. How do I feel about the allegation that Alan made passes at a sixth form girl? Do I believe it? Why didn't whoever-it-was use the even more fascinating information that Nick and Alan share a house and could be said to be living together? Surely worth a spiteful comment, yet Nick wasn't mentioned. And who gave the story to the paper?

The first one is easy. No, I don't believe it. I did mention it yesterday, wondering who could possibly have dreamed up such a tale, but he just smiled rather wistfully and said: "Whoever it was gave me more credit for ooomph than I've got at the moment, thanks"

The second question is harder. The field is wide. Politics? Teaching? Theatre? Name your suspect.

Since that first visit I have seen Alan every day. Next time I called Nick was there, politely friendly but obviously not overjoyed at my presence. I no longer care. Alan wants to see me and it's his business and his alone, so Nick may suffer me with as a good a grace as he can muster.

Whenever I arrive Alan is almost catatonic with depression, yet astoundingly, by the time I leave he is alive and awake again. Watching him come back is an extraordinary experience, as if right before my eyes a dimmer switch is slowly turning on his light. And so far I have never failed to find the dimmer switch.

Nick was there last night but I talked to Alan in his room. I have booked tickets for a Brahms concert next Friday, and Alan is due to visit me this evening for a supper – which, you will not be surprised to hear, has taken me most of the day to prepare. What a difference motivation makes! I have just spent several hours happily chopping things and mixing things (an occupation not best suited to *moi*) simply because Alan Box is to eat them. What a wimp I have become. I don't recognise myself these days.

We will start with avocado and cottage cheese, followed by Tuna baked with eggs and cheese and mushroom sauce and topped with potatoes, followed by fresh fruit and cream. Healthy and simple yet, I hope, giving the (correct) impression it has all taken a great deal of thought and care.

He is due in ten minutes. I have been ready for thirty. Restlessness and impatience have driven me to you while I wait. It's better than biting my nails.

There goes the telephone. Don't go away.

Saturday: After the events of the past few days, I have at last time to think them over carefully and reassess the situation as it now seems to be.

After my frantic phone call to you on Thursday night (howling into the phone like a crazy thing), my journey to you was awesome. No insurer would have insured me. In fact I don't remember one second of it, and am only amazed that I was *compos mentis* enough to leave your number on our notice board here, since I'd been distrait enough to turn off my mobile.

Now I've had time to think, I realise that what happened was foreseeable to anyone with half an eye (not me, apparently, because I failed to see it at all) for Nick would not have wanted Alan to come to me on Thursday, and Alan is at the moment susceptible to whomever he is with. So of course he would have changed his mind once the first panic was over, and panic alone can have convinced him that Nick was right.

He had said: "I'm sorry Hannah, but Nick thinks I'm in no state to drive, so I'm having to let you down. I'm sorry"

I hadn't offered to fetch him. Somehow it seemed important that he come under his own horse power, and he must have changed his mind within fifteen minutes because it only took me ten to close down my email to you, write a message on the board in the phone room, put the supper in the fridge, pack a toothbrush and *leave!*

He was shocked at missing me. His voice when he phoned your number was distressed. By that time he was also disappointed. We agreed to eat the now refrigerated supper on Saturday instead, and he was to ring me yesterday evening at 5 o'clock to arrange the time, so when his call didn't come as promised I knew something was wrong. He is meticulous about these things.

I went out to dinner with Anne and her husband, but the evening was disastrous. They were too nice to complain, but I imagine sharing a restaurant table with a cardboard cut-out is far from entertaining. I remember talking and laughing, but what I talked and laughed about escapes me. I almost hope it escapes them, too.

So this morning I rang Waterloo Road. Nick answered. I asked to speak to Alan but he said he wasn't there. When I asked where he was, Nick said he was afraid he couldn't tell me.

"Why not?" I asked, surprised.

"Because I've been asked not to."

"Who by?"

"I can't tell you that either."

I was stunned. Then I asked if it was Alan himself who had given those instructions.

"I can't tell you Hannah. I can't tell you anything. I'm afraid I can't even talk to you," and he hung up.

Too astonished to be angry, I stared blindly at the phone, and considered all the possibilities. One of those was that Bill might have taken him away to his old hotel or even back to Wakefield. So I went back to the privacy of my room and rang the hotel. No Mr Box was registered there. Next I tried the hospital where Alan had been given his treatment and his brain scan.

Yes, he had been admitted. Yes, certainly I may visit, and yes, he would like to see me.

I found him white-faced and anxious. His headaches had become intolerable and he was to undergo more tests during the afternoon. He seemed pleased to see me. During the hour I spent with him, he said he would probably be going home to Waterloo Road next day.

I thought hard and carefully. The truth, that Nick and possibly his father had refused to tell me where he was, would eventually have to be told since once he had arrived home I would certainly be barred from visiting.

So I made up my mind and said: "I have to tell you, I'm afraid, that Nick has obviously been told not to speak to me or tell me anything and will certainly have me barred from the house."

Alan grew quieter and whiter than ever. He closed his eyes. "So if you want to see me from now on," I continued "it will be up to you to make contact. I can't contact you any more unless you give me your mobile number."

He nodded.

There was a pause while this slowly sank into the air about us. Then I said: "So if you don't, I shall take it you'd rather not, and I'll vanish like the morning mist"

Alan frowned, swallowing as if his throat were constricted.

"Please don't vanish," he said "Please Hannah don't go".

I touched his arm. "Not if you don't want me to," I promised, "but I think we should sort all this out. The situation is completely ridiculous – three grown people pulling you apart."

He nodded. He was very upset. He accompanied me to the door. We didn't kiss, just looked long and hard at each other.

On the way home I called at Waterloo Road. Nick was there, obviously surprised to see me.

"Can I come in? We need to sort this out"

He led the way into the kitchen and stood facing me. He was fiercely angry. "You come in here," he said, and his voice wavered breathlessly. "You come in here playing Mrs Fix-It as usual. Playing God. Who the hell do you think you are?"

I was taken aback but told him I didn't want to argue, and could we work it out between us for Alan's sake. "No," he replied "and I don't want you to come here any more"

"Don't worry, I won't."

He smiled mirthlessly said "Good!"

"But I don't know what I've done," I cried.

He explained in great detail but I didn't understand any of it. I was immature, a child. I didn't live in the world, had lost touch with reality. "You're not real," he told me. "You asked me to have him, so I did, and you were supposed to leave him to find his own feet. Why didn't you?"

I stared blankly and spluttered a bit. "But Alan wanted to see me"

"How do you know?"

"Because he kept on saying so."

He shook his head and pursued his lips in obvious disbelief, then cried out in sudden exasperation. "You're the same, both of you. You're as bad as each other. You're both just kids, living in Cloud Cuckoo Land."

I said I thought that sounded rather nice, and laughed, which made him even angrier. "Oh, I've seen you together," he said. "You're just kids. You share the same tastes, like the same music...all that..." and he waved dismissively.

I told him they sounded very good reasons why one should see a person, not keep away.

By this time my brain was hurting and I remember little more, except that he accused me of not consulting him, of taking over, taking the law into my own hands. But I was growing tired of an angry young man who obviously had no intention of talking himself into reasonableness, so I asked once again if we could work it out "for Alan's sake," I said.

Once again he said no, so I moved to the door.

"Goodbye," I said. "I won't be back, but I'll give it one last try. Can we work it out for Alan's sake?"

"No," he said. So I left.

That was yesterday. Today Alan has returned to Waterloo Road. Once more I'm reconciling myself to life without him.

Things change so fast I am dizzy with it. Thank God for all the sane things in life that *stay the same!* What would I do without you all now? Love, H

ooOoo

Christabel Fraser

FROM   Hannah Pascoe
TO: Chrissiefras@coolmail.net
SENT: 21 September 2008
SUBJECT: !!

Blessings on all laptops! Lucy came last night. She is as amazed as we are. Her verdict is that Nick is jealous because he's gay and fancies Alan himself. Well, it is I suppose the first explanation that springs to mind and the only one that makes any sense, but I feel somehow there's more to it somewhere. There was a deep hatred for me personally, a venom which was the more disturbing for being unexplained. I simply didn't know what had caused it.

Then there is Bill and his stunning *volte face.* One day I'm the light of his life, an angel sent from heaven ("God, what would we do without you, Hannah?") and the next I am villainess *extraordinaire* with the blackest possible heart. Was it that he felt more for me than I thought, and then found his son to be his chief rival? Or was he just being obsessively possessive about him, or did he feel that by seeming to abandon Alan last June I had shown the true quality of my *paper maché* wings? A fallen angel in reality?

Or does he now like Nick better than me? Surely not! Bill Box is a womaniser, as I can readily prove after all his flattering attention years ago in Leeds – and recently, come to that! So why is he now joining with Nick in rejecting me? Is jealousy enough? I don't recall ever being jealous to that extent. Perhaps it takes some people that way, but if so Bill and Nick must be suffering to an equal degree, because the very same sense of hatred and violence has overwhelmed me from both.

They both hate me, and I don't understand why. It is all mysterious and horrible.

I still have tickets for Friday's Brahms concert. I imagine Alan won't be coming, but Janine is prepared to join me at the last minute. She is generous to play back-stop!

Friday The concert was good but I didn't enjoy it, worrying all night about why Alan failed to let me know. He sent no message at all. It isn't like him. Something else has gone wrong.

TEXT MESSAGE from Hannah Pascoe to Christabel Fraser.

"Just heard Alan in hosp in Intensive Care. Don't know why yet. Am off there now to find out. Love, H"

Saturday Have spent all day in the Intensive Therapy Unit willing Alan back to life. He walked under a bus. He is now going to live, so I've come home to bed. I am very *very* tired. Will write again as soon as I can. H

ooOoo

60

Christabel Fraser

FROM   Hannah Pascoe
TO: Chrissiefras@coolmail.net
SENT: 27 September 2008

SUBJECT: Intensive care

Now Alan is out of danger I have time, breath and energy to tell you what happened. It's taken me until now to realise just how extraordinary everything is. For the first day or two I just plodded on, going from crisis to crisis, asking no deep questions but accepting things as they came.

One of the first things Alan wanted to know was how I knew he was there.

How indeed? How did I ever know when he needed me? Luck? Being in the right place at the right time? Good guesswork? Or perhaps God hit me on the head with it. (He has a habit of doing that). There are times when this affair smacks of the slickest stage management.

After the concert on Friday I was too tired to write more than one paragraph to you, so took myself to bed with hot chocolate and a book about murder in a tea shop which I found impossible to read. At about half past eleven the house phone rang on the landing, immediately outside my room. A call at the hour was bound to be an emergency, so I answered it.

"Hannah, sorry to ring so late," Myra said, "but I had to tell you. I've sent a text, but know you often turn your phone off in the evening. I've just been working with Nick Wadham and he must have had a row with your boyfriend because he's left and Nick has told him not to come back. I nearly said 'What again? You're too sodding good at kicking your friends out,' but I didn't because it dawned on me just in time that he doesn't realise how friendly you and I still are, and that I know all about it. I was afraid if I let on he'd shut up. As it was he didn't say all that much, and then only because I asked how his lodger was getting on. He got very disturbed and muttered something like 'Gone away', but

279

I didn't want to say any more although something was obviously the matter. I pretended not to care, but asked casually where this chap had gone then, and Nick said he didn't know but he'd gone out without his car because it was being serviced, and he'd taken a small suitcase. Nick definitely gave me the impression it was a matter of Good Riddance on his part. I couldn't ask any more because we were both called, and then it was time to come home and Nick left rather smartly. But I thought you ought to know Alan seems to be homeless again."

I absent-mindedly said thank you, thinking through the implications of it all. We chatted on for a few minutes, then said goodnight and I sipped my chocolate in deep thought.

Then I rang the hospital, saying I was sorry to be so late but I was worried about Alan Box, and had he any further appointments with them. The nurse said yes, next morning.

I didn't sleep. By 8.30 I was up, dressed and organised, waiting for a civilised moment to ring the hospital again with a message for Alan when he arrived. At ten o'clock, after several cups of coffee and a good bit of nail biting, I finally made the call.

"I'm afraid he's not here," the nurse said. "He's in the Central Hospital, Ward 23."

"What for?"

"Sorry, I don't know. I just know that's where he is."

I rang the Central Hospital and was put through to Ward 23. A woman's voice said: "Intensive Therapy Unit". I asked if Alan Box was there and she said yes. She asked if I was a relative.

"No," I said "Just a very good friend. What's happened?"

"I'd rather not talk over the phone. If you come in I'll explain"

"I'll come now," I said.

Twenty minutes later I was ringing the bell for admittance to some closed white doors. A nurse came out, followed by a doctor obviously on his way somewhere else. I explained who I was and the doctor said: "Good! Perhaps you can tell me if he'd been on anything. Any tablets of any kind?"

I thought hard, but said he was definitely on some hefty painkillers of some kind as he'd been having bad headaches, but I didn't know which ones.

"Yes, I know about those," he said. "But was he taking anything else?"

I said I really didn't know. "How is he?" I asked.

The doctor made a rocking motion with his hand and pulled a face.

"Hard to say," he said. Then he walked briskly away and left me with the nurse, who told me to follow her.

"Be prepared, He won't look like Alan."

He didn't. I burst into tears.

The nurse found me a chair and brought me a cup of tea, then she sat with me and told me what she knew. He had been knocked down by a bus at eleven o'clock the night before. His suitcase had been found with him, with his painkillers and overnight clothes. Amazingly, his wallet had still been in his pocket with the hospital appointment card, so they knew who he was. She asked me some questions which I answered as well as I could, and then left me alone with Alan.

He was wired into machines and there were tubes everywhere, in his nose and mouth and over his heart. One side of his head had been shaved and there was a plaster over it. His left arm was bandaged and there was a cage over his feet. The doctor came a few minutes later to test Alan's reflexes with an instrument like a biro, but there was no response. Then he shouted "Alan," very loudly in one ear. Alan's right hand twitched very, very slightly.

When we were alone again I began to talk, to rub his good arm and his hand. I sat beside him through the whole of the day, talking, talking, talking all the time. Every ten minutes or so the nurse came to check his pulse and breathing and to chat to me. She was wonderful. Sometimes I had to leave while they changed dressings or turned him over, but the staff were always tirelessly kind.

I made a deal with God. "If you will let him live and be normal and happy, I won't ask anything for myself. Only please don't let him die."

At one o'clock I left for half an hour, to breathe outside air and to buy myself some coffee, but I returned to my post as soon as possible. I couldn't bear to be away.

There was another family doing the same. A middle-aged man had taken an overdose. His wife and son and daughter-in-law sat or stood by his bed talking, telling him things, just as I was doing. Occasionally we met in the visitors' room while nurses were busy with our patients, and by the end of the day we were exchanging stories and even jokes, wishing each other well. There was an air of solidarity, of comradeship. Sometimes we stopped talking to smile at each other and ask how we were doing.

By degrees Alan began to move. At first it was hardly perceptible, a change of position in one hand, the slight turning of the head, the smallest possible frown. So I continued to stroke his hand and his arm with firm fingers, to talk, talk, talk, and by mid afternoon he was moving quite positively. Once I sang to him and he frowned, which made me laugh and share the joke with the nurses and with my neighbours. They thought it was funny too, and I promised to tell Alan when he came round. "Now I know what he really thinks of my singing," I said.

Sometimes I had to wipe his mouth and chin with tissues, and felt how vulnerable he was and how he would hate such humiliating dependence. I knew I would never tell him all I was doing, but to me it was a privilege, and there was nowhere else I wanted to be.

After lunch there was a telephone call from Bill, who had just discovered where his son was. The nurse asked me if I would speak to him, but I violently shook my head. Tears were very near. She put her hand on my arm.

"I don't think I can manage it," I said, but she thought it was important to try.

"Will you stay with me?"

"Yes, I'll stay with you," she said, nodding solemnly, so I went to the desk and picked up the receiver.

"Hannah?" Bill's voice was tentative. "It seems I have to be grateful to you. How did you know?"

"I phoned his usual hospital"

He didn't ask me why I had done that, or how they had known.

"How is he?"

"I think he's going to be all right. Beginning to show signs of life. I don't know how you feel about me being here, but it doesn't matter anyway because I'm staying"

"I suppose I've got to be pleased, haven't I?"

I said nothing.

"How long will you be there?"

"As long as it takes," I said, mentally adding "All night if necessary."

"Will you ring me when you get home? I'll be down as soon as I can."

I said I would.

He thanked me again and said goodbye, and I wondered why he wasn't already driving down the motorway at 120 miles an hour. Soon afterwards Alan's ex-wife Elizabeth rang. Bill had told her the news. I didn't speak to her myself but decided to ring her later as well as Bill.

By early evening Alan was fighting me, trying to pull the tubes out of his mouth. I had to grip his hands tightly to force them back. He'd grown quite strong over the last two hours. Now and then he choked a little and the nurses explained he was now trying to breathe on his own, so the tubes could soon be taken away. I went to the loo and by the time I returned one of them had already gone. His colour was better.

By nine o'clock I knew he was going to recover. Only a question of an hour or so, the nurse said, and he would have regained consciousness. I wasn't sure that I should be the first person he saw.

But it was getting late, the nursing staff were changing shifts and I was so tired the prospect of staying possibly for several hours more was daunting, after the varied shocks of the day. And perhaps, I thought, it would be better not to be the first person he saw after all, for he may not have wanted to come back.

So I went home to Marlbury Road and telephoned first Bill and then Elizabeth. Bill said he would be down next day (Why hadn't he come this day?). Elizabeth simply said "Thank you, Hannah, for being there." She sounds very nice.

I slept heavily and next morning rang the dental surgery to say Alan had had an argument with a bus and was in Intensive Therapy, so if they didn't mind I would be taking the day off to be with him. They were very sympathetic and said: "Of course you must."

Alan's nurse had suggested I go back to the ward at half past nine next morning, and I arrived just as the clock was striking. The man in the next bed had disappeared (I didn't ask where) but Alan was sitting up. He was trying to read a newspaper by holding it in one hand. His head looked strange with one half shaved and plastered, and there was still a cage over his legs. But the tubes had gone and as I walked into his field of vision he raised a wobbly hand in salute. Everything about him seemed insecurely attached.

I sat beside his bed. "You look a sight better than you did yesterday," I told him.

He concentrated with some difficulty. "You were here yesterday? How long for?"

"A while"

He shook his head. "I didn't know."

"Of course you didn't. You were spaced out, I tell you, and a very bad time you gave us"

"Sorry."

I smiled at him happily. "Do you remember anything about what happened?"

"Not really. Bits." He stared through me and then changed the focus of his eyes till they met mine again. "I had some things with me but I don't know where they went. Credit cards and things"

He seemed worried about them, so I found a nurse, who explained that his personal belongings were locked away safely with an inventory. But because he was still anxious, the nurse brought his bag and the list and we went through them together, ticking them off as we found them.

The next two hours were disturbing and at times faintly comic. His voice would grow quicker and lighter like a boy's, speeding on and on, like a recording tape played faster and faster until finally the sound disappeared altogether and only his lips moved. Then his eyes closed and for a few moments he slept, only to wake and begin the whole process again. Sometimes he grew very angry with me and shouted, but nothing lasted long.

He worried about everything, and I worried about him. I was, still am, afraid of serious brain damage, but because they operated at once he has a good chance of recovering completely. The nurse told me he had an extradural haematoma and very nearly died.

At lunchtime two porters came to wheel his bed to another ward. I accompanied him down miles of corridor, into lifts and out again and along even more corridors until we reached a high walled room with a dozen beds, where men in plasters or on crutches moved slowly about in slippers and dressing gowns while others sat morosely in chairs. They watched closely as the porters transferred Alan and his belongings to a bed in the corner. A very young student nurse welcomed him and asked politely chatty questions.

Then a doctor came, so I had to leave, but as I moved to the door she followed and placed a detaining hand on my arm.

"Do you know what happened?" she asked.

I shook my head. "Not really. He's been talking a lot, but not about the accident, more about his state of mind before it. I'm afraid most of it didn't make sense"

"Do you think he did it deliberately?"

I looked down at my toes, considering. "I honestly don't know, but it wouldn't surprise me. In fact I think probably."

"You know him well." It was not a question but a statement.

"I think so," I said, "so far as one can ever be sure of these things, yes I suppose so."

She nodded. "Would he have been taking anything?"

"Painkillers for headaches. I don't know what sort."

"Yes I know about those. We've managed to get his notes. Anything else?"

"Not that I know of, but I don't actually live with him so I can't be sure. He has been very depressed, though."

She pursed her lips, nodded dismissively and smiled brief thanks, then she turned away. I left the ward and came home. Bill was due to arrive shortly and I preferred to be elsewhere when he did. The nurse has given me the ward phone number and she took my own.

The girls here in the house are being wonderfully supportive. Clare asked me in for coffee and I told her all about it. I had to borrow her tissues. Then Sarah knocked on my door and I went through it all again, this time with my own tissues. Louise will be home quite soon, so perhaps I should lock my door or we will all run out of tissues.

How lucky I am to have found this place. Isn't life a gas? Love, H

ooOoo

61

Christabel Fraser

FROM   Hannah Pascoe
TO: Chrissiefras@coolmail.net
SENT: 2 October 2008
SUBJECT: Progress

Things don't stand still, do they? I've kept away from Alan while his father was there, only visiting when I knew it was safe – easy enough to do, as Alan has become strangely childlike and tells me every detail of his day. His memory plays tricks. Sometimes he searches for simple words, and the effort of dredging up a name or a quite ordinary noun frustrates him so much that he thumps the bed or his chair, and his anguish is equally frustrating for me. I have to restrain the impulse to finish his sentences for him, and sometimes the temptation is too strong and I give him a word here and there. He is always grateful and nods his thanks.

His head wound and his cut arm are healing, but his leg was broken and is now in plaster. The hospital social worker came to see him after his father left for Wakefield, asking questions about where he will live and what he will do for money. Alan has been talking it over sensibly.

"I haven't got anywhere," he said. "Nick won't have me back." I didn't ask why. If he chooses to tell me, he may, but I won't force the choice on him. One would guess, however, that he confronted Nick with his behaviour to me. There may be plenty of other reasons, but for now I don't much care what they are. It's the future that concerns me, not the past.

There is, of course, the chance that his father may suggest taking him back to Wakefield with him, but Alan won't hear of it. There is a powerful bond between them, but they find it impossible to live together, probably because the characteristics they have in common are the most explosive when mixed. "Pour the mixture into a bunsen burner, light the blue touch paper and retire…!" So I mentioned as casually as possible that Clare is buying a house with her boyfriend and if all goes well hopes to be leaving Marlbury Road in about six weeks time. Did he fancy living in the bedsitter next to mine?

The coincidence struck him powerfully, as it had struck me only a few days ago, and he seemed to like the idea. It would now be a matter of getting himself out of plaster and onto his feet in time. He said his father wouldn't be very happy. An understatement, I believe!

I explained there was a spare bed in my kitchen/diner if he needed somewhere quickly. He smiled, nodded and said thank you, and although I cursed my often fatal impulse to leap in with ideas before people are ready for them, I think the knowledge has made him feel just that bit more secure.

I shall continue to visit every day, but only if he wishes it. Every day as I leave we make arrangements for the next, and always at his request. Of course there is the fact that he has so few other visitors. Max and Ruth have been, and a colleague from his school, but I appear to be the only regular caller. So, lacking better company, he is obliged to put up with mine! The nurses are friendly and welcoming.

I am away from home a good deal now and there are countless messages left for me, let alone the numerous texts. Twice the messages were from Bill, asking me to ring back. Two evenings ago there was a note from Louise to say: "The old fart wants you to ring, no matter how late. Come up and see me afterwards, no matter how late." So I dialled the Wakefield number and was hectored for several minutes by the old fart himself on how I was to stay away from Alan because I was a bad influence on him. I pointed out that my mobile was just about to run out of juice, whereupon he rang off – not before reminding me, however, that when Alan gets better he may not want me any more.

"I am perfectly aware of that," I replied, "but it's my problem and his, not yours."

Then I ran upstairs to Louise and wept out my anger and hurt and frustration into a cup of hot chocolate and a slice of walnut cake.

Now I'm off to bed. Tomorrow is another busy day. Love, H

ooOoo

62

Christabel Fraser

FROM   Hannah Pascoe
TO: Chrissiefras@coolmail.net
SENT: 16 October 2008
SUBJECT: Patterns

Life has developed a pattern. Either I go to work and drive directly to the hospital for the evening, or I drive straight to the hospital in the morning and stay for the day. I see Sarah or Clare or Louise between times, spend my working lunch hours with colleague Anne and assorted dental nurses, make countless phone calls to friends and sent so many texts I've had to recharge the mobile battery twice already. Then finally crumple into bed and watch the telly from there until either it stops or I do. A bedsitter has many advantages!

Last week Bill asked Alan if he really wanted this closeness to me. Alan said yes he did. Then Bill rang Michael to tell him he must stop me visiting the hospital, but Michael said it was nothing to do with him as I am no longer his wife, but that in his opinion Alan was lucky to have me. Bill then rang Lucy with the same command, and Lucy immediately told me, so I sent Bill a note requesting him to leave my daughter alone but suggesting that as both he and I had Alan's best interests at heart we should perhaps work together in a civilised fashion.

He wrote a strange reply, explaining, not very coherently, why he had never liked me. I nearly wrote back to say that, in view of the dazzling impression to the contrary he's given me in the past, in future I shall be unable to take either his favour or his disfavour seriously. However, after struggling with a strong desire to enclose a small bomb in the envelope, I decided that silence would be more dignified.

As the ultimate throw, Bill has now suggested to the doctors that Alan was receiving a visitor who had a bad effect on him, but the doctors simply asked Alan if that were true or if he wanted me to carry on visiting and he said no and yes in that order, which was one in the eye for his dad. But Bill's opinion doesn't concern me just now. If Alan wants to see me he shall see me, and if he doesn't he won't. He's improving fast, still on crutches but his head and his cut arm are healing nicely. We sit in a kind of conservatory to enjoy the sunshine even when the wind is cold. He has been moved twice to other wards, and I think the time will come soon when the doctors have to let him go.

My car is getting so used to the journey from work to hospital and from hospital to home that it will probably carry on taking me round the same corners and along the same streets even when the reason has disappeared.

I know (as Bill has rightly implied) that as soon as Alan is well he may not want my company any more. Acknowledgement of this has been part of the Alan package all along, one of the risks deliberately taken from the start. And if he chooses to take Clare's room when she leaves, the risk will be even greater.

Janine and Myra have independently asked me the same question – "How will you feel if Alan comes to live there, gets fully better and then falls for someone else?"

"Terrible," I answered. He may never get fully better. He may get better and realise he loves me, or he may get better and fall in love with someone new, but the most likely of these is the last. It won't be pleasant, but nothing is certain and right now he's showing every sign of preferring me, so I'm not crossing any bridges until forced to do so at gun point.

Yesterday he told me we would very probably finish up together. I was outwardly calm but inwardly swimming in the blissful conviction that he is completely right, and it must be true, but I know how quickly he can change and how deeply I believe him each time. He is totally convincing because he always means what he says at the time – and I am always totally convinced that his mood today is the definitive one that's going to last forever. Fortunately a part of me remembers being taken in before, and holds aloof.

I am on an emotional roundabout, but prepared to cling to my bumpy ride for as long as I have to.

Meanwhile, Lucy rings frequently and is a delight, Janine and Myra have both visited Alan (separately and together) on days when I couldn't. And Timothy rang the other day to say he's back in Paris and would I like to visit them? The thought of leaving Alan even for two days is frightening and painful, but seeing Timothy after what seems like a long period of abstinence will be a solace for the soul – quite apart from the blessings of a change of scenery and petrol fumes.

Janine has promised to cover the hospital visits, so the patient won't feel abandoned. He might even miss me, you never know! Meanwhile, all love, H

ooOoo

Christabel Fraser

FROM   Hannah Pascoe
TO: Chrissiefras@coolmail.net
SENT: 23 October 2008
SUBJECT: Gaye Pareee

Paris is wonderful, Chrissie. I flew direct from Bristol Airport and we seemed to come down at Charles de Gaul almost as soon as we had taken off. No time for more than a glass of wine on the journey, and there was Tim waiting for me at Arrivals. He was kind and charming, and the break has done me good. I met the cast of his current show and was treated impressively by the producer, who kissed my hand with true French elegance. I ate delicious things in the classic kind of restaurant near Montmartre, mooned along the Seine and stared into shops on Rue Lafayette. Francine is very French. She cooks. She was also very friendly and kissed me on both cheeks in a most continental way.

Michael and the divorce were mentioned briefly but not dwelt upon. Tim has obviously decided that I am coping very nicely with the situation and the less said…etc etc. This is mildly ironic since he and Francine are not married at all and, so far as one can tell, have no plans to be.

The Decree Nisi was granted last Thursday, immediately after my arrival home. I spent the day in solitude, communing with my soul and with God. There was little to say to either but much to ponder on. My feelings have been oddly blank, my reactions mostly cerebral. How can the severance of a 35 year marriage be so apparently painless? Is there something wrong with me?

There is very little cash to divide between us, but we are to share the proceeds of the house, when sold, and I am to keep my cottage in Padstow. Margaret has a flat of her own not far from Clifton, so Michael won't be homeless, and I am free to live in our house for as long as it remains unsold.

I shall be sixty next month and entitled to a pension, which will not only be small but will deprive me of sickness benefit. I'll be scared to miss even one day's work. And since I don't want to return to acting, I shall just have to publish a book instead. How about "Starving in a Cornish cottage"?

I am asked occasionally how the writing is going. With thoughts of my emails to you, I reply that I am now very prolific – a fact with which I am sure you will not argue.

The hospital can't keep Alan indefinitely, beds are few and patients numerous, but they can't actually turn him out with nowhere to go. Clare almost has her house, with only a week or two to go before completion – barring the normal hazards of conveyancing, that is! She is so nervous about things going wrong at the last minute that the rate of baths has increased two-hundredfold, so one has to take advantage of an empty bathroom whenever it's there, since it may not be there again for some time.

She gave in her notice to our beloved landlord yesterday, and I went to him immediately, to ask if Alan could have her room. He wasn't too sure. Why is he, Alan, in hospital, and why has he nowhere else to go? Most important of all, how was he going to pay?

I told him Alan was a perfectly normal person in rather abnormal circumstances, and that whatever else may or may not happen, the rent money would be sacred. So in the end Roger said yes, but he would like to see Alan as soon as he is free to come and go, which could be very soon. He walks with crutches and expects to change them shortly for sticks. He has seen a psychiatrist and a counsellor once or twice, but everyone seems very pleased with him. I shall be allowed to take him out in the car tomorrow. The social worker is keeping a strict eye on his progress and won't allow him to leave until he has somewhere secure, and preferably supportive, to go.

Thank you for offering to visit him yourself. And for your invitation to both of us as soon as he is free. On Alan's behalf I happily accept. All love, H

ooOoo

64

Christabel Fraser

FROM   Hannah Pascoe
TO: Chrissiefras@coolmail.net
SENT: 1 November 2008
SUBJECT: More progress

Have you been missing me?

I've been taking Alan out in the car every day. He came home with me several times but Roger was out so they didn't meet – a blessing in the circumstances, as Alan wouldn't exactly fulfil a landlord's dream requirements yet. Clare, however, showed Alan her room and he seemed impressed. Incidentally, so did she! Next week he is to be allowed here overnight, and will certainly be discharged immediately afterwards.

Cookery is now forced upon me. Alas! Only those who know how I detest it will appreciate the power that can persuade me into it, recipe books, greengrocers, delicatessens and all.

The race is on between Clare completing her house purchase and the hospital forcibly turning Alan out of his bed, but the reality of having him next door seems too wonderful to come about. A fantasy. Common sense warns me of all the slips and hummocks to be encountered on the way. He changes his attitude to me subtly from day to day. Is it his two accidents which have had such a destabilising effect on his emotions? Or has he always been so volatile? There is no-one I can ask.

I believe he regrets his divorce, but I am not jealous of Elizabeth. If I had to lose him to another woman, the only truly acceptable one would be his wife, albeit an ex one. There would be a rightness, a completeness about it. But Alan is certain her answer would be no. Certainly he finds it difficult to respond to love *per se.* I asked him the other day if it was me he failed to respond to, or just any woman?

He replied: "Any woman," then added: "I have to say that wasn't always the case, so I hope it's only temporary!"

I laughed "That's all right then," I said, "When you start being capable again perhaps you'll warn me."

I'm still not sure what happened between him and Nick. There is a large and obvious question mark hanging over all his relationships, but although we talk a lot and discuss many things (some of them extremely intimate) Nick is not one of them. The only relevant detail to emerge is that Nick issued an ultimatum. Alan could only stay at waterloo Road if he agreed never to see me again, at which point he packed his bag, walked out of the door straight under a No 49 bus. It's something that he was angry enough at the ultimatum to walk out, but it's difficult to know for sure.

ooOoo

65

Christabel Fraser

FROM   Hannah Pascoe
TO: Chrissiefras@coolmail.net
SENT: 6 November 2008
SUBJECT: ??

Alan is staying with me. Hallelujah!

Some amazing things have come to light during the past week. The world at large has been revolving as usual but I haven't asked any questions about it because my own bit of it has been full enough without additions. But I have to work at the surgery so at least know which day it is, and Jan phones every now and then to tell me other vital things, like whether there's a war on or if an earthquake is on its way.

Yesterday Karen called here and actually found me at home, which surprised us both! It was lovely to see her and even lovelier to hear what she had to say. Firstly, the source of the disgraceful story in the Cosmos was (need I say?) Mark Hatchet Jaw, who I am happy to say has now been ditched forever. He said he was jealous of me and Mel and the stage in general, so decided to get his revenge on 'us wot seduced her away'. He received a cheque in payment for the story, in his capacity as the horse's mouth. I wish it had been a boot in the backside.

Karen found out because he told her. He's proud of it, the unlovely sod that he is, and revenge is no good unless people know that's what it is! But astonishingly, the very nastiness of the story has worked agin 'im.

297

Celia's parents were so upset they dropped the idea of any kind of action, and Steve Hobday has told Alan that Councillor Wimbrook was more or less apologising for the story, so Mark's weapon of mass destruction turned into a fizzled squib.

Even the quoted school was puzzled and angry, since Alan had a first class reputation as a teacher with no hint of a blemish to sully his pure name. They made noises about suspending him, but since the story wasn't backed up by the girl in question who was as angry as everyone else, they decided to keep quiet instead. They even considered taking legal action themselves, but desisted when they saw it would simply cause more bad publicity, rather than less. Just shows what could have happened if the girl hadn't taken a firm stand – and how one malicious whisper by a pupil or employee and someone's life and career are damaged, even destroyed entirely.

How furious Mark must be to have his bomb fail to go off. He will be even angrier when he realises he missed the wonderful target of Nick Wadham. What fun he could have had. But it's his own fault for acting on the spur of a moment's wrath without completing his researches.

Karen is now happily settled in the flat she shares with her friend Vicky and looks forward to a stagey future. The great news is (and she could hardly wait until her trendily booted foot had crossed my threshold before exploding with it) that after being an extra for W W once or twice, she auditioned for the part of Mel's long lost daughter and got it. She starts next week. What a lucky girl she is! Most aspiring actors her age have to sweat for years through drama school, and suffer hours and hours of journeys and horrible digs as they work their way up from bit parts.

To do her justice she fully realises her amazing

good fortune and filled my flat with an hour of glorious and wonderfully infectious enthusiasm. I won't expect to see her very often. She has other fish to fry. Let's hope they're not sharks.

Alan has met landlord Roger, and Clare's room will be his from next Saturday. Contract signing and exchanging are so random and suspenseful that Clare won't be sure until the day actually dawns whether her house is truly hers and moving day is really moving day. However, she has to go now, even if it means dossing on the pavement, as her room is *bespoke!*

Meanwhile, Alan stays with me. He is getting used to the feel of the house and the people, the stairs, the telephone, the smell of it all. He manages his sticks with great efficiency and will soon be able to hurl them away altogether, his hair has grown long enough to hide his scars with an all-over crew cut, and his arm has completely healed though still tender. For me the experience is a strange one. It combines the roles of friend, nurse and *quasi* lover, and although I am vividly conscious of his presence all the time in my kitchen/diner, all desire for him is restrained by the very love which arouses it. He is not well enough for anything more.

Nowadays the strength and force of passion inside me lies beneath a calm, apparently passionless outside. I am too scared of showing my real feelings. Because of this I've wondered whether, if and when the moment of truth finally arrives, I shall be capable of letting myself go, or whether this habit of holding myself in check will carry itself through to the *denouement* (whatever that might be) and spoil it.

I never knew I had such self control.

We have arranged a week's holiday and depart for Padstow next week. Until then, every spare moment is taken up with working at the surgery, trips in the car to the hospital outpatients department, pleasanter trips to more agreeable places, and cooking.

Life seems to have changed a bit lately. Best love to everyone, H

ooOoo

Christabel Fraser

FROM   Hannah Pascoe
TO: Chrissiefras@coolmail.net
SENT: 11 November 2008
SUBJECT: clotted cream

Tomorrow, Chrissie, we leave for Cornwall. Is it Frabjious Day or isn't it?

Alan officially moved into Clare's room yesterday. Until the last minute he was being checked and re-checked by the hospital, so the out-patients department has become disagreeably familiar. And although he now walks quite happily with only one stick, I feel they've been watching him for other things as well. What those things are I'm not sure. They haven't taken me into their confidence. No status! But certainly, once he's gone they will sincerely hope he stays gone.

Me too! His hospital wards may have given me some romantic moments, but I'd rather spend future romantic moments away from the smell of soap, antiseptic and cottage pie. Besides, whenever I fetched him away for car trips it was necessary to take him back again, and now it isn't. Leaving him at the door while I drove away was frustrating and painful. His shoulders always had the wistful droop of small children being dropped off at school – I suspect for much the same reason.

But that's all over now. He stayed with me for four days before Clare finally departed with the last plastic bag and the last pair of shoes. Then another day while Landlord Roger went over her room with sweeper and disinfectant, and finally we moved Alan's own plastic bags and shoes into the empty space. After waiting for so many weeks to have him on the other side of the wall, the fact that after four nights on my side of it he's not moving closer but further away seems more than a bit ironic!

How very neat and handy it has all been, each piece of the tale dovetailing into another like a nicely designed jigsaw. But the picture on the jigsaw has a faintly surreal element. Nick's Cloud Cuckoo Land not in my head but in the design itself.

Tonight we're going to Janine's for supper in celebration, and tomorrow we depart down the M5 to Padstow. Fortunately I am now so organised, both Alan-wise and Padstow-wise, that the packing has been either done or arranged over the past day and a half. The desk is covered in lists.

When we come home there will be the business of rehabilitating him to normal living. He has lost confidence, but at the same time hates being dependent, either physically or mentally. And the very fact of his dependence and gratitude could now become a pistol to my head. What sort of mutual relationship can survive such an uneven basis? How much more satisfying it would now be to find myself grateful to him instead.

Thank you for your invitation the week after next. Most of my friends are turning up trumps and issuing invitations with gratifying speed. I suspect it's the irresistible appeal of wounded hero and devoted

Florence Nightingale that's done it!

The Decree Absolute happens next Thursday. Even now its only effect is an odd sensation somewhere at the back of my brain, but exactly in what way it is odd I can't tell you, because I don't understand it myself. An extension of the surreal Cuckoo Land?

To be honest, I suspect that I simply ***don't believe it!*** It is all happening to someone else. Meanwhile I seem to have become exclusively Alan-minded and tunnel-visioned. Perhaps this holiday will de-tunnel me. I'll send you a post card and some clotted cream. Love, H.

ooOoo

67

Christabel Fraser

FROM   Hannah Pascoe
TO: Chrissiefras@coolmail.net
SENT: 15 November 2008
SUBJECT: !!!

It is a chilly but beautiful day here. Padstow out of season is as entrancing as ever and the cottage far, far more so. Alan is here, and although he still hasn't attempted to put whatever he feels for me on a physical basis, I am grateful for the little I am given. The mixed messages are still hard to interpret, but I know quite well that to take advantage of his present state would be bordering on emotional rape. .

I neither expect nor discount that sort of change in the relationship. I'm simply waiting on events. After all, I've been existing with on/off signals for a long time, and as we all know, sex changes everything. Its effect is instant, and once changed, a relationship can never go back to where it was. Only once was there a moment that could have taken us forward into new territory, but as usual with my tender moments, nerves got the better of me and I was overcome with an irresistible desire to giggle - an unfortunate tendency at the best of times but trebly so at this one.

We went to Jan's flat for dinner then early next morning threw food, goods and selves into one car and left for Cornwall.

Life here is quiet and gentle. I love him more every day. I would do almost anything to bring him back to his normal self – the Alan I knew during Ruth's campaign – except one thing. If he ever chooses another woman I shall have to leave – not as a threat to hang over his head but because I am entirely incapable of living with it. He has known that from the first and we've discussed it several times. He tells me I'm strong, envies the courage he sees in me, yet I know both strength and courage have their limitations, and seeing him with someone else would take me beyond them. Perhaps once I could have done it, but not now. Now he tells me every day how dependent he is, how much he needs me.

Unless and until that Other Woman turns up, the idea of leaving is unthinkable. I told him yesterday that the decision to separate would have to be his, and he says he understands.

This cottage has always been special, even more so now because it belongs entirely to me, part of the divorce settlement. It will have to keep me in my old age – an insecure business in this country and climate, especially in our present economy with pensions in doubt for everyone. I might have to sell it, but meanwhile intend to enjoy it as fully as life allows – which today means very fully indeed!

I am happy and sad at the same time because, while I know Alan needs me at the moment, I am never quite sure how deeply or how lastingly. Fear is always lurking somewhere.

Not today though. Definitely not today. The sun is shining, the surf at Harlyn Bay is magnificent, the boats in the harbour are gleaming in bright watery reflections. The tide has come in, the estuary is full of sea and my cottage holds us both in cosy security.

Today I feel blessed. H

P S   This morning we were walking down the steep street from the cottage to the harbour and passed an ancient figure in a long woollen coat and a headscarf. She looked hard at Alan and then at me, and she leered. "Ah, ee'm 'aaaandsome," she told me, nodding her head. "You want to look after 'eee," "Don't worry, I'll do my best." I laughed and told Alan he had just received the Good Housekeeping Award for 'Aaaandsomeness. He didn't seem very impressed, but I bet he was really!

ooOoo

68

Christabel Fraser

FROM   Hannah Pascoe
TO: Chrissiefras@coolmail.net
SENT: 2 December 2008
SUBJECT: Many many thanks

How can I thank you enough for the wonderful birthday tea you gave me? Being sixty didn't seem to me like cause for celebration. To say it isn't a pleasant thought is the understatement of the year. Yet you made it as pleasant as it could ever be, and having Alan there with us, part of what feels more and more like a family group, made it perfect. And how nice of you to put six candles on the cake – a symbolic gesture needing so much less puff for blowing purposes. Even nicer was the deliberate down-playing of the horrid fact that I may now apply for my bus pass.

Sarah was not so sensitive, but as she went to a great deal of trouble for me I couldn't possibly complain. I had told everyone I didn't want a fuss made of this particular birthday as it would be a sort of rather painful watershed, ramming home the disagreeable truth than Alan is allying himself (at least temporarily) with an Older Woman. Ten years older in point of fact. So when Sarah invited us upstairs to her flat for dinner that evening, I agreed quite happily.

Alan and I arrived home from your tea party in time to draw breath before the promised comfortable meal with Sarah. Unfortunately, Sarah being the girl she is, that is not what transpired! Her door opened instead upon a scene I was very definitely not prepared for, and not at all happy about. Festooning the room were banners and balloons, gaily fluttering and all bearing the legend "Happy 60th birthday". And beneath them, also gaily fluttering, was the entire population of 47 Marlbury Road. Every single man-jack of them. Every girl-jack I should say, except that included in their number was our own revered landlord. And the minute I set foot across the threshold they all started singing and cheering.

Substitute the number 30 for 60 and it would all

have been enormous fun, and part of me realised it was and enjoyed it all. But another part was – what? Distressed? Aghast? Embarrassed?

I did *not* want to be 60, and there I was, faced with an indelible truth that could never, ever be rubbed out.

I am now a Senior Citizen, divorced and in love with a man ten years my junior.

The evening ended with one or two of the guests (including me) drinking rather more than they (we) should and one or two of them (*not* me) dissolving into sentimental tears. But both Alan and I recognised the early warning signs and, after all the proper noises of appreciation and gratitude, duly made our escape. We were both tired, and I was full of wine and thoughts.

I am (obviously, to judge by the tone of these missives) introducing him into every sphere of my life – Lucy, Janine, Myra, even the surgery where he sometimes comes now to fetch me at the end of the day. We go to the cinema and concerts, and the joy of coming home together is beyond description. The depth of satisfaction is so great that at each new thought of it a core of warmth begins somewhere in my chest, to grow and spread until I am enveloped in a vast contentment.

The local Lib Dems have claimed him. The unexpected arrival of not only a potential candidate but Ruth's experienced activist from last May, what's more, has created a buzz of hope in the ward. There is no election here next Spring, but they obviously intend to keep a firm hold on Alan for the following year. My sentiments exactly!

Christmas is closer than I realised and life has been so full of Alan that future dates have been submerged in present ones, but something will have to be done about it all before long.

How did you think he looks? His hair is growing, he

no longer needs dressings on his leg and he's thrown away his stick, so although I keep an unobtrusive eye on him, he is getting more and more independent. He occasionally cooks for me, which is exceedingly pleasant. He takes my washing to the launderette and always has a cup of tea waiting for me after work. He drove to Ossett last week to see Dominic and to bring home some of his belongings, but for the time being he mostly uses mine.

His scar has almost disappeared under the curls, and he is browner and fuller now in the face. In fact he is beginning to look younger than ever, which is exceptionally annoying of him. You are very kind in assuring me that I look no more than 50, if that, yet what good is it when Alan is 50 going on 30? This is against all the laws of physics and, if continued at the same rate, will eventually put him in nappies when I'm buying my zimmer frame.

Unfair!

There is one flaw in my contentment. It is a large one and arouses an insecurity every bit as deep as his presence arouses satisfaction. We still have no physical contact, apart from the usual friendly pat on the back. I can't even seem to notice it, for the thought of rejection terrifies me. Yet I wonder if he thinks my apparent calmness springs from lack of passion.

Sometimes I sit with him, watching television or listening to music, and am astonished at my own self-discipline. I didn't know I had it in me, and am giving the performance of my life!

Is it a mistake?

There are Christmas parties to come, and visits to the theatre, and WW is organising a New Year's Eve party, although I would really rather spend it with Lucy or Timothy or Alan, preferably all three. Meanwhile Louise and Sarah entertain us both to wine and nibbles, and drop in on their way home from work to share cups of tea and gossip. Louise especially is a good friend. She notices Alan's improvement from day to day. Last week she watched him leave me teasingly at my door and winked at me. "Can I be bridesmaid?" she asked.

I wish!

I said nothing, though. There is a constant ache of fear in me, despite the happiness his presence brings, and I wonder how long I can keep up this emotional marathon, requiring superhuman patience and endurance? The answer is, of course, that I will keep it up for as long as I am required to keep it up – or as long as my strength holds out, whichever is the shorter. So why do I waste time wondering?

Bill apologised to me last week for his behaviour and is polite again. That is, however, as far as it goes, and I suspect the apology was more to keep on good terms with his son than to appease me. I accepted the apology but will never feel easy with him again. In fact I avoid him if possible. He has, however, suggested that Alan spends Christmas in Ossett, which doesn't bode too well for my own festive season. With Dominic and Bill in the race, I expect to come in a bad third. I shall, however, have his company before and afterwards, and have been invited to Lucy's for Christmas itself, so refuse to feel downtrodden. Timothy and Francine have held out hope they may join us, which would make Christmas almost perfect.

This will be my first Christmas as a single person. The greetings cards should provoke some pretty comments. Michael and Margaret will be married by then. Do I send them a Christmas card? And what do I do about a present?

There ought to be a Book of Etiquette for divorced or remarried persons – viz. What to do with an old wedding ring? Doesn't life become complicated as soon as one steps outside hitherto accepted rules? Love, H.

ooOoo

69

Christabel Fraser

FROM   Hannah Pascoe
TO: Chrissiefras@coolmail.net
SENT: 16 December 2008
SUBJECT: Wedding

Michael and Margaret were married yesterday. I was working at the surgery. Most of the dentists know both of them and I was disturbingly aware that half a mile away at the registry office a provoking number of them must have been guests at the feast!

Lucy was there. Tim flew over from Paris for the day. The knowledge was hateful and the sensation definitely eerie. In fact the whole thing was surreal, and with everyone away for the day I don't think I have ever felt so *alone.* Lucy rang me later, in tears, but Timothy went straight back to France.

Sarah came later in the evening, fresh from a day with boyfriend Number 220-something. She sat with me for an hour or so, sharing my bottle of wine, and she made me laugh. She always does. Her view of life is invigorating, her personality clear and unimpeded, which acts upon me like a prism so I see everything from a fresh and often highly coloured angle. Her hair at the moment is bright canary yellow with black roots. Today she wore a very small, very tight black skirt, black tights and fur-topped ankle boots.

She rescued me from a little tomb of self pity.

I sent Michael a card, addressed to him but including both in good wishes. I did this with clenched teeth as a positive gesture of politeness rather than from genuine good will - now that the time has come I don't seem to have any. In fact, I very much hope he gets so bored that he will long for the old haphazard life with me. And that, of course, is pure spite.

Did you know I can be spiteful? I didn't until yesterday. But Alan comes home again this evening, so perhaps my darker instincts will be soothed away in the glow of his presence.

Your Christmas card is in the post. Last night I spent several hours with an address book and writer's cramp. Why is the penning of envelopes and "Love from Hannah" so much more tiring than any other kind of penning? In this case, of course, there has been the added chore of putting in my new address, which will almost certainly arrive too late to stop everyone sending my cards to Park Close.

The school where Alan did his supply teaching last summer advertised a permanent post a month or so ago, short listed him and has now offered him the job, starting January. He heard the news immediately before he went away, so he departed with a glad smile! The "Cosmos" story of the sixth form girl was revealed for what it was – fiction from beginning to end. The "No smoke with fire" adage is wonderfully pernicious and very hard to counter, a fact seemingly well known to most tabloid newspapers.

Alan was delighted on both counts. He made several friends on the school staff, one of whom apparently visited him once or twice in hospital although I never saw her there or even knew she existed.

This time his absence has seemed even longer than usual.

My love to Pete and Suzie. Please thank her for her card and tell her she's very clever. Love, H

ooOoo

70

Christabel Fraser

FROM   Hannah Pascoe
TO: Chrissiefras@coolmail.net
SENT: 22 December 2008
SUBJECT: Nearly Christmas!

How about this, then? A huge bouquet of Christmas roses arrived today from Tim and Francine. They won't be coming to us this year after all but will be staying in Paris because there is a big production looming for which a lighting engineer is urgently required. I couldn't decide what to give him because he seems to have everything he needs or wants anyway (except possibly for undivorced parents, and even that has never been stated) so I finally sent an engraved leather wallet for each, with matching leather photo frames. Life can be very difficult!

You can tell it's Christmas. Parties are like buses. They all come at once. I took Alan to one last night at the WW studio and introduced him to Robert and the cast. I even introduced him to Tom, who eyed him cautiously and asked in a stage whisper, and out of the corner of his mouth, if "that was the latest acquisition?" with heavy emphasis on the "that". Since he has known for some time of Alan's existence, I understood the question to be casting serious doubts on my taste.

I said "yes and no", which shows how far I have progressed in the world of politics!

Karen was there too in her new capacity as Mel's illegitimate stage daughter. It's extraordinarily pleasant to watch someone's dreams coming true. I wonder if the *fact* of Mel, as opposed to the *icon* version, will spoil her dream of him, for reality rarely lives up to our anticipation of it, does it? I now have to hope Mel doesn't take advantage of her extreme youthfulness and break her vulnerable little heart. I introduced her to Alan as the man she had saved by courageously coming forward with her testimony, and she stared up at him with those wide, celestial blue eyes, looking fresh, dewy and delectable. Her long blonde hair is silkier than ever, like the spun threads of old fairy tales. She looks impossibly young.

Nick Wadham was not among those present – a fact I had established through Janine before setting out, or we wouldn't have been there either. Some people I am not yet ready to see. Besides, how embarrassing for everyone in the circumstances!

It was a good party, though, as parties go, and it was more than agreeable to be back with my mates. I didn't know I was missing them. They kept asking me when I'll be working in the theatre again, and I have to admit that for the first time I was tempted. Everyone was nice to me, kind and charming and wishing to have me back on set, which Robert seemed to suggest was not entirely unthought-of, and was I interested? I said I'd think about it, and asked Alan for his opinion. He said it was of course up to me, but rather implied he hoped I wouldn't.

Meanwhile he was being monopolised by a New and Bright Young Thing, another recent addition to the storyline, who kept him animatedly enthralled with stories of her past. Myra and I were talking nearby and we both raised our eyebrows in astonishment when the Bright Young Thing offered Alan her phone number.

Of course he said yes. What man wouldn't? Besides, how rude it would have appeared to say no. I didn't ask any questions but was relieved when he explained later that her father is a Liberal Democrat and she herself wants to know more about the local party organisation.

I bet she does, I thought. Alan is becoming an attractive proposition again. The girl, however, has a brash sort of not-quite-prettiness which I would not expect Alan to find appealing. I give him credit for better taste. Her name is Lisa.

He has gone to Ossett for Christmas. I won't see him again until December 28th, but the festive season comes between times. Maybe it will be festive enough to keep me from a lovesick decline.

See you on Boxing Day. Meanwhile, have fun. H

ooOoo

71

Christabel Fraser

FROM   Hannah Pascoe
TO: Chrissiefras@coolmail.net
SENT: 6 January 2009
SUBJECT: We're back!

Christmas was pretty good, despite being Alan-and-Timothy-less. Boxing day with you was, as usual, fantastical! Many many thanks for the welcome, the prezzies, the dinner and the pudding – not to mention the combined warmth of Frasers in which I was enwrapped for the whole of one magical day! I am so glad you liked your fur bootees, and I can now visualise you as you plod about the house in them. As for my pictures, they are hanging on my sitting room wall even as I write, in a spot where they can be gazed upon for inspiration.

New Year's Eve was celebrated with Lucy and Andy and their friends. For some reason I didn't enjoy it as I should have done and was quite ready to come home after midnight to solitude and deep thought. I poured myself a last glass of wine and drank it sitting up in bed, working my way backwards over the past year and allowing myself a little hopeful planning for this one.

Alan came back looking better than ever. He walked in to a surprise, an urgent message from Heather Coxe followed by a press announcement. One of our Clifton Ward councillors has resigned for un-named personal reasons. There will be a by-election in early February. Would Alan agree to be candidate?

Of course he said yes. And now he is in top gear, happier and more energetic than I've seen him for years. He is also being extremely charming to me, of which I do not at all complain! I have promised my help, naturally, and seem to have agreed to man a committee room (sorry – to Person a committee room!)

Our conversations are as lively as ever. Livelier, perhaps, because he is livelier, and thoughts and questions are sparked from each other like lasers which ignite the imagination with imagery and concepts and anecdotes lasting sometimes far into the night. The relationship has never been so exciting, wanting only one thing to make it perfect. But all the time he grows more caring, tender and sympathetic, so I sometimes allow myself to hope everything will at last come about!

He buys new clothes and shows them off. His eyes

are bright and he laughs.

Park Close is up for sale. Michael and Margaret have their flat, so the house will soon be empty save for the pieces of furniture which are mine and which will have to be stored.

How sad and sordid these things become.

My job has settled nicely into pleasant routines, and Anne, who is my particular friend, is stimulating and agreeable both in and out of the surgery. We generally have lunch together. She thinks Alan has a nice face. She also agrees that he seems to be getting younger, so it isn't just my fancy being influenced by chronic insecurity. He often comes to the surgery with messages or to accompany me home, and sometimes simply because he's passing the door.

The political organisation has moved efficiently and quickly, so Alan is now Official. How strange that only a few months ago I was the ward member introducing a newcomer. Now not only is he more integrated than I ever was, he is the Star, the lynch-pin around whom everything and everyone else revolves.

Human nature being what it is, some members are likely to be less pleased than others. Grateful though they are to have him drop into their net in such a tidy way, I know too well how often noses can be put out by successful interlopers. All will not be sweetness and light within this pie, however appetizing the social crust!

Must go. I have new duties to perform, things to do, people to see – in this case, footslogging around the streets of Clifton. Love, H

P S A strange female voice on our phone has just left a message for Alan. She said she had the book he wanted and could he ring back, no matter how late. Having climbed out of the bath, he did so. The strange female

315

is a colleague from the school where he begins teaching tomorrow, and she will bring the book later this evening, after his return from canvassing.

P P S. Owner of voice delivered book as promised. Caught sight of her on landing. Very young, with blonde hair tied back in a high ponytail. She was in his room for some time. Heard them laughing. Brain tells me too young to be threat, but guts tell me otherwise. I have a cold, sick paralysis, can't sleep, can't write.

Why do I think the world has stopped? Hannah, be sensible! H

ooOoo

72

Christabel Fraser

FROM   Hannah Pascoe
TO: Chrissiefras@coolmail.net
SENT: 7 January 2009
SUBJECT: World's end

The world has stopped. I am very sick and can't stop crying. Alan told me this evening that he has been seeing Lisa and Cathy over the past two weeks and he is in love with Cathy. She is the teacher who brought the book. She is also the colleague who visited him in hospital, the colleague, in short, with whom he worked on supply last year.

How did my body know? It did. Intellect told me differently, but guts were wiser.

I sat in silence while he told me, then said what I

always knew I would say.

"I shall go then. Michael hasn't sold the house yet, so I can still live in it."

Alan looked stricken but undeterred. I knew he wouldn't attempt to stop me. "I've told you from the first," I said. "I simply can't stay. I haven't got that sort of courage"

Then I rang Michael, who said yes of course I can live at Park Close for as long as I wish. He was very concerned and would have made unflattering comments about Alan but I stopped him.

"He can't help falling in love," I said. "Nobody can. I couldn't, and neither could you."

Michael snorted. "He's not in love," he said. "He just fancies her, that's all. It can't last, you know that."

But I don't know that. I prefer not to demean my own relationship with Alan by believing he could throw it away for such a light thing as a passing fancy. Have I meant so little, that he could take such a risk for something so transitory?

And what has he told Cathy about me that she feels no qualms about coming to his room, next door to mine, late in the evening. That I am just a Good Friend? I try not to feel devalued, but with no success. I *am* devalued.

I can't sleep so I'm writing to you, but I can't write either so I'm not sure what to do next. Start packing perhaps?

I don't think I have ever known such pain. H

ooOoo

Christabel Fraser

FROM   Hannah Pascoe
TO: Chrissiefras@coolmail.net
SENT: 8 January 2009
SUBJECT: Moves

It's all happening now. I gave in my notice to Roger this morning. It was my day off, so I could cry all through it without having to face anyone with ruined eyes and bulbous nose. I'll go back to work tomorrow as usual. Now I'm planning how to transport back to Park Close in one journey all the things I spent months bringing here piecemeal. The flat is very full, of associations as well as belongings.

I don't want to go. This has been my home in a new and irreplaceable way, and I have imprinted my own personality on it.

There are hideous complications with the election now, too. Do I leave them all to manage without me? Or do I continue to support Alan in his campaign?

My removal is causing so many unanswered questions in everyone around me. To some I am telling the truth. They deserve nothing less. Janine and Myra, Clare and Sarah, Anne at the surgery – all of them are wonderful. And Lucy is amazing. Nobody has said very much, but they have all done the only thing they ever needed to do. Just *been there!*

Thank you for your call, and for your invitation. I shall come as soon as possible. Yours, H.

P S   You ask how I know that what Alan feels for Cathy is love. Despite everything my friends tell me, in some way impossible to describe, I am transferring my feelings for him into what I believe are his feelings for her. I seem to be closer to him than to myself, and imagine his happiness with such vividness that it crushes me.

He is with her now. This morning he ran down the stairs to his car and drove to school knowing he would see her there. In half an hour he will be home again.

I can't bear it. H

ooOoo

74

Christabel Fraser

FROM   Hannah Pascoe
TO: Chrissiefras@coolmail.net
SENT: 14 January 2009
SUBJECT: Moving again

Well, here goes Chrissie – tomorrow I move back to Park Close. I've spent all day preparing for it. In consequence, my room is full of the usual cardboard boxes and black bags, yet there seems to be a mountain of *stuff* still to be packed. Where did it all come from? Where did I stow it in such a small place?

The last few days have been a private sort of hell. I awake believing I'm still in some terrible dream, yet I behave normally. I still laugh and go to work and talk to patients, and all but close friends believe I am moving because the house is empty and I have to live in it while it's for sale. It's like a sort of re-run of the first weeks of leaving Michael. One morning now I shall wake up and find that the whole of this last year has been one long nightmare.

Alan is charmingly sympathetic and helpful. While I still live so close it is easier to be friendly than unfriendly. Anyway, I love him so much the idea of spoiling my last few days with him is unthinkable. I need him to be loving and caring for as long as possible, because very soon he won't be there at all. Tonight I am not thinking about it. Tonight he is to cook a meal for us both and we'll share a bottle of wine, and I will forget for a few hours that he loves someone else. I don't ask about her. To think about her even for a second is quite impossible.

He has promised not to involve her in his election campaign. That, he says, is my territory. So I shall help Heather run her committee room as arranged. Why should I let her down, after all? None of this is her fault.

11 o'clock We have spent our evening talking, Alan and I. Talking, listening to music, talking and then talking some more. The music was sometimes lyrical, sometimes noisy, with brass bands and jazz bands and full orchestral works, but it was always harmonic and exciting. We had Elgar and Shostokovich and a bit of Debussy, with songs from Les Miserables and some James Galway thrown in. And because we'd been drinking we sang along and beat time, and cried together. I didn't want to come to bed because he'd been so perfect, but even as I sat on his bed and thought that very thought I remembered those times in the past when he had given me a gently romantic lunch or evening out, and I'd realised too late that he had only been saying goodbye.

It isn't only actors who exit stage left to slow music and sobbing audience.

I should now be asleep. There's an early start

tomorrow for both of us. Alan, with Lucy and Andy, will be helping with the removal. The van comes at ten.

From your rather tired Hannah.

ooOoo

75

Christabel Fraser

FROM   Hannah Pascoe
TO: Chrissiefras@coolmail.net
SENT: 18 January 2000
SUBJECT: Thank you

Thank you, my best of friends, for the last two days. Without you I would certainly be dead. Your phone calls every three hours tethered me.

I never knew such pain existed. The risk of suffering has been part of the programme since its beginning, and I thought I knew the price I would probably pay in the end. But the intensity of the pain when it came, the sheer ferocity and power of it, has nearly knocked me senseless.

It was intolerable, so I wanted to kill myself. If you hadn't intervened I would certainly have done so.

But sense is returning and the fierce rushes of agony are not constant now but only intermittent. I can wander about the house with at least a vague sense of purpose, and have begun to move the furniture, change things, turn our family home into *my* home, removing chairs, tables, mugs, so that in time the house will be unrecognisable.

But Alan and Michael are impregnated into the very

walls of this place, and both are mocking me with the bitterness of reality. Both prefer someone else, one of whom is half my age. Cathy is thirty. And I have left each one in turn so he could be free for a new woman. Twice in one year I've done the same thing.

I am either unbelievably stupid or criminally insane.

But how did you know? What prompted you to ring when you did? When I woke up that first morning, here in my old bedroom, it was not a question of "**Shall** I top myself?" but "**How** shall I top myself?", and when the phone rang I was actually scouring the bathroom cabinet for codeine and aspirin, and anything else I could lay my hands on. Then, for two whole days your call every three hours gave me something to work towards. How did you know?

Astonishing how writing clears my head. Time and again I've begun in despair and confusion, but the act of writing, the necessity to order my thoughts and be at least a tad coherent, forces me to consider questions like "Where next?" And where next is of course, in this case, an election which I have promised to see through to its conclusion. There is the challenge of canvassing, and a decision to be made. How far do I wish to take it? Do I really, secretly, need to see Alan so badly that I will rush around ringing doorbells in the hope that he'll be in the pub later with the rest? I may tell myself I enjoy the excitement of campaigning and admire the people doing it with me, so why should I deprive myself of this new and exciting life? And this will be entirely true. But am I simply putting my head into one noose after another, begging for more and more pain?

Perhaps I'm a masochist – or am I just stupid and stubborn?

Whatever the truth, the reality remains that I have given up my home in Clifton because of Alan, and feel a sense of injustice at also giving up a new and fascinating social life with a purpose and an end product.

I like canvassing and I like Heather Coxe. Alan may go and boil his head!

Until then, love, H.

ooOoo

76

Christabel Fraser

FROM   Hannah Pascoe
TO: Chrissiefras@coolmail.net
SENT: 27 January 2009
SUBJECT: Where now?

After my phone call last night I am left with little to say except to describe the thoughts that came to me during the night as I lay staring at the ceiling. I slept between 4.30 and 5.30. All the other hours were spent thinking around the whole situation and making decisions. These particular decisions are important ones – for my self esteem if for nothing else!

I apologise for another panic call. It might be easier if there could be an end in sight, but the only prospect I have at present is of more and more hurdles in an endless procession stretching away for months and months, perhaps years!

I know of course that I could run away, but only from certain areas of pain which would simply be replaced by different ones, and made worse by my own sense of cowardice. Besides, unless I leave this city altogether there is nowhere to run to. I work in Clifton, ten minutes from Alan's home, which was my home before it was his. The shops were our shops, the banks were our banks, every road and turning and set of traffic lights has been walked up or driven down or stopped at by both of us for months. The house at Marlbury Road is still full of my friends and I don't want to lose them. Even Wayside Walk has been spoilt by the girl Lisa, whom I never wish to see again but almost certainly will, because there is no easy way of avoiding her – except by never going back at all. And politics would have to be given up permanently and entirely.

I can't escape Alan without abandoning the whole of my present life. So what's to do? Flight or fight? At present all my energies are taken up with trying to do both.

After canvassing last night, as promised, Alan was bouncy and friendly, full of vitality and confidence. He suggested we go for a drink on our own, so I accepted what appeared to be an olive branch. If we could keep up such civilised behaviour, I thought, it may be possible not only to survive the election but even to enjoy it. It was pleasant to be sitting on bar stools once again, discussing the evening and the people and the tactics, and the books we had read or were about to read.

He invited me to the count of votes as his guest. I of course agreed with pleasure.

Then he lobbed his hand grenade.

There would be a party on election night and he would very much like Cathy to be there. Did I mind? "It isn't as if you won't have a position of some importance," he said.

I was stunned, so shocked that all I could do was nod and say I had rather expected something of the sort. And I was more than half way home before the real impact of the blow came down on my mind with staggering force. Then I was violently, unprecedently angry.

He had gone back on his word.

I telephoned from home and we talked until my phone ran out of charge – if "talk" describes such a lethal confrontation. I don't think either of us really knew what we were saying, or cared if it hurt. I know I was incapable of describing what was truly on my mind, and spent the rest of the night bemoaning the things I *hadn't* said, the replies I was not quick enough to make, the points I failed to bring home.

But his words burnt into my brain and memory. I shall never forget them.

He said that for the first time he felt for Cathy the same depth of commitment I had felt for him, and the words went straight to my core of hurt and humiliation. Had the past year of devotion and care, of love in spite of everything his father could throw at me, meant so little that he could compare it with a completely new, untried relationship? How could he possibly know? And how dare he even try to guess?

Last night I was faced with a dilemma. (a) I could leave the election, renounce my place at the count and vanish forever, or (b) I could insist on Cathy not being at the party. Or I could allow it all to happen, stick my nose and chin in the air and carry on.

The first just seemed to be simple cowardice, childish sulks, not worth serious consideration. To insist on Cathy being excluded when she had probably been invited already would be giving Alan a lasting grievance.

If things are to be disagreeable, I prefer them to be so on my terms, not on his!

I shall therefore continue as I have begun. But I shall do it in my way and in my time.

Janine and Myra and Lucy will all be at the party, not for Alan's sake but for mine. My own rent-a-mob! I have stopped crying and am beginning to believe I won't cry any more because my tear ducts must have run out of tears. If only I could forget how fulfilled he sounded. "I think you want it to go wrong," he had accused.

I had laughed. "Of course I want it to go wrong. Do you think I'm superwoman?"

I suppose if I loved him enough I'd be pleased for him. But I'm not. I'm not big enough for that kind of altruism. Yet I know I love him enough to want him to prove himself true!

The paradox is screwing me up. Goodnight, H

ooOoo

77

Christabel Fraser

FROM   Hannah Pascoe
TO: Chrissiefras@coolmail.net
SENT: 29 January 2009
SUBJECT: Yet more

Immediately after writing to you (at 6.30 am) I wrote a card to Alan which I delivered by hand to his door one hour later. As it was Sunday, I simply came home again and went back to bed, lying there for some time looking at my life.

The card had said "Go and love and be happy, only please don't ring me because I'm busy breaking out of a beastly chrysalis and butterflies are delicate things."

It had come to me, in the enigmatic moonlight and against a damp pillow, that he must be free to go (freed by me, that is, for he is free with or without my blessing – in that there's nothing I can do about it anyway!) because hooks only fester and turn septic. How can one human being successfully control the emotions of another? There is, of course, the not so gentle art of manipulation, but manipulation is the source of even worse things – deep resentment and hatred – and in the end it destroys the one who pulls the strings.

Not for me, then!

I also told him I would continue to work for his election and be present at the count, and that Cathy must come to the party as arranged.

No, I am not superlatively generous and forgiving. I am playing for points. If Cathy does the noble thing and stays away for my sake, she will be the superlatively generous one – and I have no desire to give all my cards away just yet. If anyone is to look noble, at least for the time being, it's going to be me. What I do later is another matter, and if they conclude from my words that I'm willing to kiss Cathy and be friends, that is their little problem!

Alan has ignored my wishes and broken a promise. Two weeks ago he agreed not to introduce her into our mutual political world. Now that he's done so, with apparently no regard for my own well being, he can take a few risks with hers.

Society has always smiled upon the sight of older men with young girls, thinking of them admiringly and with tolerant amusement as "wicked old dogs," But women with younger lovers are, even after years of feminism, somehow made to feel foolish, even a bit disgusting. Perhaps Nature takes care that the species is continued by making only child-bearing women sexually and socially acceptable. If that is so, the stigma of homosexuality is also explained and we are left with a question. Are Nature's built-in taboos stronger than all the de-conditioning which is now washing over us like fumigating spray?

But gays are at least *out* and proclaiming their right to a full and happy love life. Would they campaign as hard for 60-year-olds, for whom an overpowering passion goes unrequited because gentlemen prefer fecund young blondes?

Cathy is older than she looks, by the way, but is still 30 years younger than me. That's *half my age!*

It's true that "what goes around comes around," since I clearly recall dismissing Bill Box as a piece of pulchritude because he was too old. I am therefore hoist by my own petard!

There have been some interesting comments on my new situation, but friends are predictably partisan and I'm taking their remarks with a pinch of salt. Karen said Alan wasn't everybody's cup of tea anyway, and would have been quite out of bounds for her as she "couldn't have done that to me." (Obviously a girl of taste, discernment and strong moral fibre). I found her comment particularly interesting in view of Alan's penchant for young women with long blonde hair, and Karen's own penchant for Older Men. And I'm astonished that one of them at least didn't run true to form. Perhaps one of them did. Since Karen will certainly never tell me, I shall never know.

Another remark was from Sarah, who, when I told her of Cathy's age, shrieked "What?" very loudly down the phone and stung my ear. "She's not!" I replied that indeed she was.

"But that's disgusting!" she said. "He's old enough to be her father." Then she said "Yuk!" and make vomiting noises.

I pointed out, rather mildly and with some amusement, that Alan now looks very much younger than he is, but Sarah was unconvinced. "He's too old," she said again firmly.

Be all this as it may, there is no changing the present truth - that Alan, as was always to be expected, has chosen a younger and prettier Cathy instead of an ancient holder of bus passes.. And now all there is left for the ageing bus-pass-holder to do is bear an unbearable reality and somehow make an intolerable future tolerable again by changing her priorities.

A tall order, Chrissie. Yesterday it wasn't even possible. But yesterday was the end of the world. Perhaps today is DAY ONE of a new world. Who knows? H

ooOoo

78

Christabel Fraser

FROM   Hannah Pascoe
TO: Chrissiefras@coolmail.net
SENT: 5 February 2009
SUBJECT: We keep plodding on

I haven't written because I was too busy and too miserable, if misery is the right word to use. It isn't really. Hurting, yes, to an unexpected degree, yet getting myself to work and back, talking to patients, laughing with colleagues, as though I've learnt my part and speak the dialogue with automatic precision. But I have been an actress, after all, albeit an unwilling one, and the show of daily life has to go on, if only because if I didn't force myself to work I would simply stay in bed and starve. Now I have a state pension there's no longer any sick pay, but loss of money was a boring irrelevance in face of the total, very nearly fatal, desire to incarcerate myself forever.

All that, though, is beside the point, which is that I've kept going because that's my normal *modus operandi, "…grimly to plod, head bowed into the slatey rain, clutching the slender rope, the marker in the mist…"*

Had there been the smallest hitch during the days at work, though, I would have collapsed into stupid, helpless tears and been sent home. But there weren't any hitches. Everyone was cheerful, friendly and unquestioning, and nobody was sympathetic −which would certainly have undone me – because nobody was really aware that there was anything to be sympathetic about. Anne knows more than the rest, but takes me at face value unless it's safe to do otherwise, and she asks no questions. A wise and tolerant woman.

Once I went canvassing, but only once and only then because I had specifically promised to do so. I intended to keep out of Alan's way. Heather was the only person to witness my downfall when I caught sight of him and paid the price, so now she knows enough to understand why I was walking to my car blinded by passionate tears. She invited me into her car instead, and there we sat while the windows misted and my tale of woe unfolded.

"I could have got through it," I sobbed, "if he hadn't gone back on his word. But she won't know anyone and he'll cart her around introducing her to everyone. I can forgive him falling in love, but not bringing her here when he said he wouldn't."

Heather was suitably bracing and had one or two

pithy comments to make on "bloody insensitive, selfish bastards of men" who hadn't the smallest idea of what it feels like to be someone else, and I was so heartened by this that I grew more angry and less sorry for myself – always a good exchange.

"But why does he have to do it *now?*" I demanded with considerable heat. "If he gets in he'll have hundreds of things to take his stupid female to. He'll be awash with them. But no, he has to choose the one thing I was doing and ruin it for me. It's not fair."

We agreed it wasn't fair, she assured me she would be with me at the party, and looked forward to meeting my daughter. Then I said a warm and grateful goodbye and came home, where I've done much serious thinking.

Two days from now is Polling day. I am armed and prepared, filled with resolution and hellfire defiance. Nobody, I tell myself, will ever play games with me again, and those who try will find there are more ways of kicking teeth than by using Doc Martin boots.

Last week I rediscovered the piano. Chopin has had hell knocked out of some of his sonatas.

Up the rebellion, H.

ooOoo

79

Christabel Fraser

FROM   Hannah Pascoe
TO: Chrissiefras@coolmail.net
SENT: 6 February 2009
SUBJECT: Over and out

It's over, Chrissie. I did it! So did Alan, but that's by the way. The weather for polling day was cold but dry and I was dressed for the part in new jeans, knee boots and a brand new fur-cuffed and fur-collared leather jacket suitably emblazoned with a new and very large gold rosette. Heather's house was organised for The Day with tables covered in paper, rosettes, full boxes, empty boxes, lists and even more lists. On another table Max was busy collecting numbers from tellers and transferring the information onto his computer, printing out sheet after sheet of lists and coming up with new statistics every half hour. There were pens and calculators and maps, and a telephone which was either being spoken into or roundly cursed for ringing.

There was tea, and coffee and biscuits, fish and chips, pasties and people – people knocking and coming in, people coming in without knocking, people in a hurry, leaning on chairs drawing breath, and always Heather chasing people out again saying there was work to be done and there would be no hanging about chatting while she was in charge.

Bill, to my absolute and fervent relief, was not there at all. He is apparently in bed with bronchitis. It was my private opinion that if bronchitis didn't carry him off, frustration would, for here at long last was his beloved and much recovered son fighting his own by-election without his father's help and support. What's more, looking fair to becoming an elected member of an ancient city council – *still* without his doting father's help and support.

My heart bleeds!

I saw Alan twice. He looked spruce and energetic on his tour of polling stations, and although I tried to respond to his overtures I found it impossible. The sight of him hurt my eyes.

Heather was wonderful, cheerful, normal and encouraging.

By the end of the day I was tired, more from excitement and tension than from the physically and emotionally draining work itself. The last hour was quieter, so I drove back to the house to change my clothes. I was given a ticket permitting me to enter the hallowed place where votes are counted and dies are cast and where Alan's future would be settled for him, and was officially named as his guest in default of a spouse. Had his father been present he would of course have taken my ticket, but I had more than a suspicion it was Cathy's person, rather than mine or even his father's, that Alan wished to see standing beside the long counting tables. The only response that awoke in me, however, was the word "Tough!" I had earned my ticket.

The count itself was exciting and absorbing, which in fact made it a just a little less painful because I was too busy to be nervous. Not that I wasn't aware in a hideous way of whatever Alan happened to be doing, but the result of this awareness was the facility to always be in a different place doing something else at the time. Like moving around a stage set, I was careful where I placed myself. Training comes in handy. There was also the fascination of watching little white rectangular pieces of paper unfolded and counted into 50s. After a while I became mesmerised by endless Xs and lost count, but as I wasn't the one doing the final counting this mattered to nobody but me.

Heather has a talent for calculation, so before the proceedings were three-quarters over she knew Alan had won. So did I. The Xs had proclaimed it.

He was obviously elated. His victory speech was gracious and challenging, full of quiet resolution and a sort of just visible fire, as though the furnace door was fractionally opened now and again to give a flashing glimpse of what was in store. He thanked us all, the helpers and the police and everyone whose votes had placed him where he now found himself – in a position to work like hell.

I wondered what had happened to the hopeless man I had found in Station Road, scarred both physically and emotionally, almost catatonic, and with scarcely the will to change. I remembered him as he had been, sitting head down, eyes fixed at his feet or on his clenched hands, rocking slightly in despair and a deep, black misery.

He is unrecognisable, but the change hasn't helped me, has it? I found myself hungering for the new Alan instead of the old with a different kind of desire. And as I watched, I thought of the emotional energy I had invested, the time, the devotion and the complete concentration of all my resources. I realised someone else would be reaping where I had sewn, and knew that in believing it was all done sacrificially I had been deluding myself.

I was still contemplating this when we left the hall in triumphal array, Alan to go with his agent to the Council House, (at least he had the sense not to tote me with him this time for publicity purposes) and myself to Lucy's flat where Janine would be waiting for me. Together we all drove to Heather's house in Kingston Road. Cathy was waiting in her car. She saw me and smiled shyly. I introduced her in a perfunctory way to Lucy, but removed myself thereafter from her presence. When Alan made his entrance, to jubilant cheers, I stayed with Lucy and Jan while he went from group to group with Cathy at his side. Lucy was very funny and we laughed a lot.

Then Lucy, Jan and I went home, and they all said agreeable things about me and disagreeable things about Cathy. They left me at last, conscious of courage at having withstood a more than usually testing experience. And proud of myself.

I hadn't spoken to Cathy or to Alan. The sight of them together gave me an extraordinary pain in the eyes. Like a too-bright light. So I didn't look at them.

Alan is now a Councillor and I need never see him again. And tomorrow I leave for Padstow with Lucy. I'll send you a card. Love, H.

ooOoo

80

Christabel Fraser

FROM   Hannah Pascoe
TO: Chrissiefras@coolmail.net
SENT: 22 March 2009
SUBJECT: How now?

Is it a relief, you patient star, not receiving massive missives every day or so? It must be six weeks since the last one, but while no positive events are taking place in my outer world, positive things are certainly going on within.

I am keeping myself to myself as far as possible, sidestepping invitations (for I find them hard to refuse once given) and staying quietly alone to re-assess myself and my life. Certain people I always see. Louise and Sarah call or meet me at lunchtime on working days. Lucy is in constant touch and Jan whisks me off to concerts and theatres, but mostly I drive to work three days a week and stay at home for the other four, reading, playing the piano and writing.

Yes, writing. What will become of the result is open to question, but I am finding the process of channelling thought and emotion into one positive creative act marvellously therapeutic.

This is just as well. There have been some mighty strange repercussions to my coming home, and I seem to have a few friends here and there. Not many, and those I have lost are not worth keeping anyway. Losing even one, though, is hurtful and frustrating and fills me with a sad kind of anger.

Mary Quantrill didn't at first approve of my leaving home. Having noted Alan's frequent visits here beforehand, she leaped to the (I suppose inevitable) conclusion that it was me who was the runner-off, and Michael the wronged husband left to mope alone. Then as I left and Margaret appeared more and more frequently on the doorstep, poor Mary didn't quite know what to think and was completely foxed when I returned alone – *sans* husband, *sans* lover, *sans* everything, to live in the house while it's for sale.

I suspect she still blames me in private, for she is of that order of law-abiding citizen who sees the woman's role as unquestioning and subservient, born to spend a lifetime ensuring her man's happiness at the possible (probable) total cost of her own. But she can't actually say so because she is naturally polite, and I am still Maisie Mitchell-as-was and her next door neighbour, so we continue to exchange coffee mornings now and again, and remind each other it's dustbin day. And once she took my washing in when it rained. Perhaps one day she will tumble to the fact that it is the wronged husband who has married again, not this particular scarlet woman! Or that blame rarely lies with one person only.

But while she may be bending on the surface, she

hasn't yet unbent enough to invite me when hubby is there. Does she think that so long as I remain unattached I shall be hungrily eyeing up every pair of trousers within reach? Including hubby's size 42? In point of fact, I suspect it's hubby's own decision to keep me at arm's length. He probably disapproves of me to such an extent that he's discouraging his little missus from consorting with loose women! Loose *stage* women, moreover! Perhaps he thinks divorce is catching.

Fortunately, the neighbours on the other side are more cheerfully forthcoming now than they were before. Soon after I came home they told me how they'd wished to be friendly, but had held back because Michael was "a bit stiff, like, you know," and that as I was sort of famous they hadn't wanted to impose. Now, however, free of both fame and stiff husband, the way is clear for them to offer help and lively gossip – which they do. Bob put some shelves up for me last week.

Tom has been. He didn't telephone first. "If I had, you'd have told me not to come," he said, extending a bunch of daffodils and a book of limericks.

"Thank you, they're lovely," I cried, welcoming him with delight, "but I didn't know you liked limericks."

"Ah, but you see I knew you did."

I looked at him properly for the first time and knew how single-minded I had become.

"At least I know you don't take sugar in your coffee," I laughed, and kissed him on the cheek.

He had come to take me out for lunch, he said, to the place of my choice. I would instantly have chosen the Buttress, but every sense rebelled against it. I hadn't been there since the lunch Alan and I had shared in May, almost a year ago. Because I hesitated, Tom said "Didn't you use to go to that place down by the river?"

I nodded, chewed my lower lip and frowned at him.

"A few ghosts to lay, are there?"

"One or two."

"Well, it's a lovely day, the sun is shining and the company is cheerful. Do whatever you want to do, Han, but you couldn't have a better day for ghost-busting."

I grinned at him suddenly. He was absolutely right.

"Okay, let's go," I said, reaching for my jacket.

The water was brightly speckled with March sunlight and the air was surprisingly mild. I breathed in the familiar smells and looked up at the familiar sky between the riverbank trees, and was glad I had come. Only the heron was missing.

"He'll be back," Tom said. "He's probably courting."

"Do herons court in March?"

"No idea," he grinned. "I only know I do, and in April and May and June and July…"

"And August and September and all the days up to Christmas," I finished. "You're a reprobate."

"Fun though, isn't it?"

I laughed.

"The trouble is," he went on, "that because you call me a reprobate you never take anything I say seriously"

"Of course not. I'm not daft."

"Aren't you?" and he touched the end of my nose with the tip of his forefinger.

We continued to talk nonsense until he left for home later in the afternoon. I felt better for seeing him.

Two weeks ago I drove into the city, and sat rather uncomfortably in the public gallery of the Council Chamber, to see and hear Alan in his seat below me make his maiden speech. With a sense of *deja vue,* I once again watched the Lord Mayor enter with his slow and stately tread, preceded by the man in a wig and gown holding the big stick called a mace. I heard the questions, which could easily have been exactly the same ones as last time, and was just as bored because I still didn't fully understand any of them. And I witnessed various chairmen of committees stand aloft on the dais talking in barely comprehensible jargon about their reports. I heard again the ribaldry, the sometimes witty, sometimes ponderous wise-cracking between the benches and across the chamber, and I watched while members stood to make their speeches in front of an audience who, as always, read newspapers or chatted among themselves, or even walked to and fro. I was alone and wondering why I had come, but when Alan rose to speak I was amazed. He was funny and compelling and the room was silent to listen to him. When I heard the applause as he bowed to the Lord Mayor and sat down among his exultant group, I murmured "That's my boy!"

Cathy wasn't there.

Then I drove home and spent the rest of the afternoon in silent contemplation.

It has taken these weeks to bring my thoughts to a point where they could bear, even for a second, the image of Alan with Cathy. The first bars of a love song were enough to send me reaching for the radio to switch it off, the sight of lovers in the street caused me physical nausea, television plays were impossible unless they were macho murders, which left me with the sole but constant companionship of Classic FM and Radio Three. I now have an in-depth knowledge of strange, esoteric modern works, of hitherto unheard of operas and massive symphonies. I have learnt to love Neilsen and can listen to chamber music of all kinds for hours. But opera has its quota of lovers. And Beethoven's Late Quartets are definitely, certainly and positively *out*!

Some songs are acceptable. There are splendid ones expressing the grief of lost love, and there are cynical songs expressing doubts about this whole love business anyway. But worst of all are the ecstatic, blissful songs from man to woman, and these I cannot listen to, for I have become bound into, integrated with what I imagine are Alan's responses, and sometimes seem to feel them more vividly than my own. Perhaps even more vividly than Alan does himself. His love for Cathy becomes real for me, and I seem to see through his eyes, hear with his ears, and experience a depth of passion which I am almost certainly transferring from myself to him.

I am feeling what I imagine he would feel *if he were me*. But of course he isn't me, so am I experiencing not only the severest pain of loss but a jealousy deep and burning because, in a funny sort of way, I am jealous of *his happiness?*

It is as if I have gone through my life without knowing the joy and satisfaction of a really deep passion returned in kind, and that, having had my own passion awakened, I am now seeing the object of it experiencing joy and satisfaction with someone else. So I am not so much jealous of Cathy as jealous of Alan enjoying Cathy. What a nasty person I have become.

Things haven't stood still in the outer world either, for there have been several offers on this house. The problem with selling one's home over one's head is that one is obliged to keep said home tidy at all times. Everything is looking lovely and clean and shining, with new wallpaper in the hall and new paint on the banisters (done while I was in Padstow) and there are flowers in every room, and a whiff of coffee whenever prospective buyers are due. All the usual games we play. And everyone is enthusiastic. One or two of them seemed aware of whose home it is, and there was the lingering suspicion that they were here to view the owner rather the house. Be that as it may, several have been, have seen, but have not been conquered. Not that I care very deeply. The house must, in course of time, be sold, but I am in no great hurry to leave it again.

I have had another approach from Robert. Would I care to bring Maisie back to Wayside Walk? I thought hard but once again said no. It's a mistake to go back.

There was also an invitation from Clifton Ward to stand as candidate next year. They are either very hard up for prospects or I put in a better performance than I thought – or perhaps Maisie still has a pull of her own. I said no to that, too. I enjoyed electioneering, but could never be seriously dedicated enough to be a real, live, responsible councillor. If I ever stood for election it would be in the hope of losing by one vote, because to win would be, for me, the ultimate disaster. It would be an even greater disaster for the party machine, although the machine doesn't seem to realise this, because I haven't the kind of mental computer politicians seem to be born with. Thick reports confuse me, formal committees bore me and jargon is meaningless to me. And frustration and anger at things not done that should be done would cause more pain than I now have stamina for. To sit at a table tackling vital matters strand by strand by agreement and consensus is one thing – to stand firm against the bitterness of opposition and personal hostility would seem to be such a waste of what energy I have at my disposal, not to mention precious hours and days, that I may well give up in frustration and despair. But never let it be said that light-hearted Hannah Pascoe could feel such passion for the world and its future.

The party machine has had a narrow escape. Besides, there must be other ways of changing the world's destiny, ways that involve the talents I do possess, not the ones I don't. (As well might I join an orchestra for the love of music without knowing how to play any of the instruments).

And anyway, how could I possibly sit beside Alan for one minute on the council benches. An unthinkable thought!

I've spent one or two weekends in Padstow and will go down again in the summer. Once the house is sold I shall be there permanently.

Michael comes to see me most weeks, to make sure I am well and to do odd jobs about the house, and for a while I found his presence disturbing. It came to a head a few weeks ago.

It was a traumatic, cathartic experience.

The cause of my intense preoccupation (Alan) having vanished from sound and sight, I discovered that it, his very existence, had been a veil coming between me and the rest of life. He, it, had obscured facts which now stood revealed in all their grisly squalor and awfulness.

I knew I had lost both Alan and Michael. What I failed to understand until that moment was that all the pain of divorce and of Michael's remarriage had been covered over, anaesthetised. In order to save myself from it, I had thrown every particle of energy and concentration – and passion – onto Alan. He had absorbed it. But now, without his constant presence, the anaesthetic was wearing off.

I was at last grieving for Michael. The pain I was so disturbed at not feeling at the time was now washing over me in a vast, drowning tidal wave.

It had been coming slowly and progressively, but its denouement was sudden, sharp, bitter and frightening. For several weeks I missed his integrity and cool humour, his comforting solidity and the familiarity and warmth and friendliness of marriage so much and so violently that I hardly knew what I was doing.

One evening I found myself screaming about the

house, tearing my hair and my clothes, my skin, shrieking to Michael to come back. Screaming that I should never have let him go.

"What have I done? I need you. Please Michael, come home, I need you"

Then, quite suddenly one day, the terrible keening passed and I was quiet, exhausted and empty but filled with a new kind of peace. I had accepted my mistakes, and my loss, and grief had turned to resignation.

Now I am waiting.

My feelings for Alan have changed. If he came to me now I would refuse him. How could I ever trust him again? I still love Michael, but the time has passed for us. He has a new life, and we have both entered a new phase.

So I'm waiting. I don't know why or what for – possibly for a moment when the door to the past has finally closed and a new one appears in front of me. Until then, I am your loving H

P S. I was just about to send this when Michael appeared at the door with a cheque for £4,000 – my half of an insurance premium that has just matured. And by this morning's post there has arrived a brochure for P & O cruises. One of them is for a round-the-world trip starting next January. I shall take it.

ooOoo

81

Christabel Fraser

FROM   Hannah Pascoe

TO: Chrissiefras@coolmail.net
SENT: 8 June 2009
SUBJECT: Greetings from Padstow

This is to tell you, Christabel Fraser, that for the first time for many months I am happy! There is no real reason. My home is sold and I am living here in the cottage until my life is finally sorted out. The new owners admired it all but left me in no doubt that the instant the house was theirs they would gut it, demolish it and remove all trace of my existence in it – so wherever I finally decide to live it will **not** be within striking distance of Park Close. I couldn't bear seeing my home violated. Of course this also means they won't be putting a plaque on the wall saying "Maisie Mitchell lived here". So much for fame!

My work with the dentists, though pleasant, was only a method of earning money for the time being. There was no sense of vocation, no absorbing incentive to cease what I was doing in order to do something else instead, so gainful employment being still required after the finances have been sorted out, I intend look for work here in Padstow.

Myra told me yesterday that Beatrice Rudge has died. I am sad because I loved her, and because I hadn't visited her as often as I could have done, but the knowledge of her death was comforting in a strange sort of way, as though she may be closer to me now than she ever was as a breathing human person.

I have also heard from Ruth, who phones now and then, that Alan's affair with Cathy is over, and I don't know how I feel. Relieved of some crushing jealousy, but annoyed that I'd been jealous for nothing. He had, after all, exchanged me for something transient, and what that says about Alan, as well as about me, is a whole new question. Was Michael right in his

344

judgement that what Alan felt was not love but simply fancy, or is he, Alan, now suffering the same kind of grief I've just been through?

I don't expect to find out, and just now have no desire to do so. Alan's problems are his own and not mine, and I'm not sticking my head into any more nooses (What's the plural of "noose? It can't possibly be "nice"?). I am an addict coming through a nasty addiction and I'm not risking even one little sniff.

Last week Timothy and Francine paid me a surprise and extraordinarily welcome visit, turning up in the middle of the afternoon. For once the sun shone upon us all in a spectacular sizzling heatwave. For a few hours Francine and I walked together on the cliffs and she told me how Tim had taken the news of his parents' divorce. There had been, she said, a few tears, but he had recovered his balance very quickly and understood that although Michael and I may not be physically together, he had in fact lost neither of us.

They had turned up in the middle of the afternoon so we all went out for cream teas. The tide was high so we watched the boats bobbing in the harbour and smelt the fore-runners of evening meals being cooked in the myriad of restaurants that surrounded us. Later we enjoyed a Chinese take-away and drank two bottles of wine between us. As the effect of alcohol on Timothy is a tendency to discuss philosophy and the world view of things, while the effect on Francine and myself is to turn us into giggling morons, the evening conversation was interesting! Happily we were two to one, so no damage was done.

They had brought sleeping bags, which eventually took up the entire space of my hobbit-sized living room, but seemed more than happy with the arrangement. I did suggest one of the many B&Bs that dot the vicinity, but they preferred to "doss", so "doss" they did.

It was wonderful to have them here. They insisted on taking me out for breakfast, so I revelled in bacon, eggs, mushrooms and fried bread. And coffee. Gallons of it. Far more than I usually drink, but how often do I have my lovely son under my roof.

They had visited Michael and Margaret en route to me and Francine had said the same thing to them. I am deeply glad of this. More than anything, I want to keep my family together – including good relations with Michael as far as possible.

Two days ago Andrew the troubadour drove himself down in his old and muddy Ford van, bringing fresh tomatoes, courgettes and some early strawberries. He hoped I was well, I assured him I was, and after staring down into his tea cup for a while, he said: "You must look after yourself you know. If there is anything else I can ever do for you, please let me know."

I was touched. "Thank you Andrew, I'll remember that," I said gratefully.

I told him about my round-the-world cruise, booked for next January, and he said "Don't get shipwrecked, or eaten by bears, will you?" So I laughed and said I didn't think that was likely on a large, British cruise ship. "I am much more likely to over-eat and get so fat they'll have to roll me down the gangway."

He smiled, and flexed his fingers like a pianist ready to attack the keys. Then he said: "Are you going to stay on your own? Would you ever think of marrying again?"

My reply was carefully considered. "At the moment," I said, "I can't imagine sharing my life with anyone again, but I suppose, if I'm honest, it would be nice to think there's a possibility that I might marry again one day. Let's say I'm not ruling anything out."

He looked up suddenly, then away again. "I know

there's an age difference, but that doesn't bother me. If I thought it wouldn't bother you I'd ask you to marry me."

I was amazed, and really very moved. "Thank you," I said at last, "What a wonderful thing to say. But it wouldn't be fair. You're not forty yet and deserve better from life than me."

Andrew smiled and shook his head. Then he murmured: "Oh well!" and kissed me gently on the lips. He left as quietly and unobtrusively as he had come.

I stood for a long time staring out of the window and thinking of the many ironies that surround us all. A ten year difference between Alan and myself had been too much, yet here was a man thirty years my junior willing to marry me. And I was deeply and immensely grateful.

Then yesterday there was yet another visitor. Tom climbed the alleyway steps to my *bijou* residence and rang the doorbell, and a lovely surprise he was too, with his comforting, humorous, kindly air. He stayed for most of the day and we walked the Camel Trail to the bridge and looked back at Padstow from the screen of trees. Cyclists passed cheerfully by and walkers smiled and said "Good afternoon," and I was glad Tom was there to enjoy it all with me.

Before he left he held me by the shoulders and we looked at each other, eye to eye.

"Don't ever be lonely," he said, shaking me slightly then kissing the tip of my nose. "You know where I am."

I smiled and kissed his cheek in return. "I do, Tom, and thank you."

I'd been happy to have him there with me, but was strangely relieved when he left. Despite my words to Andrew I am still learning to be self-sufficient, resisting the conditioning of years which tells me that

Woman is only valuable when she Has A Man.

The man, if ever there is one, who shares my life will be just that – a sharer – not someone on whom I depend for ultimate wellbeing. And I'm happy with that. It's a quiet sort of happiness. The past sixteen months seem to have hurtled me from the comfortable, secure, socialite life of mother, wife, actress and flirt into a place where I've had to meet difficult truths, and make unpleasant discoveries. In short, to be honest with myself for once. It was painful but no doubt good for my soul.

These truths and discoveries are still being made, but they no longer surprise me.

Tom was pleased about the cruise and said it was the best thing I could do. I told him I wanted to go as far away as possible for as long as possible, to a place where no-one knew me and no-one could find me.

"An excellent idea," he had said, "just as long as you eventually come back. I don't think this country is ready to do without you just yet." Then he climbed into his smart shiny black Mercedes and drove away, leaving me to my cottage and my solitude.

Yesterday I drove to Trevose Head and breathed the strong, fresh air with no trace of petrol fumes, only the smell of grass and salt and seaweed. Everything passed across my vision in a kaleidoscope of thoughts, images and recollections. There was a flurry of emotion, responses passing across me like clouds over the landscape, and then there was peace again. I realised Alan had told me from the very beginning all I'd needed to know, and that I should have understood how impossible it would be to change him simply by loving him. I saw how a dependence on someone when in a demeaned state is a humiliation one would prefer to forget about as quickly as possible, in which case the last person Alan would want in his life at its peak would be the person who saw him at its nadir. And I saw how I had given him permission, also from the very beginning, to use me without giving any return.

I had said: "I'm not asking you to love me, only that I am allowed to love you." He merely did what I asked of him, fulfilled his part of the bargain. What more should one expect?

And he is alive and well, which is all I asked of God. He, too, fulfilled his part of the bargain I made when Alan had one foot in the hereafter. I remember my words only too clearly. I had said: ""If you will let him live and be normal and happy, I won't ask anything for myself. Only please don't let him die."

Right now I seem to have let go of it all – of everyone – Alan and Michael and my long-dead parents, of past shames and failures, disappointments and half concealed resentments. In fact, as far as one can ever do so, of my entire life until now. In one way I feel astoundingly young, fresh like a very small child newly washed and dressed and running simply for the joy of running. But in another I feel old, full of years and accumulated wisdom.

There are tentative offers of work in Australia, where I could spend time with my elusive brother as he flies his plane somewhere in the Aussie outback. He would, I knew, open up a fresh new world for me. I know there is a door open should I choose to go back to Wayside Walk, so starvation is not yet on the agenda. But for the moment I don't choose to do any of those things. Life is too new, and I am too new, and I have a cruise to prepare for and a brother to seek. This morning, misted with spray and the sting of sea, I felt a sudden small shiver of excitement and anticipation. Only a few months from now and I will be setting off to encircle the globe. I mean to explore every last corner of it.

Meanwhile, I will always be
Your undeserving but very grateful friend,
Hannah

P S My *magnum opus* is not finished, and can't be yet,
since I haven't finished living it, but when it's written it
will be dedicated to you.

P P S I'll send you a card from Fiji.